FATHER

ELIZABETH VON ARNIM

BRITISH LIBRARY

First published in 1931

This edition published in 2020 by
The British Library
96 Euston Road
London NW1 2DB

Cataloguing in Publication Data
A catalogue record for this publication is available from the British Library

ISBN 9780712353182
e-ISBN 9780712367905

Text design and typesetting by JCS Publishing Services Ltd
Printed in England by CPI Group (UK), Croydon, CR0 4YY

CONTENTS

THE 1930s

- **1928:** Virginia Woolf gives a lecture that states women needed £500 a year and a room of their own; a version of the lecture was published as *A Room of One's Own* the following year.
- **1929:** the total fertility rate (the average number of children born to a woman over her lifetime) falls below 2 for the first time. It remains below 2 until 1943.
- **1930:** the average age at first marriage is 24.3 for men and 21.3 for women.
- **1931:** *Father* is published.
- **1931:** the census shows that there are approximately 1.7 million more women than men in the UK, about the same difference as 1921. The 1931 census was destroyed in an accidental fire in 1942.
- **1931:** 34.2 per cent of women in the UK are considered 'economically active', a term used by the Labour Force Survey to include those in work and those looking for work. The number rises by only half a per cent by 1951.
- **1936:** Elizabeth von Arnim publishes *All the Dogs of My Life*, the closest thing she wrote to an autobiography.
- **1937:** the Matrimonial Causes Act extends the right of women to divorce their husbands, no longer requiring incest, sodomy, cruelty, etc., to be an additional offence to adultery. (Men could already divorce women for adultery, without additional offences.)
- **1939 (September):** the outbreak of the Second World War.

ELIZABETH VON ARNIM (1866–1941)

The author known today as Elizabeth von Arnim was born Mary Annette Beauchamp in Australia in 1866 and moved with her family to England when she was three years old. Her cousin, born more than twenty years later, was the renowned New Zealand short-story writer Katherine Mansfield, whose real name was Kathleen Beauchamp.

The author name 'Elizabeth von Arnim' was never used during her lifetime. Her works appeared as 'By the author of *Elizabeth and Her German Garden*', which was her first, very successful novel in 1898. Later, her books appeared as being by 'Elizabeth' (inverted commas included) and only when she was republished in the 1980s was she given the name by which she is best known now, Elizabeth von Arnim.

The surname came from her first husband, Count Henning August von Arnim-Schlagenthin, making her a countess. They lived in Berlin, and it was here that she wrote her heavily autobiographical first novel, which led many of her readers to believe she was German. The couple had five children, but in 1908 Arnim left her husband, whom she referred to as the 'Man of Wrath'. He died a couple of years later, and in 1916 she married Earl John Francis Russell, the brother of the philosopher Bertrand Russell. Her second marriage also entitled her to use the title Countess. This marriage was equally unhappy, and the couple separated in 1919. She would use the marriage as the basis for her 1921 novel *Vera*.

❦ ❦ ❦

For more than four decades, Arnim wrote comedies, tragedies, and tragicomedies with equal skill. She is perhaps best remembered now for the poignant and touching novel *The Enchanted April*, but deserves to be known for her wide range of work. In *Father*, she combines the comic and the poignant with wit and hidden depths.

PREFACE

Elizabeth von Arnim is perhaps best known for her 1898 work *Elizabeth and Her German Garden* and her 1922 novel *The Enchanted April*. *Father*, one of her later novels, is a deserving inclusion in the British Library Women Writers series. The novel revisits one of the most striking themes of von Armin's works: the importance of a garden in a woman's life. When *Father* was published in 1931, the theme of freedom through access to the natural world joined with the fate of the 'surplus' women who remained unmarried in the interwar years.

The eponymous father appears very little throughout the novel, and yet his presence is felt on almost every page. We begin with Jennifer, toiling away for her emotionally distant father, being given the news that he has unexpectedly remarried. This leaves Jennifer free at last to pursue her dreams of moving to the country. By casting off her restrictive London life and embracing nonconformity, her life begins to change dramatically. As might be expected from an Elizabeth von Arnim novel, the comedy is sophisticated and unexpected. A borrowed coat and a pile of sardine cans provide light relief. However, there is always a string of unintended consequences which leads to the dramatic conclusion of the novel.

On the surface, the detailed comedy, richly drawn characters and romantic interest lead the reader to expect a tale of a zany spinster with a neat and satisfying conclusion to her story. But at the heart of the novel is the escape from a heavy-handed father and suffocating urban existence. Her liberation from domestic constraint brings her to the happiness of the garden. It also brings her to towards new and fulfilling human connections. While the ending seems neat, there is a sting in the tail when we consider the reality of Jennifer's new life and the consequences of our actions, both large and small.

Lucy Evans,
Curator, Printed Heritage Collections

CHAPTER I

Mother said, dying, "You'll take care of father, won't you—"

"Always," sobbed her kneeling, heartbroken daughter.

"Don't leave him, Jen."

"Oh mother, I promise—I won't ever. Not ever, ever—"

No; one will never leave father. But what if father, not left, meticulously attended to, taken care of, obeyed and cherished, after twelve solid, faithful years of it, without saying a word to a soul comes back to tea one afternoon with a new wife? Then, isn't one released? Hasn't one completed one's job? Can't one with a clear conscience, indeed must one not, hand him over, and at last, at last—oh, how glorious!—be free?

Father, however, didn't seem to see it that way. He appeared to take it for granted that his daughter would continue about him as before, side by side with his new wife, on the ground that homes were the natural places for maiden daughters; and when she reminded him that she was thirty-three, he merely inquired with acerbity, for in his heart he was thinking she ought to have been married and out of the way long ago, whether being thirty-three altered the fact that she was a maiden daughter.

He was, that is, doing his duty by her; and, as sometimes happens with duty, the doing of it made him cross.

Now the last thing father had meant to be on his wedding day was cross, so naturally, when he found himself being it, he became much crosser, and at last, as will presently be told, there was quite a scene.

To begin with, though, all was blandness. There wasn't a cloud at the tea-table. Father was very pleasant indeed, if faintly apologetic—not embarrassed, for he was never that, but there was a faint flavour of apology in his manner, which was perhaps not to be wondered at, since his new wife was ever so much younger, one could see at once, than his daughter, and he sixty-five.

"You mustn't think, Jennifer," he said after tea, which had been the oddest meal of her life, as he called her into the back diningroom where, protected by folding doors from anything that might be going on in the front one, they had worked together so long—she the obedient handmaid waiting on his thoughts, taking them down as they emerged from him, typing and re-typing them, over and over again with dogged patience typing a single paragraph, a single sentence, sometimes for days working on a single sentence till it was, in father's eyes, as near perfect as it could humanly be got,—"you mustn't think, Jennifer," he said, "that I've sprung this on you unfairly."

Pleasant, he thought, surveying this workroom of his, this back diningroom looking on to the backs of other diningrooms in the parallel street behind, with its cold neatness and sombre, rep-covered furniture, its type-writing table for his daughter between the maroon window-curtains, its big writing-table for himself, with the revolving chair from which he dictated,—pleasant to leave it for a while. He hadn't had a holiday for years; not since, now he came to think of it, poor Marian's death. There had been too much to do to think of holidays. Years slip by remarkably quickly when one is busy. And Jennifer, too—his eyes came back to the sturdy, heavy, shortlegged figure—pleasant to have a change from Jennifer. She was losing, he had noticed lately—since, that is, he had become acquainted with her who till that morning was Miss Baines—her freshness a good deal, and soon, if she didn't take care, would be a regular old maid.

Father didn't like old maids; not to be shut up alone with, most of every day, in the back diningroom as well as at meals, and he couldn't help feeling relieved to think that this stretch of his life was over. Yet he admitted, making the best of things, that if his daughter weren't an old maid, or weren't that which would certainly presently become one, neither would she have been living at home, efficiently helping him in his work. She had been very useful. She would still be useful. It cut both ways, he thought, trying to console himself for her continued presence in his house, now that he could do without her.

"You mustn't think, Jennifer," he therefore said, in case it should happen to be exactly what she was thinking, "that I've sprung this on you unfairly."

"No, no," she reassured him, looking at him without seeing him, so much dazzled was she by what she did see; but if ever a thing had been sprung on someone, was it not this on her? As to unfairly, what did she care about unfairly, when she was free?

She blinked. Through and beyond father she saw doors flying open, walls falling flat, and herself running unhindered down the steps, along Gower Street, away through London, across suburbs, out, out into great sunlit spaces where the wind, fresh and scented, rushed to meet her, and the birds, and the stars, and those glorious vague beings in the Bible called sons of the morning, sang together for joy. Father, provided for; she, with a clear conscience, free; the twelve years during which youth had been ebbing away, the years shut up in the back diningroom at a typewriter, with no hope that anything would ever be different and no thought of anything but sticking to her promise and taking care of the helpless, gifted man, finished and done with—what did they matter now? Not a jot, thought Jen, her wide-open eyes shining with the reflection of what she saw through and beyond father. She could *feel* the wind—she could *feel* it, the scented fresh wind, blowing up her hair as she ran and ran …

"*Oh!*" she exclaimed, taking a long breath, and clasping her hands; for really she couldn't help it—she, so quiet always, so careful never to show the least excitement, nor any wish, couldn't help just that one small cry.

Father naturally thought it was a reproach, or the beginning of reproaches. It might well be that it was. Many reproaches, also those in his own writings, began with precisely this exclamation, and he was aware that the occasion was one on which grown-up children are apt to make unpleasant comment.

But he hadn't brought his daughter into the back diningroom, and left his young bride alone with empty teacups, in order to be reproached. Far from this, his motive in taking her aside had been to assure her, before proceeding on his honeymoon, that what he had done would in no way make a difference to her, and that her mind might be at rest. This was what decent fathers in the circumstances did. He was a decent father; his intentions towards her, whatever his private wishes might be, were good; and, aware of this, his eye, as he looked at her when she clasped her hands and so ominously exclaimed, grew cold.

Of course he knew his marriage was sudden, and also he knew it might be called secretive; but how much better if all marriages were sudden and secretive, and accordingly undiscussed beforehand. These things should be taken simply, considered father. They were not important, except to the two persons concerned, and should be accepted without fuss. Father hated fuss, and the flapping of feminine wings. Also, he long had needed more relaxation in his life of work than the astringent affection a daughter could provide, and latterly had been quietly making up his mind to get it. No one could say he hadn't properly matured in widowerhood, with twelve years of it, austere and withdrawn, to his credit. Besides, was he not an artist? And should not every side of an artist have its proper outlet? If proper outlets were withheld too long, the need for them inevitably became apparent in the artist's work, and unbalanced it.

Not that father was of those who think they ought to fall in order that they may rise, to wallow in order that they may emerge. He disliked anything violent; his nature was a quiet one; his habits solitary. But, quiet as he was, and solitarily as he preferred to live, from time to time, being human, he had yet a kind of itch, a kind of gnaw, a kind of—who shall describe exactly what father had? Anyhow it got into his work; especially in spring, in the nesting season, when even the sparrows in the sooty backyard seemed to have secured something denied to him. And lately he had been conscious that those parts of his books which had to do with love, from March onwards loomed out of all proportion to the rest, besides becoming steadily more lush, more full, and conspicuously, of, as it were, sap.

Father abhorred sap; he shuddered at written lushness. On no account must his work be permitted to sag away from the Greek serenity, the Elizabethan simplicity, which was what so deeply endeared it to his small, fastidious public. And when a reviewer said of his last book, obviously referring to the love scenes, "Mr. Richard Dodge's style"—he was spoken of as Mr. Richard Dodge, because there are many Dodges—"is curiously broadening," it was the last straw.

Broadening. Detestable word. Detestable symbol of a detestable thing. In the interests of his style, having accidentally found Miss Baines he woo'd her; in the interests of quiet and talk avoidance, he married her without telling anybody but herself. She was so young that she thought a secret marriage an immense joke, and also she easily did what she was told, for it saved, she thought, a lot of trouble, and also, again, her age was the age of hero-worship; so that when father, the great Richard Dodge, celebrated in two continents, the chief hero of her relations, who belonged to an eagerly literary set, suddenly loomed into her life and without loss of time began to woo, she was awestruck. It never would have occurred to her to refuse him. That very morning father had married her; and, as such a thing as getting married hadn't happened to him for a long while, he had been feeling almost excited, very nearly buoyant, quite apart from, and in addition to, his satisfaction at knowing that his style would now cease to broaden, now that he would have a domestic outlet for breadth, and his love-scenes would once more become exquisite rather than lush.

What simple remedies life provided, he had been thinking, pleased, at tea, a meal during which his daughter had behaved quite well; what agreeable simple remedies. A young wife, four weeks on the continent—he was taking her to Norway—and a return, purged and detached, to that which was most important to him in the world; good work, without a word in it which wasn't the exactly, the beautifully, right one.

And now here was his daughter going to do her best to spoil it; starting, he was afraid, a scene. Fuss, after all, was not going to be spared him.

“Surely,” he began, forestalling what she might, disagreeably, be about to let loose on him, “surely on my wedding day, of all days—”

“Oh, but I’m only trying to *realise*!” she interrupted, her hands pressed tightly together, her eyes bright and wide open.

“My dear Jennifer, there’s nothing for you to realise,” he said, a little stiffly because of having to be patient. “This will make no difference to you. Do you suppose I would allow a newcomer, however dear to me, to oust my daughter from her rightful home?”

Certainly his daughter should never be ousted. She had looked after him dutifully and well from the day her mother died; and of late years, once he had trained her to the needful unremitting application and accuracy, she had been most helpful in his work. Grateful was an odd word to use in regard to their relationship, thought father, but he was grateful to Jennifer; and being grateful, being a decent father, he had firmly made up his undoubtedly reluctant mind,—for every man prefers to have his young wife to himself,—that so long as she was unmarried, and he was alive, she should never want for a home. Could any parent say more? He doubted it. Would most parents in his position say as much? He doubted that too.

Yet here she was exclaiming, in answer to his kind and reassuring words, her eyes, he noticed, unusually bright, filled, he feared, with the light of imminent unseemly criticism, “No difference? No *difference*, father?”

“No difference at all. Don’t be foolish, Jennifer,” he said, trying not to speak too sharply, it being his wedding day; but indeed her words sounded exactly like the first words of fuss. “Except,” he continued, “that sometimes now in the evenings you will be able to talk to another woman, instead of playing chess with me, our daily life will go on just as regularly as before. Three people instead of two. Really, Jennifer, that’s all it amounts to—and of course the immediate fact that I shan’t be here to dinner tonight, nor in the house for the next few weeks. Make your arrangements. Give your instructions. I’m afraid,” he went on rather quickly, as she seemed to be about to open her mouth, “my absence for a time is inevitable, but it will leave you undisturbed in making the necessary alterations in regard to—well, rooms. And it's not as if you won't have plenty of work to keep you busy. I'm taking Netta to Norway, and during my absence there's that fifth chapter to be gone through again—a most important chapter, as you know, with alterations which need great care. Set your mind at rest, my dear," he finished, giving himself a pull in the direction of proper paternalness, and bending forward and lightly kissing her on the brow—that was what fathers kissed daughters on, and for years now he had been thoroughly tired of brows—"set your mind at rest, and while I'm away get on with that fifth chapter."

There; he had settled Jennifer; said what was right; behaved as a father, in the circumstances, should. And following up the kiss with a brief pat on her rather heavy shoulder, her solid, unvirginal shoulder—he had often wondered why Jennifer, a spinster, should be so solid—he began going towards the door.

❦

She, however, went quickly after him, and laid her hand on his sleeve. "But, father—" she said, her face close to his.

What a pasty creature she was, he thought, in spite of his annoyance noticing, from long practice as an artist, her details. All his heroines were rosy—freshly, delicately, dewily rosy, because of Jennifer's opaque and colourless skin. Her eyes, too, he thought, coldly examining her, weren't blue like his, or brown like her mother's, but hazel, and father had a theory that people with hazel eyes were really all a little mad, or at least became mad before they had done. True, Jennifer had shown no signs of madness up to now,—was, on the contrary, oppressively steady and quiet and uninteresting; still, people with eyes like that weren't altogether to be trusted. The best thing about her was her voice, which was remarkably and quite unusually agreeable; but as he didn't particularly want to talk to her—what in the world would he have to say?—it wasn't of much use to him. And the next best thing was that she had really very pretty, even, white teeth, which lit her up surprisingly when she smiled, changing her face, indeed, altogether.

The trouble with Jennifer was that she didn't smile; or so rarely that one almost forgot she could. She should do it more often. It was her duty to make the best of herself, if only because his eyes so frequently were obliged to rest on her face. Besides, it was every woman's duty to make the best of herself, and Jennifer's not doing so no doubt accounted for the fact that she was still on his hands. Off those hands she ought, of course, to have been long ago; yet if some man had reft her from him before he was ready, as now, for her to go, it would have been extremely awkward, father knew; he couldn't have run his house without her; his work would have suffered considerably; in fact he was unable to imagine what would have become of him. Those conditions, however, were over now. The moment was ripe for a husband to come along and r—

Father, who had been looking at his daughter with a hostile eye because of that hand on his arm, a hand objectionably firm, as if determined that he shouldn't get out of the room till fuss had been made and endured, here suddenly left off seeing her, and stood slowly rubbing his nose up and down between his thumb and forefinger, which was what he did when searching for a word; because what, he wondered, was the infinitive of reft? It must have one. All verbs had one. Now what, now what, he asked himself, forgetting the face so close to his and the hand on his arm, forgetting even the charming creature patiently sitting alone with crumbs and teacups in the next room, could possibly be the infinitive of reft?

So well did Jen know this trick, and the accompanying sudden blankness in his eyes, that from long habit she nearly let go his arm and looked round for her fountain pen, in readiness to fix the precious word the instant it was caught. Instead, however, she did a thing that was very unlike her, and unlike, too, anything anybody had ever done to father before, with whom few were friends and none took liberties—she shook his arm; not much, but unmistakeably.

Brought back by this extraordinary behaviour with a shock to the present, and to the menace of his daughter's attitude, he stared at her for a moment in astonishment, and the instant she opened her mouth to speak checked her. Whatever she was going to say, father, roused and offended by the familiarity of that shake, was determined she shouldn't say it, and stiffly withdrawing from her detaining hand he informed her, with no further attempt at benevolence, that what she had to do now was to waste no more time but go upstairs and see about the things he ought to take with him; and he continued, turning his back on her and once more making for the door with his curious, shuffling tread, "I've told you I mean well by you, and I now add to that that I leave in half an hour. There's nothing more to be said."

"Oh, but there is, there is! Father, you must listen—"

There; she was beginning again; coming after him; coming after him out into the hall, where everybody could hear. What preposterous conduct was this? Couldn't a man marry a second time without bringing a hornet's nest about his ears? And if anyone had a grievance, wasn't it he, who had a maiden daughter to support and put up with, and was shouldering the burden of two women in the kindest, most uncomplaining spirit?

"Well, now, what is it?" he said, this time with unconcealed irritation as she, following close on his heels, once more put her hand on his arm—caught hold of his arm in fact, actually holding him back who had a bride waiting and a train to catch. "Surely anything you wish to say can wait till my return?"

"No," said Jen, a note in her voice he had never heard before. "No. That's just what it can't do. It's most important, father, and you positively *must* listen."

Here it was, then, upon him, the fuss he had wished to avoid; and in the hall too, just outside the door behind which, not quite so patient now, and beginning to wonder a little, sat among crumbs and teacups the lovely late Miss Baines. This on his wedding day, thought father; on his wedding day to have a daughter who stuck to him like a burr, and a burr with a grievance. How one's children, for whom one had done everything, ended by being nothing but troubles! They should, of course, be somewhere else by the time they were thirty-three, and not still at home, reproaching their fathers.

"You don't really think I can *stay* here?" asked Jen, her eyes very bright. "Now that you've married again? You must see that I shall have to go?"

Father stared at her. He was astonished. These were quite different words from those he had been trying to prevent. He was so much astonished that he could hardly believe his ears, and stood quite still, making no attempt to get rid of her hand.

"Go?" he repeated, staring. "Go where?"

"Oh, I don't know yet—how can I know? I haven't had much time to think, have I? But I can't stay here," said Jen quickly, with an eagerness and animation he wasn't aware the solid creature was capable of. "There isn't room for two women in this house. It simply wouldn't hold us both."

No; that was precisely what he had been thinking. Though he never, being a decent father, would have said so, it was perfectly true. The house, except extremely awkwardly, couldn't hold them both. No house had yet been built which could hold, in peace and comfort, a maiden daughter approaching middle age, and a young second wife. But that Jennifer should see this at once, and clearly, was the last thing he had dreamed of.

He was cautious, however; he felt his way; he wasn't going to be led on into showing his real wishes. "What exactly do you mean by 'have to go'?" he inquired therefore, not committing himself. "Are you suggesting, in spite of what I have been at pains to assure you, that you are being driven from your home?"

She let go his arm, and picked up one of his heavy hands, which hung, when he wasn't using them, oddly inert at his sides, and holding it in both hers said, "If you could see into my heart!"

"I'm glad I can't," said father coldly, determined to proceed carefully. She was talking differently, behaving altogether differently, from her usual tranquil, taciturn fashion. She seemed, he thought, to be bursting; with reproaches, as he had till now supposed, doing his best to prevent the explosion, but it appeared as if he had been wrong, and she were bursting with something else. Strange of Jennifer, he thought, after years of calm, to burst into animation on his wedding day.

"But it's full of nothing but congratulations," she said, earnestly. "For everybody," she added, her rare smile suddenly lighting up her face.

He looked at her, still uncertain. Without her smile, these words might well be taken as acid, as sarcastic, as what the deposed—well, not the deposed, but the supplemented—do say on these occasions. She was, though, undoubtedly smiling, besides pressing his hand with what, also undoubtedly, appeared to be affection, and it did look as if she were, as she had said, congratulating.

Strange, strange, if this were indeed so; and, in a high degree, felicitous. But father was full of doubt. Not so easily did women make way for each other. And what about leaving him, to whom she must naturally be much attached?

He lifted his free hand, and slowly rubbed his nose. It wasn't a word he was searching for this time, but a clue to Jennifer's readiness to go. Probably somewhere at the back of it, he thought doubtfully, there merely lurked the ingredients of a more complicated scene than the one he had been staving off.

"The last thing I wish," he therefore said, not trusting her, feeling it safest to continue to insist on his benevolently fatherly intentions, "and the last thing Netta wishes, is that you should imagine you're not wanted. This is your home, Jennifer. Netta and I both want you to know that."

"It's very nice of Netta," said Jen, another smile breaking her face up into dimples, of which, very wastefully considering her plainness, she had three. "It's very nice of Netta," she said—Netta, of whom till an hour ago she had never heard!—"but she can't possibly want a stepdaughter years older than herself for ever hanging round."

No; that was precisely what he had been thinking—or rather feeling, for prepared to do his duty he hadn't put it into so many words. But that his daughter should say it was really very unexpected. Of course if she were sincere and candid, she was being astonishingly sensible. He had always known she was sensible, but not that she was astonishingly sensible. Was he making discoveries, after over thirty years? Did Jennifer really possess the gift of knowing exactly when to go? It was a great gift; the most valuable, perhaps, of all in a family. And to go pleasantly into the bargain, leaving the atmosphere behind her clear of the slightest trace of acrimonious smoke. …

Still—

Father, looking at her and slowly rubbing his nose, clouded over again. For, after all, to possess the gift wasn't enough. There had to be somewhere to which one went; and where was Jennifer to go? He, with his new responsibilities, certainly couldn't afford to keep her anywhere except at home. His books didn't bring in much. Though everybody had heard of him, not many read him. And if one mouth more to feed at home wasn't serious, it became very serious when the mouth was somewhere else.

So he looked at her, his face fallen into gloom. Years ago he had, for one reason or another, withdrawn from further contact with his own relations, while as for Marian's, regarded as refuges they were quite useless, being undesirable, scattered and poor. Where, then, could she go?

"This is idle talk," he said, with the acidity of disappointment. "Even if I wished it, which I emphatically do not—do you hear, Jennifer? I say I emphatically do *not*—what would you live on? Now that I have Netta to think of, I couldn't possibly—"

"Oh, father—as though I'd dream of it!" she interrupted quickly. "Why, I've got my hundred a year of mother's, and there's an immense amount of good living to be got out of a hundred a year for those who know how to manage—me, for instance. I'm quite sure that all I'll have to go in for is judicious eliminations."

Judicious eliminations. Where had she got such an expression from? She hardly ever talked. He had vaguely taken for granted that she knew only such words as he dictated to her. Judicious eliminations. Ridiculous.

He pulled his imprisoned hand free. A hundred a year. Yes, he remembered she had that; Marian, very foolishly as he had felt at the time, had left it to her. But what nonsense to suppose she could live on a hundred a year. How could he, Richard Dodge, well known in two continents, praised and admired, if little read—and he was little read only because the number of people capable of appreciating perfect writing was limited—allow his daughter to try to? In decency he couldn't. If people saw his daughter spending her time in doing what she called judiciously eliminating—

No, there was no escape for him. Saddled, he was; saddled. The relief he had for a moment supposed was going to be his was mere mirage. She should have married years ago.

"You talk like a child," he said, angrily because he so much wanted her to go. "A hundred a year for a person unpractised in poverty is starvation." And it was at this point that he advanced the thesis, in exasperated tones, that home was the natural, the only place, for maiden daughters, and that she irrelevantly remarked that she was thirty-three, and that he asked whether being thirty-three altered the fact that she was a maiden daughter, did not, indeed—he was too deeply disappointed to be polite—if anything make it worse; and as by this time his voice had grown loud, it could be heard all over the house, including the front diningroom, where she who but such a little while ago had been rather fortunately, as she gradually began to think, still called Baines, was becoming more and more possessed by the idea, while she listened to the voices in the hall, that her distinguished bridegroom and his elderly daughter were having what most people would call a set-to with the gloves.

She sat listening. How unlike his books this was, she thought, alarm gathering in her young eyes, those books which her relations admired so much for their serenity and their bland beauty, and which she, too, carried away by the prevailing enthusiasm of her family, had read, and thought so wonderful. Ought she, she wondered anxiously as the sounds grew louder, to do anything about it? She hoped not. She was no good at all at separating fighters. When her dog fought, it was her practice to flee and wait. Still, her distinguished bridegroom was really making a great noise, and if he had had four legs, and a tail and things, ten to one somebody resourceful would have rushed out and peppered him.

Hesitating, but deeply impressed by the way he was talking, she did at last get up and creep to the door, and presently, after a further period of attention and uneasy listening—for though it was a good thing, she was sure, that there should be beautiful books, was it a good thing, she for the first time doubtfully asked herself, to marry the people who wrote them?—she opened it a slit, and nervously put her charming head out.

"There now," said father to Jennifer, very angry indeed—fuss, fuss, fuss after all. He had done everything a man could to escape just this.

"*I* wasn't making a noise," Jen retorted—actually retorted, and gaily too. Never within his recollection had she retorted, let alone gaily.

"I hope," hesitated the enchanting young person in the door, opening it a little wider, and looking at her pink bridegroom and her pasty stepdaughter with anxious goodwill, "there isn't anything I can do? Because if there is"—she paused helplessly, gazing at the pair—"I don't believe I could."

CHAPTER II

Jennifer laughed as she thought of this scene a week later, when, having worked hard and conscientiously since the departure of the honeymooners at re-arranging the house and disentangling the important fifth chapter, she slammed the front door behind her and ran down the steps, off for the Friday to Monday into the country—off, indeed, for the first unhampered holiday of her life.

She had made up her mind. She knew what she was going to do. No good arguing, she realised in the hall on the wedding day, when her delicious new relative, all eyelashes and alarm, came out of the diningroom prepared, in the interests of harmony, to do what she could. Better pretend to give in and agree. Departure could take place later—flight, if necessary. Flight probably would be necessary. There came a moment, she imagined, in the lives of most unmarried daughters, and perhaps in other people's too, when they must either bolt or go permanently under. Bolting would be what she would do—departure, that is—with the same secret suddenness with which father had got married. There was much to be said, she too now perceived, for secrecy and suddenness in family affairs. It saved talk, and averted obstructions. Besides, if she bolted, father, who was, she was perfectly aware, longing to be rid of her, would be able to put all the blame on her, and while being infinitely relieved and pleased really, would yet have the satisfaction of calling her heartless and ungrateful.

All this she saw in a flash when Netta nervously emerged from the diningroom. What she had to do at that moment was to agree to everything, and get the couple off in time to catch their train. When they were safely gone she could make her plans at leisure, for they weren't coming back, father had said, for a month. Silly of her to have argued, and made poor father cross. She ought at once to have seen the line to take.

She did see it, however, in a flash when Netta came into the hall looking so anxious; and breaking away from father's anger, and cutting short the indignant descriptions of herself that he was giving his alarmed bride, she had hastily kissed him—how extraordinary it was of her to do that, only she and he knew, but at that great moment she would have done anything—and rushed upstairs and got his things together. Trains won't wait. Travellers must catch them. Happy people like honeymooners must certainly catch them.

Just at the last, when the taxi was at the door, Netta hadn't seemed to want to catch anything very much, and Jen had had to encourage her with cheerful words. It would never do for her suddenly to jib, and refuse to carry out her part in promoting the family happiness. Everything clearly depended on Netta, who had so miraculously descended on Gower Street like some blessed unction from above, smoothing out the dismal ruts life there had got into, willing, for some reason Jen hadn't had time to discover, to take on father. Jen, her heart very warm towards her, had given her an affectionate, grateful goodbye hug, and then found that Netta didn't let go. She went on clinging. Jen had had to disentangle herself. There, waiting impatiently, was father; there, waiting expensively, was the taxi. "Oh, but you'll *like* it!" she had assured Netta, in answer to she didn't know what unspoken doubt, anxiously urging her towards the front door; and then for an instant had wondered what it was that Netta was going to like.

Well, but she was going to like father, of course. She would like him very much, Jen was certain. He would be quite different with his young wife from what he had been with his stodgy daughter. Look at him, helping her into the taxi so carefully, he who always got into everything first. Probably she, Jen, hadn't an idea how nice father could be, given really attractive material to work on. That slender loveliness he had married, that delicate, honeysuckle beauty, would probably bring out sides in him no one had yet seen. A man had to be given a chance, thought Jen, as she stood on the steps benevolently watching the departure. Father hadn't had much of a chance with her, she knew. She was tired herself of her dull face, her serious, dull face, and she only saw it occasionally, so what must father be, who saw it all the time? Oh, Netta was going to be very happy with her distinguished and devoted husband. They were all going to be very happy—Netta with father, father with Netta, and she herself (was this a proper thought to have? She hoped so, for she had certainly got it) so gloriously without either of them.

"Goodbye! Good luck! Bless you both!" she called out—very familiarly, father considered, who was wholly unaccustomed to being blessed by Jennifer—waving her handkerchief with the strange new exuberance which so much surprised and disconcerted him.

And he would have been still more surprised and disconcerted had he known that she went back into the house singing.

Singing. At the top of her voice. She who never so much as hummed, who never even wanted to hum, and wouldn't have done so on any account, because father hated noise.

No noise was allowed in that house. If Minnie the cook, who had been with them fifteen years, and Maud the housemaid, who had been with them seven, wished to laugh, they had first to shut all the doors. If street musicians tried to ply Gower Street with music, on such occasions as they came near enough for him to hear, father went out himself and injuriously addressed them. Cats hymning their loves, and canaries voicing their despairs, were abhorrent to him. Dogs he detested, and wouldn't suffer to cross his threshold. The house lived an almost inaudible existence. In silence its daily routine was gone through. Quiet voices and soft footsteps were fixed habits. The doors had the best-oiled hinges in London. There was a clock on the stairs which ticked rather coarsely, and there was the inevitable tapping of Jen's typewriter, but otherwise all was subdued, muffled, reverential.

And now here was Jen singing, and audaciously singing, like some exultant thrush on a fine spring morning, as she hurried into the back diningroom to tidy up her day's work, and for the first time saw that dull spot not as a prison, not as a gloomy frame within which sat an ageing girl doggedly performing duties that would never end, but as a jumping-off place from which one flung oneself into glory. Incredible that only that morning she had had no idea how close she was to bliss! One should trust more, she thought as she trilled, as she rouladed, as she scuttled the papers away into a drawer as if they were no longer of the least consequence. Why had she given herself up to such blank resignations? Nobody could tell what Providence had up its sleeve. Just one single day, not even a whole one yet, and here she was with father happily provided for, her promise to her mother faithfully kept, her duty honourably discharged and done with, and, stretching out ahead of her, the whole of life waiting to do what she liked with.

Papa is wed, and I am free,
O blessèd state of liberty!

she sang, the words coming into her head from she didn't know where, ready fitted to what seemed a most inspired and admirable tune.

The house shivered to hear it. Minnie the cook, alone in the basement because it was Maud the housemaid's day out, felt her blood go curdled at these sounds. What was happening upstairs that afternoon? What was Miss Jen about, making a noise like that?

Minnie had already noticed several other unaccustomed noises since tea—the master, for instance, being angry in the hall, and Miss Jen actually answering back. And she had seen things, too—from the kitchen window she had seen a taxi driving away with the master and a lady in it, and Miss Jen waving her handkerchief just as if there hadn't been a row a few minutes before. And the lady—what was she doing there? No lady ever came to the house, yet this one had certainly got in, because Minnie had seen her getting out, and you can't get out, she reasoned, if you haven't first got in. The front door bell hadn't been rung, though, or Minnie would have answered it. How she had got in Minnie couldn't think. All she knew about her was feet—tiny ones, with high heels—going down the steps, and very thin legs like a child's, and a back being helped by the master—funny to see him helping anybody—into the taxi.

These things she had noticed—impossible not to, in a house that went by clockwork—yet no idea of their true meaning entered her head. Such an explanation would never have occurred to her who had assisted at the laying out, so many years ago, of her poor dead mistress, and had seen her young lady growing sober and spiritless before her eyes, and watched her master growing old and bald; and it wasn't till Jennifer began to sing that she became definitely uneasy.

Perhaps she had better go up and see what was wrong. It wasn't like her young lady to sound happy like that. It gave Minnie as much of a cold turn as if a mouse had sat down in front of her and started hallelujahing in her face. There was the tea to clear away. She would have to go up anyhow. She would fetch it out of the dining-room, and have a look at her young lady on the way, and see if she weren't feverish.

"Minnie—what do you think? Father's married!" Jen called over her shoulder when she heard her passing the back diningroom door, breaking off her song and looking round at her more excited and wide awake than Minnie had ever seen her.

"*That's* no news, Miss," said Minnie quietly, pausing and scrutinising her young lady's face with anxious concern. Was she sickening for something? No one, thought Minnie, who wasn't, would think of such a silly thing to say as that.

She therefore humoured her, as one humours those with temperatures, and said quietly, "*That's* no news, Miss. Since I known 'im 'e's been that."

"But he *is*, I tell you," cried Jen, banging the drawer to on the manuscripts, and going over quickly to Minnie and giving her sleeve an excited tug. "All over again. Quite fresh and new. This very day."

And Minnie answered, incredulous, still not sure this mightn't be the beginning of measles, "If it's true, it's nothing to sing about, Miss, and if it ain't, then I think you'd best go to bed, and take a couple of aspirates."

And Jen said, "But it *is* true. She was here this afternoon. They've gone to Norway. They won't be back for a month."

And Minnie said, "Then it's a disgrace."

And Jen said, laughing at her shocked face, "Oh, poor father—don't you want him to be happy?"

And Minnie said, very stern as she thought of father's bald head, and those spindly child's legs going down the steps, "Not at 'is age, I don't. Nor that way, neither."

❦

But that was a week ago; last Friday, to be exact; and Minnie had come considerably into line since then, and though she talked darkly of no fools like old fools—she begged Miss Jen's pardon; what she meant to say was no gentlemen like old gentlemen—threw herself into the cleaning of the house with vigour. And when, a little afraid of how she might take it, Jen broke to her that she intended setting up on her own, and was going to spend each week-end during father's absence scouring England in search of the smallest, cheapest, and remotest place to do it in, Minnie, to her relief, wholeheartedly sympathised.

All stepmothers, according to Minnie, who had only seen this one's legs, were cruel, and Miss Jen—indeed there was nothing to laugh at—had much best go before she was driven out. Minnie's sole concern seemed to be that where she went should be respectable, for this setting forth alone into the world was a ticklish business, she said, and Miss Jen hadn't an idea how many wicked people there were about, waiting to prey on a young lady. How should she, shut up all her life working the way she did, and not seeing a soul except that old Sir John What's-his-name, when he came to dinner once in a blue moon? And she went down to the kitchen, and fetched a paper called the *Sussex Churchgoer*, a weekly publication with which she, very churchy and born in Sussex, solaced her Sunday afternoons, and suggested that Jen should study its advertisements.

No addresses, explained Minnie, were permitted to appear in its columns which were not personally known to and recommended by the local clergymen. Miss Jen couldn't go wrong in Sussex, said Minnie, if she kept well inland and trusted the *Churchgoer*. There wasn't a county in England nor a body of clergy to touch it, if one avoided its coast, Minnie assured her, for a young lady who had to leave home because of a stepmother, and wanted to be quiet and safe.

❦

So Jen, on that bright first day of freedom, went to Sussex, a bag in one hand, an umbrella in the other, and the *Churchgoer*, with pencil marks against the most likely addresses, pressed tightly under her arm. What did it matter where she went, she thought, so long as it was country? She longed for the country, had longed for it all her life, with a violence nobody would have imagined could exist in the quiet figure bending over a typewriter and industriously tapping. Her mother had longed too, but had had to do the best she could with window-boxes instead. Father wouldn't budge from Gower Street. He was like Doctor Johnson in his affection for pavements. The time of roses, or of the harvest moon, was nothing to father. He had no wish to smell hot grass on a summer day, or the young leaves of silver birches in April. He could apprehend these things without moving from his comfortable revolving chair, and he did apprehend them, embodying them in exquisite description presently to be copied out by Jen, who wondered sometimes, as she copied, whether it were better to know without having felt, like father, or feel without having known, like herself.

Certainly she knew which was the more painful. In Gower Street he stuck, and therefore she stuck too. In Gower Street her mother had lived and died, thwarted but uncomplaining, pining for the country, and never getting there, seeking solace in her window-boxes; and Jen, inheriting the longing and the window-boxes, had suppressed the one, and tended the other with pious, melancholy solicitude.

But there is little real satisfaction to be got out of window-boxes, especially in winter; and often, as she took her afternoon exercise in the London streets—father was punctilious in regard to exercise, regarding it as essential to health and good work, and sent her out daily to take the proper amount, while he, in another direction (for there had to be some relief from her company), and by himself, (for he was a man who didn't like his friends) took his—often she had thought, lingering outside the flowershops and gazing through the windows at their lovely treasures, "Shall I *never* be anywhere where things like these grow? Where I might even grow some of them myself?"

It seemed impossible; the idlest of dreams. And now, positively, she was going to—going to live where she liked, and grow what she liked within the limits of her hundred a year, free to satisfy every wish so long as it didn't cost much. Oh, all her wishes were so cheap, she said to herself, as she went into the Post Office where her savings were, on her way to Victoria, and drew out twenty pounds so as to be ready for anything. A dandelion would do instead of a rose, if she couldn't have a rose. She was, she was sure, infinitely flexible, able to fit into the humblest little corner and enjoy herself in it, if only she could be in it alone. Freedom, personal freedom, the right to be alone, was what she wanted, and what she now so miraculously had got; the power to behave naturally, to make one's own arrangements, to decide (it seemed a little thing but was, she was certain, the whole difference between vigour and wilting) what one would do next. Never yet had she been alone, and never, since her mother's death, except in her bedroom, relaxed and natural. How could she be natural with father, who had always had the whip hand of her, if only for the reason that, like other parents, he had got there first? And as for relaxed, she would like to see herself relaxing in his presence. On his wedding day, the shock of suddenly being freed had produced an audacious liveliness in her she had never shown before, and how angry it had made him! From the very beginning, long before he became her sole care and duty, he had imposed pretences, forced her to take cover in insincerities. Yes, father; no, father; she could hear her hasty, anxious agreeing when she was a child.

"Sign here, please," said the clerk.

She signed, and looked, smiling, at the young man, not seeing him, absorbed in her bright thoughts. Miraculously all that was over, and here she was on her own feet, responsible to nobody, healthy, inconspicuous, and with two pounds a week certain for the rest of her life. Could happiness be more complete?

He smiled back, because Jen's smile, so sweet and transforming, was very apt to produce another in response. She didn't see that either, and gathering up the notes tucked them into her blouse and continued on her way to Victoria, still absorbed, for she was thinking how tragic it would have been if she had had to go on being father's prop and stay till she was too old to know what to do with freedom when she got it.

But she hadn't had to. It had arrived in the nick of time, just when she was the exact right age—young enough to adore the fun of adventurously setting out like this, without an idea where she was going to sleep that night, and old enough for no one to be able to say that living entirely alone wasn't proper.

Not that she would care, if anybody did say it—*Papa is wed, and I am free.* … The words, the tune, wouldn't go out of her head. They danced triumphantly round and round. Her feet kept time with them. Nobody in the world now had a right to say anything to anything she did. *O blessèd state of liberty!*

In all England there wasn't a happier creature than Jennifer as she got out of the train two hours later at Amberton, which was the nearest place with a station to the addresses she had chosen in the *Churchgoer*, and having asked a porter the way walked off briskly along the road, through beech woods, which leads up on to the downs in the direction of Benendon St. Michael, and is one of the most beautiful in Sussex; a road white with dust that morning, for it was August, and there had been no rain for many days.

❦

The porter at the station called her mum. Satisfactory; most satisfactory.

He took her for a mum, of course, because of her figure, which father had liked so little that all his heroines were almost consumptively thin. It delighted her to know how usefully now this figure, of which she too had thought poorly till then, was coming in. Thanks to its solidity and weight, she would be taken for somebody's widow, and those who let lodgings would applaud her, rather than criticise, for being alone.

Great were the advantages, perceived Jen, twirling her umbrella as she gaily stepped out, hardly feeling that she was carrying a bag so much was she exhilarated, of looking like a mum and yet not being one. There wasn't a single mum in the world she would have changed places with that morning—poor, tethered creatures, all taking care of some man and his house and servants; while as for the advantages of being plain, what could be more evident? Why, she couldn't have done anything by herself if she had been Netta, for instance, and had had to take all those eyelashes about with her wherever she went. What would have become of her? Nothing good, she was certain; nothing lastingly good, like freedom. Such eyelashes were doomed to attract notice and rouse acquisitiveness, and their owner's melancholy fate was capture. Oh, many and precious were the compensations of the homely, she thought in great contentment; and a sudden steep bit of road seeming to dare her to show her mettle, she grasped her bag and umbrella more firmly and broke into a run, and ran part of the way up it, slowing down presently for want of breath, and arriving panting, but amused by her own absurdity, at the top, where the woods on that road leave off, and the open downs begin.

❦

On the Sussex downs that day it was very beautiful; it would have been impossible to find anything anywhere more beautiful, and even persons accustomed to beauty would have had to stop and look.

Jen wasn't accustomed to beauty, and she stopped dead, and such breath as she still had after running up the hill was taken away. She stood and gazed, her mouth a little open. It seemed to be half England she saw from up there, lying shimmering in August ripeness at her feet. Far away sparkled the sea, and its saltness was mixed with the other scents which came, all honeyed, to meet her, and wandered over her face, and kissed her throat, lifting her hair behind her ears, playing about the back of her neck, and behaving exactly, though she didn't know it because of never having had one, like a lover.

She put her bag and umbrella down in the grass by the road, and took off her hat so that this sweet air should cool her forehead. She held her arms away from her body, so that it should encircle her with freshness. Just in front of her the road nosed its way gently between fringes of flowers whose names, prisoner of Gower Street that she was, she didn't know—frail lilac things on slender stalks, little pink things in tufts close to the ground, vivid yellow things with bees swaying on them, brilliant blue things crowded round by butterflies, starry white things, their faces turned up boldly to the sun—all living and shining in a world made wholly that day of light, and scent, and colour.

Her face was sober with wonder. Those years in the back diningroom, like some dark tunnel through which one emerges into sunshine, had ended for her in glory. All the time she had been so miserable, she had really been heading straight for this. She was awestruck. Such great and unexpected blessings should bring forth fruit, she vowed, and she would show her gratitude by seeing to it that they did. Solemnly, bareheaded, she lifted up her face to the splendid light, and vowed there should be fruit, though not yet quite knowing what sort of fruit, on a hundred a year, could best be encouraged; but there must be kinds which would flourish even on a poor soil, if tended with determination.

Father had said—but then he was angry because he so much wanted to get rid of her, and didn't see how he decently could—that nobody unpractised in poverty could live on a hundred a year, except in acute discomfort. Well, she was going to show him that one woman, anyhow, not only could live on it happily, but also, in some way presently to be decided, make her life fruitful; show him, that is—she hesitated, passed her hand over her thick, pale hair, and put on her hat again—if he would come and look.

But father—

❦

Doubts assailed her as to father's ever wanting to come and look. She stooped and picked up her bag and umbrella, smiling, but also sighing, at the thought of how little he loved her. In fact, little was putting it too high; he didn't love her at all. And she smiled because, if he had, she wouldn't now be free, for love, she judged, must be a great imprisoner, a great cutter-off of liberty; and she sighed because, just for a moment, for the briefest moment, it seemed as if love, with all its imprisonments and cuttings-off, must yet be sweet.

Impossible, however, to have it both ways, she told herself as she walked on towards Benendon St. Michael. Such freedom as hers, magnificent and complete, was bound to include freedom from love. And seeing that she hadn't got love anyhow, that since her mother died she hadn't had a scrap of it, and had grown quite used to doing without things like kisses and soft words, what did it matter?

It didn't matter; it mattered less than nothing; and the day getting hotter, and the road being sunny now all the way, she soon left off thinking, because almost immediately, walking on those shadeless heights, she entered into the peace of perspiration, and everything except consciousness of physical well-being went out of her head.

Hardly ever in London had she been able to get really hot, really into that happy, dissolved, and relaxed state of body which so felicitously at the same time dissolves, relaxes, and pacifies the spirit. Once, desperately, on a July afternoon, when the morning's work had gone wrong and father had been cross, she had managed to perspire herself back to patience by taking an omnibus to the foot of Primrose Hill and then walking very quickly up and down its asphalt paths in the sun ten times without stopping. But this she had found both dull and conspicuous, and she laughed as she thought of her dogged determination not to leave those slopes till she perspired, the I-will-not-let-thee-go-until-thou-bless-me attitude, the time it took before the wretched place did bless her, the astonished faces of the people she met, of the people on seats who kept on seeing her striding by, and the steadily increasing distrust of the policeman at the bottom of the hill.

Well, no more would she need go in search of stretching. Both the cottages she had marked in the *Churchgoer* had gardens, and in whatever garden she ultimately anchored, whether in one of these or in some other of whose existence she wasn't yet aware, she was going to dig; and, digging, perspire; and, perspiring, be happy. And presently, she supposed, the contours father deplored—she had seen him deploring, though he never said anything, whenever his eye dwelt on her figure—would disappear; those contours she was now finding so useful in giving her dignity, in giving her a presence, in causing porters to call her mum, and which she had, after all, inherited from him.

Father had a very conspicuous contour in his middle.

❦

At Benendon St. Michael, the cottage advertised had a garden described in the *Churchgoer* as pretty, with plenty of fruit and vegetables. At Cherry Lidgate, a village four miles farther on—she had carefully looked them both up in an ordnance map—the cottage advertised had a small orchard as well as a garden. Really her only difficulty would be to choose which one she would have.

True, each had what some people might call a drawback—easily to be overcome, however, Jen was sure, who on that bright morning of escape felt capable of dealing with the drawbacks of the whole world. Besides, it was precisely the drawbacks which made the cottages cheap; and though, in spite of what father had said, she didn't doubt she could live well and comfortably on a hundred a year, especially if she grew vegetables and then ate them, she yet felt it desirable that as little as possible of her income should go on rent.

These two cottages were far the cheapest in the *Churchgoer*. Everything else was either too dear, or not a cottage at all but a family wishing to bestow loving care on somebody who was an invalid or feebleminded. Nearly everybody in the *Churchgoer*'s advertising columns seemed to be full of loving care, and wanting to bestow it. The milk of human kindness ran down its pages as though, thought Jen, they were some holy beard. Even the cottages, and certainly the lodgings offered, had an ointment-like flavour about their description; and what with this flavour, and the *Churchgoer* being a publication devoted entirely to the doings and needs of the Sussex clergy, she wasn't surprised that both the addresses she had picked out should be those of clergymen.

Father didn't care about clergymen, who, for their part, judging from the allusions to his works in clerical papers, rather violently didn't care about him; but if their cottages were watertight and cheap, she would as soon live in one of them as in anybody else's. She was without prejudices. Fate, represented by Minnie, had thrown the cottages of clerics in her way, and they would do as well as other people's. She had no objection to clerics. Neither had father, who didn't care about them in the sense that he didn't mind them one way or the other. A bland indifference to their doings, indeed to their existence, was, and always had been, father's attitude. Churches, creeds and dogma were nothing to him. They had been left out of Jen's upbringing, and accordingly were nothing to her either. She had never spoken to a clergyman in her life; she hadn't been christened, but registered; on her head no bishop had laid hands in Confirmation; and the extreme tolerance of complete want of interest in anything to do with orthodox religion pervaded the upper floors of the house in Gower Street, while, in the basement, Minnie the cook continued passionately christian.

❦

Out of this pagan atmosphere, so entirely empty of clergymen, came Jennifer that August morning, and approached the village of Benendon St. Michael filled with desire to become, if she possibly could, the tenant of a vicar. More: if persuasion could do it, she desired to become his tenant then and there—for then and there, she had realised during her two hours' quiet thinking in the train, was what she certainly ought to aim at, and if persuasion should avail her nothing at Benendon St. Michael, then she would go on to Cherry Lidgate, and try the other man.

She hoped, however, that she wouldn't have to go on. It seemed evident that these vicars couldn't have advertised merely in order to refuse. And why should they refuse? Here was a steady, reliable-looking applicant—think how respectful the porter had been!—who might well be a widow, and anyhow would undertake to behave like one, with twenty pounds inside her blouse, and able and willing to pay the rent in advance. Why, they would probably jump at her, and she would secure what she wanted this very first week-end. That, of course, thought Jen, a wave of optimism washing over her, would be perfect, for then she could use the other week-ends the honeymoon lasted in getting her nest ready, so that, having kept her promise not to leave Gower Street before the newly-married pair's return, and having duly welcomed them and handed over the house and servants to Netta, she would be able to announce to father that she had got a home, that he needn't give her a thought ever again, and, certainly to his relief and perhaps with his benediction, come away at once, and start her lovely new life.

Alight with confidence, she walked the remaining six hot miles to Benendon St. Michael, and towards the end couldn't believe there weren't sixteen of them. Who could have dreamed, she thought, that miles could be so long? It was a good thing she was full inside of hope and determination, for by the time she had done four, though her spirit, because of all this hope, was as brisk as ever, her feet weren't, and began to get in her way a good deal, and by the time she had done five, it was plain to her that of the two cottages the first she came to would be the most suitable. But it was, in any case, the better one, having the great advantage of being furnished—simply but adequately, said the *Churchgoer*—and of costing, even furnished, only as much a week as the Cherry Lidgate one was to cost with nothing in it; so that, except that it hadn't got an orchard, and after all orchards weren't everything, it really was the more desirable of the two.

Yes; the first one for her, thought Jen, whose chief desire now was to leave off having to walk. True, there was its drawback, or rather that which some people (not herself) might regard as such; but the other one had a drawback too, and a much worse one, because at least at Benendon St. Michael the drawback halved the rent, while at Cherry Lidgate it had no apparent effect on the rent whatever, and was just pure drawback. All one had to do in order to secure this first one, with its simple but adequate furniture, for five shillings a week, was to play the organ at the children's services on Sunday afternoons. If one were not willing to do this, one could still have the cottage, but it would cost twice as much.

Well, there was nothing in organs, thought Jen, who hadn't yet played any, but didn't see why she shouldn't begin; they were very like pianos, except that they had pedals and stops, and she could play pianos. Who wouldn't be willing to take on an organ, and halve the rent? She felt perfectly willing. Besides, one sat down to play an organ, and the idea of sitting down in a cool, shady church, was beautiful to her as she trudged along and the sun beat on her shoulders. As for pedals and stops, you trod on one and pulled out the other. There could be no real difficulty. She declined to believe that an ordinary sensible woman wouldn't be able to deal with them if she gave her mind to it. Shut her up alone with an organ for a reasonable time, and she felt sure she would emerge its master.

The farther she walked, the surer she became; and when at last she arrived at Benendon St. Michael, and, inquiring for the Vicarage, dragged her feet, which seemed curiously and very painfully to have outgrown the shoes which that morning had fitted them so comfortably, to its door and rang the bell, she was ready to promise to play anything, if only, in a cool place, she might sit down.

❦

The Vicar was out; but the neat maid, who opened the door, dressed already in her afternoon black, for it was only a few minutes to lunch-time, said he was bound to return almost immediately—and, "Won't you come in, mum, and wait?" she added, stepping aside invitingly.

Mum, again. Jen sighed with pleasure. And she was yet more gratified when she found herself left confidingly alone in what appeared to be a study. So she did look trustworthy, she did look like the kind of person vicars would want to let their cottages to, in spite of her warm disorder and the state her shoes were in. That her reliableness should pierce through disorder and dust was really most reassuring.

The maid, having politely asked her to sit down, and again told her that the Vicar couldn't possibly be long, because he was never known to be late for meals, shut the door and went away, and Jen, sinking into the chair beside the writing-table, put her bag down on the carpet beside her, propped her umbrella against her knees, and thought how delicious it was to be able to rest in a nice, cool, shady place like this.

It was the coolest and shadiest place, she decided presently, that she had ever been in; and it seemed to become cooler and shadier every minute. The room faced north, and close up to its single tall window grew some of the yew-trees which, she supposed, would naturally collect round clergymen. Yew-trees, churchyards, clergymen—they would hang together, surmised Jen, acknowledging, even as she surmised, that she was ignorant. Photographs of people who looked like wives hung on the walls, interrupted at intervals by photographs of college buildings, and of groups of persons dressed alike—boy scouts, volunteer rifle corps, cricket elevens, football teams and such, within the middle of each group an older individual taking evident pains to show that he felt jolly. There was a singular cold smell about, which, she concluded after a period of interrogation, was the smell of abstinences—the smell of not being smoked in, not being laughed in, not being loved in; very like, in fact, the smell, or rather the absence of smell, which till now had pervaded the back diningroom in Gower Street. So that she concluded the clergyman she was waiting for had lost his wife, if he had ever had one, and lost her a good while ago, and that if he had ever had any children he hadn't got them now. For some reason, too, she was sure he was a dry and stringy man.

Quietly she sat, trying not to look at anything in the room too particularly, its owner being absent and his possessions at her mercy; and just as she was repeating to herself for the tenth time that the coolness was pleasant, was deeply refreshing, and unconsciously, as she said it, buttoning her alpaca jacket, what was still left of her warmth suddenly altogether left her, and a slow and most disagreeable shiver trickled, like iced water, down her spine.

That was the worst of getting very hot, she thought, shifting uneasily in her chair—unless one either put on some thick things, or had a bath, one suddenly became so very cold. Naturally she couldn't have a bath, nor could she put on anything warm, for she had left her coat at home, not supposing she would need it on such a fine summer's day.

It vexed her now that she should have left it behind, for she didn't want to get a chill and be laid low at this exciting and wonderful moment. It would be the most stupid thing in the world if she were to have to take to some strange, inhospitable bed that night, and not be able to get out of it again on Monday morning and go back to Gower Street to continue her duties.

Colder and colder she grew as the minutes passed, cold with the icy coldness which succeeds perspiration. She fidgetted and shivered, and vainly tried, by holding her arms tight across her chest, to keep a last shred of warmth in; and presently, as the Vicar still didn't come home, and her discomfort, while visions of pneumonia and the ruin of all her hopes played about her imagination, became acute, she gathered up her courage and rang the bell, and when the maid appeared told her she thought she would go outside and wait in the sun, and call again later.

"I've left my coat at home," Jen explained; and described how hot she had got walking over the hilly downs, and how she was gradually becoming chilled to the bones, and how the sun in the village street would warm her again.

The maid, on hearing this, was full of understanding. She was a kind-hearted girl, with a rheumatic mother whom she nursed on her afternoons out; also she was generous and easygoing, and as she had few things of her own to lend was free-handed in lending other people's; and it seemed only natural, the lady being so pleasant and so cold, to find her something to put on, rather than let her go wandering about the village.

"Oh, *dear*," she exclaimed, sympathetically. "Wait a minute, mum—" And she ran and fetched a coat from somewhere down the passage, bringing it back with a face of concern, and wrapping it round the shivering visitor, even buttoning her into it.

Kind girl; nice girl, thought Jen, accepting it thankfully, and not inquiring whose it was—supposing, indeed, that it was the maid's.

But it happened to be the Vicar's winter coat, and he, when he arrived home ten minutes later, and found a strange woman in it, didn't like it at all.

It prejudiced him against Jennifer from the first.

She, intent only on her errand when at last he appeared, forgot, as one does, what she was wearing, and it entirely went out of her mind that she had anything on which wasn't her own. Who thinks of clothes and appearance, who is a single-minded creature concentrating solely on renting a cottage? Therefore, forgetting it, she said nothing about the coat, and every minute the Vicar became more prejudiced; in fact, as time passed and still his caller didn't explain, so deeply prejudiced did he become that he found it difficult to speak.

He sat on the other side of the writing-table, not looking at her, his narrow head slightly bent, while she told him the purpose of her visit, and was increasingly provoked by his inability to say the only thing he really wanted to say, which was, "Why have you got my coat on?" He knew the Duke would have said it at once; he knew the garden-boy would have said it at once; and it added to his annoyance to have it brought so disagreeably to his notice that he belonged to the in-between class which couldn't be simple, and was called—he had always disliked the word—middle.

"So I thought," went on Jen, still hopefully, though slightly dashed by his unresponsiveness, "I'd be willing to play the organ at the children's services."

"Really," said the Vicar, who wasn't listening, his thoughts all on his coat.

"And then the rent would only be five shillings a week," she continued.

"Really," said the Vicar.

"Well," said Jen, after a brief pause during which she felt definitely surprised, "you say so yourself in the advertisement."

"Really," said the Vicar.

"Well—*look* at it," she said, holding out the *Churchgoer*, and pointing to the place.

The Vicar didn't look. His head remained bent sideways, his fingers played with the gold cross which hung on his hollow-looking waistcoat, a waistcoat that nothing he and his cook did could dilate, for he was naturally hollow. Why had she got his coat on? The question absorbed his whole attention. He couldn't possibly listen, or think of anything else, till he knew the answer to that.

A man, in that quiet place, of many inactivities, and possessed of a cook of gifts, a man frequently fed and almost always leisured, he had developed, as time slid by, a faculty for being easily upset. But he was upset silently, as became a clergyman. His resentments padded about inside him with muffled footsteps, and not once in recent years had got out and made a real noise, his wife having been dead some time.

On this occasion, too, his resentment was muffled, in spite of the unusual, the monstrous fact that a strange woman was sitting before him, inexplicably clothed in his own coat. How had she come by it? How dared she not mention it, and apologise? He would discharge Annie, who must know about it, that very afternoon.

What the world was coming to he found it impossible to conceive. And always, each time he tried to lift his head and look at his objectionable visitor squarely in the face, and say, "Why have you got my coat on?" he found he couldn't.

Jennifer thought him a very queer man. Perhaps, however, it was the habit of clergymen to be queer, and sit with their heads turned the other way. How should she know, she who hadn't come across a single one till now, not to speak to and be in the same room with, because of father's being a pagan? And for all she knew, this averted attitude, this extreme reserve, was the usual practice of vicars in dealing with people they hadn't met before.

Perhaps, too, this particular one was shy. His was a remote parish; he lived, probably, the life of a recluse, and no doubt had, with the passage of years, become tongue-tied. Still, shy or not, it did seem odd to announce publicly in a paper that you want to let your cottage, and then go dumb when somebody comes along and wishes to have it. It made it difficult to arrive at agreement. At this rate it would take years to become his tenant, the word *Really*, which was the only one he had as yet emitted, wouldn't get them anywhere; and the day was half over, and soon she would have to be looking for a lodging for the night.

So, overcoming her surprise, and thinking that perhaps she hadn't made herself clear, she leaned forward a little in the hope of catching his averted eye, of seeing his face round its corner, as it were, and once again explained, in the simplest language, her need of a cottage, her desire to live in the country, her willingness, to play an organ, her wish to tend a garden, and the apparent suitability of the one, full of fruit and vegetables, which he had advertised. Politely did Jen talk—politely, and, she hoped, sensibly, in what father had himself admitted was a pleasant voice, finishing up with a request, also most polite, that she might be allowed to go and inspect the property.

"Really," said the Vicar once more, his mind full of one thing only, and deeply inattentive to her words.

"It isn't an unusual request?" asked Jen, beginning to think that perhaps he wasn't quite normal. "I don't see how I can take it if I haven't seen it."

"Seen what?" asked the Vicar absently, fingering his cross.

"Your furnished cottage," said Jen patiently. "The furnished cottage you advertised in the *Sussex Churchgoer*. Last Saturday's. This one that I've marked—"

And again she held the *Churchgoer* out to him, and pointed.

"How can I take it," she inquired, patient but plaintive, "if I haven't seen it?"

But he, coming suddenly to the surface, now jerked his head round and flashed inimical pale eyes at her. "It's not to be let," he said curtly. And it wasn't. Not if he had fifty cottages, all on his hands and he starving, should this woman have one. His coat. His winter coat. Sitting there inside his coat, without a word of explanation …

"Not to let?" repeated Jen, blankly. "Then why—"

"It-is-not-to-be-let," he repeated very distinctly, emphasising each word, "and I am wasting your time."

He got up quickly, crossed to the fireplace, and put his finger on the bell.

Dismissal. Plain, and—yes, surely rather crushing dismissal.

Now why?

Perplexed, she sat staring at his narrow black back, at his bony, big-knuckled finger on the bell. It almost seemed as if what was the matter with the Vicar wasn't shyness, but hostility. It almost seemed as if he disliked her.

But why? Why should he dislike her, when he didn't know her? Did one ever dislike people until one knew them? And what had she said, except that she wanted to rent his cottage? What on earth had she said, except that?

Jen became low-spirited. She became almost as low-spirited as she used to be in the back diningroom. This was the very opposite of being jumped at. It seemed to her now extraordinary that she should ever have imagined she would be. If she produced such an effect on clergymen, then she had better give up the other cottage too, for the other vicar, and for the same mysterious reasons, might also regard her with aversion. Yes—aversion. No good hiding the fact. Aversion was in every line of that turned-away back, of those raised, warding-off shoulders.

She sat drooping. How disappointing, she thought, her head inclined to sink on to her chest; how tiresome. And she was so hungry. And her feet had grown so enormous. If only she knew what she had done!

"Do you mind telling me," she said, drawing herself up again, and earnestly addressing what she could see of him, for the case seemed to call for earnestness, "if I have offended you?"

The case seemed also to call for immediate departure, and as she spoke she began to get up.

But her foot caught in something. Oh, yes—the coat; the immense coat she was buttoned up into.

"Dear me—I was forgetting this," she said, disentangling her foot from its folds, and pushing up the long sleeves, which hung well below where her arms left off, so as to get at the buttons and undo them. "Your maid very kindly—"

She spoke in jerks, busy with the stiff buttonholes.

"I was so cold," she explained, fumbling. "After getting hot. I walked from Amberton. I hope you don't mind. Oh, here she is," she went on, turning to her friend the parlourmaid, who appeared in the door looking a little flustered—perhaps because of the violent ringing of the bell. "Thank you so very much for lending me your coat. I think it has probably saved my life."

"*Her* coat? *My* coat," flung the Vicar, over his bristling shoulder.

"*Your* coat?" echoed Jen staring, pausing in the act of pulling it off.

Light dawned on her. Light dawned on her face as well, which broke into its sweet, transforming smile.

"Ah, why didn't you tell me?" she asked, her voice full of laughter, but full, too, of chagrin. "Why didn't you tell me? I'd so infinitely rather have had the cottage than the coat!"

❦

"Perhaps," thought the Vicar when she had gone, and he sat down at last to his delayed and accordingly ruined luncheon, "she wouldn't have been a bad tenant, in spite of her bad beginning—" For he had seen, over his shoulder, his visitor's attractive smile, and had been taken by it as those few persons who saw it invariably were taken; also, he had no other applicants for the cottage, which had been standing empty, and he having to keep it in repair, for some time.

He consoled himself, however, by reflecting that she probably had an objectionable husband, who would have come down for week-ends and not attended services, and no doubt a destructive child or two; and on Annie's bringing the coffee, in the interests of discipline and of keeping his word to himself, he gave her notice, and then spent the afternoon wishing people wouldn't force him, by their actions, to do that which only ultimately led to his own discomfort.

❦

Outside the village, Jen was sitting down. She sat on a milestone, her feet in the long, cool grass by the roadside, thinking. It was two o'clock, and she was hungry; but its being two o'clock made her chiefly remember that more than half the day was over, and she didn't yet know where she was going to sleep that night. In lodgings, she supposed. Probably she would have to go back to Amberton. All that long way.

She drew her dusty shoes thoughtfully backwards and forwards through the grass to clean them, looking at them without seeing them, for she was still seeing the Vicar. Her face, which had quickly sobered after leaving him, broke into laughter again as she remembered the coat, and herself in it, and that flash round at her of pale, infuriated eyes; and if anyone had been passing along and looking at her he would have thought, "What a *lot* of dimples!"

Not that dimples were of any use to Jen, who was of course aware she had them but had long considered them sheer waste in a face like hers—as meaningless as words stuck down alone without their contexts; yet it was after seeing them that the Vicar had begun to relent, and father, on the few occasions she showed them, each time had definitely warmed towards her.

Her dimples, then, could be more useful than she knew, and sitting on the milestone reflecting on the slightness of the happenings on which our fortunes depend, and how the wearing of a coat had changed the entire lines of her future, she yet had no idea that in her interview with the Vicar if she had chanced to begin, instead of finishing, with a smile, her conduct in regard to the coat would probably have been overlooked, and she might by now have been lunching with him as his accepted tenant.

She knew nothing of this. What she did know was that she was hungry, that her feet were steadily growing bigger and her shoes smaller, that the afternoon was ripening, and that the other cottage, the only remaining string to her bow, was four ghastly miles farther on. Yes—and when she got to it, when she had walked all the ghastly miles, suppose she made some silly mistake again, and said something, or did something, which annoyed this vicar too? How did she know what words or actions annoyed or didn't annoy vicars? The coat, of course, she could see would be likely to annoy anybody, but how could she tell what other things there might be which vicars wouldn't be able to stand? Clergymen were unexplored territory to her, and if she were unfortunate enough to give offence a second time, her weekend would have been wasted, and she would have to struggle back somehow into Amberton, and go into lodgings till it was Monday morning, and her jaunt was over, and Gower Street had to be faced again.

She stooped and opened her bag, and took out some biscuits she had prudently brought with her, and began to eat. Father, she reflected munching them, had been right to wave clerics aside from his life. What she had seen of them up to now she didn't at all like. For her next weekend's search she would study the advertisements in a secular paper, and have nothing more to do with the *Churchgoer*, which had involved her in this expedition. But, while she ate, a robin perched just above her in the hedge watched her brightly, his head attentively cocked, and in a field opposite, cows, grouped beneath a grove of oak-trees, lazily swished their tails in the shade, and dotted over the deep blue of the sky a few white summer-clouds, fat and radiant, hung like suspended, heavenly sheep, and the adventurous road, curving away between hedges sweet that day with traveller's joy, flung its fragrances in her face as it passed, and she couldn't but acknowledge that the *Churchgoer* hadn't done so badly for her after all, bringing her up here and setting her down to eat biscuits in the middle of such beauty.

She did acknowledge it. Whatever happened, she had had a marvellous day in exquisite places; and, feeling much better after the biscuits, she spread the *Churchgoer* out on her knees, and prepared to give her whole attention to what it had to say about the cottage at Cherry Lidgate.

Here is what it said:

> *Unfurnished four-roomed cottage To Let immediately. Five shillings weekly. Good garden. Suit childless couple. Must be church people. Man willing to cut grass and dig occasional graves preferred. Apply Rev. Ollier, Cherry Lidgate, Sussex.*

Not very promising, really. She considered it, her head on one side, while the robin, his head on one side too, almost as if he were impudently imitating, considered her. No, not very promising; and she couldn't now imagine why she had, on first reading it in Gower Street, supposed it would do. Was it because she was tired now, and her confidence had been shaken by the interview she had just had with the unpleasant priest, that the drawback she was aware of, but had disregarded, should suddenly seem so immense?

She sat leaning her elbows on her knees, her eyes fixed on the brief sentences, and went over them one by one and carefully weighed them. After all, she told herself, though it was true she wasn't a couple, on the other hand she was childless, and though it was true she wasn't what could be called church people, she felt she could behave as decorously as anybody in a pew—yes, and without becoming entangled in insincerities either, for who so able wholeheartedly to join in hymns, if they were of praise, and wholeheartedly to say prayers, if they were of gratitude, as one who lately and wonderfully has been set free?

No, this wasn't the difficulty; nor was it the not being a couple; nor the cutting of grass, for she would enjoy doing that. The difficulty was the graves. She couldn't dig graves. She knew she couldn't, however occasional they might be. Graves were, she was afraid, a drawback not to be got round, an obstacle altogether insuperable. And yet, she tried to reassure herself as she sat staring down at the *Churchgoer*, that last sentence only after all expressed a preference, and a preference based on the hypothesis that there would be a man in the cottage. If, now, she argued, the man weren't there, he couldn't dig graves, and it followed that if she got the cottage the grave question would at once cease to exist. But would the Rev. Ollier see it like that? Would she be able to help him to? If he didn't, or if his preference for the kind of person mentioned were strong, then goodbye to the Cherry Lidgate cottage too—it was not for her.

Why, oh why, she passionately inquired, flinging back the wisp of hair that had fallen across her forehead, and in doing so catching the robin's bright and interested eye—"Darling!" she interrupted herself to murmur, blowing him a kiss—why, oh why, had she allowed herself to be wrapped in that vicar's coat? Or, being wrapped, forgotten to explain? His was the cottage, furnished, and with fruit and vegetables, and only an organ to play once a week—a finnicking business compared to graves—in which, she was certain, fate had really meant her to live. And so cheap, too, compared to this one, which hadn't a stick of furniture in it. Even if she succeeded in somehow getting round the graves, her hundred pounds the first year would have the most awful holes made in it by things like a bed, and a chair, and a kettle, and heaven knew what else besides. Why, oh why, had she been such an idiot as to forget to explain at once about that coat?

Well, no good sitting there regretting. She must be up and doing. Having come all this way, she must at least make a try for Cherry Lidgate; and as the afternoon wouldn't last for ever, and she still had four miles to' go, she had better be getting on.

So scrambling with some difficulty to her swollen feet, she got on; and, as she painfully trudged, reminded herself how at this hour on this day a week ago she was aimlessly taking such exercise as the detested London streets could give, without a notion that when the same day came round again here she would be, up in what, compared to them, or indeed compared to anything, was surely heaven; and in this way, renewing her appreciation of her great good fortune, she took fresh courage.

There wasn't much to grumble about, she thought, holding up her head and putting her best foot foremost. But even her best foot was by this time very bad, and she had to use the umbrella she had twirled so gaily a few hours earlier as a stick to help it along. The bag, too, had begun to hurt, chafing her fingers and growing steadily heavier, and the four miles, advance with what doggedness she might, continued to stretch and stretch on ahead instead of ending, while such signposts as she came to, however long it had been since she passed the last one, still said there were three more miles to Cherry Lidgate.

That was because she had lost her way. She lost it twice in the hot, intricate lanes deep sunk between their hedges, and not till half-past four, covered with dust, limping, and at her last gasp, did she, turning a corner, see a church, see a house next to it behind a high garden wall, see a gate in the high garden wall, and, most heartening, most delightful sight of all, see the gate being opened at that very moment by somebody she at once, and rightly, concluded was the Rev. Ollier.

CHAPTER III

He, called so in the advertisement for brevity's, and therefore economy's, sake, had no idea that the deliquescent figure's goal was himself. Nor had he any idea that during the whole time he was leisurely lunching, comfortably smoking, pleasantly occupying himself among his roses killing greenfly, attentively considering the sky in hope of rain and, having considered it and found no hope, going in to tap the barometer and remark on its obstinate height to his sister Alice, who, as was her habit when he said anything, sniffed—he had no idea that during the whole time he had been doing these things, up there in the sunflecked, stony lanes, threading its painful but determined way through their intricacies, the figure he now beheld was bearing slowly down on him, slowly, surely, and inescapably, he would have said could he have seen into the immediate future, as Fate. There it was, come five hundred yards nearer while he, in his study gazing idly out of the window, wondered whether his sermon for the following Sunday were too short, and decided that no sermon could ever be too short; there it was, come another five hundred yards nearer while he, reminded by the rose-bushes his eye was resting on, of their battening, ferocious greenfly, turned to his bookshelves and for a space pored over an article on aphis in his gardening encyclopaedia; and though at three o'clock, when, feeling he ought to resume parochial duties in spite of having no real business till four, he took down his hat and departed to the village in conscientious search of work, the approaching figure was still two miles away, by a quarter to five, on his returning home to tea cool and fresh from a funeral, it had managed to get as close as the corner of his garden wall, and round this corner, just as he was in the act of opening his gate, Jennifer loomed, and on seeing the black-coated, dog-collared man took fresh courage, for who could he be but Ollier?

At the sight she broke into a kind of tottering run, in case he should disappear through the gate before she reached him, and having got close to him she dropped her bag on the path, straightened herself, heaved a great, pleased sigh, and said, "*Oh*, what a relief!"

Naturally Mr. Ollier, who had observed her unsteady approach with surprise, was startled. He paused in the act of unlatching his gate, and gazed inquiringly at the heated lady before him. The happy circumstance—at least, he had frequently been told by his sister Alice that it was happy—of having an influential godfather had made him a vicar long before the usual time, and though he had been at Cherry Lidgate over two years, he still wasn't quite twenty-seven when Jennifer appeared round the corner and dropped her bag with, he thought afterwards remembering it, a symbolic gesture of dropping anchor in port, at his feet.

But at the moment he was merely startled, and looked at her nervously.

"Are you Mr. Ollier?" he heard her ask in a voice he even then noticed was singularly delightful.

She asked the question softly, as if it were almost too good to be true that the very first person she came across should be the man she wanted, and that she needn't walk any more; and she smiled at him as instinctively as everybody else smiled at him, for Mr. Ollier roused goodwill, he inspired trust, and little children thrust their hands into his unasked.

At her question he laid hold mechanically of his speckled straw hat. It was pushed back rather far off a forehead which had, during the last year or two, in spite of his being so young, become much higher. They were a bald race, the Olliers, and his sister Alice, who was fifteen years older than himself, had long been obliged to re-stock her hair from shops—greatly to her disgust, for she hated subterfuge, but how could she, being a woman, she asked indignantly of Lady Higgs her neighbour, who was rich and had her confidence, go about bald? And Lady Higgs said she couldn't.

"Yes," said Mr. Ollier very politely, at Jen's question; and such was his diffidence, born in him to begin with, and vigorously fostered by his sister Alice during his brief and cloistered life, that almost his answer had been, "I'm afraid so."

She inquired if she might speak to him. He courteously replied, "Of course"—and indeed anybody, at any time, could always speak to Mr. Ollier. Whatever he was doing, he left off doing it to be spoken to. He was a patient and attentive listener. He was the most amiable of young men. And his profile, which was weak, as perfect amiability probably must be, had that about it which turned the meekest among his acquaintances into persons with wills.

Hence he was much liked. He restored flagging self-respect, he revived decaying character. People known to their friends as lambs swashbuckled directly they got with Mr. Ollier. All down-trodden wives, all creatures of broken spirit or chronic anaemia, perked up when he appeared, and felt, as they happily bullied him, that there was kick in them yet. Indeed no man had a sweeter, more modest nature; and his Christian name was James.

"But if," he continued after another courteous but nervous glance at his visitor, "it's about the parish nurse's post, I'm afraid we filled that last week."

"Oh, nothing of *that* sort," said Jen, much pleased.

Her face lit up even more. It charmed her to know that what she looked like was a parish nurse. Why, that was almost better than being taken for a mum by the porter! Evidently she need never be afraid of having her respectability, her solidity, doubted. She could do as she chose in the matter of living alone, and even, if she were hard put to it to make ends meet, might take in a male lodger; and nobody would say a word.

"It's about the cottage," she said, smiling again at Mr. Ollier, and full, she couldn't have told why, of confidence that he wouldn't turn her away, while he for his part, who always instantly saw the best in everybody, was already aware that she was a pleasant-looking woman beneath her dust—a nice, if dilapidated, woman, young still, and with a strikingly sweet smile and voice. "The one you advertised in the *Sussex Churchgoer*."

"My sister advertised it. Do you know of anyone who wants it?"

"Yes," said Jen. "Me."

James stared at her through the enormous spectacles which hid his kind and rather beautiful grey eyes. The Olliers, besides being early bald, early went into spectacles. That was because, unless they did, they ceased round about the age of twenty-five to be able to see. James's were enormous, with tortoiseshell rims. Alice's were *pince-nez.*

Through these great spectacles, which made him look like a dragonfly, he stared at Jen, and reddened uncomfortably, for he hadn't thought of anyone who wasn't working-class inhabiting the cottage—a cottage not at all fit for a lady, with no bathroom or anything, and what there was out at the other end of the garden. It embarrassed him greatly that his tired and dusty visitor should want something he felt he couldn't give. He would so much rather give than not give. It was extraordinarily difficult for him to say No—so difficult, indeed, that he never did say it, and left refusals to his sister Alice.

But the funeral at which he had just officiated had reminded him of his pressing need for a man in the cottage by the church, who should be able occasionally to supplement Burridge, the parish grave-digger. Burridge, father of many children and therefore not lightly to be dismissed, had taken to having bouts of drink which lately had coincided, and awkwardly, with demises. It would be a great relief to everybody if there were a man living in the one available cottage whose job was to lend a hand on these distressing, if happily infrequent, occasions. Even while, that afternoon, he was reading out the great words of the burial service, though he tried to keep off secular thoughts and concentrate only on their melancholy splendour, he hadn't been able not to hope that Alice's advertisement would soon bear fruit. And here it was bearing it already, but of the very last kind he wanted.

Therefore all he at the moment could find to say, as he stared at his visitor uncomfortably, was, "Indeed." And she, quite certain, somehow, that she was going to live in Cherry Lidgate and that this was her landlord, so certain that it seemed a pity to waste time talking about it, said, "If it isn't too far, might I go and look at it? I'm tired, and don't think I could walk much more."

"I'm sorry you're tired," was his evasive, though sympathetic, answer. She did look extraordinarily exhausted, poor thing, and all anyhow what with heat and dust; and that she should be exhausted and all anyhow made it seem worse to refuse to give her what she wanted. Still …

"I know," said Jen, shifting a little impatiently from one aching foot to the other—for why have to bother to explain when she felt so sure she was going to live in that cottage?—"I know I don't fit in very well with the advertisement, but I've thought it out, and isn't it an advantage only having one person in a place instead of two? There's so much less wear and tear, to begin with."

"Indeed yes," agreed the unhappy young man, his forehead wrinkled into lines of trouble. "But really I'm afraid—"

"I'm sure you *needn't* be afraid," said Jen encouragingly. "And if you're thinking about preferring it if the man cuts grass and sometimes digs graves, none of that would apply, would it, if there wasn't a man?"

She heard herself talking to him like this with surprise. They might have been friends for years, he might have been her younger brother, so easy did she find it not only to be natural but almost, she perceived, saucy with him. That last remark of hers had been quite nearly saucy. She being saucy! It astonished her, for she didn't then know that it was James's outstanding characteristic to let loose naturalness in other people, and draw from them such sauce as they might contain.

"Indeed it wouldn't," he said, as gravely as if she had said something sensible. "But you know, really—"

And catching at the word apply, before she could speak he told her that his sister was the person to apply to, not himself. "My sister sees after these sorts of things," he explained.

"Oh, I'm sorry," said Jen, who genuinely was. She would so much rather have settled everything with the brother. She had an odd and distinctly gratifying feeling that she could do as she liked with him, a feeling of power which curiously raised her opinion of herself. Absurd, of course, she recognised, and nothing in it really, but how pleasant, how refreshing, and how hitherto outside her experience!

"Not at all," he assured her, supposing she was apologising for troubling him. "Would you care to come in and speak to her? Though I really am afraid—"

Well, leave it to Alice, he thought, breaking off and opening the gate so that the strange lady might go in. As she walked beside him up the path, he carrying her bag and umbrella, he saw how badly she was limping, and remarked, concerned, that she seemed indeed to be very tired.

"Yes—I've walked from Amberton," said Jen.

"From Amberton? But that's ten miles."

"Yes. And I lost my way twice, so I should think I've been about fifteen."

"In this heat!"

"Yes. And I who haven't walked, not really, for years. Perhaps," she added, smiling up at him, for, having short legs, she barely reached to his shoulder, "that's why I feel I must have this cottage. So as to be able to sit down, so as not to have to walk any farther. I don't believe I could. Besides, I must live somewhere. Everybody lives somewhere. Even dogs."

"Of course," he agreed, his forehead sent into deeper puckers than ever by this speech. "Only they don't—"

It seemed harsh to point out to her that though everybody lived somewhere, including dogs, they didn't necessarily all do it in Cherry Lidgate; in fact, very few of them did, as she would see for herself if she were able to take a stroll round the tiny parish. So he didn't finish his sentence, because how difficult to be harsh to someone so dusty, so footsore, so much marked by heat and fatigue, and who was also a woman. Impossible, quite impossible, James found, to be harsh to women, even when they weren't footsore. From his cradle he had been trained to this attitude, highly convenient for those women who, like Alice, had to do with him, brought up carefully to think of them, because of their physical weakness combined with their function of child-bearing, as sacred. Alice had seen to that; Alice who, though she didn't herself child-bear owing to not yet having had occasion to, felt that if such occasion arose she could do so as well as anybody, and was therefore just as sacred really. Sacred, but at the same time pitiful little fellow-pilgrims,—so in his heart James thought of them—gallantly shouldering the responsibilities and pains of motherhood, carrying, while he in his unmenaced man's body was so safe, the heavier share of the burden God had inscrutably thought fit to lay on the human race. Taken altogether, that is. Taken singly they sometimes didn't perhaps seem quite like that. Taken singly, they sometimes seemed almost tough. Alice, for instance; and Lady Higgs, up at Burdon Manor.

He couldn't honestly say there was anything weak or pitiful about either of them.

"But after all," he thought, turning from the image of these two to the travel-worn, limping lady beside him, and looking down at her sympathetically, "they're our mothers, poor things. That is," he amended, recollecting that this poor thing, if tortuously, had conveyed to him that she was single, "many of them."

Still, whether mother or only potential mother, he didn't see how he could let her have the cottage, and walking up the path beside her he fell silent, so painful was it to him not to be able to give people what they wanted, so ignoble did it seem to take refuge, as he was about to do, behind Alice. What, though, could he do? There wasn't another available cottage in the parish. If he couldn't have some sober fellow at hand, ready to step into Burridge's place when he was incapacitated, public opinion would sooner or later force him to get rid of the poor chap; and then Mrs. Burridge, and the annually lengthening queue of little Burridges, would be turned into the street.

He couldn't turn a whole family into the street. He couldn't possibly do an inhuman thing like that. Alice must explain. Alice didn't mind explaining, and saying No. He would go and fetch her, and get her to settle this wretched business. And, averting his eyes from the, to him, highly distressing spectacle of hopefulness about to be dashed, he led his visitor into the drawingroom, and asked her to sit down.

"I'll go and find my sister," he said, making for the door.

"I can't think why," said Jen plaintively, dropping on to the nearest chair. "You do perfectly."

"Oh, but she can tell you all about it," he said, hurriedly going out; and he comforted himself with the knowledge that if the stranger were to see the cottage and its inconveniences, she would be the first to say she couldn't live in such a place.

❦

Alice was on the lawn, beneath the great cedar. In front of her was the tea-table, with the tea not as hot as it would have been if he had been punctual.

He wasn't punctual, because of having been held up by the stranger, and Alice, who wouldn't begin any meal, not even tea, without him, so as to cure him—which it had—of being late, was looking severe. In fact she was looking very severe, for she didn't like tepid tea, nor did she like sodden scones; and the one sensual enjoyment in her restricted spinster-life being food, it was important that this legitimate pleasure, really the only pleasure which was at the same time both acute and respectable, shouldn't be spoilt.

Here was an entire meal—not, it is true, one of the major meals, but yet a meal prepared with care and costing good and expensive material—spoilt, and nobody able to enjoy it. Waste, waste; Alice detested waste. And therefore, her own rule of never beginning before her brother arrived, forcing her to sit looking on while the scones, originally delicious, and the tea, originally fresh and excellent, got into the condition in which they became just waste, she naturally was put out, and when at last he came hurrying across the grass she vigorously showed it.

"*Really*, James—" she began in a voice sharp with vexation, at once snatching up the teapot and filling the cups.

But he interrupted her—he, interrupting, when no one in that house except herself ever dreamed of doing such a thing!—and said, almost before he reached the table, "I wish you would go indoors, Alice, and tell a lady you'll find in the drawingroom that she can't have the cottage."

Alice stared at him, the teapot suspended motionless in her hand. "What lady shall I find in the drawingroom?" she asked. "And what cottage are you talking about?"

"Well, there's only Rose Cottage, isn't there, and I don't know who she is, but she saw the advertisement and wants to take it, and I can't possibly—not *possibly*, you understand—allow her to," said her brother, working himself up into an immense outward show of determination because of how little determined he felt inside, and grasping the back of the chair meant for him to sit on, and rocking it backwards and forwards to emphasise his words.

Alice, resuming her pouring out, and ignoring his request that she should go indoors, merely sniffed.

"Dear, dear—aren't we grand," was her comment. And she added, pushing his cup towards him, "Allow, indeed!"

But he, strangely—for usually he instantly came to heel, being courteous, being patient, being, also, weak—took no notice of her reminder that she in that house was the one to allow or not, and went on quickly, bolstering himself up with his own words, knowing that if he didn't he would be so sorry for the poor, dusty creature with the charming smile waiting hopefully in the drawingroom, that he might be led into doing what he was sure he oughtn't to do—he, bolstering himself up with quick words, went on to explain that he couldn't have a single woman in the cottage, that he must have a man in the cottage, a man who would keep the churchyard nettles down, a man who would dig graves in case—well, in case, for instance, Burridge's wife were to die, because it was impossible decently to ask a man to dig his own wife's grave, wasn't it, and besides, Burridge had begun lately to drink too much and be unreliable in getting the measurements right, and he hadn't told Alice because it had been too unpleasant to talk about, but when poor old Mrs. Bleach was buried the other day she had turned out at the last moment to be a foot wider than Burridge had allowed for, and the parish had been a good deal alienated from him in consequence, and it was quite likely, if he wouldn't give up drinking, that he would have to be dismissed, and what a disaster that would be for his wretched wife and all those small children, but if there were someone handy who could step in when he wasn't able to do his duties people probably wouldn't worry, not so long as the graves were punctually dug and were the right size, so that it was important that one, at least, of the persons who took Rose Cottage should be a man, and the applicant waiting indoors had given him to understand that she was unmarried, besides being a lady, and would Alice go in and tell her the thing was out of the question, and perhaps give her some tea, for she had walked a long way, poor woman, and seemed very tired.

To all of which Alice, who had never, she thought, heard such a rigmarole, replied in her brief, effective way, "Bosh."

"You don't understand," he said, gathering up his mouth into as much firmness as possible. Really Alice was—but he had better not let himself begin thinking what Alice was, except that she was his sister, whom he was bound to love.

"Bosh," she said again, suddenly immensely calm in the face of so monstrous an accusation. She not understand? If she didn't, then in that house, she would like to know, who did?

She asked him this, and he, sticking to his point and gripping the back of the chair very tight, and both of them forgetting the stranger waiting in the drawing-room, said she didn't appear to, anyhow not in this case.

"Oh, *bosh*," said Alice, with immense contempt. "Sit down and drink your tea, James. If it's cold and nasty, it's your own fault."

He stood looking at her, not moving. Didn't he know, all too well, what he was talking about? And it really was rather repulsive, the way she said bosh. How much he wished she wouldn't. Still, she had always done it, ever since he could remember, and he was afraid she wouldn't now leave off. It was a habit dating from childhood, when she, fifteen years older and for a long time enormously bigger and stronger, had greeted his fumbling efforts at self-expression with the disconcerting, the paralysing word. Fortunately, since he had taken orders she hadn't said it in public; in public she only sniffed, and sometimes so faintly that no one but himself was ever aware of it—out of respect, he supposed, for his cloth, certainly not for anything else about him. And though he continued to practise his unselfishnesses and little chivalries on Alice, at the date of Jennifer's appearance on the scene he was finding it, though not yet facing that he was finding it, increasingly difficult.

"It isn't bosh, Alice. I wish to goodness it were. Burridge is quite often now the worse for drink."

"Indeed," said Alice, her bright little eyes, like illuminated black currants, fixed on his face. "News to me. Of course you know it's wrong to make accusations unless one is sure of one's facts, so I hope you are sure of yours."

"I'm only too sure. I've heard him myself singing while he digs."

"That's not a sign of drink, is it? Is there any reason why the poor man shouldn't sing at his work? And for goodness' sake don't keep on rocking that chair like that, James."

"Inside graves?"

"Why not?" asked Alice, aggressively liberal-minded because he wasn't. "If his work happens to be graves?"

"No decent man," said her brother, flushed with the effort of standing up to her, and not knowing what to do with his hands now that he had let go of the chair, "would sing when he's digging a grave, unless he's been drinking more than is good for him."

"Bosh," said Alice.

"I'm sorry you don't agree. I think you would have if you'd heard him. After all, we're supposed to be decent people here, and there are some sorts of songs which are not very decent anywhere, and quite disgracefully indecent in graves. Burridge's songs are that sort."

"What have you heard him singing?" asked Alice, curious.

"Nothing that I'm going to repeat to you," he answered.

"Because you can't. There *isn't* anything to repeat," she retorted. "And it's ridiculous and childish to make accusations that you're not able to substantiate. Besides, it's wrong. People get imprisoned for doing that," she finished, angrily eating one of the leathery scones.

"I didn't say I couldn't substantiate them. I said I wouldn't," said her brother, showing a surprising amount of spirit.

"Wouldn't!"

Alice paused, scone in hand, and stared at him a moment. Then she issued a command. "Tell me at once, James," she said.

"I'm sorry, Alice, but I'd rather not."

"Tell me at *once*," she repeated, impatiently.

With an immense effort he screwed himself up to defiance point. "I shall not," he said, seizing hold of the chair again.

"Hoity *toity*!" was her amazed comment.

She stared up at him as if she were seeing him for the first time. Never had he refused a request of hers before, let alone not obeyed a definite command. But indeed, said James to himself, how could he tell her? She would only instantly ask him what sort of influence did he suppose he had, then, on the congregation committed to his charge, if a member of it could get out of hand so terribly; and this was precisely what he had been painfully asking himself. For what the abandoned Burridge had been singing, lustily throwing out clay preparatory to the burying, a month before, of a lady parishioner who till only a few days previously had been having her windows and boots cleaned by him, and been looking through the windows and walking about in the boots just as though she were going on for ever, and had very unreasonably and unfairly dismissed him from his post on the ground that she couldn't see through the windows or show herself in the boots, which was nothing to do with him, but just death coming on, declared Burridge—what he had been singing were the following words, to a tune which kept time with the activities of his shovel:

'Eaven or 'ell, 'eaven or 'ell,
Which it'll be 'oo can possibly tell?
'Ip, 'ip, 'ooray, al-le-lu-yay,
Don't you wish now you'd been gooder, old gell?"

Of course, James couldn't and wouldn't tell Alice that. Most of the things he told her he was sorry for afterwards, and of this he wouldn't hear the last to the end of his days, he was sure. For it included his own lapse from duty in not reporting the man at the next vestry meeting, and Alice would never understand, she whose views were all so clear and definite, the immense secret difficulty he was constantly having in reconciling the claims of justice and mercy. He couldn't reconcile them. They persisted in clashing. Honestly he tried to, and each time was forced to give up, and plump for mercy. So that, happening to go through the churchyard and hear the profane and heartless song, what had he done? Not his duty, certainly; not that for which he was consecrated, appointed and paid. But, pretending he hadn't passed that way at all, that he had heard nothing and seen nothing, he had slunk off on tiptoe among the tombstones as if he were somebody guilty, concerned only lest Burridge should catch sight of him, and so he be forced to report him, and then he would be dismissed, and his poor, harassed, perpetually child-bearing wife, and endless string of little children, be thrown out homeless on the world.

"I can't help it," he thought, holding on to the chair so hard that his knuckles showed white, and meeting his sister's eyes as bravely as he possibly could. "I'm not going to tell her. She'd only take it up herself, and start doing things in the interests of decency and propriety. I've told her too much already. I've always told her too much about everything. It's because she got into the world so long ahead of me, and I've never been able to catch her up."

And Alice, incensed by his refusal, incensed by his unnatural attempt to assert himself and overrule her, incensed by her spoilt tea and ruined scones, incensed by James altogether, whose fault everything was including her now being so very angry, was roused to violent opposition to every one of his wishes, and made up her mind on the spot that whoever the woman was who wanted the cottage, short of being what in the village was called fast, she should have it. Just to teach him. Just to let him see.

❦

She got up. She gave him a look which ought to have cleared his mind as to her intentions, but didn't because he never saw it, his eyes, in the silence which succeeded his refusal, sinking before hers; and wasting no more words on him she walked off to the house.

He, even after a life-time with her misreading her behaviour, supposed she had gone to turn down the stranger's application, that being the only reasonable, the only possible course to take in the unfortunate circumstances, and sitting down with a sigh, partly of relief at being alone, partly of concern for the stranger's disappointment, began abstractedly to drink his cold tea and munch a scone, while he considered the difficulties and confusions of life.

"It's a bore. It's a *bore*," he muttered to himself. Somebody was always being hurt and thwarted; somebody was always having to give up, so that somebody else might have. The poor creature in the drawingroom, where would she drag her dusty feet next in search of shelter? he wondered. Poor woman. Yet what could he have done? He wished women weren't so pitiful—that is, the ones who were pitiful, not the ones like Alice. Alice wasn't pitiful at all, and, contradictory as he was, he wished she were. If she were, she might put herself in other people's shoes, and now, having performed her unpleasant duty and turned the poor woman down, she would offer her the use of one of the many sparerooms in the Vicarage for a few days, till she was thoroughly rested and had some notion of what she wished to do next.

But Alice wouldn't. He knew it wouldn't so much as enter her head—not from unkindness, because he was sure she was really a thoroughly good woman, but from want of imagination,—and presently the weary stranger would be forced to continue on her way.

Well, he was at the bottom of that, after all. It was he who had said he couldn't possibly let her have the cottage—said it to Alice, because he hadn't the courage to say it himself. Was it cowardice? He expected it was, but he couldn't help it, he found it quite impossible to disappoint. Alice fortunately didn't, otherwise the parish would have been seething with a perpetual shilly-shallying, with a constant and entirely ineffective dodging about between everybody's wishes. Made differently from him, Alice could and did say no, and she said it with decision and finality, sweeping objections, entreaties and laments out of her way with the thoroughness of a broom vigorously wielded. In there, in the drawingroom, she was doing it at this moment; he did hope that it was at least accompanied by cups of tea.

And looking up at the sound of footsteps, he saw both his sister and the stranger come out of the house by the garden door and go off together, the stranger apparently a good deal recovered from her fatigue, and Alice ostentatiously swinging a key he recognised as the key of Rose Cottage, down the path that led to it through the churchyard.

CHAPTER IV

Jen couldn't believe her eyes when she first saw Rose Cottage—and indeed in anybody's eyes, who should have been passing and not gone inside, it would have seemed extremely attractive. For one thing, you could hardly see it for roses; hence its name. And it had a thatched roof, and latticed windows, and a little garden with a brick path to its porch, and an orchard sloping part of the way up what she presently learned was Burdon Down, and really it was exactly like the cottages artists paint.

Was she going to get all this—the roses, the thatch, the lattice and the orchard—for five shillings a week? For about what the milk bill in Gower Street used to come to?

It seemed impossible. But she was. And she got it solely because Alice Ollier was in a temper with James, her brother.

Snuggling in a hollow, the garden was finished off on the churchyard side, with a suggestion on so hot a day of admirable coolness, by an edging of tombstones. An immense yew-tree grew near the low, dividing wall, and beneath its shade Burridge, who had inhabited the cottage during the brief period before his family increased, wanting something to sit on on summer evenings and being, when he wasn't drinking, thrifty and resourceful, had made a seat out of a disused memorial slab, text and all. If you sat on this seat long, especially on a warm day, the green mould in the lettering came off on you, and you went about unconsciously announcing in reversed order, to those who cared to run and read, that you were not lost but gone before; and James, a natural non-interferer, was still wondering, as he had wondered when he first saw the thing fitted with rustic wooden arms and a back which plainly showed the use it was put to, whether he ought to take some firm sort of line about it and have it removed on the ground of its profanity, or merely pretend he hadn't yet noticed it.

There were two little gates to the garden, one leading into the churchyard and convenient for graves, the cottage having been lived in chiefly by people who dug them, and the other out into the lane that meandered away, between high hedges, to the village in one direction, and up on to Burdon Down and the house of Lady Higgs on the other. Both these places were over a mile off on either side, so that it was a lonely cottage, completely out of earshot should cries for help ever issue from it; and naturally James, aware of its drawbacks and of all the things it hadn't got, had never dreamed of anyone living in it except a robust labourer and his wife.

It was Alice who, observing its roses, had lately been thinking, in view of so much picturesqueness, Why labourers? and from that had proceeded to ask herself, Why not a gentleman? Labourers' wives were always having babies, and accordingly always not being able any longer to squeeze into the tiny place. She was tired of the coming and going in that cottage. Even in the short time she had been at Cherry Lidgate three couples had come and gone. Why shouldn't some quiet man, a writer or a painter, or even one who was merely fond of roses, take it—perhaps for week-ends, if he didn't care to be there always? Such men do exist, and do quite often need bolt-holes. A man of good education, else he wouldn't see how pretty it was; and of simple tastes, else he wouldn't like having to fetch up the water from the well in a bucket, nor that what she called the conveniences should be at the other end of the garden; this was the sort of person who might, she thought, be attracted. Somebody safe and proper for James to talk to—not, that is, a woman; somebody friendly, who would come round and smoke a pipe of an evening, and shake James out of the groove he was getting into, somebody not too young, because of the quiet, and not too old, because of the conveniences. And though it was true that she had put the advertisement in the *Churchgoer* so as to avoid unnecessary discussion with James, she had at the same time, unknown to him, put quite a different one in the personal column of *The Times*, which might be expected to produce results in a day or two.

And now the last thing in the world she had wanted to happen, or James either, had happened, and the cottage had gone not only to a woman but to an unmarried one.

All James's fault. He shouldn't have goaded her. Naturally incensed by his behaviour, by his ridiculous sudden attempt to defy her, what could she do but offer it to the stranger at once on entering the drawingroom?

"Good afternoon. I'm Miss Ollier. I hear you wish to look at our cottage with a view to taking it," she said in a burst, almost before she was through the door. "If you'll come with me I'll show it to you, and if you like it you can have it."

And when the thing was settled, which it was in ten minutes, and Jen, undaunted by either the inside, or the pump, or the conveniences, and delighting in the fact that it was remote, had pulled out six pound-notes and paid six months' rent in advance, and they were walking back to the Vicarage together, where she had left her bag and umbrella, Alice, having cooled down, began to be uneasy.

She began, indeed, to be very uneasy. The cottage wasn't fit for any woman alone, and especially not for a woman who was a lady. She would for ever be up at the Vicarage complaining, or trying to borrow things; or she would want to be sociable, and even, though so unattractive and stumpy—she glanced at the new tenant sideways—might set her cap at James, who, in spite of being such an obvious goose, yet because he was in a nice house and good position had already, since they lived there, been assailed by predatory women, and Alice had had to beat them off.

She had succeeded up to now because they didn't live, as this one, who of course too was predatory, was going to, next door; but could one beat off a woman, if she were determined enough, who lived so close? Alice, again glancing sideways at her companion, took comfort in the fact that she wasn't by any means all she might be in the way of looks, besides being well past any youth she might ever have had. It wouldn't be possible, Alice thought seeking reassurance, for James to be attracted by this Miss Dodge, as she said she was called—and probably was, conceded Alice, otherwise suspicious, for no one would be Dodge unless obliged. She didn't seem to be the sort of person who sets her cap at men, she told herself. A solid person she seemed; a quiet, solid person with short legs. And the legs didn't even match each other, for she limped as she walked.

Still, Alice didn't trust unmarried women an inch. Naturally they all wanted a good home, and not having to pay for it; and men—the comfort she had taken forsook her again—were great fools. Especially James. Indeed yes, and was he not a great fool, she thought, her anger flaming high again, bringing this on both of them! The letting of the cottage to somebody they neither of them wanted in it was all his fault. Why couldn't he keep a civil tongue in his head, and not provoke her by refusing to tell her what she had a perfect right to know, and by looking so superior, and treating her like a child? James, her young brother, whom she had not only dandled on her knee, but, ever since their father died, ruled entirely! She wouldn't have been provoked if he hadn't provoked her. It was entirely his fault for baiting her. She never got angry unless people made her angry. The whole responsibility for what she had just done, and for anything that happened as a result, must be on his shoulders. She washed her hands, said Alice to herself, full of exasperation and doubts—she washed her hands. People should think twice before, by their conduct, they force other people to get angry. Let her alone, and she was as good-tempered and easy-going as anybody. …

And when Miss Dodge had gone, taking herself and her bag off to the village inn for the night, when she had gone unhindered by any invitation to have tea first, let alone stay in one of the Vicarage's sparerooms as James, Alice knew, would have suggested, he being soft and squashy and an easy prey to strangers—when she had gone, assuring Alice, who stared at her stonily as who should say, What on earth do *I* care?, that she hoped to see about furnishing the cottage next day, Alice at once went in search of her brother, so as to tell him what she thought of him for compelling her to do what she never, in this world, otherwise would have dreamed of doing.

❦

She found him in the rose-garden, snipping dead roses off with the small pair of scissors he carried about for this purpose in his waistcoat pocket. The garden was blandly golden in the afternoon light. Rooks cawed. Not a leaf stirred. It breathed peace. But in James's mind at that moment was little peace, for he was thinking while he snipped, his back turned so that he didn't see Alice approaching, how really unbearably high-handed she was becoming, and that something ought to be done about it.

But what? He snipped and snipped, and wished he knew. Impossible in a vicarage to have rows, even if he had been the sort of person who doesn't mind having them. If she had indeed let the cottage to the stranger—she had certainly taken her to look at it—it was exceedingly wrong of her, and not least wrong towards the poor lady, who wouldn't realise at first what she was in for; but, wrong or not, it was impossible to have a row about it, and also, faced by the accomplished fact, it was really rather useless for him to mind. What was the good of minding the actual and the finished? It had always seemed to James, other considerations apart, that to allow oneself to be upset because something has been done which one considers a pity, or even considers disastrous, is to double the misfortune. Why throw after what is already gone one's own good temper and serenity?

He asked himself this once again, as he snipped his roses and tried to pull his thoughts into the direction of peace. Alice, he knew, objected to an attitude which, she told him, was weak-kneed and anaemic. But was it? He couldn't help thinking it was merely sensible. A few weeks ago he had lost a five-pound note, and because, when he had done all he could to find it and hadn't succeeded, he then put it out of his thoughts and didn't interminably lament, she upbraided him, asked him if he imagined he was made of money, and told him roundly that he was unfit to be trusted with any.

Of course he was aware he wasn't made of money, and he disliked extremely losing five good pounds—his own pounds, after all—but what was the use of fretting over them when it was plain that they were irretrievably gone? Now, when it appeared from her first words—she made him jump, suddenly speaking to him from close behind—that the cottage was irretrievably gone, in spite of his having just been thinking that something must be done to check Alice's high-handedness, faced by yet another accomplished fact he saw no use in adding to the annoyance of not having the kind of tenant he had hoped for, an extra, and much more corrosive, annoyance with his sister. She shouldn't, James said to himself, be permitted to disturb the peace of the summer afternoon; it would be an insult to the quiet roses, and the lovely, tangled, pensive sweetpeas. In fine weather, really people oughtn't to quarrel. And besides, what about God, and his own priestly promises? Being a priest did lay an obligation on one to put up with things; so he proceeded once more to put up with Alice, and when she at last stopped talking, having said a great many things which seemed to him really almost puzzlingly perverse and illogical, for she appeared to be blaming him, and very angrily, for the fact that she had let the strange lady have the cottage, he merely mildly asked, as he continued unperturbed to snip, "Did you discover what she wants to do here?"

"Live," snapped Alice, peculiarly annoyed at being asked that which she was asking herself and hadn't been able satisfactorily to answer; and peculiarly annoyed, too, at the way James was taking it lying down, after all his boastful talk about not going on any account to let the cottage to anybody but a married couple.

That was the worst of James: he invariably ultimately knuckled under; and though this flabbiness was of course convenient, it made it impossible not to despise him. He ought to show more fight when he was attacked. Wasn't he a man? Anyhow to look at him he appeared to be a man, yet it was like hitting out at just a ghost, at just emptiness, telling him what she thought of him and teaching him a lesson. He didn't mind having a lesson. He hardly seemed to know he had been given one. What can one do with such persons? If they don't mind, if they refuse to be aware, they fade beyond one's reach, and become, in a very cowardly and reprehensible way, thought Alice, unassailable.

"What is her name?" asked her brother, his back turned to her, engaged with his roses but feeling impelled to fill up the silence she had fallen into.

"Dodge," said Alice briefly.

"Dodge," repeated James, not because it made any impression on him, but just so as to say something. "She must be very poor, I'm afraid," he added, "to wish to live in such an inconvenient little place."

"Bosh—poor. If she's poor, why is she fat?" asked Alice. "I've never heard of being fat and poor."

"Well, I didn't mean actual want," said James, snipping.

He was indisposed to discuss the new tenant's figure. Alice, who measured the same from her neck to her waist back and front, and considered that so would all women if they were really good and attended to their duties, admired persons, he was aware, of a flat build. He didn't. He was quite sure that curves were comfortable things. All women should have them—kind curves, soft curves, curves against which one could lay one's head when tired of everything, and go to sleep. He concealed this opinion, however, from Alice, who was knobby, and couldn't of course help being knobby, though he did think she needn't, because of having them herself, admire knobs; and turning his inward eye away from the pleasing undulations her words recalled, undulations he had at once noted as a salient feature in the new tenant, he asked, so as to make conversation as the moments passed and Alice, behind him, though she didn't speak didn't go, and he felt it was nicer to say something than to seem to ignore her as if he were vexed about the cottage, "What references have you got?"

She was taken aback. Till that moment she hadn't thought of them. References. Of course no one let their cottages straight off without asking for references, without finding out something, at least, about a prospective tenant. Now see what James had forced her to do, through annoying and flustering her! It was only her hurry to show him he couldn't order her about that had made her forget to ask for them.

But she wasn't going to allow him to suppose he had cornered her. "References?" she therefore retorted, "You ought to have thought of that before."

"Before what?" asked James. "I don't understand, Alice," he added, pausing in his work but not turning round. Always he would rather look at his roses than at Alice; always he would rather look at almost anything than at Alice.

"Bosh," retorted Alice, more emphatically than usual. "You understand perfectly. You know quite well it's all your fault, and now you want to shift the responsibility on to me. References! Can't you trust people?"

He began to snip again. What a mercy it was that Alice was only his sister, and not his wife; for so at least, though he had to listen to her during the day, he hadn't got to during the night.

"Can't you?" she repeated, determined to make him answer.

"Yes," said James. "Of course I can, Alice."

"Well, then," she said, defiantly.

❦

Nevertheless, though she held her head up and defied him, in her heart she was very uneasy, and when next she saw James, which wasn't until that evening at dinner, she was extremely short with him; so short that she hardly said more than Yes and No, taking no notice of his attempts at general conversation.

James was conciliatory; Alice was hostile; and the meal was extremely uncomfortable. In the intervals between his snubbed politenesses, James reflected how little such things as good food, and prettily arranged dinnertables, and luxurious surroundings were worth when the person one is obliged to be with is cross, and Alice, conscious of the smoothness with which, thanks to her untiring efforts, the wheels of his household ran, of how, thanks to her, he had no worries and only comforts, of how, in a word, he owed her everything, sat angrily considering the shape of his head and ears.

Being incurably civilised, and of that type of character which prefers, having cut its losses, to be cheerful and forget them, James refused to be discouraged, and continued to do his best with the opportunities for amenities provided by such actions as offering bread and suggesting butter; but the results were poor. Alice shook her head and said No, or nodded her head and said Yes, and, as the meal progressed, waved his attempts to give her second helpings impatiently aside; and that was all.

It afflicted James, and Alice knew it, to eat meals in silence, but she saw no reason why he shouldn't take his turn at being afflicted. Therefore, except for monosyllables, she steadily held her tongue, and she only said the monosyllables because of what the parlourmaid might otherwise think. Certainly she wouldn't converse. Did one ever hear the like, that a man could behave as if nothing had happened when he knew the tenant he had said he wouldn't have had yet been foisted on him, and when he knew what his sister thought of him for forcing her to do this foisting? Such want of character, such slackness of grasp, was really dreadful. It would be a long while before she got over this, thought Alice, impatiently snapping off bits of toast. Never again should he be given the chance of making her act hastily. In future she would be ice and immovableness when he started trying to get the upper hand, and not allow herself to be driven by natural indignation into impetuous action. She had got the upper hand this time, or rather she had retained it, for at no time during his life had he had it, but at what a cost! Here was this woman from nowhere—positively, she had been so much rattled that she hadn't even asked the creature where she came from, let alone demanded those references—settled on them, and Alice already disliking her. She was bound to dislike her anyhow, seeing that she had got in only through being a bone of contention, but her dislike was intensified by the two unpleasant facts that she was a spinster, and James was a fool. A fool, a spinster, and propinquity. What mightn't, thought Alice, result from such a combination? Men never, she was sure, knew when they were well off, and what she had seen of them had convinced her that just contrast was sometimes enough to bring about most undesirable situations—just newness, just the attraction of something different, and, as often as not, and certainly it would be so in this case, something, as they no doubt discovered all right when it was too late, ever so much worse.

Well, she would take no risks, she would keep a very watchful eye on her weak brother. If she hadn't been a person who prided herself on never going back on her word, and if it had been possible to bring herself to allow him to crow over her, she would have called that very evening at the *Three Jolly Shepherds*, and told the woman the bargain was off—given her back her six pounds, and stopped her from getting the furniture she had talked of buying in Amberton next day.

But Alice couldn't do that. She couldn't depart from the principles of a lifetime, nor could she possibly eat humble pie before James. Impatiently she waved his polite offer of more pudding aside; impatiently she watched him having more himself—so like him to keep her sitting there longer than usual while he had twice of everything, just when she was in such a hurry to get away; for she had made up her mind to walk over to Burdon Manor after dinner, and tell Lady Higgs what had happened, and ask her what she thought of it. There would be a full moon to come back by. There would be dusk to go by. She would take the short cut across the fields, and not pass Rose Cottage—which she didn't want to see again for a long while, thank you very much, said Alice to herself.

And now James was holding her up by taking an immense piece of cheese. James was always so tiresome with cheese, going on and on in a sort of vague way, not really wanting it, she was sure, but just emptymindedly eating it because it was there on the table before him.

Alice sat fuming. So dense he was, so dense, she thought, to be able to go on eating endless cheese when what had happened that day might quite likely change their whole lives. If she wasn't watchful, that is; if she wasn't very watchful. In that quiet village, where nothing ever was different, the coming of a stranger was anyhow an event, and when the stranger was a spinster, with no apparent *raison d'être* for living there such as writing or painting, the event might well be called stirring. Certainly it would stir the parish. The thing to aim at was that it shouldn't stir James. True that if it did, thought Alice remembering the new tenant's appearance, he must be really morbidly stirrable. Still—propinquity; a bachelor and a spinster; separated only by a handful of tombstones. …

She would ask Lady Higgs what she thought. Rich and sensible and friendly, Lady Higgs was a valuable asset in Alice's life. To her she was accustomed to go whenever there was anything particular to talk about. Lady Higgs would forgive her for interrupting her at such an hour, Alice was sure, when she heard that what was wanted was advice. For really if Lady Higgs thought this an occasion on which principles might be laid aside, Alice would after all go back on her word, seeing how desirable it was that she should, and the first thing next morning call at the inn and tell Miss Dodge she was sorry, but she couldn't let her have the cottage. No explanations—merely hand back the six pound-notes, and good morning. Without anything in writing, what could the woman do? Nothing. She would have to go somewhere else. And to James Alice could say, even if it wasn't true, for while she was about it she might for once relax a little all round, that the applicant couldn't face the conveniences, and had gone away.

And now coffee; she had got to sit through coffee. It was her own arrangement, that coffee should be served at the table, and not carried after them into the drawing-room, so here she was forced to go through with it from start to finish. James could never drink his coffee and have done with it, like an ordinary mortal, but must sit and sit, interminably fiddling round in the cup with his spoon long after every scrap of sugar must have melted, and as likely as not beginning all over again with a second cup, when at last he had finished the first one.

Usually Alice liked second cups too, for she had trained her cook to make very good coffee, but not tonight, not with such vexation and uneasiness in her heart, not when just to be kept sitting at the same table as James and his amiable face, his unalterably amiable face and great soft eyes—doe-like, thought Alice, and had anyone ever heard of doe-like eyes in a man?—and see him behaving as if there were no need to worry or to mind anything ever, just to be kept sitting there, when she was itching to get away to Lady Higgs, while he interminably chased the sugar round in his cup, gnawed at her so maddeningly that if she hadn't been a clergyman's sister, and he a clergyman, she thought it quite possible that she might have leaned across the table, snatched the cup away from him, thrown what was in it in his face, said one of those words with dashes in their middles which appear to give relief, and rushed out of the room.

Quite possible; and very horrible. He had brought her who, left to herself, would be as good as anybody, to this state. Whatever Lady Higgs advised, whatever ultimately was done in regard to the cottage, James anyhow wouldn't, for a long while, be forgiven.

❦

But Jen, full of the delight which is the portion of those who have got what they want and to whom nothing, therefore, is impossible, settled everything for everybody by going to live in Rose Cottage that very night.

The key was in her pocket; the place was her own; why waste a moment unnecessarily lodging anywhere else? There wasn't anything in it, but she would soon get hold of a few things to go on with. It was extremely dirty, but she would soon get hold of somebody to clean it. Nothing seemed, and nothing was, beyond her powers in her joy at having got exactly what she wanted on the very first day of her search; and forgetting all about being tired, she set to work to get into her home with such energy that by the time Alice was taking the short cut across the darkening downs that evening to Lady Higgs, if she had gone a little way to the right and peered over the edge of the high ground at the back of the cottage she would have seen a light shining in its window, and if her eyes had been able to pierce through walls she would have seen Miss Dodge on her knees, in an immense dishevelment and excitement, unpacking, from a wooden case, the immediate necessities of the moment.

The landlord of the *Three Jolly Shepherds* had been her unexpected helper. Himself jolly, though not a shepherd, when she arrived limping at his inn and asked for food, and told him she was the new tenant of Rose Cottage, he flung himself at once, heart and soul, into her affairs. Was not Burridge his best drinker? Was not the advertisement Miss Ollier had put in the *Churchgoer* a direct menace to his excellent customer's position as grave-digger, and the thin edge of a wedge which would ultimately oust him from the parish?

The landlord thought it the best news he had heard for a long time, that Rose Cottage should be safe in the hands of a lady who, being single, wouldn't be likely to increase and overflow as other tenants had. By nature friendly, he became doubly so in his pleasure, and not only sent a vigorous widow of his acquaintance called Jones round at once to scrub and clean, but after Jennifer had had some food and washed and tidied, himself drove her in his ancient Ford to Amberton, and advised her, for she struck him as enthusiastic rather than experienced, as to the sorts of things she positively must have at once, and the sorts of things which could follow next day by carrier.

How it came about that a single lady—she had briefly outlined her situation—had got the cottage, he couldn't at first understand; but by the time they reached Amberton, and she had talked very pleasantly most of the way, asking intelligent if optimistic questions about all she saw, and had smiled more often than she hadn't smiled, which was what women were intended to do by God Almighty when he made them, the landlord held, instead of looking at a man as if he were a sinning worm and they the Day of Judgment, as Miss Ollier did—by the time they reached Amberton, he had come to the conclusion that young Vicar, showing spirit at last, was at the bottom of this, and that now the village would see some fun.

For that sister of his wasn't going to let him and her comfortable home go easily—the whole parish was unanimous on this point. Hadn't it seen her shoo off any ladies who weren't grandmothers, and cut them short when they came along and wanted to be friendly? Perhaps she didn't think this one mattered; and when the lady first came in to the *Shepherds*, covered with dust and dragging her feet, he hadn't thought much of her himself. But a wash and brush up, and a cup of tea, had done wonders, and she had as nice a way with her as any lady he knew.

He'd be much mistaken if young Vicar hadn't spotted it too, and had let her have the cottage so that she should be close at hand for him to fall back on when that sister of his was too much for him. But it isn't in nature, reflected the landlord, for a man to fall back often on a woman without wanting to marry her, so the village could look forward to a lively and exciting time.

Young Vicar, kicking out at last! The landlord chuckled gleefully. All men should kick, he was of opinion, when petticoats get above themselves; and in this case he knew there wouldn't be kicking allowed without a lot of fighting on the part of the petticoat involved, so that there would be some pretty battles now round at the Vicarage, and he only hoped young Vicar would keep his end up.

❦

Rejoicing in the prospect of a bit of excitement in that quiet place at last, and having deposited Jen, and such indispensable things for the night as could be crammed into the Ford, like a kettle and matches and candles and a mattress—the bedstead was to follow, with the rest of the larger objects, by carrier next day—on the Rose Cottage doorstep, he drove quickly to his inn to spread the good news among his faithful band of nightly drinkers.

They received it uproariously. Cheers and laughter shattered the holy calm of the summer evening. Burridge drank the lady's health, the health of the unmarried lady coming to live in the cottage which used to be his, and which had seen so many people come to live in it, and after nine months go away again because it had grown too small; and he embroidered this theme with all his own peculiar and inventive ribaldry, so that the roysterers roared, and the landlord, who loved a joke so much that he didn't mind who or what it was about, slapped his thighs in delight, and even into the Vicarage garden, where James was sitting alone on his favourite seat near the churchyard wall, these sounds of unbridled, and he was afraid drunken, merriment penetrated.

Softened by distance, they yet got there; and to have got there at all showed, thought James, how shatteringly loud they must be close. Alice had disappeared after dinner without a word—very cross, he was afraid—and he sat by himself, smoking his pipe and listening ruefully.

Burridge at it again, he was sure. Burridge letting himself go in his nightly rip, while his wife, poor fruitful soul, was putting rows of children to bed. Was he, James, much good if he couldn't keep his own grave-digger in order, and protect him from what was certain to happen to him sooner or later, now that it wouldn't be possible to house an assistant who might do his work for him when his bouts occurred? It was no use, of course, being annoyed about it, but he did wish that Alice hadn't—

He stopped in the middle of his sentence, arrested by a thought. Didn't Alice, when he asked her what had become of Miss Dodge, say she had gone to the *Jolly Shepherds* for the night? If so, and he didn't see where else, tired out as she was, she could go, there, at the back of all that drunken brawling, the unfortunate woman must at this moment be.

Intolerable of Patterson to allow it, when he had a lady lodging in the house. Really, thought James, hastily knocking out his pipe and getting up, he must go across at once, and stop it.

But even as he got up he hesitated, fingering the bowl of his pipe, and flushing. He wasn't much good at stopping things—he knew that well enough. They were all very nice to him; all his parishioners, including Burridge, were extraordinarily nice to him; yet he didn't seem to have the least authority.

Not that he wanted it. He hated authority, and having to have it over people who were a thousand times better than he was, was abhorrent to him. Could anything, he asked himself even at this moment, be more absurd than that he, who knew nothing, except perhaps a little about gardening, should be set up above men old enough, and wise enough he was sure in the richness of their experience, to be his father? Whenever, conscious that as a priest it was his duty, he had screwed himself up to mild criticisms of the behaviour of his flock, they listened politely, goodnaturedly, and almost, it sometimes appeared to him, sympathetically, as though aware of what the effort cost him, and having listened continued to behave exactly as before. His experience had been that he couldn't change them; and the most weakening doubts crept round quite often in his mind as to whether they in fact needed changing. This full-blooded, jolly acceptance of material joys—wasn't it in itself a tribute to God's abounding mercies?

Still, there was a limit to what could be winked at, he said to himself, and the unfortunate Miss Dodge, in some horrid little hot bedroom at the *Shepherds* being kept awake, when she was so much exhausted, by what he was certain was ribaldry, had to be considered too. He must do something about it; he must at once deal with the situation; he must go and—

Encouraging himself with visions of what the poor lady must be enduring, with a great show of firmness he stuffed his pipe into his pocket, and was just going to force himself to visit the roysterers, and somehow silence their brawling, when he was again stopped short,—arrested, this time, not by a thought, but by something he saw.

It was a light, bright and steady, shining away down there through the trees, in what could only be the window of Rose Cottage.

CHAPTER V

Well, that was a funny thing, thought James, standing still and staring. The empty cottage with a light in it. What could it mean? Had some tramp got in, and was intending to sleep there? If so, he would go and tell him he couldn't, for he was bound, he felt, during his tenant's temporary absence, to protect her property.

It seemed to him, though, impossible that any sane man should wish to sleep in a dirty, cobwebby cottage when there was the lovely warm night outside, and all God's stars. Still, people did seem curiously to cling to stuffy indoor places, even when they were tramps, so no doubt that was what was happening down there. He must go and dislodge whoever it was; point out how far more pleasant, as well as wholesome, the nearest haystack would be, and gently urge the injudicious intruder to go and sleep in it. And this time, setting forth to do his duty without hesitations, he jumped over the low wall into the churchyard, and threaded his way quickly among the familiar tombstones to the yew-tree which stood sentinel, black against the velvety darkness of the star-strewn sky, at the little gate leading into the Rose Cottage garden.

Softly James opened the gate and walked up the weedy path, tiptoeing along in his thin-soled evening shoes, hoping to catch the man unawares,—for really he should be reprimanded before being told to leave; and when he got close to the porch, what was his surprise to find the door flung wide open, and the light being allowed to stream out unhindered on to the tangle of roses which hung about it, as though it didn't matter in the least if anybody saw.

Here was a bold tramp, thought James; a tramp quite careless of discovery. Probably he had been told the owner of the cottage would stand anything, he said to himself with a rather wry smile. Indeed this was very likely, he thought, aware of the impression he produced, but if that were what the fellow believed he would find he was wrong this time. And pulling the roses out of the way, neglected roses which trailed almost to the ground and hung over the entrance to the porch like a curtain, he prepared to deal firmly and simply with whoever he found inside.

❦

But he found nobody inside. He was looking into a perfectly clean, bright, empty kitchen, smelling of soapsuds, free from cobwebs, its iron cookingstove, for years so rusty, shining with blacklead polish, a pail filled with water on the floor, a kettle standing on the only chair, and in this kettle, its lid having been taken out, was a bunch of roses. That was all. Nothing else. No tramp, no anybody. Just cleanness, brightness, emptiness, and complete silence.

James stood staring, holding back the creepers with one hand. The tenant, he thought; the tenant, already in possession. What extraordinary, what admirable decision of character! And those roses in the kettle—just what he would have done with a kettle himself, if he had had one. Astonished he stared, the freshness of much scrubbing soap in his nostrils. Was it possible that, dead tired as he had observed the strange lady to be, she yet had scrubbed the place out alone and unaided? No, she couldn't have. When he saw her that afternoon she could hardly stand. Somebody must have helped her; somebody was being more kind than he was; and who, if not Alice? Not that he imagined Alice had scrubbed, but he did jump instantly to the conclusion that she had directed others to do it—sent down the maids from the Vicarage, been busy engaged in benevolence, during the absence which he had attributed to bad temper, before and after dinner.

Of course. His heart, which warmed at the slightest sign of kindness, at once glowed towards his sister. He took back everything he had been saying to himself about her, and heartily begged her pardon in his thoughts. How nice of Alice. How, really, what one would expect of her. She was short with him and snubbed him, but beneath her husk—no, that wasn't a pleasant word—beneath, rather would he say, her sometimes slightly harsh manner and her favourite disconcerting monosyllable, was, after all, goodness. Just as with everyone else he came across, go deep enough, and wait long enough, and there was God.

And inspired by her example to do what he too could in the way of neighbourliness, he called out—rather timidly, for it was so quiet down in the hollow, the noises the *Jolly Shepherds* were making all blotted out by the intervening high ground on which the Vicarage stood, that his voice sounded startingly conspicuous—"Miss Dodge!"

And after a pause, a little louder and inquiringly, "Miss Dodge?"

And then, taking courage, quite loud, "I beg your pardon—but can I be of any use to you, Miss Dodge?"

Jen heard him. She was on the other side of the cottage, the side where the orchard was, engaged in dragging the mattress she had bought in Amberton across the grass to the apple-tree under which she proposed to sleep. Full of excitement, she pulled and tugged the thing along, for surely it was a great moment in her life, the first night she had ever slept out of doors? Mrs. Jones, the woman who had cleaned up for her, had gone home, and Jen, supposing it quite easy to carry a mattress into a garden and place it beneath a tree, had laid hold of it in a spirit of confidence, and begun to tug.

Almost immediately she found it wasn't as easy as she thought. Surprising how heavy the thing was—or was it that she, used for years only to clicking away with her fingertips on a typewriter, had nothing but the most miserable flabby muscles in her arms? She would soon, of course, alter such a state of things, and quickly acquire properly useful arms—and legs as well, and feet that could carry her about anywhere she chose to go for as long as she wished, without doubling their size inside her shoes; but meanwhile it was really extraordinarily hard work dragging the mattress across the grass, and she had had to stop every few yards to rest, and still had quite a long bit before she could reach the particular tree she had set her heart on, when she heard, through the stillness, the tenor voice she already knew as the Vicar's, the amiable, rather sheeplike tenor voice, calling her name and asking if he could be of any use.

The very man. "Oh, *yes*!" she called back relieved, and instantly dropped the great heavy thing. "Please. Do come round here, won't you? I'm in the orchard—"

And so it chanced that James, with only stars to chaperon him, helped Jen prepare her bed for the night.

❦

It was exactly what he would have liked to do himself—sleep out of doors, that delicious weather; and though he knew he couldn't, because of Alice, whose idea of what was fitting for a clergyman was that he should behave at all times as if the entire parish were gathered round him in a ring looking on, he rejoiced to know that there was going to be one happy, free human being so near him doing it. In his own hot bedroom presently, he would think of the new tenant lying out there lapped in coolness, her face upturned to the spreading branches, the dew falling softly on her closed eyelids. It made him think of his happy undergraduate days, when he used to dream through long afternoons moored in a canoe under the willows of the Cam, with nobody to criticise or reproach him. Eagerly he took hold of the mattress. She had chosen a perfect place to sleep in, he thought, carrying it after her to the apple-tree. The sun wouldn't be able to wake her too early there, because of the shoulder of Burdon Down. What a nice woman. First those roses in the kettle, and now this sleeping out of doors. He was sorry he had grudged her the cottage. Alice had been right to let her have it. He would tackle Burridge with more determination, and insist on his mending his ways, and then all would be well all round; for certainly a woman who liked filling her kettle with roses, and sleeping out of doors, was an acquisition to any parish.

Enthusiastically James laid out the mattress in what he judged the exact best spot beneath the tree, flattening out the surrounding long grass and nettles by trampling on them, spreading the blanket she fetched from indoors, and plumping up the pillow. If she were as wholesome, and natural, and delightful as this first act of hers seemed to point to her being, then perhaps she wouldn't mind, as a different kind of woman would mind, the cottage's drawbacks, especially seeing that Alice and he would be so close by, ready to lend a hand. Suppose, now, instead of having got hold of the wrong tenant, Alice had got hold of the precisely right one? What did it really matter about Burridge? Up to then it hadn't mattered, so why should it in the future? Besides, he would tackle him. Rather. Of course he would. The very next day. Tell him he couldn't go on like that. Tell him—

"Is there anything more I can do?" he asked, when he had made everything as comfortable as he could, and greatly hoping that there still might be something.

The tenant said No, in the extraordinarily attractive voice he had noticed that afternoon, but how very kind he had been, and wouldn't he sit down and rest from his labours, and talk awhile. And it being only ten o'clock, he didn't see why he shouldn't. And as there was nowhere else to sit, unless on nettles, he sat on the mattress, side by side with her. And though he knew that from the point of view of parishioners it would have been better if he had been sitting on a chair, as there wasn't a chair he obviously couldn't sit on one.

So down he sat, and at his companion's suggestion lit his pipe. This, thought James, was true enjoyment. He gave himself up to it, wondering what Alice would say if she saw him, and deciding boldly that he didn't think he cared much. And they began to talk—at first in their ordinary voices, but soon dropping into undertones because of the beauty, the immense, absorbed, hushed beauty of the night, with the moon, a day past its full, beginning to sail over the top of Burdon Down behind them, and part the apple-leaves with silver fingers. And presently they didn't even talk, but sat quite still, just as if for years they had been easy friends, and together they watched the great yew-tree on the other side of the little sleeping garden brushing its dark and solemn head across the stars, and listened to the cry of an owl, floating from somewhere very far away towards them on the silence.

To Jen, who in her life had hardly known what silence was, it was a revelation. She listened, dissolved in a kind of awestruck joy. It seemed to her as if she were in the presence of perfect holiness, as if she were close to the very feet of God. She who had been trained irreligiously became, in this beauty, religious. She wanted to worship and fall down; she wanted to praise the Lord her Maker. And forgetting James, who anyhow was very easily forgotten, under her breath she murmured, *And the Glory of the Lord was revealed*—for father had seen to it that she studied the Bible carefully, it being, he assured her, English literature at its best.

James's heart gave a thump. That she should say what he so often said to himself on similar occasions struck him as very wonderful.

He turned his head, and looked at her in the dark. "You feel that?" he whispered.

No one ever said aloud any of the kinds of things he was so constantly thinking, because no one in the parish, not Alice, not Lady Higgs, not anybody, ever seemed to see the things he saw. If they thought as he did, if they saw what he did, they never mentioned it; and to have things which are precious to one eternally unmentioned makes one, he had long discovered, lonely. These August nights, for instance—quite remarkably and unusually beautiful, warm and velvety as he had never known them, ushered in each evening by the most astonishing variety of splendid sunsets—nobody had said a single word about them. They might have been February ones, for all the notice they got. Sometimes he climbed up to the top of Burdon Down towards evening, and stood staring in amazement at what looked like heaven let loose in flames over England; but always he stood alone, always there was no one but himself up there, and no one afterwards, when he descended from his heights, seemed to be aware that anything unusual had been going on. As far as Alice was concerned, and she was the person he saw most closely, God needn't have bothered to fill the year with magnificence, or invent a single sunset. For her the hedges in May foamed with white sweetness, and the buttercups turned the fields to glory, in vain. On her the wonder of the first real spring morning was lost. While as for when the daffodils trooped out in March and took possession of the world, she saw in this recurring miracle merely a sign that lamb would now be in season, and hastened to order it, roast, for their Sunday dinner.

Of course, thought James, afraid, yet hoping, he might be judging them wrongly, it was possible that she, and Lady Higgs, and the rest of the parish, did feel these things, but what was certain was that they were no more alluded to than if they had been improprieties. Nice to know the days were lengthening; nice to know the winter was over; that was as far as, in speech, anybody went. And he had sometimes thought that if only he could find someone who would talk about them, talk about them with real enthusiasm, he might feel less cut off, less by himself. It was extraordinary how lonely one could be, deep down inside oneself, just for want of a fellow-gloater. Talking wouldn't be enough; what one needed was someone who would gloat. A fellow-gloater must, James long had been wistfully certain, be an immense addition to one's own enjoyment. And now, suddenly, such a one seemed to have walked from nowhere into his life.

Was it possible? It must be. The way she had said that about the glory of the Lord, the awestruck catch in her voice …

His heart leaped responsive; but all he did was to grip his hands rather tighter round his knees, and turn his head and whisper, "You feel that?"

"Feel it?" Jen whispered back. "*Feel* it?" And after a pause added softly, "You know Gower Street, I expect. Well, it's where I've lived till to-day."

And she began to tell him, in a low, hesitating voice, because she kept stopping to listen to the silence, of what it had been like in Gower Street on summer nights, while away deep down in the country she had always known there must be this; and how she had ached with longing for it, how she had ached and ached with longing. And she talked to him as simply and easily as if he were her friend she had known for years. And it wasn't only because of the mattress, and the moonlight, and the intimacy which steals over people who sit side by side under these conditions, it was because of something about James himself.

What was it? she wondered, turning her head to look at the hunched-up figure. In the darkness of the tree they were sitting under she couldn't see his details, but she remembered that when she first met him that afternoon she thought he had a funny, quaint sort of face, kind and undecided, as if he wouldn't be able very easily to make up his mind which side to take when there were sides, because they all seemed to him so good, and, behind his enormous spectacles, she had noticed rather beautiful and embarrassed grey eyes.

He wasn't embarrassed now. Perhaps being in the dark did away with that. And he had a most restful effect on her. She sat blissful and relaxed, conscious that no effort of any sort was needed, and no being cautious and on her guard, as she had had to be so constantly with father—able to let the night's loveliness enfold her without being disturbed and interrupted by somebody else's personality. This man's personality didn't get in the way of one's happy thinking, it didn't come between her and what she wanted to attend to. With him she might talk or say nothing, as she felt inclined, and whatever came into her head she might say, and it wouldn't matter. He was as comfortable to be alone with as one's own bedroom, she thought. It was as if she were by herself, except that, agreeably, she wasn't. It was as if nobody were sitting under that apple-tree with her, except that, agreeably, someone was. Perfect, said Jen to herself; perfect. The very man to sit under a tree with in the dark.

She looked at what she could see of him with immense goodwill. Indeed it was deeply refreshing to be just simply natural, and not engulfed and lost in someone else's personality. With father, she had never once, in her whole life, been natural. Probably no obedient creature, she thought, could be so, no creature whose time was spent carrying out orders, and dodging round as the shadow and echo of another human being; no person, that is, who was in any way a slave.

Gazing at her tiny cottage lying bewitched at her feet in the moonlight, she said to herself that perhaps in order to get the fullest flavour out of life people should live neither as slaves nor slave-owners, but each apart in a little house, each independently in a place so small that it was the merest covering, the merest lid, like her own cottage—a place giving the least possible trouble to keep going, needing the least possible amount of one's precious time spent on it; and from it issue forth to their work, and to gregariousness, and to friendship and talk, and to lovemaking too if that were what was wanted, but always going back to the freedom, and healing, and self-development of solitude. How was one to think, if one was never alone? Or find the quiet necessary for realising how deeply happy one was?

She said something of this to her companion, and her voice seemed to him the very voice for a man to sit with in the dark, under an apple-tree.

He was leaning forward on the edge of the mattress, with his back almost to her, listening with absorbed attention more to her voice than to what she was saying, and thinking how like she was, flowering through her voice into beauty in the darkness, to some butterflies he had come across in the Swiss mountains the summer before. When they were folded up they were grey, mothlike creatures that one might easily overlook, but directly they opened their wings they became the loveliest things in the world, all rose-colour or heavenly blue. So had she been to him in the daylight that afternoon,—an ordinary woman, not in any way noticeable; but now listen to her, opening into beauty on the wings of her voice!

Entranced he hung on each sentence. How beautiful a speaking voice could be, he thought. He hadn't heard many in his life; in fact, he hadn't heard any, in women, that were definitely beautiful. Agreeable, well-bred—those were the best he had come across, and all the others were in different degrees, greater or less, on the whole afflicting. But this one—oh, he would like to listen to it for ever. It was so exactly suited to the occasion, falling on the night like the sound of water softly lapping in places set about with ferns, or like the sounds doves make, cooing in green enclosures. Could such a voice ever say bosh, James asked himself? He doubted it. Such music belonged only to kindness, and fair words. And when, in addition to being beautiful, instead of making the sort of conversation voices usually do make at a first meeting, and sometimes go on making at every subsequent meeting, it told him without any preliminaries what was really passing through its owner's mind, James felt as much refreshed as if, on his long continued spiritual drought alone with Alice, the blessed rain of real companionship were at last descending.

❦

He wondered what her Christian name was. He hoped it was something lovely, which would make up for her being, so disconcertingly, Dodge.

Dodge. That, of course, was her father's fault, and she couldn't help it. But he did want to be able to say some name, at least in his thoughts, which would go with the music of her voice. Presently he would ask her her Christian name. He felt so happy, so easy with her, as if he could ask her anything, and yet be safe from a snub.

But she was wrong about the little houses, one for each person, scattered over the world. He was sure that a state of things like that couldn't possibly work, for not only was society based on co-operation, but everybody almost had their Alices in some form or another. Also, might not such an arrangement easily lead to selfishness? And what about families? There had to be families. The world couldn't go on without families. Nor was he at all certain that, personally, he would like to live by himself in a little house, because companionship, if it were of the right kind, was probably one of the best things in life—in fact, undoubtedly was; and how could it be companionship, if most of the time it left off?

He said something of this, though loth to interrupt the queer, sweet music, and she answered, with a slight note of surprise as she recalled the appearance and brusqueness of Miss Ollier, "Do you love your sister so *much*?" and James, who hadn't been thinking of his sister, was brought back by the name with a jerk, and frowned a little—he couldn't have told why—and said, "I ought to. She has devoted her whole life to me." To which his companion, with genuine and obvious sympathy, unexpectedly replied, "How awful."

This startled James. Had he been saying something which sounded disloyal to Alice? But the vaguely outlined owner of the lovely, comforting voice didn't seem to think so, and proceeded to tell him of devotions—she called them concentrations—she had known; of her mother's on her father; of her own, not at all from her heart, but because she had promised it, also on her father; and how she didn't know which was the more enslaving,—to concentrate on somebody, or be concentrated upon oneself; but she was sure that both were bad. "One has to be free," she finished, as if taking it for granted that he would think so too.

"Spiritually, certainly," said James, who, except from Alice, felt he didn't want to be as free as all that, and could picture mutual concentration, under the right conditions, as a very happy thing indeed. What, really, in the whole world could be a happier thing? Under that apple-tree, in the scented darkness, it seemed to him that there was nothing to touch such a state.

"Spiritually—certainly," he therefore said, conceding that much freedom, but reserving all the rest, all the things he could so well imagine, the dear warmth and solace of some sweet, bodily presence, kind hands that gently touched, eyes that understood.

And Jen, smiling, retorted, "Clergyman."

And James, smiling too, said, "Well, that's what I am."

And Jen told him that till that day she had never spoken to a clergyman in her life.

And James said that she must have, because of being prepared for Confirmation.

And Jen explained that she hadn't been prepared for Confirmation, nor confirmed, nor christened, because of father's attitude towards the Church and its creeds, which was one of complete absence of interest. He wasn't hostile, he merely ignored; so that none of the usual rites had been performed on her.

"I hope you don't mind?" she asked, suddenly remembering that he, as a clergyman, probably would mind, and rather wishing she hadn't told him.

That was silly of her, she thought, to tell him. It might prejudice, not him, for already she somehow knew he was never prejudiced, but his sister against her; and suppose, when the six months for which she had paid rent in advance were up, just as the snowdrops were flowering, and the blades of all the bulbs she was going to plant were cleaving the soil, she were given notice to quit?

Now why hadn't she held her tongue?

For a moment she wondered why she hadn't, but was almost immediately aware of the reason: in the company of Mr. Ollier no tongues were ever held. Round him, she felt, they freely and happily wagged, and whatever they said, whatever indiscretions they spilled out, would be with him for ever safe. This was an endearing quality, she thought, for there could be no greater relief than to get rid of one's indiscretions in safety, and know that they would never come back on one. And she said to herself that Mr. Ollier must be a perfect treasure to his friends.

"It's not too late," remarked James, answering her question as a clergyman should.

"What—to be confirmed?"

"Yes. Nor is it too late to be christened."

"I don't think," said Jen, shaking her head, "I could start my career here by being christened. Not at my age. Imagine—fonts, and things."

"No, no," James assured her. "Of course you couldn't, and nobody wants you to. I was only telling you the facts. And just now, when you said this loveliness tonight was like—"

He broke off, and not till after quite an appreciable silence did he go on. "That showed," he said, "that whatever your father's attitude may be, your own is certainly religious."

"Is it?" she murmured, her eyes fixed on the unearthly beauty lying beyond the dark shadow of the tree. "Well, perhaps. I expect you know. And it's true that all this last week I've been wanting to say prayers."

"I hope you did say them, then," he answered, as in duty bound.

"I think I did. Something anyhow kept on bubbling up."

"And why particularly this last week?" he asked, passing over her curious description of the act of prayer.

"Because I've been happy. Suddenly, and utterly unexpectedly. Oh, it has been so wonderful! I didn't know—I never guessed—one could be as happy as that."

And she fell silent, gazing at the intensely still garden, where in the moonlight each separate leaf and blade of grass was smitten motionless. And James too was silent, because of the rapture in her voice. What could it mean, he thought, suddenly strangely depressed, except—

"I suppose," he presently said, dejectedly, "I mustn't ask what it was?"

She turned to him, called back from the contemplation of her bliss. She had forgotten he was there. Everybody was continually forgetting that James was there.

"What what was?" she asked.

"Why, what was making you so very—so extraordinarily happy this last week."

He thought he knew. He was afraid he knew. When a woman talks about being happy with that sort of wonder, really of ecstasy, in her voice, what could it mean except, somewhere, love? And his heart seemed to miss a beat waiting for her answer, and seeing that six hours ago he had never set eyes on her this struck him as really very strange.

Why should it matter to him so much, that which he felt sure she was going to tell him? Well, he hated engagements, for one thing—other people's engagements, that is. They were selfish and exclusive, they destroyed old friendships, and prevented new ones. He had seen it happen so often, the complete leaving out in the cold of everybody except the two absorbed people concerned, and he had been feeling so certain of this friendship, so confident that he and his lovely-voiced tenant were going to be close friends. Had he then been led to this orchard, to this apple-tree, to this intimate sitting whispering together in the dark, only to hear that she had just got engaged to somebody else?

Life all over, thought James, as bitter as it was in him to be. Life was a bully. It deliberately disappointed. It raised hopes, only to dash them. It dangled, only to withdraw. Besides, she ought to see other men first—though, as she obviously wasn't a young girl, he didn't know why he should suppose she hadn't already amply done so.

"I expect I shouldn't have asked that," he said, aware, and far more acutely than ever before, of his extreme personal loneliness. "Please don't tell me if you would rather not."

"But there's nothing I wouldn't tell you," Jen said, herself surprised that it should be so. "I think it's very odd," she added, pondering this strange fact. "I don't know why I feel like that, but I do."

"That's just what I've been feeling about you," said James; but he said it mournfully, for what was the good? What earthly good was it, if she had only come down there to mark time till her marriage?

He drooped over his clasped hands. Such things as he had been imagining, such delightful, exquisitely consoling things, didn't happen. Manna no longer dropped out of the skies when one was starving. Strangers with adorable voices didn't come round corners and march straight into one's intimate life; and if they did, there was always Alice, who wouldn't like it. Yes, that was his lot: always Alice. He had better settle down to it, and leave happiness to other people.

"You may think it a queer reason for wanting to say prayers," he heard his companion say, "but it was because my father married again. The other day. Quite suddenly. And the prayers were all of thanksgiving."

"Your father?"

Slowly James revived. Slowly he sat up straight. Her father. Nothing in people's fathers marrying, except satisfaction. When fathers married, daughters were freed.

Warmth stole down his spine. His heart seemed to fill out to its proper size again. "And so you were able to get away, and put your little house theory into practice," he said, seeing the whole situation in a flash, understanding with the quickness of a fellow slave.

Eagerness came back to his voice as he twisted round sideways towards her and smiled an enormous smile, for his mouth was capacious and seemed, when he smiled, which was as rarely as Jen, because with Alice one didn't smile, to reach almost anywhere. She couldn't see it in the dark, but she knew, from his tone, that it was there.

"Yes. It's most wonderful. I never could have left him if he hadn't done it. And you know—after a bit—one feels—one wants—"

"Oh, *doesn't* one!" James agreed with all his heart; adding, in case this might sound as if he were tired of his own condition, "I mean, I can imagine if I had a father, that after a bit—"

"Yes—after a bit," nodded Jen, as he paused. "One doesn't, because one can't, but, after a bit, one would like to."

His own thoughts; his secret, obscure, suppressed thoughts, coming out and frankly putting themselves into words.

He pushed himself up an inch or two nearer, overwhelmed by a desire to take her hand—no, not quite overwhelmed, for he didn't take it, but how much he wanted to!

"I've got a hundred a year, from my mother," she went on. "Just enough to prevent my buying more things than I need, and then having to waste precious time looking after them—just enough to live on and yet be free from possessions. It's a great thing, to be free from possessions."

"A hundred a year?"

His happiness was a little damped, and his capacious smile gathered itself up into seriousness again. He and Alice, particularly he, between them had two thousand a year, what with the money their mother had left him, and his stipend, as well as a rent-free, charming old house with a magnolia all over it, and a delicious garden; and though he adored the courage which could regard a single one of these many hundreds as enough, it did seem to be the result of inexperience, and he was afraid for his friend.

Yes, he was now very certain that she was his friend. They had leaped, all the usual delaying insincerities and feeling-round cut out, straight into real friendship. She wasn't entangled with anybody else, neither was he. For what after all, he thought defiantly, was Alice? Their course was clear and open, there was nothing to prevent—

Besides, when people tell you what their income is, it makes an immense stride towards intimacy. He only didn't respond with the amount of his because he was ashamed of its size compared to hers. Yet how much pleased she sounded with her poor little hundred a year, how confident that it was enough. He wondered, anxious for her now that she was his friend, if her pleasure and confidence would last when she got to grips with daily life, and if happiness could exist for an educated woman among the discomforts and fatigues which must surely attend such a pittance. How could there be happiness, if there was no time for it? And how could there be time in a day filled with hard bodily labour? She had said the cottage was so small that it could be kept clean with hardly any trouble; but what about cooking? And what about the water having all to be dragged up from that beastly well? A sordid life, he feared it was going to be, and her hands getting spoilt, her little pretty hands—oh, he had seen them in the moonlight when she was pretending to help him drag the mattress—while he a few yards away, up in his vicarage was lapped in comfort; he, a man, a strong, young man.

As though reading his thoughts, she said, "There's such a lot of time—enough time for everything on earth that one can possibly want to do, and hours and hours over for being happy in, if only one has very few possessions. I'm sure possessions are the devil." And she added that she begged his pardon for mentioning the devil, but that, it being dark, she had forgotten for a moment that she was sitting with a clergyman, and James laughed and waved her apology aside, and said that after all the devil was one of his special subjects.

"There's my cottage, clean already," she went on, proudly gazing at it as it stood among its moon-pale roses, the bright light shining from its open door, "and all because it's so small. Yet it really was rather dirty, as perhaps you know."

"Indeed I do. Quite unfit for you."

"Unfit? Why, it's perfect. But it *was* rather dirty, and in spite of that, one woman could and did clean it out from top to toe in three hours easily."

"*You* weren't that woman, I hope?"

"No. I was in Amberton—buying this mattress, and a few things I had to have."

"In Amberton? You went back to Amberton?"

"Yes, Mr. Patterson took me in his car."

"How very wonderful you are," murmured James.

"I think Mr. Patterson was very wonderful, the way he helped."

"And my sister sent somebody round to clean while you were gone?"

"No—why should she? Mr. Patterson sent Mrs. Jones."

It hadn't been Alice, then. She hadn't, after all, done anything. Yet, in a strange place, and tired out, his new friend had managed to get hold of people to do what she needed.

"I think you're extraordinary," he said in a low voice, after another silence.

"Why?" she asked, interested, for nobody had ever called her extraordinary in her life before.

"Knowing exactly what you want, and getting hold of people to help you, and doing everything so quietly and quickly. I spend hours, hesitating. I don't seem able to move a step without worrying whether the other direction wouldn't have been the right one."

"I think one's mind gets made up very quickly if night is coming on, and one hasn't got anywhere to sleep," she said.

"But to see a cottage, take it, have it cleaned, and be in it with a kettle and a bed, all between tea and supper, is really a remarkable achievement."

"Not a bed," she smiled. "Only the beginnings of one. The rest of it is coming out tomorrow."

"Well, enough of it to go on with, anyhow. Are you always like this? Do you always decide instantly, and instantly proceed to carry out?"

"I don't know. I've never been free before. But when one has had dreams, and suddenly there's a chance of making them come true—"

"But fancy this being your dream—this wretched little cottage. How I wish it were nicer for you!"

"I tell you, it's perfect."

"And I tell you I'm mortally afraid you'll see tomorrow that it isn't. Mortally. Because then you'll go away, and I shall have lost—"

He stopped abruptly, and didn't tell her what he would have lost. It was all very well feeling happy and easy and as though one could say anything, but there were in fact things one didn't say—not too soon, not at one's very first meeting.

And she, smiling in the darkness at how simple he was, and at how quickly they had made friends, said she would never go away, unless she were turned out; and he, after a moment, for he had to compose himself on hearing this and not say the things that leaped to his lips, went on very soberly to tell her that the garden was in an awful state, as she would find out, and she must let him send his gardener down to clear out the weeds for her.

"I'll let you do nothing of the sort," she said. "Thank you, of course, and all that, but I want to do it myself from the beginning. If you *knew* how I've longed to be shut up alone with a garden and a spade! I brought a spade and hoe back with me from Amberton. Mr. Patterson said they could wait, and that I needed other things more, but there's nothing I need more, and I'm going to start on the nettles the first thing tomorrow morning, and then I'm going to make borders, and then I'm—"

"But—are you so fond of gardening?" eagerly interrupted James, who loved it with passion, and, in his household, loved it alone. Hardly did he dare hope she was as fond of it as she sounded, and he had to know at once, he couldn't wait. …

"Fond of it!" echoed Jen.

She turned to him, bending forward a little, and repeated, her voice full of amusement at the inadequacy of the words, "*Fond* of it, did you say?"

Silence fell upon James, complete and blissful. The perfect friend. The sharer of enthusiasm. The fellow-gloater. Found at last.

❦

A sound of distant wheels and hooves, coming along the road that led over Burdon Down and drawing gradually nearer, mingled in his consciousness with this bliss. Somebody was driving very carefully and slowly, as well he might, down the steep, stony, chalk lane. A two-wheeled cart. One horse. James's mind mechanically registered these impressions, while his ears listened to what Jennifer was saying, and his heart glowed with his own extraordinary good luck.

She was explaining that she actually hadn't done any gardening yet, because in Gower Street one doesn't garden, except window-boxes, which were, as he could imagine, highly unsatisfactory things regarded as practice; but this hadn't stopped her from reading nurserymen's catalogues, and studying manuals, and planning what flowers she would grow if ever she got the chance,—a weakening literature, she admitted, and one she hadn't indulged in very often, because it made her dream dreams instead of attending to her duties. Those luscious descriptions of exquisite flowers—what was the use, she asked, while James listened with one ear, and with the other to the approaching wheels, of reading them, and getting all stirred up and excited? Her duty lay indoors among ink and paper, and no good thinking of what was going on in places where there were roses. But each year, towards the middle of April, somewhere towards the end of the month, a lilac-bush in the next door backyard, a single lilac-bush left over from days when God still had some sort of say in Gower Street, began to bloom, and it was amazing how difficult this made it for her; not difficult to stick to her post, because there was never any thought of being able to leave that, but difficult, exceedingly, to concentrate on what she was doing. Fortunately, father never would have the window open, so she was spared the intoxication of the scent, the divine scent that had drenched all the spring mornings of the world since the first lilac flowered in Paradise. Father, who wrote about April so beautifully—

Yes, father wrote.

Yes—books, of course. Novels. Very wonderful novels.

"Is your father by any chance Richard Dodge?" asked James, putting two and two together, but his attention much distracted because of the approaching wheels. Who could be driving down that lonely road at such an hour?

"Yes—that's the man," said Jennifer.

"I haven't read him, but I've heard—"

"Yes, that's what most people say. And I should think especially clergymen. Father's writings must be anathema in vicarages. Long before they became improper, they've been profane. I'm sorry if you mind. Perhaps I ought to have said I was his daughter, to begin with. Only then your sister mightn't have wanted me to come here."

"Why should I mind?" asked James, now hardly listening at all, his voice dropping lower as the wheels drew nearer. They were quite close now, and seemed to be slowing down—almost they seemed as if they were about to stop. Yet why should they stop just there? Why, in that lonely lane—

"Well, that's a comfort," went on Jen, pleased. "What was I saying? Oh, yes—I was going to tell you that father^ who writes so beautifully about April, never wants to open a window and let it in. Isn't that queer of him? He writes marvellously about flowers too, with a quite exquisite appreciation, but won't have a single one in the house. Don't you think that's very odd?"

For answer he suddenly gripped her foot, which was the bit of her nearest him, and whispered, urgently, "Hush."

"Hush?" repeated Jen, surprised. She too had heard the approaching wheels, but she was used to wheels, and thought nothing of their approaches.

"I want to listen," he breathed, gripping her foot tighter.

"Well, you needn't hurt me," she murmured, dropping her voice to a whisper because his urgency was impressive. She tried to get her foot away. It hadn't recovered from the miles and miles of hot walking it had done that day, and here he was clutching it as though it weren't a tired and tender thing at all, but just something to hold on to in a moment of what was evidently excitement.

"*Please*," was all he said to that, his head bent, intently listening.

The wheels had stopped; no mistaking it. They had stopped at the gate that led into the garden from the lane, and somebody was climbing down out of what he was now sure was a high dogcart, and, probably surprised, as he had been, at the bright light streaming through the open door of an uninhabited cottage, was coming to investigate.

Of course. He ought to have thought of that door and shut it, or else put out the light. But he hadn't at first intended—a man can't tell beforehand that he is going to spend the evening sitting under a tree with a lady—a man can't very well begin by putting out a lady's lamp—

How awkward, though, how terribly awkward, for him to be found there; he, the Vicar, on a mattress, in the dark, with the new tenant. He couldn't cross that stream of light and get away into the churchyard, he couldn't move from the shadow of the apple-tree without being seen in the bright moonlight, and his being discovered in such a situation would be all over the parish by the morning. Alice would hear. What would she think, and say?

James's own thoughts began to move at a great pace, and suddenly were lit by a flare of rebelliousness. Why shouldn't he sit there? What harm was he doing anybody? What harm was there in two fully grown, responsible people sitting out of doors together on a summer evening, even if it were a mattress they were sitting on?

But he knew that though there wasn't any harm—not really, not unless one made harm—such behaviour would offend what the Scriptures called *these little ones*; and the world appeared to be packed with little ones, all being offended by the simplest things. Indeed, thought James, his brain working at twice its usual speed while he hung suspended over the yawning moment, the simpler one's conduct was, and the more natural, the more deeply offended did the little ones seem to become. The countryside swarmed with little ones. The other vicarages were full of them, and Alice was the biggest little one of the lot. One imagined one was talking to an adult, and, the moment one said something self-evidently true, one found the person one was addressing wasn't an adult at all, but only a little one, being offended. He knew very well that his being where he was would violently offend even the least of the little ones, and therefore that it would be a disaster for him to be discovered.

"I think someone's coming in at the gate," remarked Jennifer.

"Oh, *hush*!" implored James.

"I wonder who."

"For heaven's *sake*!" implored James.

"Shall I wait, m'm?" asked a man's voice, loud and unembarrassed, out in the lane.

"Yes. I shan't be a minute, Riley."

Riley. Lady Higgs's groom. And the other voice—Alice's.

Now all that remained to James was to put his trust in immobility and luck. If he and his companion were absolutely motionless, if they behaved like two wild animals taking cover, if they lay *perdu* among the leaves and hardly breathed, Alice, coming up the path, intent on the light and the open door, mightn't see them. The real danger would be when she left the house, having found nobody, and perhaps began looking about in the garden. …

"Sit quite still," he breathed, himself gone rigid. "Don't move a hairsbreadth—"

"But it's only your sister," Jen whispered, as Alice advanced into the river of light.

"Oh, good God—but that's just *why*," whispered James.

❦

Alice, as James had expected, walked up the path looking neither to right nor left, her eyes fixed on the open door and the light. As he had done an hour earlier—positively he had been sitting there a whole hour, and he thought it was five minutes—she pushed the tangle of creepers aside, and stood on the threshold staring in; and, also as he had done, having observed the signs of occupation, and the tidiness where that afternoon, when she showed it to Miss Dodge, had been cobwebs and grime, and the clean smell of soapsuds in place of damp frowst, and the pail of water set ready by the stove, and the kettle, lid removed, filled with roses, she called out, surprise and question in her voice, even as it had been in his, "Miss Dodge? Are you there, Miss Dodge?"

To this there was naturally no answer, and the two, breathlessly watching from their dark place beneath the apple-tree, saw her, after hesitating a moment, go in, and heard her inquire, her voice more muffled for she had evidently advanced as far as the foot of the little staircase, whether Miss Dodge were upstairs.

Miss Dodge naturally wasn't upstairs; the silence in the cottage was complete; and Alice stood listening, much puzzled.

James, in his dark shelter, the tension relieved for a moment, let go Jen's foot, and turned and caught her hand.

"She'll be out again in a minute," he whispered quickly, drawing himself up nearer to her. "She may begin looking about in the garden. Don't stir, will you. I'd get into the most *awful* row if—"

"No, no—I won't move," Jen whispered back, bending close to his ear—almost with the gesture of a mother protecting her babe. Which was rather what she felt like, for in the last few seconds she had completely grasped James's situation. He was afraid of his sister; and Jen, who knew all about being afraid of the person one lived with, immediately flung herself heart and soul into the business of aiding and abetting him against Alice. Besides, on her own account she was disposed to frustrate Alice. Couldn't a woman leave her door open, then, on a fine night, without Miss Ollier coming along to find out the reason? And oughtn't Miss Ollier, anyhow, to have been in bed long ago? The church clock had lately struck eleven; what was she doing, Jen asked herself, hostile now and entirely on the brother's side, gadding about in wheeled vehicles and coming into people's cottages at such an hour? With her hat on, too—her daytime hat; a navy-blue hat, its front trimmed by an aggressive, stiff, upstanding, bellicose bow, which, Jen began to think, must be symbolic. Even in the afternoon, pleased as she had been with her for letting her at once have the cottage, she had in some instinctive, subconscious way, she now remembered, feared the hat; and to go on wearing it right into what was so soon going to be the middle of the night, did suggest qualities which must be terribly oppressive to live with—vigilance, energy, a reluctance ever to relax and lay aside armour.

Clothes, Jennifer was sure, must often give away what a woman was like inside, and it was fairly evident that Miss Ollier's inside was very like her hat. It must be, or her brother wouldn't be so much afraid of her. Poor young man. Poor, kind, nice, simple, young man. On what rights, she would like to know, was based this everlastingly recurring domestic tyranny going on behind the neat front-doors and decently shrouded windows of people's homes? She, who had so newly been released from it, wholeheartedly was on the side of those who still were captives. Clearly the man by her side was still a captive, and equally clearly he always would be if nobody came to the rescue and saved him by marrying his sister. In her own case the miracle had happened, and young Netta had come along and taken on father, but she was afraid it didn't look as if it would in Mr. Ollier's case. Women easily married old men, but men didn't easily marry elderly women—especially not if they were, thought Jen, Miss Ollier. And the young man by her side, living in his beautiful, magnolia-covered Georgian house, a house surely built only to enclose and cherish happiness, was so kind, so gentle, so ready, she was certain, to fall back all along the line before any attack—because people did fall back before attacks if they were courteous, if they were kindly, if they preferred the graciousness of giving in to the winning of sterile domestic battles, if, that is, they had a true knowledge of what really mattered, of what really was precious—

"*Now*!" whispered her companion, suddenly interrupting these reflections, and jerking himself closer.

Jen started. For a moment she had forgotten …

Yes, there she was again; there was Miss Ollier, pushing the creepers on one side, and standing with the light behind her looking out into the garden. Oh, but how awful if she turned her head that way! Would she smell the pipe? Would she see them? They could see her so plainly themselves, with eyes accustomed to the darkness, that it seemed impossible she shouldn't see them—if she looked—if she turned her head—

❦

Crouching they watched, holding their breath, pressed shoulder to shoulder; and a thrill, such as he hadn't had since he was a child playing perilous games of being hunted and escaping, ran along James's veins. This really was wonderful, this hiding from Alice with somebody willing to hide too, instead of, as he had hidden in his melancholy childhood, all by himself—wonderful, but how dangerous. Obviously, it was terribly dangerous; much the most dangerous action of his life. Strangely worth it, though. He hadn't been so close to a woman, except his mother, since he took orders. He could feel her heart beating against his arm. It was extraordinary to remember that he had only met her that afternoon. Why, he seemed to have known her always. …

Of course, if Alice were to take it into her head to come up the slope to the orchard, they would be done for.

He couldn't imagine what would happen.

He didn't dare imagine.

But meanwhile, how wonderful this was, sitting so close to his friend that he could feel her heart-beats.

He shut his eyes. The sweetness and the danger of his position went completely to his head. Starved was what he had been till tonight, he thought; nothing but bones, emotionally; a perfect skeleton in the matter of love. Nobody ever kissed him. Alice's goodnight peck wasn't a kiss. Religion by itself wasn't enough—you couldn't kiss religion. Setting an example was a barren business—you couldn't kiss an example. And oh, what good was it, being continually manifestly spotless for all to behold, when it didn't warm one's heart? What a man wanted in life—well, he wasn't twenty-seven yet, and there was a good deal of it still before him, and he had been feeling more and more distinctly lately, as this lovely, hot summer proceeded on its teeming way, with all which he beheld, whichever way he looked, recklessly mating and bringing forth, that what a man wanted in life wasn't only Alice.

So he sat with his eyes shut, and when he opened them once for a second, and saw the listening figure on the path below swimming indistinctly in a haze, he shut them again—for there was no good in looking at something that swam indistinctly—and kept them shut. The peril of his position grew vague as a dream. Love—that was what a man wanted; needed; simply had to have. Kind love. Sweet, smiling, gracious love. In one's house like sunshine, filling it with light; in one's garden like roses, filling it with fragrance. Ah, how he could imagine it! How well he could imagine it, the sort of heaven there would be about a man all day—and all night too, if, by the blessing of God, one happened to have married Love. …

Giddiness came over him. Tighter he held the hand in his, closer he pressed against the heart he could feel beating.

Somebody whispered, "She's going. Look—"

Who was going? Where?

From the depth of his sweet dreaming, he came sighing back to life.

Yes—Alice really was going, straight down to the gate, and without turning her head, he saw, his eyes blinking as if he had been roused from sleep. She could be heard, presently, getting into the dogcart; and presently the wheels could be heard, beginning slowly to crunch the stones again.

Clearly now was his chance. He knew it. All he had to do was to leap up, hurry across the garden and through the churchyard, and he would get home first, and be sitting in his study when she arrived, as though he had never left it.

But he ought to go at once. Every instant those wheels were drawing Alice nearer the Vicarage, every instant that he lingered made it more difficult for him to be home before she was.

Yet how reluctant was James to move. It really seemed as if he couldn't, as if to tear himself away was impossible.

"Run," whispered Jennifer—still whispered Jennifer, just as if the woman in the dogcart could hear, for she was unable at once to shake off the panic she had been in on this poor, bullied young man's account.

She sat up straight. She dragged her hand out of his. She gave him a push.

"*Run*," she whispered again. "Run—*run*!"

And instead of running, without saying a word James turned, seized her in his arms, and to her abysmal, her speechless amazement, with violence and desperation, and what seemed to be a terrible interminableness, kissed her.

Then indeed he did run, fleeing across the garden and up through the churchyard as though the devil were after him. What had he done? He didn't know; he couldn't think; his mind was roared through by a whirlwind of confusion, his blood pounded in his ears.

Breathless, with thumping heart, he reached his study and threw himself into a low chair. There, his arms hanging nervelessly over the sides, and his hair damp and ruffled, he gave himself over to agonies shot through with exultations. Tomorrow—in the daylight—when he saw her again—would she ever, ever—

And there Alice found him when she came in a minute later, his long legs stretched out anyhow, his face strangely flushed, his eyes, she could see even through his spectacles, wild.

She stared at him a moment. Her own vexation with him faded away, and all the advice Lady Higgs had given her about keeping her end up, and not standing any nonsense from a brother so much younger than herself.

"I believe you're going to have 'flu," she pronounced at last, her voice shrill with foreboding. "Or else something you've eaten has seriously disagreed with you. Don't move, James. Now don't *move*, I tell you. Sit still, now, while I fetch my thermometer, and take your temperature."

CHAPTER VI

While this was being done to James, and he far too greatly agitated to notice or object, Jennifer was sitting on her mattress beneath the apple-tree in a state of high indignation. Her hair was in a tumult, and her face was hot. Also, one of her eyebrows had been scratched by James's spectacles, and hurt.

She hadn't, strange as it may seem, but it is nevertheless true, been kissed by a man in her life before—except by father, who, when it came to kissing, didn't count—and was of opinion, as from a violently hostile angle she considered what had happened to her, that if this was lovemaking, then she didn't think much of it. But it wasn't lovemaking. It was gobbling—just gobbling, she said to herself, outraged, thumping her clenched fists on the mattress; as if one were a plate of food, with no say in the matter, and no wishes, and bound to be gulped down, whether one wanted to be or not.

How entirely revolting, she thought. How unspeakably revolting, this rifling, not of beauty, which might be understandable, but, so much worse, so deeply humiliating and unpardonable, of her helpless and unassuming plainness. Mr. Ollier, on whom she hadn't set eyes till that day, and whom she had been liking so much till the dreadful moment when he turned into a satyr, merely because it was dark and he could forget what she really looked like, and they were alone and close together, and she was a female, and he an evidently sexually-starved male, had flung himself upon her as if he were snatching food at a railway station between two trains, too hungry and hurried to bother about the quality of the food, not caring what it was, so long as it would temporarily stay his pangs. So, she supposed, shocked and bitter, were kitchen wenches attacked by lustful farm-hands. Could a woman be more profoundly mortified? And was it credible that a clergyman, of all people, should behave so?

"He ought to be *unfrocked*," she said to herself somewhere round midnight, again thumping her clenched fists on the mattress, the word coming into her mind from God knew where.

Then, feeling that her face, at least, could be washed clean of him, even if her consciousness couldn't, she jumped up and ran down to the cottage, and sought solace in the pail of water set by the kitchen stove for quite other purposes by clean, unruffled Mrs. Jones in the innocent hours of the afternoon.

With angry splashings Jen washed, as if trying to sluice off the very memory of James, and when she had got rid of his kisses, anyhow physically, she blew out the lamp and went back to the orchard, and lying down on her mattress, or rather throwing herself down on it, for all her movements were violent with indignation, she tried to compose herself to sleep. He shouldn't spoil her sleep, she thought, clenching her fists again; he shouldn't unfit her for all the work she meant to get through next day.

But, naturally, she wasn't able to compose herself; and for a long while she did nothing but toss about furiously, telling herself that never had woman been more humiliated. "If it were dark enough, *anybody* would do for him," she said aloud in her wrath, again thumping the mattress. Well, she didn't intend to be the any woman. He would have to find someone more accommodating. She hadn't come here, she hadn't picked out Cherry Lidgate as the background for her new, beautiful life, just to be insulted, dragged in dirt. And though in her heart she knew the young man was incapable of insult, of dragging anybody in dirt, how was she, being so angry, to reconcile this deep, smothered conviction, with kisses of such dreadful ravenousness that they had forced the horrid thought on her that she was food being gobbled?

Oh, it spoilt things, it spoilt things! she cried passionately, hot, angry tears squeezing themselves through her tight-shut eyelids, as she lay on her back vainly trying to go to sleep. So kind he had seemed, so gentle, so incapable of violence—and then look at him. How could she stay there, with him for her landlord, and living just round the corner? Who could have believed that, having found exactly what she wanted, the whole thing was going to be smashed up?

Somewhere about dawn, exhausted she at last fell asleep, and then slept so heavily that the sun was well above Burdon Down and shining warm on her face through the branches of the apple-tree, and Mrs. Jones's little girl, as arranged the evening before, was coming up the path with the milk, before she woke.

At the sound of the gate clicking she opened her eyes, and stared up at the green leaves, and bits of dazzling blue sky showing through them, above her. What was this? What had become of the curtained window of her bedroom in Gower Street, and the chest of drawers in front of it, which was what she saw every morning the first thing?

A bee, already heavy with honey, was droning in the warm air. There was a smell of fruit, of apples ripening in the sun, of apples rotting in the grass—the luscious smell of high summer. Nothing could be more unlike Gower Street; nothing could sound and smell more different.

Slowly she remembered where she was, and why she had all her clothes on, and all the circumstances of her going to bed in that place; and she wondered, as she lay still a moment watching, her head turned sideways, Mrs. Jones's little girl carefully carrying a jug along the path below, that she should have been so much excited. For a great calm was now upon her, a delicious feeling of being new—as new and untouched as the fresh young morning itself. Sleep had held her in its arms, and smoothed out all yesterday's furrows. The night was gone, and out of its blackness had come this golden flower of day, with leaves rustling in the sun, and Mrs. Jones's little girl bringing the milk for breakfast.

Absurd, absurd, she thought, those nightmares she had had of furious resentment, grotesque to have been so angry. She no longer wanted anybody to be unfrocked. Too much fuss was made about kissing and such things, it seemed to her, restored and wholesome. Women, with their concentration on their tiresome selves, and their easily upset virtue—why should they imagine the heavens were falling if they should happen to be grabbed at and kissed with gusto? Wasn't that, according to father's writings, who, after all, was a wise and experienced man, what they were chiefly made for? And did it much matter one way or the other, a little accident—she felt now it had been only a little accident, brought about by a combination of circumstances improbably recurring—like that? Anyhow she couldn't be bothered to worry over it, or over the impassioned clergyman. She had other things to do, many other things, many happy, jolly, sensible things, this wonderful new day. Poor young man—let him keep his frock, and go his way with God's blessing.

And stretching herself, she sat up and shook the hair back from her face, and tidied it quickly with both hands; and directly she moved, Mrs. Jones's little girl, prim and clean in a pinafore on the path below, saw her, and stood still and stared.

❦

"Hello!" Jen called, pausing in her tidying, and smiling down between her raised hands.

"Hello?" piped Mrs. Jones's little girl in a tiny, interrogative voice, nervous but polite.

"Did you ever know such a lovely morning?" inquired Jen, beaming at her.

Mrs. Jones's little girl, who hardly knew anything except lovely mornings, so persistent had they been that summer, and the memory of the mornings of her few other summers being blotted out by what seemed to her immense chasms of time, had no idea what to say to this, so said nothing, but stood, very shy, first on one foot and then the other, with both her diminutive red hands tightly grasping the jug of milk.

"Well, I'm sure you didn't, whatever you don't say," said Jen, scrambling to her feet and pulling her clothes straight.

Her clothes felt uncomfortable and scratchy, after having been worn without stopping for twenty-four hours, and she wanted to do so many things at once—take them off, wash, put on her dressing gown while they aired, and have breakfast—that they only got a very hurried and sketchy pulling straight.

Mrs. Jones's little girl watched nervously. Her mother hadn't prepared her to find the lady in bed out of doors, and then getting up and shaking herself ready for breakfast as if she were a dog. No one could tell what a lady like that might do next, so she watched her nervously, and only just managed to stand her ground when the lady ran down on to the path, almost jumped down on to it, and stooped and kissed her.

"Darling," said the lady. And added, kissing her a second time, "Good morning."

This was very distressing, because some of the milk got spilt, and her mother had told her on no account to let that happen. She stood her ground, however, desperately clutching the jug, and said nothing; nor did she say anything when the lady, looking at her wrist watch, asked her whether she didn't think it terribly lazy of her to sleep till eight o'clock.

"Isn't that a dreadful waste of a fine morning," Jen said, smiling at the serious, small face with its sweep of lowered eyelashes, and hoping the little girl would look up and show her what her eyes were like; for they must, thought Jennifer, be very sweet eyes if they at all matched the rest of her.

The little girl, naturally unable to commit herself to an answer to this question even if she had known one, only hung her head, very shy, and remained silent; and Jennifer, taking the jug from her and thanking her for having brought it, said goodbye and went indoors to get breakfast ready.

No goodbyes, however, could dislodge the little girl until she had been given back the jug. Her mother's orders were, "Bring back the jug," and bring it back she would, whatever happened. So that she was still standing there, still shifting from one foot to the other, and still hanging her head, her fair hair like a cloud of spun gold hiding her face, five minutes later when Jen came out to eat her bread and butter in the porch.

"Hello?" said Jen, inquiringly.

"Hello?" repeated the little girl, in a hasty, conciliatory pipe, though without looking up.

"Not gone home yet?" asked Jen.

No, the little girl hadn't gone home yet, but had such difficulty in putting this obvious fact into words that she could only make small, inarticulate noises.

"Wuff—wuff—wuff—" said the little girl, anxiously; or seemed to say.

"What, darling?" asked Jen, straining her ears.

"Wuff—wuff—wuff," said the little girl again; or seemed to say.

"Well, then, if that's so," said Jen, after a moment's attentive but unfruitful listening, "come and have breakfast with me, won't you? I'll go and cut some more bread and butter. Darling—*do*. We'll sit on the grass over there, and have a picnic."

But the little girl's face grew so red and alarmed at this that it was plain the idea of a picnic was abhorrent to her. She plucked at the corner of her pinafore, her head hanging lower than ever; and when Jen said, "Don't you want to? What is it, then, darling?"—for though she manifestly didn't want to stay and picnic, neither did she seem able to go away—when Jen said, "What is it, then, darling?" the little girl lifted a finger, with an obviously immense effort, and pointed it at the jug standing where Jen had put it down on the floor of the porch.

"Wuff—wuff—wuff," said the little girl, very anxiously; or seemed to say; and took a cautious step nearer.

"Oh—the jug. Do you want to take it back? But I haven't got anything to put the milk in," said Jen. "Yes, I have," she added quickly, laughing with sudden glee as she stooped and picked it up—"I've got myself." And she drank all the milk at a draught.

"So simple," she remarked when she had finished, gasping a little, and looking at the little girl who had forced herself to come quite close. "Now it needn't stand about getting flies into it, or going sour. But I'll have to have some more this afternoon. You'll bring me some, won't you? There—take your jug," she said, holding it out. "No, wait a minute—I'll wash it out for you."

But the little girl didn't want it washed out, and wouldn't let it go again, once she had got it, for anything in the world. Hugging it to her chest, she trotted off quickly down the path, with an uneasy glance over her shoulder half way to the gate, as if she were afraid she might be being followed.

"Don't forget to come back this afternoon," Jen called after her; adding, something inside her suddenly tugged at by the grace of the small, fleeing figure, whose hair, caught by the sun, was turned to glory, "little *love*."

She stood a moment shading her eyes, watching the child open the gate and with punctilious conscientiousness stand on tiptoe, when she was on the other side, so as to reach over and latch it again properly. Children; how sweet they were, thought Jen. What precious, lovely things. Of all the treasures in a beautiful world brimful of treasures, they were the most precious and lovely. And they went on. They weren't like roses, only there in summer; they didn't, like hyacinths, only adorn the spring. Bulbs were all very well, but children—

She broke off these thoughts, a curious wistfulness in her heart; and the last flutter of the pinafore having disappeared down the lane, she sat down on the step of the porch, and began to eat her breakfast of bread and butter.

But while she ate, smiling at the remembrance of the child's beauty, as unconscious as the beauty of the morning, she also sighed.

Now why did she sigh?

A little surprised, she asked herself this, and could find no answer.

❦

During the next few hours she was very busy, for the carrier from Amberton came out soon after breakfast with the rest of the things she had ordered, and they had to be unpacked and arranged. In the afternoon, she decided, she would begin her attack on the weeds, and do as much as she could towards their extermination while she was there this week-end, in spite of having to be interrupted by going back to Gower Street on Monday morning. Better get started on them as soon as possible, she thought, going out every now and then, in the middle of her unpacking, to have another look at the rank things. They fascinated her. Obviously, she argued, their very luxuriance was an earnest of what the soil could do, given a proper chance; obviously anything one put into it would flourish.

And not only did the weeds flourish, but toadstools, of which in the darker corners there were flocks, seemed to be enjoying themselves a good deal. And so were snails and slugs enjoying themselves,—fat, prosperous, and many. And what could this exuberance, this vitality wherever she looked, point to, except that the soil only asked to be permitted to give results? That which, she reasoned, so tremendously nourished one set of things, would equally tremendously nourish another set of things; and her imagination, unshackled by knowledge, leapt along excitedly into a next year's April jewelled with tulips, followed by a summer paradise of pinks, and roses, and sweet-peas. Jasmine-muffled lattices; she would have those, of course—the lattices were there already, and only needed muffling. Sweet William with its homely cottage smell—those, too, in masses. Violets dim, and pansies freaked with jet—oh, it was all going to be so wonderful, she thought, sighing with happiness.

There would have to be a good deal of spadework first, though, she realised, but her spade was there, standing in a corner of the kitchen, ready unpacked and only waiting to be used, and what satisfying, strengthening hours lay ahead of her in its company, what healthy hardening of her muscles, and growing ability to carry mattresses about without having to be helped! By the way, that mattress was still out under the apple-tree. Her gaiety clouded over at the remembrance. Across the bright looking-forward of mind, a shadow fell. In spite of having decided that the odious business last night didn't matter, wasn't to be allowed to smudge her day, at the thought of the mattress it came back and worried her again. Really it had been rather horrible—the *feel* of it had been so horrible, the dreadful, hot closeness, the sudden revelation of—

She thrust it aside. She shook it off, as she had done on waking up. She didn't know, didn't want to know, of what it was a revelation. And stopping on the path—this was in one of the interludes in her unpacking, when she was out in the garden—she deliberately lost herself in the consideration of a quantity of brambles she had just caught sight of.

More work, here. Much hard work, here—the sort that would take up all her attention, and effectively blot out unpleasant imaginings. With what sort of instrument, she asked herself, could one hack one's way through such an apparently impenetrable mass of brambles? Spades wouldn't do it; nor would an ordinary billhook—a tool she had met for the first time the day before at the ironmongers, and been persuaded by him to buy. Something much sharper and stronger would be needed to deal with this, and something with somebody very strong and determined using it. The weeds, the toadstools, the snails, the slugs—those were soft things a woman could get rid of by herself, with patience; but the crowd of brambles, mixed up in such a tangle with what seemed to be gooseberry-bushes, mightn't they be more than she, unhelped, could manage?

Slightly dismayed, Jen contemplated them, her head on one side. How very lazy the last tenant must have been; how really wickedly neglectful. No wonder the young man the night before, during that pleasant period of friendly talk before he turned into something that wasn't a young man at all but a sort of dreadful animal, had offered to send his gardener to clear the ground for her. Naturally she had refused, because she wanted to do everything herself; but she hadn't then seen the brambles. Now that she had seen them, it seemed really disastrous that, by his behaviour, he had made it impossible for her ever again to accept help from him.

Idiotic young man. Tiresome, ridiculous young man. Even if he were, beneath his decent clergyman's coat, a sort of wild animal liable to sudden outbreaks, why couldn't he, in the presence of a stranger, have kept himself, for once, in leash? And been a comfort to her? And been somebody she could always, in a difficulty, fall back on?

Again she shook herself free of thoughts of Mr. Ollier. She didn't want to think of him at all; not now; not ever. Cleared out of her mind he was going to be, as utterly as the brambles were going to be cleared out of her garden. And, frowning at the monstrously flourishing masses, she concentrated her attention on deploring that the last person who lived in the cottage should have been so lazy.

❦

As a fact, the last person who lived in the cottage hadn't been lazy at all, but merely a man with the clear realisation, natural in an assistant grave-digger, of the rapid passage of time.

This realisation had paralysed him, as it had paralysed his predecessors, and hence the brambles. What was the good of anything? had been his attitude, he having seen for himself how, before one could turn round, people who seemed to have been just born were ready to be buried.

"What's the good," he used to inquire of his wife, when she tried, in her need of vegetables, to goad him to garden, "what's the good of 'avin' truck with livin' things? They only dies." Adding that his business was to put in corpses, not potatoes—see?—and that if she didn't hold that blinking tongue of hers—for though he lived next door to a churchyard, he yet swore—he'd soon show her which of them she was—see? Sometimes winding up, while he filled his pipe, by remarking that the only things, as far as he could make out, that never did die were corpses; which left her, being incapable of reasoned argument, frenzied but dumb.

Jennifer didn't know, as she unpacked in the quiet cottage, how many people had quarrelled in it, nor would she have been able to imagine that the sweet silence had ever been broken by sounds less harmonious than the tunes the robins were singing, perched just outside her open door. It was peaceful enough now. The wranglings and the angers had all rumbled off, like spent thunderstorms, into far-off places, and the robins piped, and the summer leaves rustled, and Jennifer undid her parcels, and put things tidily in such places as there were, just as if the little house had never been anything but the dwelling of an unmarried gentlewoman, and she at peace.

Busily she worked at settling herself in; cheerfully the robins piped their tiny tunes to her. One of them even hopped on to the bedstead the carrier had dumped down in the porch, where it considerably blocked up the way, and after watching her inquisitively as she tried, about one o'clock, to light the stove so as to cook some dinner, sang its song quite close to her.

She left off striking matches a moment to watch it, enchanted. It, in its turn, watched her; and presently, having finished what it wanted to sing, hopped nearer, jerking its head on one side as it stared with the easy familiarity and interest that made robins, of all birds, she thought, those one would be least surprised to see dropping in at tea-time to call. The robins were going to be her friends. She would encourage their familiarity with crumbs. She would keep a bowl of water in the porch for them to come and drink from. What a lot of things she was going to do—happy, out-door things she thought, once her cottage was in order, and she had got to know, for instance, the ways of this stove! It was a pity it chose just that first morning, when she was so specially busy, to refuse to light.

She began striking matches again, but for a long while struck them in vain. She used up nearly a whole box, and burned most of the paper her parcels had been wrapped in, before the fire was alight enough to cook on, and she rather wished Minnie had happened to be there that day—only, of course, for that one day, that necessarily fussed and busy day of settling in. It would have been a comfort not to be held up by having to get food ready. At the Vicarage, she dared say, that licentious young man, looking as if butter wouldn't melt in his mouth, was sitting down, all unruffled, to things like legs of mutton. Well, let him. Now why wouldn't this stove draw? Tiresome of it, when there was so much to do. The morning had slipped by at such a pace that she didn't seem to be any nearer tidiness at the end of it than she had been at the beginning. That bedstead, for instance—it still was cluttering up the porch. Something would have to be done about it; it couldn't stay there, bruising her shins every time she squeezed past it to get out, and fatiguing her spirit with the effect of disorder it produced. Somehow it had got to be carried inside; and not only inside, but up the tiny staircase to the bedroom. She ought never to have bought the thing, she said to herself, as on her knees she blew into the obstinate stove. Here she was, going to be obliged to waste precious time going into the village directly after dinner, so as to find a man to come and help her carry it upstairs. What did she want with a bedstead? What was this tradition, accepted, as so many other traditions, without examination, that one should sleep raised above the ground? Why should one sleep raised above the ground? She had slept only on a mattress the night before; not well, it was true, but that was because—oh, there she was back again at that unpleasant Mr. Ollier and the mattress. …

Impatiently she shut the stove door, the fire having at last caught, and getting up began breaking eggs into the frying pan. Was it because she was, really, an old maid, she asked herself, that she seemed unable to stop thinking about something she had decided wasn't worth thinking about?

Was it because, during her prolonged and sheltered life with father, she had been so completely cut off from any possible lovemaking, that when it did come upon her it gave her such a shock? Evidently it had given her a great shock, or it wouldn't keep on cropping up in her mind. Against her will, against the convictions of her commonsense, which told her the whole thing had been an accident of juxtaposition and a moonlight night, up it kept on cropping. Perhaps she would be more sensible when she had had some food. After only bread and butter for breakfast, perhaps dinner was what was needed for the final blotting out of Mr. Ollier from her mind. Why, if she went on like this, she would be forced to begin to suspect that that insulting embrace had, in some shameful way, stirred up hidden emotions in her. …

Hidden emotions? The thought was most unpleasant. She put it from her, jerking up her chin defiantly. She had no emotions, hidden or unhidden—unless it was the emotion she now felt at the prospect of dinner.

❦

Dinner was eggs and bacon. Mrs. Jones had brought her a neat pile of rashers from the village shop the evening before, and some eggs freshly laid by her own hens. These were the things to fix one's mind on, Jen thought—the pleasant frizzling of bacon, the fun, even if it did take up time, of cooking one's own dinner; and with a return of cheerfulness she laid the little table, spreading it with one of the two napkins she had bought in Amberton, and putting the roses, no longer now in the kettle but in a jug the carrier had brought, in the middle of it.

Dear, simple things of life, thought Jen when, admiring her handiwork, she sat down to dinner. Wasn't she *happy*. Wasn't she just *perfectly* happy. She had flowers, she had sunshine, she had solitude, she had eggs and bacon—absurd to let her pleasure in these things be clouded by a foolish and highly artificial notion that she had been insulted. Who could insult her, if she declined to recognise insult? Besides, the last thing the poor young man had intended, she was certain, was to insult. A repressed clergyman, breaking loose in the moonlight—that was all there was to it. And nothing, either, to do with her. She had merely happened to be present.

"For God's *sake*," said Jennifer, beginning to eat her eggs and bacon, "let's be sensible."

❦

Afterwards, when she had finished, and had lit a cigarette, and was quietly smoking, she felt quite different—as calm as she had been that morning on waking up. Sleep and food; they focussed everything. She must remember that. Next time anybody annoyed her, she would first go to sleep, and then eat eggs and bacon.

Anyhow she could now placidly plan her afternoon, without being continually interrupted by irrelevant and unpleasant thoughts. Presently, when she had washed up, she would stroll round to the village—there wasn't any hurry, there wasn't the least occasion to rush at things the way she had been doing all the morning—and find a man who would come and carry the bedstead indoors for her and set it up in the bedroom. The same man could then bring in the mattress, which was an eyesore of tumbled disorder out under the apple-tree. It was all quite easy and simple. No need to hustle, as she had been doing till dinner. An immense leisure was now to be hers for ever, and it was entirely her own silly fault if she upset it by rushing at things.

Her elbow on the table, her mind filled with peace, her eyes dreamy as she gazed out through the open door at the sunny garden, she sat resting, and presently wondered where father was at that moment, and whether he were loving being happy as much as she was. She hoped so. Dear father. Funny how much her affection for him had increased since he had gone away. Really he was a dear old man, when one came to look at him impartially, and from a distance. A distinguished dear old man, too; a father to be proud of.

Always, of course, she reflected, blowing smoke rings, she had been proud of him in a muffled sort of way, but not always, close up to him, had she been able to see that he was a dear old man. Here, sitting in the peace of her own cottage, quiet after her morning's labours, she clearly perceived father's real innocuousness, his fundamental simplicity, and felt very warm towards him. By his work he helped to make the beautiful world even more beautiful—for those, that is, who weren't clergymen—and of how many people, she would like to know, could one say that? Undoubtedly he was a father to be proud of. When she came down here to live for good, she would bring the copies of his books he had given her on birthdays and at Christmas, and would put them, in a glorious row, on the window-sill. He had had them handsomely bound for her, and each contained a suitable autographed expression of paternal goodwill. They would lend a great air to the place. In that small, bare room, they would be the only things which were splendid. Yes, he was a distinguished father, and she did hope Netta would like him very much. Netta was so charming that he was bound to be happy, rid for ever of his taciturn, undecorative daughter. Happy and soothed herself, Jen wanted the whole world to be happy and soothed; and especially father—that queer recluse, that queer disliker of almost everything, and certainly, till Netta came, of quite everybody, whose fife, devoted entirely to perfecting his art, had been such a strange and solitary thing.

She mused, her eyes on the hot little garden beyond the tangled roses, but not seeing it. What a very odd marriage it was—that girl, and father. Where had father found her? How had he persuaded her to marry him?

And with some surprise—for everything had happened in such a hurry, and she herself had been so much absorbed in her own affairs that there had been no time either to want to know anything or to be told—she realised that she hadn't an idea.

❦

Later, she went down to the village, in search of a man who would clear the porch of the bedstead.

At first she didn't want to go, feeling, after the good meal and the hard morning's work, disinclined for the hot walk, and sat watching the lane at the end of the garden hoping some man would pass to whom she could call for help.

But nobody passed; neither a man, nor any other human being. The lane, which led only from Burdon Down to the village, and was a short cut to nothing but Lady Higgs, remained empty and unused. Grasshoppers chirped there, and swallows skimmed; the sun beat blindingly on its white chalkiness; its edges were sweet with flowers; and grasshoppers, swallows, blinding light, and flowers had it all to themselves. Throughout the hour during which she sat watching, nobody had occasion to take the quickest way to Lady Higgs, nor had Lady Higgs, for her part, who, though not a man, would have at once, had she appeared, been asked by Jennifer to be the vehicle of a message to a man, any occasion to take the quickest way to Cherry Lidgate. (She, indeed, never had such occasion, there being another road to it, longer but good, and her advance towards the Vicarage, when she called on Alice, always being made majestically in a Rolls.)

Jen therefore kept her eye on the lane in vain; and about three o'clock, giving up hope, she fetched her hat from upstairs and set out herself, plunging into the white hotness outside as if into a scalding bath.

The village drowsed in afternoon languor. Its men, except an ancient one long past exertion, were away working in the fields and hedges. A few women, having finished washing-up, were sitting, the necks of their blouses undone, at the open doors, trying to get a breath of air. In the little schoolhouse, imprisoned children were droning lessons, and their reluctant voices floated sleepily out into the street through the open windows. Mr. Patterson, on inquiry at the *Jolly Shepherds*, was having his daily nap, and couldn't be disturbed. Mrs. Jones was nowhere to be found—not that Mrs. Jones, or any other woman, could have got the bedstead up the stairs, but she would, Jen felt, have known where to find a man. A man was what was wanted. Mr. Ollier would have done perfectly, and he just round the corner, two minutes' walk away on the other side of a cool churchyard, instead of at the end of over a mile of white glare. But he had put himself beyond the pale of helpfulness, or of anything else that was neighbourly and friendly. Oh, bother Mr. Ollier; there she was thinking of him again. …

Discouraged by finding she had dragged through the whole mile of heat only to have to drag all the way back through it without having got what she came for, she left a message for Mrs. Jones with the woman in the village who seemed least overcome by somnolence, asking her to send a man round as soon as ever she could lay hands on one, and proceeded to face the scorching lane again with what energy she could. She hadn't much. Her legs dragged. It really was intolerably hot. She wanted to sleep. She didn't want to do anything more that day, but just sleep. After all, what was all this hurry? Why not find some nice cool place—perhaps in the shade of the yew-tree on the edge of her garden, and just go comfortably to sleep?

Languidly, the heat of the afternoon having got into her whole body, she opened her gate and made for the yew-tree. The mattress under the apple-tree, and the whole of that side of the garden, was flooded now by sun, so even if she had wanted to, which she didn't, because beneath that apple-tree sat the ghost of Mr. Ollier, and probably would continue to sit there till he had purged his offence by apology—even if she had wanted to, she couldn't have rested there.

Yes, by the way—oughtn't he to come and apologise, or something? Wasn't that, really, what he should do, and rather soon? She hadn't thought of this before, but she did think of it now, as she made her way to the branching yew-tree in search of coolness. She imagined it was what most women, so completely non-participant as she had been, would expect, and what most men, surely, would wish to do. During her busy morning at grips with the realities, engaged in driving him from her mind whenever he thrust himself into it, this aspect of the affair hadn't struck her. But now she did begin to wonder that she had seen nothing of him, and asked herself whether things could be left in the air like this. If they were left in the air, what sort of faces would he and she make at each other next time they met? Sooner or later, a next time was inevitable. They couldn't live within a stone's throw of each other, and not, some time or another, meet. Then, if he hadn't said he was sorry, which she was sure he was, very, by now, and suggested she should forgive him, wouldn't that be awkward? For him, that is, he being shy in daylight, she remembered, and any future meetings certainly not going to be—she would see to that—in the dark. She herself wouldn't mind of course, having, since her dinner, definitely and finally decided that Mr. Ollier and his snatched kisses were of no importance whatever.

❦

Beneath the yew-tree, half buried in dank weeds, she discovered Burridge's converted tombstone, and sat down on it thankfully, pleased that in a dark corner there should be a seat, and blessing whoever had had the brilliant idea to make it of stone.

She had changed after dinner into a linen frock she had sensibly brought in her suitcase, and the precious coldness of the tombstone quickly got through its thinness, and spread relief along her body. The frock would suffer, but she didn't care. Creeping up her was comfort, and nothing else at that moment would have given her that, except just what she had found—deep shadow for her eyes, long grass and dock-leaves for her feet, and an ice-cold stone for her hot body.

Well, this was really very pleasant, thought Jen, sitting there in the quiet, her chin cupped in her hands. There wasn't a sound, except the occasional hop of a bird from dry twig to dry twig. Nothing seemed at the moment to be busy; spiders in their webs sat still, the numerous snails were all motionless among motionless weeds, and the birds, if they hopped, hopped lazily. Her eyes grew drowsy. Sleep was what she wanted. She would lie down full length, and feel the delicious coldness all along her back, instead of only on one bit of her.

Yes, that was the thing to do, and bother her linen frock getting covered with mould. She liked lying flat. It rested her far more than when she was propped up on a pillow. She would stretch herself out, and go to sleep.

And with a sigh of deep satisfaction, she did so.

Alice found her there half an hour later, when she came to call.

CHAPTER VII

Alice didn't want to call, and would have much preferred to ignore this woman, who had come barging into her ordered life and with the utmost promptitude begun by stealing a march on her; but she was determined not to make any more mistakes, and allow herself, a second time, to be swept by anger with James into conduct she would afterwards be sorry for. So, seeing that the woman was there, and actually already established, she decided that the only wise thing to do was to pocket her feelings, make the best of a bad business, and pay her a visit.

Also, she was curious. It seemed queer that the tenant should be in the cottage already. Where had she got furniture from so quickly? True, there had been hardly any when Alice looked in the night before, but the woman had slept there, so the bedroom, anyhow, must be more or less furnished. Alice wanted to know how on earth this had been managed, and without any appeal, either, being made to the Vicarage for help; and also, if belatedly, she was going to ask questions, and discover as much as she could about Miss Dodge. Clearly the more she knew the better armed she would be for the protection of James, should snares be set for him and he, if incredibly, want to walk into them. Oh, no—it would never do for her to hold aloof, and accordingly know nothing of what the woman was doing, and of what might be going on down there. She must at once establish conventional relations, and the first step towards conventional relations was to call.

Therefore Alice called. Having reached her decision, she let no grass grow under her feet, but called at once. The moment was propitious; James was safe in bed; it was the hour at which calls are customary; and putting on her hat with the navy-blue bow, off she went.

"Now you," she said, going into James's room before leaving, "are to sleep. I'm walking over to Lady Higgs, and shan't be back to tea. If you want tea, here's the handbell, but it's much best for you not to have any, and sleep instead. You know the doctor said you were to diet."

For Alice, taking no risks with James's health, which had seemed actively threatened the night before, had had the Amberton doctor out the first thing that morning. He, after prolonged examination, had said it wasn't influenza; he also said it wasn't several other things; and the more illnesses Alice, who was really anxious, suggested, the greater it appeared was the number of those James hadn't got. When pressed, the doctor did at last say it might be a touch of sun, and that, if it were, then he prescribed quiet and diet. Assuming, said the doctor, that such should turn out to be the case—was there ever a doctor like it, Alice asked herself, with his ifs and his assumings?—assuming that it were so, then James should stay recumbent, while he dieted, in a darkened room. Not necessarily in bed; a sofa would do, said the doctor, continuing to underrate the seriousness of James's condition. Ah, but he hadn't seen him, she kept on telling the doctor, as she had seen him when she got back from Lady Higgs—all wild and panting. …

But though she described, the doctor didn't listen—she might just as well not have been in the room at all for any heed he gave her. An inattentive, wandering-minded person; too old, Alice decided, to know much any more about anything, and next time there was an illness she would send for the new man from Didlington.

However, James was to have some medicine, and was to keep quiet—for a day or two, the old doctor said, but she would take good care it was for ever so much longer, and that it should be in bed that he kept quiet, and not, as the doctor suggested, merely in his room. Also he was to avoid alcohol, the doctor said. Avoid alcohol? Seeing that James never drank anything except water, this was a silly, ignorant thing to say. Any doctor worth his salt would have known he didn't drink, just from looking at him. If ever somebody had water written all over him it was James, Alice considered, who at times felt she might, perhaps, be able to respect him a little if he at least drank his glass of wine at dinner like a man.

Still, however stupid the doctor seemed to be, and probably was, he must know the symptoms of the major illnesses, and she was much relieved that James shouldn't be sickening for something awful. She really had had a shock when she saw him the evening before. Her whole life would be torn up by the roots if anything happened to James—anything finally severing, like death or marriage. Why, she would be done for. She would just sink into an unconsidered spinster, with neither authority nor background; and, if it were marriage which severed, she would be unpleasantly short of money into the bargain. Outrageous, of course, that it should be so, but that was life all over—men getting everything, even if they were fools, and women's only chance of proper recognition and power being in connection with, and through, the creatures; unless one were one of these women with so-called gifts, one of these artist-women, but she thanked God she wasn't that sort. And quite apart from the fact that she owed her comfortable home and position, and her freedom from money cares to James, having ruled him since he was a baby he had now become necessary to her very existence—something to care for and to bully, to goad and to guard, something belonging to her, an object in life. What she would do without James, Alice, in her softer moments, couldn't imagine.

Reassured, however, that anyhow it wasn't death that was going to happen to him, while as for marriage this couldn't happen to him either as long as he was shut up in his room in bed, Alice, breathing more freely, and almost in her relief blithe, decided to go and see Lady Higgs, and told James so, while not mentioning that she intended calling on Miss Dodge on the way. To Lady Higgs she would take an offering of apricots, which were at their ripest just then on the warm south wall, and she would pick them herself, choosing only the quite perfect ones, because Lady Higgs had a great deal of everything, so it wouldn't do to offer her any but the best. She picked them after lunch, and they were all ready on the hall table, filling a big basket because Lady Higgs was never offered baskets that weren't full and big, when she went into James's room to pull down his blind and tell him he was to sleep; and the basket was in her hand—really a beautiful sight, full of golden fruit, downy and rose-flushed, and sure to please Lady Higgs, who had so much fruit of her own, in glass houses and on hot south walls running into acres, that she was always being given more—when she opened the gate from the churchyard into the Rose Cottage garden, and found the object of her visit stretched out on Burridge's stone seat.

❦

At first she didn't see her, the tombstone being deeply embedded in rank growths, but something white caught the corner of her eye as she was proceeding past it, and, stopping to peer over the intervening tangle of ancient gooseberry-bushes and brambles and bindweed and dock-leaves in order to find out what it was, (for Alice, if she caught a glimpse of anything, could never rest till she knew exactly what it was) she perceived the embroidered edge of a petticoat—a petticoat visible, because the skirt which should have covered it wasn't decently pulled down, and clothing the lower part of the body of Miss Dodge.

There she lay, as flat as somebody who wasn't flat could be got to go, on her back, her face upturned, her mouth open, her legs all anyhow, sound asleep; and it was strange what an effect of impropriety the edge of white embroidery, seeing that it was only an edge of white embroidery, produced. That, and the way her legs showed. Quite a good deal of her legs showed; and her stockings weren't properly pulled up, the neat Alice, straining forward to look, and so accurately pulled-up herself, instantly noticed.

What a sight, thought Alice: all that leg; how very merciful it was that James was safe in bed.

Well, she had come to call, and call she would; and the first step to calling on persons asleep obviously being to wake them, she stepped over the detaining bushes, holding her basket high out of harm's way, and carefully freeing her skirt each time it caught on a bramble.

Jennifer slept on. The sound of the approaching Alice didn't disturb her, nor did any consciousness that somebody was standing looking down at her penetrate her heavy slumber. Lost to the world was Jen, deep in the first real sleep she had had since she left her bed for the last time in Gower Street; and Alice, resting her heavy basket on the edge of the tombstone, didn't quite know what to do.

She wasn't accustomed to call on people who weren't in upright positions, unless, of course, they were tucked up in the decency of sick beds, and she hadn't yet contemplated anyone, who wasn't ill, from this particular angle; but, on the other hand, neither was she accustomed, having made up her mind to do a thing, to permit circumstances to thwart her. She had come to call, and call she would, though certainly to have to begin by, she supposed, shaking, or anyhow touching, the person to be called on, especially this person, wasn't exactly pleasant.

She stood staring down at the recumbent figure. How very plain people looked asleep, she thought. Evidently no one had told Miss Dodge to breathe through her nose when she was a child. James didn't breathe through his nose either, but that wasn't for want of telling—it was because, like all weak people, he was obstinate; and though it was difficult for him to be obstinate when she was present, which was all day, he made up for it, she was afraid, by being obstinate when he was by himself, which was all night. She could hear him making up for it; she could hear him from her room, even though it was right at the other end of the passage. During the hours of darkness, freed from control James did as he liked with his mouth, and the house consequently reverberated.

Miss Dodge, however, was quite quiet. Although her mouth was open she made no sound, and might have been dead, in such a heavy silence was she wrapped. Indeed, her motionlessness was so complete that Alice suddenly felt a pang of fear lest something might have happened to her, and this was not a sleeping but an unconscious woman. Had she had an accident? Had she had a fit? Had she dropped down, overcome by the heat and her own fat, and fainted? Certainly, on closer examination, there was a most helpless, fallen-down, dead look about her.

How extremely unpleasant, thought Alice; and set her basket of apricots squarely on the ground, preparatory to taking action.

But what action? Lift the figure's eyelids, and examine the state of its pupils? No, she couldn't bring herself to lift Miss Dodge's eyelids. Grasp some portion of her, and shake it? No, Alice really couldn't bear to grasp any of Miss Dodge's portions. The only thing she could think of as endurable was to call her loudly by name; and this she did, first from where she was standing, at the foot of the tombstone, and then, as there was no response nor any sign of life, going along to its other end to where Miss Dodge's ears were, and there, stooping down, more urgently repeating her call.

❦

To her relief, a relief instantly succeeded by annoyance, for nobody, thought Alice, had any right to look as dead as all that without being it, Miss Dodge stirred, half opened her eyes, and asked vaguely if anybody was calling.

"I should think so," said Alice. "I was." Adding crisply, as she remembered the purpose of her visit, "And am."

"And am," repeated Jennifer in a sleepy murmur, her eyelids drooping again.

Somebody was talking to her. Who? Why?

"For a moment I thought you had had an accident," Alice continued, speaking with the severity usual in persons who find the object of their anxiety is, after all, safe and sound. Besides, why didn't Miss Dodge, now that she was awake, sit up, get up, pull her skirt down, push her hair out of her eyes, behave like a responsible human being receiving an afternoon call? There was all that stocking still showing, and the indecorously suggestive edge of white embroidery. She hadn't moved any part of her, except, for a moment, her eyelids. And they, even as Alice spoke, were fluttering, as though they were going to shut again.

"Don't do that," said Alice, sharply.

The eyelids, with an effort, opened again, but only a little, only half. Through them Jen blinked sleepily a moment at the figure silhouetted against the branches of the tree over her head, puzzling it out, trying to remember where she had seen it before, and why she herself, used to awakenings in her soft bed at home, was not only out of doors but on something that felt like stone.

"Do what?" she murmured, her limbs creeping deliciously with sleep, her brain vague and care-free.

"Don't go to sleep again. I can't stay long. I was passing, and thought I would call."

"Oh," said Jen, placidly considering this; and her divinely happy, languid brain arrived at the conclusion—not that it mattered much, not that anything mattered much—that the thought was a bad one.

"You should have resisted," she murmured, through her half-closed eyelids dreamily contemplating Alice's head and hat and navy-blue ribbon. They seemed to be a good deal mixed up in the branches of the yew-tree; probably were caught in them, like the ram's horns in the Bible—or was it Absalom? Something, or somebody, got caught in branches in the Bible; and once one got caught in branches, there one hung—and hung—and it took ages—ages—before—before—

Veils gently closed down on her brain again; the head, the hat, the branches, floated off mistily into unfathomable distances.

"What?" snapped Alice—snapped Alice sharply, as she saw the eyelids shutting again. "Really, Miss Dodge, hadn't you better wake up? Or if you don't feel well say so, and I'll call another day."

This time the voice did cut through Jen's enveloping fog, and she woke a little more completely, and gazed at the face above her.

Miss Ollier. Yes; that was who it was. Why should she have to see Miss Ollier? What had brought her there?

She blinked up at her, her mind still placid, her limbs still full of the lassitude of sleep. "How do you do," she murmured; and as Alice wouldn't answer, declined having anything to say to the absurd, superfluous question, Jen, waking up still more, began to realise the situation, and grasped the fact, painful indeed to her, that she was being called upon.

It ought to have been the brother calling, she thought; calling to apologise for what he had done the night before; and then he could have cleared that bedstead out of the way.

With a sigh she reluctantly resumed the burdens of polite life. "I've been asleep," she said, raising herself on one elbow.

"So I see," said Alice, curtly.

"Won't you sit down?"

"Where?" snapped Alice.

"Why not here?" inquired Jen, putting her feet to the ground and half-heartedly indicating the space of empty tombstone beside her.

❦

Well, Alice hadn't come round to sit among midges on a stone seat. She wasn't aware that what was being offered her was a tombstone, because James, unable to make up his mind as to the rights or wrongs of it, and shrinking from her quick, upheaving decisions, had never told her of his discovery of its existence as a seat, and it was one of the few things in the parish she didn't know about; but on principle she was against sitting on stone, and mouldy stone at that as she could see for herself, and she detested midges, which so unfairly got at one without, by making a preliminary noise, offering one the alternative of killing them, and she considered that a lady calling for the first time should certainly be invited indoors, and have a chair placed at her disposal.

Besides, she was curious and uneasy about Miss Dodge, and determined to find out all about her, and one couldn't find out nearly so much out of doors. Many things could be deduced from an examination of people's furniture—not that there could possibly be much furniture in that cottage, but there was bound to be some, got in probably during the morning, and furniture often betrayed people quite as much as their conversation. For a complete picture, one had to have the background as well. Alice, whose eyes missed nothing, got a good deal of information from people's backgrounds.

Being, therefore, plainspeaking and direct, when Jen asked, "Why not here?" she at once said she would rather go indoors.

"You can't," was the answer; as brief and almost as snappy as her own speech, Jen now being completely awake, and remembering Miss Ollier's inquisitive visit the night before. Why should she keep on turning up? It was no longer her cottage. It had nothing to do with her. "Not without squeezing a good deal, that is," she said.

"Squeezing a good deal?" repeated Alice.

Was she suggesting, this heavy-shouldered person on the seat—she was still sitting while Alice stood, which was a breach of good manners to begin with—was she suggesting that she, Alice, with her trim, unredundant figure, wouldn't get through doors without squeezing? Squeezing what, she would like to know? Not a superfluous ounce had she on her whole body; not the least bit of anything which conceivably might yield to pressure.

She drew herself up even straighter than usual. "I've been in and out of that cottage hundreds of times," she said. "Why should I have to squeeze?"

Briefly Jen explained what had happened, and how she was waiting for help from the village; briefly and coldly, because the fact that Miss Ollier should have been in and out of her cottage hundreds of times filled her with misgivings for the future, and anyhow she didn't want to be called on by Miss Ollier, not even once, let alone hundreds of times, for she looked upon Miss Ollier as a bullier of brothers, as a house-tyrant, as a person of stiff and unbending character who closely resembled the bow in her own hat, and she objected, besides, to being woken up by a visitor, regarding it as contrary to the decencies, should one find the owner of a property asleep, to do anything but go away at once on tiptoe. Also, only inquisitiveness would bring her there twice within twenty-four hours, and Jen didn't like inquisitiveness.

But while she was explaining about the blocking bedstead, and Alice was looking down at her scornfully, for what a muddle-headed creature the woman must be, thought Alice, not to have asked the carrier to take the thing indoors and upstairs for her when he was there, Jen suddenly saw the basket of apricots set down in the grass beside the tombstone, and her curt statement of facts began to falter.

A present. A gesture of welcome. Miss Ollier had brought her some fruit as a preliminary to neighbourliness.

Tripped up in her hostility, she felt ashamed. Such beautiful apricots; and so many of them. Miss Ollier was kind, then, after all. She wasn't really disagreeable. Probably she was only one of those people whose faces were the worst part of them, and it just showed, thought Jen, touched and surprised, how wrong hasty judgments were, and the quick taking for granted that people's manner and appearance were an index to their inside.

They weren't. Especially in the case of the Olliers they weren't. These Olliers seemed more different inside from outside than anyone she had ever come across. Look, last night, at the brother—outwardly giving the impression of being unable to hurt a fly, and inside capable of the most volcanic conduct. And look, now, at the sister—dragging this enormous basket of gorgeous fruit round, staggering round with it herself in all the heat, just so as to give pleasure, while still at the same time, judged superficially, appearing to be, if anything, cross.

She wasn't cross. It was only her manner. *By their fruits ye shall know them*, thought Jen, turning her eyes away from the basket, remembering that it doesn't do to stare at gifts not yet bestowed. And anxious to make amends for her behaviour, she got up and said very politely, "If you don't mind the bedstead being in the way, and would rather go indoors, do come in."

"Of course I'd rather go indoors," said Alice, picking up her apricots. "Who wants to sit on mouldy stone? It's most unwholesome."

"Won't you let me—" began Jen, before she could stop herself. She was going, instinctively, to ask to be allowed to carry the obviously heavy basket. Tact intervened in time. Tact demanded that she should continue to ignore its existence, until the moment of its presentation.

But it was difficult to ignore its existence, because it was so big, and keeping her eyes carefully on Alice's face, so as not to look at it as they stood facing each other in the knee-deep weeds, she said, with real appreciation as the delicate fragrance of the sun-kissed fruit rose deliciously to her nostrils, "I think it is so very kind of you to have come round—" and, as those do who know they are about to be given a present, she smiled with marked friendliness.

Alice eyed her suspiciously. What was the matter all of a sudden, she wondered, with Miss Dodge?

"Not at all," she said, stiffly. Dimples, too, the woman had got. Ridiculous at her age to have dimples. She hadn't seen her smile till that moment, and didn't like it one little bit. How old was she? She had seemed much older the day before—well on her way to the forties, Alice had judged. "Not at all," she said. "I only—"

"Yes—so *very* kind," said Jen, smiling gratefully as Alice stopped, supposing that the sentence, completed, was to be, "I only came to give you these."

It was quite overwhelmingly kind—Jen, whose life had been almost completely bare of presents, except those stately gifts, as a reward for her share in their production, of father's books, was overwhelmed by this one, so beautiful and so unexpected—but she did think Miss Ollier was needlessly embarrassed by her own kindness. Embarrassment was catching. She herself was feeling quite shy now of the apricots. Also, it was a little puzzling, after all, that anybody whose intentions were so amiable should go on looking so exactly as if they weren't.

"Not kind at all," snapped Alice; and they stood silent an instant, their eyes on each other's faces, Jen still smiling, though a little uncertainly, surprised at being thus snapped at, feeling that givers don't usually snap at recipients, and Alice saying to herself, with great uneasiness, that one wouldn't know Miss Dodge for the same person when she left off looking glum.

"If you hadn't a bedstead, where did you sleep last night?" she asked abruptly—abruptly, because she was thinking of the curiously transforming smile rather than of her own question.

"Oh, well, I had a mattress," said Jen; and remembering that which had happened on the mattress, and how naturally shocked her visitor would be if she knew, she turned red.

Alice, of course, noticed that at once. Her bright black eyes on Jennifer's face instantly noticed the redness, but though her alert mind darted about searching for a reason for it, it couldn't find one. Mattresses, by themselves, didn't make women turn red. There was something else, something at the back of Miss Dodge's thoughts, something connected with that mattress. But what?

In vain Alice's mind darted hither and thither, trying to discover what it could be. The one thing she knew for certain was that the tenant's behaviour, at the mention of the mattress, had become definitely queer.

And while she was scanning the face before her searching for clues, her back towards the path and the churchyard gate, a still deeper red, a really violent red, suddenly rushed across Miss Dodge's pasty features, and her eyes, looking beyond Alice, became fixed.

Now what on earth—

Alice stared at her an instant, astonished; and then, twisting round so as to see what was having this striking effect on Miss Dodge, in her turn her eyes became fixed. For there, in the act of striding with curiously long, swift, silent footsteps up the path to the cottage, she beheld James.

CHAPTER VIII

Now James had been having a miserable time. He couldn't remember anything in his life approaching it for torment—not when his father, a stern hard man, was cruel to him; not when his mother, who had been gentle, died. In immense agitation of mind, aghast at himself and yet curiously exultant—for why should he be exultant because he had behaved like a dissolute cad?—he had had to submit to being treated as if sickening for something, to endure being kept in bed and humiliatingly nursed, so as at all costs to prevent Alice's getting hold of even an inkling of the truth.

She was so quick at inklings! How often he had suffered from her uncanny precision in pouncing on thoughts and feelings he had supposed not a soul could possibly guess, and triumphantly dragging them out into the glare of her derision. Only in this case it wouldn't be triumphantly that she would drag if, by the slightest mistake on his part, the smallest momentary inattention, he were to betray that it wasn't illness that was the matter with him. There would be no triumph for Alice over this discovery, nothing but, succeeding the first shock of quite natural horror—didn't he, thinking of what he had done, feel horror himself? Horror marvellously thrilled through with exultation, it is true, but still horror?—real disaster. For Alice depended on him entirely for her comfort. Her own little bit of money wouldn't be much good to her, she would be obliged to live very differently if, for any reason, she had to leave him. Scandalous behaviour on his part, scandalous according to her high and rigid standards, would probably force her to go, and force her also to refuse any help from him; and had he not scandalously behaved? There was no doubt whatever that he had; and not only according to Alice's high and rigid standards, but according to any standards, thought the tormented James, utterly ashamed of himself, imprisoned in bed, compelled to be quiet when honour and decency demanded that he shouldn't lose a moment in hurrying down to Rose Cottage, and begging his outraged neighbour's pardon.

He, a clergyman; he, a parish priest, to have behaved like that! He, a gentleman—or supposed to be a gentleman. It really was too awful. And he didn't even dare toss in his bed, try to find some relief in twisting from side to side on his pillows, because directly he moved Alice darted across the room to put her hand on his forehead, and feel his pulse.

Ignominious; hideous. There he lay trapped, having to pretend lethargy, while the hours passed and God knew what his neighbour could be thinking of him. What could she possibly be thinking of him, first for what he had done, and then for not coming to say he was sorry?

But was he sorry?

Strange thoughts shot through James's racked brain, strange, jumbled-up thoughts. Naturally he hated having been a cad; on the other hand, ought he to regret that at last he had been a man? At last; high time too, thought James, rent inwardly by exultations warring with agonies. For during those intoxicating, all too brief moments, he had been, he felt, for the first time a man like other men—and surely it must be a good thing to be a man like other men? The distressing part of it was that he had been a cad as well; but then, never having had a chance yet to be either, was it to be wondered at that he should have become both simultaneously? A man must be given opportunities for caddishness, thought the distracted James one moment, while the next he equally distractedly repudiated the theory, if he is to learn how to avoid it. He had had none. He had been sheltered, pap-fed, not allowed to call his soul his own, earmarked for the church from his cradle, surrounded at every step since he could remember by Alice and her affection; oh, yes, he was sure it was affection, and that if he were drowning she would give her life to save him, but then he never was drowning, and meanwhile he did wish, to take a small example of the sort of thing that ultimately made existence intolerable, he did wish she wouldn't say Bosh.

Exasperated, James flung himself over in his bed,—couldn't stop himself, even if Alice did see him and rush across the room to tuck him in tighter. She had just said the odious word again. It was intolerable. He really couldn't stand it.

Yet he did stand it. When he tried not to take his medicine, and she said Bosh, he gave in at once, drinking the stuff down hastily, obediently, and ignominiously.

Medicine. What did he want with medicine? Was there ever anything more fantastic, more, really, outrageous, than because a man had kissed a woman he should have to take medicine?

But there it was. Such was the development of the exquisite and shameful moments on the mattress, and if James hadn't been a clergyman he would have sworn.

"You'll have beef-tea for lunch," announced Alice.

Beef-tea!

James perspired with the effort not to swear.

All that day he had lain trapped, forced to silence, to acquiescence, outwardly quiet while under the sheets he perspired, and Alice's claims, and his own claims, and the neighbour's claims—she too had claims now, James felt with a thrill, she had to be shielded, he had to protect her from any possible discovery by Alice of the share, so completely innocent (only Alice would never believe it), she had had in what he had done—all day all these claims whirled round and round his tormented brain, first one set uppermost and then another, and the whole lot apparently irreconcilable.

For some time past—oh, long before last night and the apple-tree—hadn't it been becoming clear to him that he, like everybody else, had claims? And hadn't he sometimes wondered, as he went about his simple duties in the parish and his simple pleasures in the garden, whether he was, then, to spend the rest of his years renouncing them, because they conflicted with Alice's? Marriage, for instance. Hadn't he too a right to marry if he wanted to? Perhaps it was the unusually fruitful summer, the hot succession of teeming days; perhaps it was his increasingly realised loneliness; perhaps it was merely that he was young and starved; but whatever the reason, he had certainly been thinking quite often lately about marriage.

He remembered this now, during the hours spent shut up in the darkened bedroom trying to reconcile everybody's claims, and he remembered how, because he knew it would be hard for Alice if he married, each time the thought entered his head he had put it from him, deciding that he really couldn't buy happiness at her expense. Besides, he had said to himself, anxious to look at the subject from as unfavourable an angle as he could, suppose it wasn't happiness that he bought? Suppose, having married, and made poor Alice, after her life's devotion to him, wretched for the rest of her days, he were to wake up and find he had only married somebody who also, every time he opened his mouth, said Bosh?

There was always this possibility to be considered. It was quite likely that he was the sort of person people easily said Bosh to—certainly, and he was glad it should be so, they never seemed to mind what they did say to him. Also, it was evident that in marrying one easily made mistakes, for he only had to look round at his brother clergymen to see that they nearly all appeared to have made them. Whether they recognised them as such or not, there the mistakes were, in their houses, pervading their lives, having to be sat with at every meal and slept with every night; and at least, whatever her faults were, nobody had got to sleep with Alice.

In this way he had tried, that summer, to put thoughts of marriage from him, a good deal helped by the fact that there wasn't anybody to marry, and had thrown cold water on their vague, general ardour. Now remembering them, as he lay with time enough, it seemed to him, to remember everything that had ever happened, far from considering them ardent he regarded them as pusillanimous, and even for a moment was inclined to smile pityingly at the poor timid things, as he who is experienced smiles pityingly at what was once his own ignorance.

A man had to take risks. Clergymen, especially, had to take risks, being debarred by their profession from any real preliminary experience; but he would be a poor sort of a man who was afraid of this, and afraid of that, before setting out on an adventure; and what could be a more glorious, perilous adventure than marriage? Well could he imagine himself setting out on it, hand in hand with his little fellow-pilgrim. She wouldn't be so very little, though, she wouldn't be just a foolish, wispy girl; but of course she would be smaller than himself, and it was sweet to think of her as little, and needing his care, his help. Hand in hand they would set out, fearing nothing because they had each other, talking gently and kindly, the perfect friends, the perfect companions and lovers, never saying harsh, ugly words—

"Now you," Alice's voice broke in at this point, "are to sleep. I'm walking over to Lady Higgs, and shan't be back till after tea."

❦

She hadn't got down the stairs before James was out of bed. Moving stealthily, lest she should hear and come back, he began to dress, his hands shaking with excitement. The servants mustn't hear either, so he couldn't have a bath; but thanks to Alice's care for comfort there was running hot water in the bedrooms, and he was able to wash properly and shave.

He cut himself shaving, and cursed under his breath, and then, startled that he had cursed, cut himself again. Well, never mind—curses or no curses, get on with it, he said to himself, hastily dabbing sticking plaster on his wounds, and then scrambling into his shirt. He mustn't lose a moment. He would need all the moments there were before Alice could be home again, for the apologies he was going to make. Never had woman been so shockingly behaved to, and never should woman be more utterly apologised to.

Alarming yet sweet duty. His heart thumped, only to think of it. He would take her some fruit—a peace offering; a basket of those lovely apricots from the south wall, and gather a bunch of sweet-peas to lay on the top.

No, he wouldn't. Somebody would see him picking them—the gardener, or somebody. He was supposed to be in bed. He mustn't forget that. Nobody must know he wasn't. Besides, he hadn't time. All the time he had would be needed, to the last second, for his apologies. Not a minute could he waste of it—it was far too precious. In his whole life there had been no time remotely approaching it in preciousness.

Had Alice really got away? How long had he been dressing?

Yes—there wasn't a sound in the house. Not a sound—only his heart, thumping. She really was gone. She was probably half way to Lady Higgs by now.

But he would just look out of the window, to see if the coast were really clear.

No one in sight. The garden was empty. The servants would be having tea.

He put his hand on the door.

He opened it silently.

"Here goes," he whispered, with a catch of his breath.

And, like an arrow released, swift and noiseless James went.

❦

Like an arrow released, too, he went up the path to Rose Cottage, aiming straight at its porch, looking neither to the right nor left; and Alice, knee deep in the weeds, after an instant's speechless staring, snatched up her basket and went after him. Even in that moment of amazement she didn't forget Lady Higgs's present, and with it tightly grasped in her two hands, held high above the gooseberry bushes, she pushed her way through the thorny tangle and got out on to the path.

"James!" she called.

Something in her voice made Jennifer follow her. In spite of the extreme awkwardness of having to face Mr. Ollier, for the first time after what had happened, in the presence of his sister, some instinct told her that she must go to his help, that in the next few minutes he would be needing a friend.

Poor young man. After all, and in spite of the apricots, she sided with him. His sister's gift of fruit was as nothing weighed in the balance against the way she called to him. No one should be allowed to speak to a fellow-creature in such a tone—as if he were a dog, thought Jen, blushing for humanity, as if he were a slave. And a guilty dog, and a sinning slave.

Prepared to stand by him in she hadn't an idea what conflict, she arrived at the fringe of gooseberry bushes a second or two after Miss Ollier had got through it, just in time to see James, who had almost reached the porch, jerk round as if he were shot.

No wonder, thought Jen, full of indignant sympathy; no wonder. It was like a whip being cracked, the way his name had been hurled after him. James. So he was James. Well, James should be backed up. …

But what was her astonishment to see him, after his violent jerk round, so obviously the jerk of some one receiving a shock, immediately return along the path towards his sister, holding out his hands and flushing, not with fear, Jennifer could have sworn, but with what looked very like pleasure.

So much astonished was she that she didn't attempt to get through the bushes on to the path, but stayed where she was, her mouth a little open. How queer, she thought, staring. She must have been wrong again—judged hastily, jumped to conclusions. Perhaps in the Ollier family, to be called out to like that was an endearment. What did she know about the Olliers really? Still—last night he had certainly seemed afraid. …

James didn't see her. He only saw what Alice was carrying: the very offering he himself had wanted to make. How kind; how thoughtful. These were the sorts of little actions James loved. And his heart, which had given a jump at her voice, immediately began to beat steadily and warmly again, because he was like that—forgetting everything, in swift pleasure at a kindness.

So, now, he forgot what Alice's feelings must be at finding him out of bed, even forgot, for an instant, why he wasn't in it, and intent only on relieving her of the basket, which was generously full, he could see, and much too heavy for a woman, hurried back along the path almost as quickly as he had hurried up it, and exclaimed, "Oh, Alice—how very kind of you! Do let me carry it."

"No," said Alice through closed teeth, holding on to it as he tried to take it from her.

"Really I must, Alice. Give it to me. It's much too heavy for you."

"Bosh," said Alice, jerking herself sideways away from him, and holding on tighter.

If only Alice wouldn't say Bosh, thought James; if only, only she wouldn't. It didn't do her justice. It spoilt things. Even over the graciousness of her gift of apricots, it cast an unpleasant shadow.

Then he saw Jen; quite close; just the other side of the bushes; and, turning scarlet, dropped the hands stretched out to take the basket, as the memory of the night before rushed over him in a burning flood.

To meet her again like this, in Alice's presence, when he couldn't say a single thing of all the things he was so full of, and was himself being said Bosh to! She must have heard the humiliating word. How could she possibly not have heard it? If ever a human being was plainly overwhelmed by emotion as he stood staring helplessly at Jennifer, it was James.

"I wish he wouldn't look like that," she thought, annoyed—sorry for him, but also annoyed. "It'll make his sister think God knows what."

But Alice was too angry, as well as anxious, to think of anything except the incomprehensible and alarming fact that here he was, up and out of doors, when he ought to have been in bed.

"James, what are you doing here?" she asked. "Are you mad?"

What a way to talk to him, thought Jennifer, at once flaming up on his behalf. Doing here? Mad? As if he weren't free to go anywhere without his sister's permission and knowledge, as if he were a little boy, and she the supreme authority!

She, so lately escaped from them herself, naturally detested supreme authorities and was ready to help anyone suffering under them. "I expect, like you, Mr. Ollier has come to call on me," she said, stepping across the bushes, and smiling at James with rather anxious welcome. "How do you do?" she said, and longed to be able to whisper, "For heaven's *sake* leave off looking as if you were thinking of that silly mattress. It doesn't matter. I've forgotten it. Stand up to her. Don't care a damn—" she who had never stood up to father, and had cared every possible damn. But then her case had been different; she was bound by promises, and his own helplessness, to father. Miss Ollier was only a sister, and the least helpless person, Jen was sure, in the whole world.

"Call? Bosh," said Alice, thrusting her, as it were, on one side. "Why are you out of bed, James?"

This to Jen sounded mysterious. She began to think that perhaps she wasn't in possession of all the facts. Why shouldn't James be out of bed? Surely it would have been conspicuous of him not to be, in the middle of the afternoon?

His face seemed to confirm her suspicion that she didn't know everything. He was evidently feeling something or other acutely, and it couldn't possibly be just that silly business on the mattress. She felt a great desire to take his hand, to show him she was his friend, and wasn't angry with him.

"I'm quite well, Alice," he said. "Perfectly well—" his eyes, as he turned to his sister, imploring her not to let out that she had taken his temperature the night before, and had had a doctor to him.

"I never heard such nonsense," said Alice, exasperated and nonplussed. "How can you be quite well, when last time I saw you you were quite ill? You must be raving mad to have got out of bed. It's your temperature up again, of course. Look at you—all flushed. Come home at once, James."

And she walked off down the path to the gate, leaving him to follow, expecting him to follow, just as if he were a perfectly trained dog.

"Will he go with her?" thought Jen, holding her breath. "I don't believe he's got a temperature. I don't believe there's anything the matter with James. Will he go? Will he? If he does, he's done for."

❦

But James, though he went, yet wasn't done for. He went, that is, as far as the gate with Alice, and there, out of sight and earshot of Jennifer, having opened the gate for her with his usual courtesy he made his stand.

Alice thought he was suddenly demented. Anybody seeing him would, she was sure, have said, "Here is someone demented"—whereas James was only being, for the second time in his life, a man. Caddish, too, again a little, he was afraid; it seemed difficult to be a man without a touch of cad. But he would try to make up to Alice for it afterwards. Somehow. How, he didn't at the moment know.

Two things were clear to him as, in much turmoil of spirit, he followed her to the gate; he wasn't going back to bed, and he was going back to explain and apologise to his neighbour. But, more sensitive to the decencies than either of the women, he couldn't allow his sister, as much for her sake as his own, to make a public scene. The scene, he knew, was inevitable, but it shouldn't take place before a third person, however strangely near to him that third person had become. No one but himself should see his sister at her worst, should see her show sides of a character which at its best was capable of gracious acts like the gift of apricots.

Therefore, at the cost of his neighbour's despising him—she must by now be used to doing that anyhow, he thought—he appeared to obey unresistingly, and when Alice said, "Come home at once, James," he went without a word.

As far as the gate he went, following her in silence, nerving himself to face the sort of thing that was, in the whole world, most abhorrent to him, and when Alice was through it, instead of going through it after her he stayed where he was, and made his stand.

Shutting the gate gently, with her on its other side, and addressing her almost as if he were in a pulpit and she were in a pew, he explained, his voice three parts conciliatory, and one part firm, that not being ill, being, indeed, quite well whatever he may have been earlier in the day, he proposed, before joining her at home, to go back and finish his call on Miss Dodge; and it was when he had got as far as this, and Alice was still too much astonished to speak, that his eye fell on the basket.

"Why, you've forgotten to leave the apricots, Alice!" he exclaimed, suddenly quite natural.

"The apricots?" repeated Alice, staring at him across the gate, and not yet having had time to grasp the significance of its being shut. "Bosh. They're for Lady Higgs."

Then it was that James became what she called demented. He saw red. He flung aside all attempts to conciliate. Because she was angry with him, she was denying her own kindness, and his neighbour, so innocent in this as in everything else that had happened, was to be punished.

He leant over the gate, and swiftly reaching out his long arm caught hold of the basket. "They're not," he said—he almost, indeed, shouted.

"They're for Miss Dodge. You know you meant them for her. Give them to me, and I'll take them to her."

"Bosh," said Alice furiously, a touch of fear, though, in her voice, for she had never seen him like this, and his hands on the basket were very determined and strong.

"It isn't Bosh. Once and for all, it is *not* Bosh, Alice," he said, his eyes flashing through his spectacles.

"Are you mad, James?" she cried, when, in spite of her struggles, he wouldn't let go.

"Neither mad nor ill," said James, tugging at the basket, "and I'm not going back to bed, and you *are* going to do the kindness you came to do. You'd better let me have this quietly."

"I won't," said Alice, setting her teeth and holding on.

"I don't want to hurt you," said James, tugging.

"How dare you—how dare you—" choked Alice, swayed hither and thither as he tugged and she wouldn't let go.

And then they struggled in silence, deplorably and monstrously, like two infuriated children, the gate between them, the only sound their quick breathing, and the soft thud of apricots rolling off the basket to the ground.

"*James*!" Alice suddenly cried out.

He had got it. He had wrenched it from her. And lifting it in triumph over the gate, he ran back up the path with it to Rose Cottage.

❦

There, in the kitchen, Jen was preparing to boil the kettle for tea, an expression on her face as of one who washes her hands of all Olliers. Almost was she in the act of shrugging her shoulders when, stepping clumsily in his excitement over something or other that was blocking up the porch, James very nearly tumbled, basket in hand, on the floor at her feet.

"Here," he said, breathless with hurry and emotions, "Alice forgot to give you these. They're for you. Take them, will you—I must go to Alice.

And you're to forgive me about last night. But I've just been a much worse cad than that. I'm a cad twice over now. I'll come back and tell you about everything the first moment I can. If you'll let me. But if you don't let me, I'll still come. Goodbye. What's your name?"

"Jennifer."

"Jennifer!"

He was gone. Out again, stumbling over the object blocking up the porch, down the path to where he could see Alice standing where he had left her, on the other side of the gate.

"Now for it," thought James, plunging forward into whatever awaited him, prepared for something awful.

Then he caught his breath, exactly as if he had received a blow in the face, for Alice was crying.

His sister crying? Was it possible? Never in his life had he seen her cry; he hadn't supposed she had it in her to do a thing like that, and it seemed as though his heart stopped beating at the sight.

"Alice—" he said, pulling the gate open and hurrying through it, "Alice—please don't. I'm so sorry. I didn't mean to be rough and hurt you—"

He took her hand, he patted it, he stroked it, he did all sorts of things to it that in its life had never been done before, and at last, as she still said nothing but just wept, in an agony of concern he timidly drew it through his arm.

She didn't resist. It was the most incredible thing that she shouldn't resist. And it was positively stupefying that she should cry.

Could this be Alice? James asked himself distractedly, wanting to cry too.

And there was her hat, with its brave upstanding bow, still defiant on her head, still symbolic of an attitude vanished so incredibly in a soft swamp of piteous tears.

He was overcome. To see Alice, whom he had known only as a tireless and apparently invulnerable despot, suddenly with all her defences down, exposed and helpless, not saying a word any more, giving up, was dreadful to him. Evidently by his unpardonable brutality, fighting for that confounded basket, he had cut her to the quick. How could he have lost his temper like that? How could he have forgotten to be decent? He hadn't dreamed that she had a quick. Absorbed in himself, he now saw, and in his own precious feelings, he had overlooked the fact that she too, like most other human beings, might at some point or another be sensitive. He had touched that point; he had smashed through her reserve; and he who could never bear to see a woman cry had now to behold his own sister, who had held her head so high and always led the way, weeping as helplessly as a hurt and humiliated child.

"I've been a *cad*," he said, as he led her, with an agonised solicitude, home. "I fought over that wretched basket like some beastly schoolboy. Alice—"

Thus James capitulated. Thus, before thrown-down defences, and what seemed complete surrender, he himself unconditionally surrendered. Haunted by the image, extraordinarily repugnant to his whole nature, of the beastly schoolboy, shocked beyond coherent expression at the effect of his lapse, his one and only lapse—no, there was that other lapse last night, but thank God she knew nothing of that—into barbarism, he lay at Alice's mercy; and when, having gone to her room and stayed there for hours, still crying he was terribly afraid, she came down to dinner very pale and red-eyed and with her right hand bandaged, he lay at her mercy more utterly than ever.

A bandaged hand. He had hurt her, then, hurt her terribly physically, as well as in her loyal, devoted heart.

The thought was unendurable to James. Flushing and wincing, he pointed to the hand and said, "Alice—? Did I—?" And when she bowed her head, his heart seemed to turn right over inside him.

Well, somehow he must make amends; but how? At dinner, which neither of them ate, he sat looking at her helplessly, while she, with swollen eyes, looked in silence at her plate. It had been dreadful to see

Alice trying to eat her soup with the spoon so awkwardly in her left hand, and dreadful to see her give up, and quietly lay it down. The beautifully starched and frilled parlourmaid didn't know what to make of all this, and stared openly, and James saw her staring, and winced again to know it was he who had reduced his sister to sit there not caring what the servants thought of her. Brute that he had been. What devil had taken possession of him since yesterday, and how was he ever going to be able to repair the strange beast's damage?

With a twitching face, he sat wondering what in the world he could do to make amends; but it wasn't till much later, till the painful evening had dragged almost to its end, and Alice's silences had begun to be broken by a word here and a word there, while with her left hand she nursed the wounded right one, that he gathered there was a way, perhaps—a way of doubtful value, it seemed to him, but still apparently containing the possibility of some sort of comfort for poor Alice: he could take her away somewhere. They could go away together, for a quiet holiday.

Gradually he was given to understand this, though the word holiday wasn't quite what she meant, he gathered—rest was more the word, a quiet rest. And presently he further gathered that the quiet rest they both needed—he, he gathered, needed it too—should be sought somewhere far away—perhaps on the Yorkshire moors, or in Scotland, or even, perhaps, abroad. Both their nerves, he gathered, had suffered from the long-continued heat. Nerves were what was the matter with them both, he gathered, ragged nerves. …

He could only gather, because she was so strange and vague and unlike herself, and her words, such as they were, came out brokenly, and at long intervals. Still, by bedtime he had gathered this much.

"But can we?" he asked, dubiously. "I'll do anything, of course—anything you feel might— But can we leave at such short notice? Who would take the services?"

Alice, he gathered, thought perhaps she might be able to arrange that.

❦

So this was why Jennifer, when she returned Alice's call on coming down from London the following Friday—she had sent a note of thanks round by Mrs. Jones's little girl the day after getting the apricots—found a strange clergyman sitting under the Vicarage cedar who, on closer examination, turned out to be her pale-eyed enemy, the Vicar of Benendon St. Michael.

She had been much relieved the Saturday before, if slightly surprised, that poor James, as she now began to think of him, hadn't kept his promise to come back and tell her, as he had said he would, all about everything, for she felt that little good would come of that. What she wanted in her new life was peace, and not to have poured out on her the strange variety of emotions which appeared to afflict the Olliers. It was a good thing, of course, that he should recognise he had been a cad—yes, that was the exact right word for his conduct on the mattress—but she didn't know what he meant by saying he had been a double one. Perhaps, being a clergyman he had an extra tender conscience, and to have an extra tender conscience, combined with a disposition to sudden caddishness, seemed to Jen unfortunate.

Anyhow, since his brief rush back with Alice's present, and his breathless apology, she had left off worrying about that silly mattress business. He had purged his offence—if it had been an offence; for, after all, all he had done was momentarily to forget himself, and better men than James had forgotten themselves before now, and with better women. These warm, moonlit nights, probably the whole of England was dotted over with people forgetting themselves. The only thing about her own case which could legitimately surprise her was that he should have been able to indulge in these activities with someone so entirely unsuited to them, she would have supposed, as herself. But summer nights no doubt play strange tricks with people who are, as poor James evidently was, in great and pressing need of affection and not getting any at home, and, besides, it had been very dark under that tree.

So she turned her attention to other matters, relieved that he didn't come back; and the man from the village, sent by Mrs. Jones, having put up her bedstead for her, and carried in the mattress which had made its first and last excursion, she told herself, into the orchard, after frugally supping on an egg, and sitting quietly afterwards for an hour on the step of the porch, she locked the cottage door at ten o'clock, and went to bed in her tiny attic very contentedly, if a little hot.

Next day, too, how pleasant it had been to hear the bells ringing for the Sunday services, and know that James was safely shut up in church for most of the morning, doing his duty by his flock. She was all for flocks, so long as she needn't belong to them herself; she was all for anything that would keep people busy, and cause them to let their neighbours alone. Secure for the present at least, she strolled happily about her property, examining its possibilities, planning its future, and presently, because her fingers itched to get at them, fetching out her spade, and in spite of its being Sunday having a little preliminary tussle with the weeds.

Yet, though she had certainly enjoyed her undisturbed morning, when the service was over and the worshippers had straggled homewards through the churchyard, and she saw, last of all, Alice come out and wait for James, and then take his arm and walk slowly away with him to their vicarage, she felt, for some reason, as she watched them disappear together, slightly ruffled.

Now why?

She asked herself this, surprised by the sensation. Well, for one thing James hadn't even looked her way. True, she had carefully got behind a tree, so that nobody should see her, a woman with a spade, a woman surrounded by slaughtered weeds, a woman manifestly Sabbath-breaking; but he might at least have tried to, after all that had happened.

Then, for another thing, she didn't like the way Alice took his arm and walked him off as though she were the only person in the world who had a say in him.

Yes—and then there was yesterday afternoon. She had forgotten it till that moment, but now, seeing him walked off like that, really as though he were on a lead, it came back to her how Alice had ordered him home, and he had at once obeyed, with the ready obedience, almost, of a dog. True he had reappeared, but only just so as to throw the present Alice had forgotten to give her on the table, and scamper off again down the path, as though he heard his master's whistle; and men, she thought, shaking her head disapprovingly, shouldn't behave like that.

No, indeed they shouldn't, thought Jen, who till so lately had been behaving exactly like it herself. But then she wasn't a man, and father wasn't Alice, and besides, what else could she have done, she would like to know, bound as she was by father's helplessness and her own vow? The cases were entirely different. A man shouldn't allow an ordinary, obscure sister to order him about.

And leaning her spade against the trunk of a tree, and wiping her warm hands on some dock-leaves before going indoors to dinner, she decided that it was both natural and proper that she should feel ruffled by the spectacle of James, who was good, being doglike to Alice, who was bad.

In spite of those magnificent apricots, she couldn't help suspecting that Alice was bad. There was nothing personal about it, she said to herself, carefully wiping her hands; it was just an instinct she had. Anybody who saw them both would, she was sure, feel the same.

❦

After dinner, which was sardines, because it was too hot to cook, and after a proper interval after dinner, so as to give James time to recover from the roast beef and Yorkshire pudding he had probably been eating, she thought, "Now he'll come," and began, because it is one's duty to look neat, to smooth her hair; and when he didn't come, and the hours passed and still he didn't, she was ruffled again—indeed, was definitely annoyed.

But really, she thought, explaining away this annoyance, it wasn't in human nature not to deplore seeing people, who weren't dogs, behaving as if they were. Especially when one liked them; especially when one wanted to be real friends, and help them to stand up to bullies; especially when they had—though this, of course, was neither here nor there—if disgracefully and illegitimately, yet with marked enthusiasm, kissed one.

Yes: why not face it? Whether neither here nor there, there was no doubt that being kissed by people did seem to make a sort of link. One couldn't, she was sure, feel quite the same towards them as one probably would if they hadn't; and that being so, wasn't it natural, wasn't it—really, creditable, to want to be able to think highly of them? And wasn't it natural to be annoyed if, by their behaviour, that desire was frustrated?

James was gritless; and she doubted whether one could ever be real friends with somebody gritless. In the long run, wouldn't one become disposed to patience, rather than to friendship? And wasn't there something arrogant about patience, something patronising, and completely incompatible with equality?

As for that sister. …

By this time she had finished the apricots, and their visible presence no longer impeded her clear vision of Alice by reminding her of a kindly act. Once more she was able to look at her clearly, and looking at her clearly she didn't at all like what she saw. It was Alice, she was sure, who was preventing James from keeping his promise. Not, she explained to that other part of herself which was always having to have things explained to it, that she wanted him to keep his promise, except on the general principle that a promise was a promise and should accordingly be kept, but she did think it indefensible that a sister, a mere sister, a nobody really, an ordinary, unintelligent spinster, without the smallest claim on somebody else's time and freedom, should interfere with a man's movements.

Wives might perhaps have a say in their husband's movements, though she certainly had never seen her mother attempt to have a say in father's, but a sister should stay in her proper place, and, if she didn't, she should be made to.

It oughtn't to be impossible, even when the sister was Alice and the brother James, for wasn't she, Jennifer, at hand to back him up? But she didn't see what she could do if he stayed timidly at Alice's side, and was afraid to show himself. No one in the world could do anything for somebody who remained invisible in what she unfairly called, being ruffled, his magnolia-covered kennel.

Late in the afternoon a different explanation of his absence occurred to her. By this time she was no longer annoyed with the Olliers, but only annoyed with herself for being annoyed, because really it was ridiculous to waste her first precious, lovely Sunday in her own home in being angry with people of whom a week ago she had never heard.

The other explanation of James's absence was that he, not knowing she was only going to be down there weekends till father had finished his honeymoon, and therefore that she would be returning to Gower Street the first thing next morning, thought there was no particular hurry, thought he could come round any time, and that his promised talk with her would keep.

But for some reason this explanation left her, if anything, rather more annoyed than before.

❦

It wasn't till the evening, till the last of the day's services was over, and the last footstep of the last home-going worshipper had died away, and she had heard the church door being locked, and then whoever had locked it going away too, and it was plain that she now wouldn't see James again for nearly a week, that her annoyance began to give way to uneasiness.

What, really, had happened to him? If ever a man meant what he said, it had been James when he declared he was coming back if she let him or didn't let him. Why, then, didn't he come? To what ignoble knuckling-under was that sister forcing him, in the beautiful benign-looking old house?

The lies the outsides of houses told! The humiliations that went on behind their tidy, smug faces! She hated to think of James, inside that one, knuckling under, but who knew better than she the anxious amiability, the readiness to placate, forced on one by living with somebody who doesn't mind being disagreeable? She, of all people, should sympathise with and understand James's difficulties, she who not only had herself diligently pandered, but for years had watched her mother pandering and continually trying at least to imitate concord, so that the level of decorum inside the house should at least be brought to the level of decorum of its polished-knockered, snowy-doorstepped outside. Yet, though she knew perfectly all about the lengths to which a family will go to preserve the appearance of peace, here for hours she had been judging James because he too went those lengths—labelling him gritless, comparing him to a dog. If he were doglike, what about herself, then, during the years with father, and what about her mother? The Gower Street house had re-echoed with their soft, propitiatory barks.

Sitting on the step of the porch in the dark, the faint stirring of a little wind from time to time threading her hair through with coolness, she saw how impossible it was for James, or for any other decent, sensitive man, faced by a woman who didn't mind what she said or did, not to knuckle under. Short of physical violence, what could he do to silence such a woman, except give in? The proprieties had to be respected. There couldn't be brawls. Especially in a clergyman's house, there couldn't be brawls.

She sat very still, her chin in both her hands, her annoyance with him all melted now into sympathy and concern—and a kind of tender concern, too, as though, by some mysterious process, that being embraced business, which had so much infuriated her to begin with, had ended by making her feel close to him, and intimate, and as if, in some puzzling and highly disconcerting way, he was part of her.

He wasn't part of her, of course. Nobody in the world, thank God, was part of her. Free and independent, set squarely on her own feet, in possession of everything she wanted because she wanted so little, she was as detached as any human being well could be from hampering affections and relationships. But she did undoubtedly feel a curious interest in James's fate, a curious concern for his happiness—exactly as if she were, somehow, involved in both.

She stared into the dark garden, considering this. It was queer. Queer, indeed, that just the fact that she had been temporarily, and accidentally, and not in the least for her own sake but merely because she represented Woman, held to a man's heart, should give her the feeling of somehow having a share in him.

If this were the effect of embraces, what a good thing people didn't usually begin by such short cuts to intimacy! For then one would probably feel as if one had shares in everybody, and barriers would be flung down right and left, and independence and personal privacy would go hang, and the world would be full of intimate secret friends, all so much tangled up in interest in each other that such a thing as a detached existence would be impossible.

"Why, it would be *dreadful*," she said aloud, giving herself a quick shake, as if to shake herself free from even the shadow of the thought of such an enslaved condition.

❦

Next morning she went back to Gower Street.

Very early it was when she locked the cottage door behind her, left the key at Mrs. Jones's on her way through the village, and set out on the long tramp to Amberton.

This time she had nothing to carry, and her feet weren't aching. Also, she now knew the way. So that, the day being young and cool, having paused a moment to scowl at the vicarage of Benendon St. Michael as she passed its inhospitable gate, she briskly stepped out, did the remaining six miles in two hours, caught the London express, and was home by eleven.

Home? No, this wasn't home any more, she thought thankfully, opening the door with her latchkey and going into the narrow, gloomy hall, which looked narrower and gloomier than ever after the vast brightness of the Sussex downs. The house was in much the same confusion of displaced furniture and rolled-up carpets as when she left it the Friday before, little progress having been made during her absence; but what progress had she not, during this time, made herself! Unexpected and developing indeed had been her experiences since last she stood on that doormat. In the short space of a single week-end she had ripened, she felt, considerably; and if the spinster who let herself in at the Gower Street door was different from the one who had let herself out of it three days earlier, it was chiefly, she candidly admitted, because of James. He had mellowed her. Difficult to make head or tail of as it was, there was no doubt that the result of her brief association with him was that she was mellowed.

"Minnie, I'm mellowed!" she all but called down the kitchen stairs, when what she meant to say was, "I'm back."

Minnie was beginning to prepare lunch, and the familiar smell of the sort of lunch one had on Mondays came up the stairs to meet her, offending a nose which had so lately been smelling only roses and fruit. Not that it mattered. Nothing in that house mattered to her any more. She could regard it now, its furniture, its gloom, its endless memories of work and silence, with the benevolent, slightly amused indulgence a newly-released spirit, about to depart and dwell for ever in light, may be presumed to feel at the sight of the discarded body of its death.

"I'm home, Minnie," she called, suppressing that other announcement; and then corrected herself, and said, "I mean, I'm back."

"Found something to suit you, Miss?" asked Minnie, coming out of the kitchen to the foot of the stairs.

"Yes, everything," said Jen, smiling down at her. "Just think—I'm in a cottage already. I've taken it. It's mine. I've been living in it ever since I saw you last."

And Minnie, glowing with justified pride in the efficiency and promptness of her *Churchgoer*, said, "Didn't I tell you, Miss Jen? There's nobody like the clergy when it comes to giving one a warm welcome."

And Jen, her face becoming suddenly thoughtful, was obliged to agree that that was true.

❦

Then she forgot James, or rather she temporarily lost sight of him in the rush of things to be done for father. She became engulfed in the preparations necessary for an unexpectedly married parent's return. The whole house had to be re-arranged to make room for the slender Netta. The upstairs part, untouched since her mother's death, had to be entirely altered, and only she could do this properly, for what did Minnie know about brides? Jen didn't know much about them either, but she could imagine that when they were young, when they were exquisite, their surroundings should somehow be made to match them.

She soon found, however, that nothing she could do would make that house match Netta. It was a hopeless business; and she gave up trying, and concentrated only on making it clean. At least it should be spotless; and the day Netta arrived, she would hide its worst bits of gloom with flowers.

Father wouldn't like that, but no matter. Some concessions must be made to Netta; she couldn't be treated as if she were a plain, thirty-three year old daughter, or an ailing and accustomed wife. Would he, wondered Jen as she flew about the house, expect that lovely thing to sit in the back diningroom with him every day while he dictated? Impossible to imagine such young grace shut up in that black bottle of a room. The room couldn't hold it. It would probably burst. And a good thing too, she thought, smiling. It was time that room burst, she said to herself, remembering her own youth worn away in it.

But, after all, it was impossible to picture Netta in the house at all. What did she know about Netta, except the glorious fact that there she was? In return for the immense benefit she was bestowing on the Dodge family by being there, her new home, if it couldn't be comfortable, should at least be spotless; and Jen slaved to make it so, shutting out from her mind everything to do with Cherry Lidgate, and all her conjectures about James, knowing that such thoughts, so bright on the one hand and so disturbing on the other, would only distract her attention, and delay her final departure into freedom.

Indeed, it gradually became her hope that if she made immense efforts, if she thought of nothing else, if she got up at dawn and stayed up till midnight, one more inside of a week might perhaps see her through; and spurred by this she did wonders. Why, if she succeeded, she would be able to spend the whole of the last week of father's honeymoon uninterruptedly at Cherry Lidgate, only coming up the day he arrived to arrange the flowers, and welcome him, and tell him the good news that she was taking herself permanently off. Yes, she would aim at that; and redoubling her efforts, she pictured his gratification, and everybody's happiness. It would be a wonderful moment, when she handed over the keys to Netta, and blessed and thanked her for becoming a Dodge.

So she worked and worked, and by Thursday night she had got so well ahead that it really did look as if after another middle of a week everything would be ready. The worst of the re-arranging of the rooms was over; the worst of the sorting and tidying of manuscripts was over too; the important fifth chapter, beautifully corrected and copied out, lay ready on the desk, together with a list of the most likely of the innumerable secretaries who had flocked to the house in answer to an advertisement she had put in the *Times*,—"Poor things," she thought, seeing them so eager—nothing being more certain than that father would have to have a secretary, and that the secretary wasn't going to be Netta.

And she went to bed on the Thursday night tired but triumphant, and next morning started for her cottage, happily sure that the following Friday would probably see her going to it for good.

❦

The moment she turned her back on Gower Street, she forgot it. Father, his marriage, everything to do with him, faded completely from her mind, so infinitely more important to her now was her own life, and what awaited her this second week-end in the romantic hollow at the foot of Burdon Down.

She couldn't help wondering what awaited her, seeing how much had awaited her there last time; and fishing James up out of the back of her mind, where he had lain quiet while she was so busy, she wondered how soon she would see him again, and how he had been getting on while she was away, and how, really, their relations, begun so unusually, would develope.

She did hope they would develope peacefully, and not interfere with her gardening. Peace and gardening were what she wanted most; though when, in the afternoon, having left her luggage at Amberton to be sent out by carrier—she had brought her belongings with her this time, and all her books, including, of course, father's, in their gorgeous presentation bindings—when, having walked over the downs, she reached Cherry Lidgate, to any one watching her it would have seemed, from the way she looked about for a possible glimpse of him, that what she wanted most was James.

She looked about, however, in vain. There was no sign of his thin, black figure, and she didn't, as on the last occasion, coming round the corner of the Vicarage wall, almost run into him. The village street lay empty, blazing in the sun. Everybody was indoors at tea. James too was probably having tea, she thought, under the cedar, in his cool garden. And she remembered that she owed Alice a call, and it occurred to her that she might as well pay it now as later, and get it off her mind; and accordingly, only stopping in her cottage long enough to tidy herself a little after her immense walk, and brush the dust off her shoes, she proceeded at once to the Vicarage, using the short cut Alice had used to call on her, the short cut through the churchyard, which landed her familiarly on the lawn instead of at the front door—but if Alice could be familiar, so could she—and, arriving unseen and unannounced, she emerged straight into the Vicarage garden, and there, instead of James, found the Vicar of Benendon St. Michael, having tea under the cedar by himself, as if the whole place belonged to him.

❦

Since, from a distance, one tall lean clergyman looks very much like another tall lean clergyman, what with their collars and all, she didn't at first realise who he was, and had come quite close before she remarked, in much surprise, "Why, it's you!"

He for his part, lifting his pale eyes from the plate he was holding, off which he was abstractedly collecting crumbs and throwing them to birds he didn't look at, was even more surprised.

He had just been thinking of her. She was the real cause of the acute discomfort he had endured lately—till, in fact, the day before, when he was able, according to his arrangement with Miss Ollier, to come over and live in Ollier's well-found vicarage during his absence, having agreed to take the Cherry Lidgate duty for a month. For, the very day after the visit of the person now standing so unexpectedly before him, his servants had left him—the excellent cook, a most rare treasure he had had for years, making common cause with the girl Annie (to whom he had very properly given notice after that affair of the winter coat), and declaring that if Annie went she would go too; adding, moreover, on his showing anger at such a senseless, and for him disastrous, determination, and rebuking her perhaps a trifle severely, that she would go at once, then, that very day, and take Annie along with her, and he could keep their month's wages for all they cared; or words—the ignorant and unseemly words servants appear to use immediately more than merely Yes, sir, or No, sir, is required of them—to that effect.

So that he had been having several most unpleasant days, spent in the midst of the sudden incredible disorder into which his house seemed at once to fall on the departure of the women, besides having to sit down to really quite appalling food, prepared for him by a widowed parishioner, temporarily come in to oblige. The woman expected him to eat it. Not only did she cook disgracefully, but expected him to eat the revolting results. Indeed he had been thankful to get out of all this, and transfer himself bag and baggage to the comforts of Ollier's vicarage, especially as Ollier, with whom he hadn't an idea in common, wasn't in it himself.

But they were only temporary comforts, he only too well knew. At the end of a month he would have to go back to his disordered home and the hideous, the impossible task for a man, of finding a cook and training her in his preferences. Black was his outlook. Black in itself, it seemed still blacker by contrast with the bright perfection of Miss Ollier's house. And his thoughts during these days—particularly during morning and evening family prayers, which, like the services of the Church, were so familiar to him that he did most of his thinking during their repetition—had been divided between envy of Ollier's luck, who in no way whatever, that he could see, deserved to have such a sister, admiration for the remarkable woman herself, whose qualities blazed at him from every polished tap and door-knob, and anger with that other woman, the stranger whose conduct in regard to his coat was at the bottom of the whole trouble.

At the moment when he lifted his eyes it happened to be this anger which was uppermost in his thoughts, so that to see the object of it quite close to him surprised him very much; and when this object said, quite familiarly, "Why, it's you," he answered very stiffly, as he got out of his chair, for to be addressed by a stranger nakedly as You affronted him, "My name is Devenish." Whereupon Jen immediately, and for the rest of her life, thought of him as Devilish—Mr. Devilish; and was obliged to admit, seeing how much this simple joke amused her, that she must have a very elementary mind.

The interview was brief, and unsatisfactory. Tea was not offered, nor any suggestion made as to sitting down; and no amount of beauty in Devilish's setting, no amount of lovely contrast of light and shade playing about him, of glowing colour in the border with the sun on it which was his background, of cool green gloom where he stood beneath the immense branches of the cedar, of prettiness in the table he had just got up from, set out so delicately, like a table in a picture—no amount of any of these things, exactly the sorts of things which ordinarily would most have charmed her, could make her want to stay with him a minute longer than she was obliged to.

Nor did he in the least desire that she should stay; indeed, his one wish was that she should go. The squat cause of all his troubles! Towering above her, Mr. Devenish, his eyes inimical, briefly told her why he was there, and that the Olliers wouldn't be back for a month; and she, having received this information with a puzzled face, her eyes questioning his though her lips made no comment, remarked, so as to say something before immediately going away again, that she had come round to return Miss Ollier's call, and was living in Mr. Ollier's cottage.

"Really," said Mr. Devenish; a comment which had a familiar ring.

"You wouldn't have me in yours, and I had to live somewhere," said Jen, moved, she didn't know why, to try to strike a spark or two out of Devilish.

But he only said, "Really," again; he wasn't to be drawn into emitting sparks; and she was back in Rose Cottage less than ten minutes after she had left it.

"Now what," she asked herself, when she was safely alone, her forehead puckered, her eyes anxious, "has that Alice been doing to my James?"

Her James.

She paused in the mechanical business of taking off her hat and smoothing her hair.

Her James.

She hadn't a notion why such an expression should have come into her head. In it had flashed, before she could stop it, before she had an idea it was anywhere about.

Her James, indeed.

She repudiated it. If that was how she was going to feel about him, all squashy and maternal and protective, then goodbye to independence and pride, and peace and gardening.

But it wasn't only squashy and maternal, the feeling at the back of this unexpected expression. It was something else. It was something that—

She took off her hat, and hung it up on the cottage's one peg. Indeed, she thought, facing the facts, the effect of being kissed on a hitherto unkissed spinster of riper years was deplorable. Properly incensed as she had been at the moment, virtuously outraged, was it possible, then, for a woman to be retrospectively stirred up?

It rather seemed as if it were. Or had she, then, been stirred up all the time?

She stood for a moment staring at the hat she had just hung up.

Whatever it was, she was ashamed of herself.

CHAPTER IX

She dug. When a woman, she sternly decided, begins to get feelings which can only land her, if not nipped, in enslavement, the best thing she can do is to go in for hard and persistent exercise. So she dug; and discovered there is much virtue in a spade.

Perseveringly used, it does wonders for the mind, she found, and by the time she laid it aside on Sunday evening—she dug openly all Sunday, defying Devilish as he passed through the churchyard on his way to officiate at the services, nor caring what anybody thought of her, set only on digging herself free and sensible again—by the time she laid it aside, she was of opinion that no woman should be without one. Then perhaps they wouldn't be quite so silly. Then perhaps they would find there were other things in life besides some man. They would find, for instance, how surprisingly delicious just bread and butter is, when one is ravenous, and, when one has laboured out of doors all day, how deep and exquisite the satisfaction of dreamless sleep.

Indeed, the simple efficacy of spades in restoring one to reason astonished Jennifer. In hot weather especially, when the earth was sun-baked, evidently there was nothing like them. Perspiration poured off her, and with it seemed to go those foolish feelings about James. You can't perspire, she realised, and worry over a man at the same time; you can't perspire, and at the same time hanker. She was going neither to worry nor hanker. The last thing in the world she could bear to develope into would be a hankering spinster.

So she dug and dug; and nothing being able to stand up against a spade vigorously handled, even when, on Monday morning, a letter came from James, a letter posted in Switzerland, and written with every sign of mental disturbance—short, scrambly, dashed off as if in fear lest Alice should come into the room and look over his shoulder, a letter without either her name or his on it, and to the effect that he couldn't imagine what she must think of him, but his sister had had a sort of nervous breakdown, and he had been obliged to take her away for a change, and the instant he got back he would explain everything—even when she got this, it only needed a slightly increased amount of slightly more dogged digging to make it slide off her, and melt too from her thoughts.

Alice, and a nervous breakdown! He was being taken in, but it didn't, it mustn't, concern her. And James, his letter, her own absurd, mixed-up emotions, were all dug out of her mind along with the dug-up weeds, and carefully laid on one side, where they would do no harm.

These weren't the things to concern oneself with in fine August weather. They were stuffy, indoor things—the sorts of things one brooded over in rooms, and thought about because one had nothing else to do, and it was raining. But the letter coming when it did—the postman, who knew the handwriting, looked curiously at her when he gave it to her—did have this much effect on her, that it made her forget to go back to Gower Street. When she ought to have been starting on her walk to Amberton to catch the London train, she was reading it; and when she had finished reading it, and had thought a few things about James and Alice, and how he seemed always to be having to go to Alice, or away with her or something, and always was promising to come back and explain everything, she reached out instinctively for her spade, as a protection, as the proper refuge from everything to do with Olliers, and went into the garden and fell to digging with increased dogged-ness; and it wasn't till well on in the morning that she suddenly remembered Gower Street, and stopped abruptly in her work, and exclaimed aloud, "Oh, my *God*!"

Mr. Devenish heard her; Mr. Devenish, who was not far off, just on the other side of the low churchyard wall, where, time hanging on his hands, he had been ostensibly examining tombstones, while really observing with acid curiosity the activities, unfeminine indeed, of Ollier's tenant.

And he mentally noted, "She swears."

❦

Well, having missed the train, having forgotten all about the train and Minnie and Gower Street, Jennifer thought, "What's the use of worrying?"—as James was apt to think on similar occasions, and settled down to enjoying staying where she was.

Much better enjoy what you had got, when by chance you had got it, instead of wasting time worrying because you ought really to be somewhere else. She hadn't meant to stay; she had conscientiously intended to go back that morning, and continue the work begun. But it did seem to her, on thinking it over, that Minnie and Maud between them could very well manage without her. She had, after all, done the most important things, sifted out the secretaries, corrected and copied the fifth chapter, and Minnie knew now exactly how the rooms were to be arranged. Why leave all this, and all the lovely, scented country, so gorgeous just then with August magnificently burning its way into September, because of that old Gower Street? There were other trains that day, but she wouldn't go in them. One mustn't overdo conscientiousness, Jen decided, resuming her digging; and she came to the conclusion that a single day, even a few hours only, would be quite enough before father's homecoming for her to give the finishing touches to his house, and fill it with flowers.

Therefore in the afternoon she wrote to Minnie, her fingers so stiff from gripping the spade, and the palms of her hands so much blistered, that she could hardly hold the pen, and told her what indeed she, Minnie, had long noticed by the time the letter arrived, that she, Jennifer, hadn't come back after all. She, Minnie, wrote Jennifer, knew what to do, and helped by Maud could very well get on without her. She, Jennifer, was busy; she was very much occupied; she couldn't possibly be spared. And taking the letter to the post, and passing the *Three Jolly Shepherds*, there, at a table on trestles set out before the door, she saw her friend Mr. Patterson, sitting in his shirtsleeves drinking beer with his wife; and on his hailing Jen with genial respect, she paused to greet Mrs. Patterson; and he remarked that it was thirsty weather; and Jen, at his words, and at the sight of the clear, cool beer on the table, became thirsty too, and found herself quite unexpectedly, and in the sight of the whole village, tossing off a great glass of the golden stuff herself, as if she had been used to it at the end of a day's work all her life; and Mr. Devenish saw her—Mr. Devenish, who was not far off, just on the other side of the street, coming out of a cottage into which, against his grain, he had been forced by the alleged seriousness of the illness of one of Ollier's parishioners; and he mentally noted, "She drinks."

❦

Mr. Devenish also saw her, a few days later, doing other things which roused first his curiosity, and then his condemnation; for in the Rose Cottage garden were many snails, and Jen, not knowing what to do with them, but sure they oughtn't to be left where they were, collected them at odd moments into her skirt, and carrying them carefully to the low wall gently tipped them over into the churchyard.

At first she had misgivings, but soon got used to it. The snails had to go somewhere, and where else could they go? The other side of the churchyard wall was the one really convenient spot. Nobody could see them. They were hidden snugly in long grass behind a tombstone; and while snails, she had read, were death to gardens, they couldn't possibly do any harm to a place so dead already as a churchyard. James wouldn't mind, she was sure, even if he saw them, which he never would unless he went deliberately to look, and God, who had made snails, couldn't, for that reason, she reflected, mind either.

So over the wall they were gently tipped; and the heap grew and grew, because it was a nice cool thing collecting snails in the shade, and whenever she wanted a rest from digging she went and fetched a few more skirtsful. And since from the getting rid of snails to the getting rid of other superfluities there is but a step, she soon, becoming callous, proceeded to eggshells and sardine-tins; and it was when she was disposing of her third sardine-tin that Mr. Devenish saw her.

Now what, he asked himself, setting his *pince-nez* more accurately on his nose—for he was some way off, up on the path to the vestry—could the woman be emptying into the churchyard? The churchyard was Ollier's, and as such indifferent to him, but on general principles he couldn't see a churchyard being used to throw things into, being used, in fact, as a dustbin, unmoved. Plainly undesirable objects were being transferred to it. The woman was getting rid of something she obviously didn't wish to keep—what, exactly, from that distance, he couldn't tell, but it would be his duty, when she had withdrawn, to go down and find out.

Already, passing on his lawful occasions between the Vicarage and the vestry, he had noticed with hostile curiosity the absorbed figure down on the other side of the wall, working at tasks which he had till then associated only with day-labourers. Whatever time of the morning or afternoon he went by, there she was, toiling and intent, and his duties in James's vicarage being as good as non-existent, and his well-fed days therefore monotonous, he got into the habit of going along the path to the vestry just to see what the woman—he had learned she was a Miss Dodge, but preferred to describe her to himself as the woman—was doing next, and always he found her obeying the scriptural injunction, and doing whatever she had to do with all her might. With too much might altogether, and too little intelligence, considered Mr. Devenish, observing her, from between the tombstones the day after he had discovered that she drank, actually on her knees cutting grass with what appeared to be a pair of scissors.

That, of course, was nothing. It neither surprised nor interested him. They were her scissors, and it was her grass, and she, being of the sex which doesn't think, naturally set about the job in the most awkward and tiring way possible. He merely reflected coldly that a woman on all fours was an ugly sight, and that a man would either cut the grass with shears, or, still better, get somebody else to do it for him.

But this, now—this throwing things into the churchyard; this was very different. It might well come under the head of lawbreaking. Certainly it would come under the head of profanity. And it was his duty, at the first opportunity, to go and look.

So he went and looked that very afternoon, at a time when he judged that she would be indoors preparing tea, for he had learned she kept no servant. But Jennifer didn't have tea, having soon dropped it out of her afternoons as a bother, and was, as usual, in the garden digging, and catching sight of the black figure threading its way down through the churchyard between the tombstones, paused in her work.

"Devilish," she remarked to herself, leaning on her spade. "Good heavens," she added the next moment, "he's making straight for the snails. Now, how ever has he—"

She watched him uneasily, aware that she had become perhaps a little free with the churchyard the last day or two, and that in her zeal to get rid of things she had been throwing objects over which, unlike the snails, couldn't be called God's creatures. For instance, those sardine-tins. Three of them were on the heap, the last one having gone over just before lunch, and nothing had been added since, to cover it up. It was lying naked and exposed, right on the top. He was bound to see it.

Indeed, at that very moment Mr. Devenish, having again adjusted his *pince-nez*, was seeing precisely this—the ignoble crown to the extraordinary mass, collection, colony,—he really didn't know what to call the horrid pile; and was contemplating it with disgust. An empty sardine-tin. Other, similar, tins protruding. Also eggshells. And the whole slowly heaving, because of the snails.

This, he thought, was too much. It was callous profanity. Thankful indeed was he that he hadn't got the woman in his own cottage. She mustn't be allowed to continue in Ollier's cottage, either. She must be dislodged. He would see that Ollier dislodged her. He would write at once to Ollier, and tell him what she was doing, and that in his opinion she should undoubtedly be dislodged. Ollier was a boneless boy, who thought of nothing except mooning about in his garden, and let his parish do pretty well as it liked, but even he would see that for God's Acre to be used in this manner was going too far.

God's Acre; God's Acre; Mr. Devenish indignantly repeated the words as he examined the revolting mass, his indignation switching from it on to James. For, positively, he couldn't be sure whether Ollier would see what an outrage had been committed. Ollier didn't seem to mind anything very much, and Mr. Devenish, who minded everything a great deal, regarded such slackness as a real scandal. Parishes like Ollier's disgraced the Church, he thought, staring at the snails. With his want of personality, he had no hold whatever on his flock, nor could have, nor apparently—this was the worst—wanted to have. Probably he hadn't a hold even over himself. Probably, if temptation came his way, he would at once fall into it, thought Mr. Devenish, in whose way temptation, the sort he was thinking of, the only sort that seriously tempted, for many years now hadn't come. Lucky indeed was Ollier to have a woman like his sister at his side; but then he had all the luck, thought Mr. Devenish getting angrier, including a quite remarkable cook. He could only hope the boy realised his blessings. He didn't look as if he realised anything. At his age, and with a face so characterless, he oughtn't to have been given a living at all. Patrons of livings shouldn't be allowed to give them to youths hardly down from Cambridge, merely because they happened to be cousins. Unfair, unfair, the way Ollier had got everything, and without the least effort. He had even got Lady Higgs—the kind of parishioner every priest dreams of; and got her, positively, by inches, for if her seat had been only a foot or two more to the north-east, it would have been in his parish instead of in Ollier's, and she would have worshipped in his church, and supported his charities, instead of Ollier's. Not that, he understood, she was particularly free in her support, but that was because Ollier was a young fool who didn't realise the importance of the really rich, and didn't know or care how to approach her properly; indeed hardly ever, so he had been told, approached her at all, leaving her cultivation entirely to his sister, who, remarkable and competent as she was—he could see that from the perfect order of her house—and in every possible way, he was sure, admirable, wasn't, owing to her sex, quite the same thing as the parish priest.

And Mr. Devenish, who had begun by being outraged by the snails, ended by being curiously incensed against James, and went off to the Vicarage to write him a strong letter then and there, describing what was being done, and suggesting that it was ultimately his fault.

Jennifer watched him go with relief. Nothing was going to happen, then; Devilish wasn't coming down to rebuke her. After all, she thought, suddenly brave as a lion now that he had gone, seeing that it wasn't his churchyard, it would have been rather impertinent of him if he had. What was he, except a stop-gap,—really an interloper? She would have pointed this out to him, if he had taken upon himself to admonish her. Oh, yes, she would have stood up to Devilish all right, she assured herself, flinging the weeds, as she dug them up, on one side almost as if they were bits of Devilish, and she were drastically dealing with him.

Nevertheless when, a few minutes later, she heard footsteps on the path at her back, on the other path, the one that led from the gate into the lane, she started violently, and clutching her spade stood quite still, hoping she wouldn't be noticed, and far too much afraid to look round.

Devilish, after all. Devilish, coming upon her from behind. How like him. How mean to cut her off, and not give her a chance to—well, withdraw. Perhaps, if she didn't move, he wouldn't see her. Really it was a pity she had put herself in the wrong over those silly sardine-tins.

But the steps on the path, having arrived at the spot level with where, among the gooseberry bushes, she was trying to pretend she didn't exist, came to a stop. She clung to her spade, and waited.

He had seen her, then. He was standing silently watching her. Mean man. Objectionable man. Making her feel all creepy up her back.

Well, she would face him. There was nothing for it but to turn, and with dignity face him.

And dropping the spade, she did turn, haughtily prepared for the worst; and there instead of Devilish, standing on the path regarding her with eyes full of hesitation and inquiry, was that lovely young creature, father's new wife.

❦

Netta.

Now how extraordinary. Now how had she found out the address. And how, why, had she come?

Jen stared, open-mouthed. That some one who ought to have been in Norway with her husband, should be in the Rose Cottage garden without him, robbed her utterly of speech.

Netta, for her part, stared too, holding on hard to a dog who was struggling in her arms—her dog; her inseparable dog; the dog on whose account she had refused to go to Norway, where father tried to take her for his honeymoon, for how could she go to Norway without her dog, and how could she go there with him when, as she discovered at the last moment, he would be made to languish for six months in quarantine on her return? The only time she had ever been separated from her dog was during the hours she was being married and taken to tea with her stepdaughter, on which unique occasion she had stretched a point, and left him in charge of a cousin called Henry, who didn't know she was getting married, and when he brought the dog late in the afternoon, as arranged, to the railway station, and handed him over to her in a compartment of the train for Hull, he got the surprise of his life.

"I say," Henry had whispered, on seeing father also in the compartment, "shall you be all right, shut up alone with that old buster?"

Doubt on her own face, Netta had whispered back, "I hope so. He's my husband."

Whereupon Henry, incredulous and horrified, could only gasp, "Good God!" And Netta, though herself assailed by doubts, feeling she ought to show some spirit, declared in Henry's ear that he wasn't a buster, but a very celebrated man, and Henry just had time to say, with every appearance of scepticism, "*Is* he, by Jove," when the train slid off, and he was left, shattered and alone on the platform.

This dog was now struggling to get at Jennifer, because he thought she was a tramp. Netta wasn't sure either but what the brown, earthy figure among the bushes wasn't a tramp—a female tramp, being given temporary outdoor relief; for she had only seen her stepdaughter during those brief moments on her wedding day when, what with one thing and another, and the way her new relations wound up by going into the next room and leaving her alone while they had what sounded like a set-to with the gloves, she hadn't been in a condition to take much notice of anybody; and holding on tight to the violent animal, she was about to ask whether Miss Dodge was staying there, when the brown person in the bushes began to move slowly towards her, and the dog's struggles to get free became so frantic that her whole attention was concentrated on preventing his escape.

This confused things a good deal for the next minute or two, and by the time they could hear themselves speak, the brown person was saying, "Netta, how in the world—!" so that of course she knew then who it must be, though the dog still didn't know any better than before, and continued to confuse things; and it wasn't possible to speak properly, really, till they had all three somehow got into the cottage, and a sardine had been fetched, and he, not being a cat, was so much surprised at being offered an oily fish that it quite took his bark away.

Then Netta, having put him and the sardine on the worn brick floor as close together as they would go, took off her hat, shook back her fair hair, and looking at Jennifer from under the long black eyelashes which so endearingly framed her lovely, candid, child's eyes, said, with that mixture of shyness and courage which had been on her face when she peeped reluctantly through the diningroom door in Gower Street at her wrangling relatives, and inquired if she could help in any way, "I've come to see you."

"But—where's father?" naturally asked Jen.

"He's at Brighton," said Netta.

"Brighton?" echoed Jen, staring. "But I thought—didn't you start for Norway?"

"Yes. But where we got to was Brighton," said Netta, putting her hat down on the nearest object, which was the stove—luckily, at that hour, not alight. "Ought I—oughtn't I to kiss you, or something?" she added, looking at Jennifer, again with that air of mixed courage and reluctance. "I'm a sort of mother of yours now, you know. I suppose it's true, though it doesn't seem likely."

"It's absurd," said Jen.

"It *is* rather funny," agreed Netta.

They kissed; Netta shyly, Jen gravely. Jen felt very grave, and much perturbed by this inexplicable visit; but grave and perturbed as she was, she couldn't but notice, as she kissed Netta, that she smelt very delicious—like freshly washed and powdered babies who should be mixed up with bunches of violets, thought Jen, sniffing appreciatively.

Then Netta said, as they stood facing each other, and the dog, preoccupied on the floor, was quiet for a moment, "I've got a day off—" and Jen was so much struck by this phrase, surely a little unusual on the lips of one not yet married three weeks, that she found nothing to say, and just stared. A day off. A day off what? She could only suppose, a day off father.

"I've got it," explained Netta, flushing faintly at the expression on her new relation's face, "because I took it. If I hadn't taken it," she explained further, feeling she must justify herself as this expression became visibly more pronounced, "I wouldn't have got it. So I—well, I took it," she finished, half defiant, half afraid.

"Do you mean," said Jennifer, after a short silence, in the voice of one hardly crediting her ears, "father doesn't *know*?"

"I expect he does by this time," said Netta, carrying it off as best she could, "because of lunch. There'll be two places laid for lunch, and when he sees one of them staying empty, he's bound, after a bit, to put two and two together, isn't he?"

And stooping down she picked up the dog, who, having learned all there was to learn about the sardine, round which for a space, outraged, he had been sniffing, was beginning to confuse things again.

"You mean, you just—" began Jennifer.

Words, however, failed her. How could anybody, she asked herself, bewildered and shocked, behave like this to father? And what extraordinary fearlessness, what independence, what indifference! On a honeymoon, too; on a honeymoon which hadn't yet lasted three weeks.

She stared, speechless. Was it possible, then, to be indifferent to father's wishes—or rather to what would have been his wishes if he had been given a chance to express them? Was it possible to do something which was bound to make him very angry, and not mind his anger? But, shocked as she was, into her heart there did creep a kind of frightened admiration.

Such courage seemed to her, who knew him, as she thought, so well, unbelievable. Father, having things like this done to him! *Father.* And by a girl.

"May I sit down?" asked Netta, looking round.

Jennifer pulled one of her two chairs forward, her eyes, fascinated, still on the girl's face.

"You're not angry?" asked Netta, letting herself down carefully, because of her arms being full of dog—and kicking dog at that, obviously wishing, now that his attention was no longer diverted, to get at Jen.

"Why should I be angry?" asked Jen, glad that that was what she looked like. It wouldn't at all do for Netta to guess that her reckless behaviour was being anything but condemned.

"One never knows why anybody should ever be angry," said Netta, with a small sigh. "At least, I don't. But they are. And I thought you seemed as if—as if perhaps—"

"That's only surprise. Naturally I'm surprised," said Jen. "You're being here *is* rather surprising."

"Well, I did ring up your house in Gower Street."

"Your house," corrected Jen.

"I can't somehow believe that," said Netta, surrounding the dog with both her slender, bare arms, and holding him close.

"It's true, though. *This* is my house."

"What?" said Netta, looking at her with startled eyes. "Aren't you coming back to Gower Street? But I thought you were going to live with us. I thought—"

"Oh, never mind that now, Netta. Tell me why you rang up."

"Because I want to talk to you. And if you're not coming back, it's a mercy I came."

"But you oughtn't to want to talk on your honeymoon," said Jen, her heart afraid.

"Well, I do. About Richard. And when the Gower Street maid gave me this address, and said it was in Sussex, I looked it up on a map, and found it was only twenty miles from Brighton. So I hired a car, and came. It's waiting in the village. If you don't mind, I'd like to ask you a few things about Richard." And Netta, shrinking but determined, arranged herself more conveniently in the chair.

Richard, thought Jen, gazing down at her. That was father. How odd the name sounded on this child's lips—so familiar, so almost disrespectful. It wasn't, of course, either of these things. The celebrated man was hers. She might even, Jen supposed with a slight shiver, call him Dick if she wanted to.

"You mean—father?" she said hesitatingly, misgivings thick upon her; for what could she wish to know, and what could she, his daughter, with either propriety or tact tell her? Besides, she was sure husbands were best not asked about.

"Well, *I* can't call him father, can I," said Netta, laying her cheek on the dog's head, as if in him were all her comfort, and looking up from this position at the discouragingly solemn face above her.

"And *I* can't call him Richard, can I," said Jen, trying to laugh. But she couldn't laugh. No sound resembling laughter emerged; and she said, suddenly turning away, suddenly feeling she had better get busy, do something, fuss round, distract Netta's attention, "I'll make tea. You must have tea—" and grabbing at the kettle, she filled it by dipping it, with a great, untidy splash, into the pail of water.

"I don't want tea," said Netta, her cheek on the dog's head. "Tell me—what is Richard *really* like?"

This was bad. This was very bad. This was about as bad a beginning as could be. Not for a daughter, Jen felt as she struck a match and tried to light the spirit lamp, still with the idea of doing something, of distracting Netta's attention—not for a daughter to tell her father's wife what he was like, nor for a wife, she was sure, to seek information of her husband's daughter. True, this wife had no resemblance to any wife she had yet seen. She was a girl, a child almost, who instead of being where she ought to be, in some jolly home full of lively brothers and sisters and dogs, had unaccountably strayed into the austere silences of father's society, where, judging from her question, she wasn't feeling as comfortable as she had perhaps expected.

Now it was of vital importance that Netta should feel comfortable.

Simply everybody's happiness depended on it. If she weren't, if she grew restive—Jen's hand, holding the match, quite shook with apprehension of what might happen to them all if Netta grew restive.

"Father's a *dear*," she said therefore, after a pause during which she was ostensibly absorbed in getting the spirit lamp to light; and she said it emphatically, trying to sound as if she were convinced.

She was half convinced. She did almost believe that if he hadn't, till then, been what perhaps might be generally called a dear, he certainly would become one with this adorable young wife. "That's what he's like, Netta," she said, throwing the match away and turning to the figure in the chair. "And an extraordinarily distinguished dear into the bargain—as of course you know."

"Oh, I know he's distinguished," said Netta, with a lack of enthusiasm that increased Jen's uneasiness. If a girl isn't enthusiastic on her honeymoon, when will she be? Jen asked herself, who knew little about honeymoons, but had certainly been led to believe that they included enthusiasm.

"Ever since I can remember," went on her drooping visitor, "it has been dinned into me that he's distinguished. My relations think there is no one like him. And I've seen it for myself, in his books. What I don't understand—" she looked up at Jen with perplexed brows"—is why it should *stay* in his books."

"Stay in his books?"

"Yes. Not come out into every-day life. Not be visible anywhere. His being so distinguished, I mean," explained Netta.

Jen, turning away, stretched out her arm and took a loaf and some butter from the shelf. Every word Netta said alarmed her more. She began feverishly to cut bread and butter.

"Well, but doesn't it?" she asked, bending over the loaf.

"Did *you* think it did?"

"That's different. He would be different with me. I'm only his daughter."

"But there's no sign of it. Not the tiniest glimpse of what I mean—of his being so wonderful," Netta said. "I've read all his books, and I used to dream how marvellous it would be if ever I could meet him. Meet him! And now I've married him," she said, sitting up straight, and looking at the busy figure in an incredulous, an almost accusing, astonishment—as if she, Jennifer, could help her having married father! Jen thought, feeling the accusation in her voice, and diligently applying herself to cutting bread and butter.

"It's funny, isn't it," remarked Netta, as her stepdaughter said nothing.

"It isn't funny at all," said Jen stoutly, but inwardly afraid. "It's wonderful. It's the most wonderful thing that could have happened to any girl. Do you like marmalade, Netta? I'm afraid I haven't got any jam. If I had known you were coming I would have had a cake for you."

"That's what I thought when I did it," said Netta, taking no notice of this talk of marmalade and cake.

"Did what?"

"Married him."

"Well, and so it was, and so it is," insisted Jen, arranging the slices of bread and butter she had cut on a plate. "It's what no one else has done, anyhow—not for ages, I mean," she corrected herself. "Just think what he is—*who* he is. Why, all over Europe and America—"

"I don't care about Europe and America," interrupted Netta. And her young face drawn into lines of perplexity, she went on, "What worries me is that he's so *different*. I can't make out why he should be so *different*. Did *you* find him different?"

"Different from what?" Jen asked, clattering the cups about. "You know, Netta, father's your husband, and I don't believe wives ought—"

"Oh, but you must let me talk," interrupted Netta, her delicate eyebrows frowning. "It's very important. You're the only person who really knows. Tell me why he's so *completely* different from the things he writes?"

Jennifer went to the stove, and filled the teapot with boiling water. "Do you think he is?" she asked, her back turned.

"Don't you?"

"Well, and if I did," said Jen, still with her back turned, picking her words, proceeding with extreme caution, "and if he does sometimes seem to be—a little different, it would only be natural. Nobody can keep up to the highest pitch the whole time. Father wouldn't be human if he did. He wouldn't be nearly such a—well, such a dear. You want him to be human, don't you? You don't want him for ever sitting aloof, up on his peak?"

"But it's when he's on his peak, as you call it, that he's what I thought I was marrying. It's when he comes off it—comes down to breakfast, for instance—that he isn't. What did you do with him at breakfast?"

"Do with him?" said Jen, going back to the table, teapot in hand. "Nothing. I poured out his coffee, and let him alone."

"But he won't be *let* alone," said Netta, frowning.

"He won't be?"

Jen, putting down the teapot, stared at the girl, trying to visualise a Gower Street breakfast at which father wouldn't be let alone. What exactly did Netta mean? She herself knew very little about wives, having only seen her mother in that capacity at close quarters, but she imagined her mother, anyhow, would have been delighted if father had emerged from his customary taciturnity at meals, and talked. For her part she had neither expected, nor wanted, nor got, conversation out of father. He ate his meals in silence. He took his exercise solitarily. In the evenings he and she played chess. A remote, aloof man, caring really for nothing, she had judged, but his work. So what did Netta mean, that he wouldn't be let alone?

"I don't know what *you* think," said Netta, leaning forward and searching Jennifer's face as though for help and enlightenment, "but *I* think there ought to be a close time for such things."

"What things?" asked Jen.

"Why, lovemaking," said Netta, looking at her stepdaughter, aggrieved and indignant.

"Lovemaking?" repeated Jen, startled. "Look here, Netta," she said hastily, turning a little red beneath her sunburn, so strange was it to think of father in these connections, "you must talk to your mother about this sort of thing, if you feel you must talk to somebody. And tea's ready. Come along—pull up your chair. Will that dog keep quiet, do you think?"

"I haven't got a mother," said Netta, without moving.

"Well then, I should say it was better not to talk to anybody. I suppose if one gets married one must expect to—to be made love to."

"But not at breakfast."

"Why not, if one happens to want to?"

"Two should happen to want to."

"Well, anyhow I'm sure it's ridiculous to try and have fixed times for it, and switch it on as if it were electric light."

"I don' t want to switch it on. I want to switch it off."

"But there's such a thing as a wife's duty, isn't there?"

"Nobody told me what Richard's wife's duty would be. He was mum as a fish about the very things I ought to have been asked if I'd mind. He simply never mentioned them. From that first day in the omnibus—"

"What omnibus?"

"The one I met him in. From that first day till my wedding day he behaved exactly like his books, and from my wedding day on he—well, he didn't."

"Oh, my dear Netta, things will settle down, and you'll get quite used to them," said Jen, busily filling the cups.

"Never," said Netta.

"Oh, nonsense. I never *heard* such nonsense."

"But you don't know," said Netta. "You simply don't understand. How would you like—"

"Listen, Netta—I won't and can't talk to you about father," said Jen, putting the teapot down with a bang. "It's not right nor decent."

"But who will, then?"

"Nobody, I hope. He's your husband, and what you've got to do isn't to talk about him, but to love him."

"Did you?"

Jen picked up a teaspoon, and began fishing a fly out of the milk. Why did Netta say these things? It really was dreadful of her to say such things.

"Of course I did—and do," she said, bending over the milk jug. Yes, she had loved father, she did love father—in a sort of way, that is. A wife's way, naturally, would be different, would be more pronounced. And anyhow duty was duty, and if one took on obligations one should honourably fulfil them. Netta had taken on obligations the day she married, and now, not three weeks later, was talking in a way that seemed to show a desire to shirk. If Netta were to start shirking, what would become of them all?

"Do come and have your tea before it gets cold," she said, trying not to sound either severe or anxious. She was so young, this girl. She couldn't be more than nineteen. Foolish to take her seriously; useless, as well as unkind, to scold her. Still, it really was frightening, how much depended on her being happy with father. …

"I don't want tea," said Netta, hugging the dog.

"Oh, but you must have something to eat before going back to Brighton."

"I don't want to go back to Brighton."

"Don't be silly, Netta," said Jen, quite snappy in her anxiety.

"Why can't I stay here?" asked Netta, leaning forward on her chair, the dog gathered close to her heart.

"Stay here?" echoed Jen, looking at her in great alarm.

"Oh, I'd *love* to!" exclaimed Netta, suddenly eager, speaking quickly. "Do let me," she pleaded. "It'll be much easier getting back in the morning. The car can put up somewhere. And you and I don't know each other a bit yet, and we'd make friends. Please. Just one night. You can't think what a *comfort*—you can't *think* what a comfort, just one—"

"Are you mad, Netta?" Jennifer interrupted; and there was that in her voice which instantly shut Netta's mouth.

The eagerness disappeared from her face as if it had been wiped out by a blow. She looked for a moment at her stepdaughter, then slowly drooped over the dog again, held him closer, let her cheek rest once more on his head, and murmured, with a slight shrug of her thin young shoulder, "Oh, well—"

❦

Then her stepdaughter, drawing the other chair to the table, sat down on it squarely, and began to be very sensible and firm.

She was now thoroughly frightened. This mustn't be allowed to go on—the girl's nonsense must be put an end to, once and for all. So, pushing one of the filled cups towards her who still sat where she was, and the plate of bread and butter and the marmalade, she informed her authoritatively—how like a governess she felt!—that she must eat something before her return journey, that on that return journey she soon would have to start if she was to reach Brighton in decent time for dinner, and that under no circumstances was father going to be left miserable and anxious a moment longer than could be helped.

It really was most wrong of Netta, she continued, trying to smile so as to soften the words—but no smile, to speak of, appearing—*most* wrong, to have come away without asking him, without even telling him. She must remember that she was grown up and married, and couldn't any longer behave as if nothing mattered except just what she happened to want to do at the moment. She was father's wife. There were things wives didn't do. There were duties, obligations. And now, instead of wasting time talking silly stuff, let Netta be sensible, and drink her tea, and tell her a little about herself; because she knew nothing at all about her, Jennifer didn't, except, of course—here she really smiled—that she was exceedingly adorable to look at. And then presently, quite soon in fact, they would walk together to the village, and Jennifer would see her safely off, and she must be very nice to poor father when she got back, and tell him she was sorry if he had been anxious, and she wouldn't do it again.

Who could stand up against such talk? Certainly not Netta, who never could stand up against anything—not for long, that is. Her cheek pressed hard against the dog, her eyes shut so as to hide what she was terribly afraid felt exactly like a tear squeezing its shameful way out through her eyelashes, she sighed and gave up. No good talking to a stony spinster. No good expecting such a one to understand the intricate surprises of marriage. Since, evidently, her fate was to be sent back to Brighton without having been given the least information and help, why bother? After all, she thought, drooping lower, clinging closer, there were always dogs. Nobody could be quite alone in the world as long as there were dogs.

"I don't believe," she presently murmured when Jennifer's admonishments seemed to have come to an end, her eyes still shut because of that disgraceful tear, her voice the voice of one who ceases to struggle, "I don't believe my stepdaughter has the faintest idea of what it's like being married."

"Well, but how should she have?" inquired Jen, pretending to be amused, though, even as she spoke, the recollection of that moonlit night under the apple-tree for some reason rushed back to her, flooded her mind, surged, scalding, into its remotest corners, and burned her face bright red.

She looked at Netta, and stirred uneasily in her chair. If it were like that—if being married were at all like that—and went on being like that—and was like that even—yes, Netta had hinted it—at breakfast—and if, at the same time, one didn't happen to love the person very much—why, then—

But—father?

Ah, no—it was quite impossible to imagine *father* ...

Later, as they walked together into the village in search of the car—Jen wondered what, among other things, would be said that evening in Brighton to the extravagance of the car—there seemed to be no kick left in Netta. Without making any further attempt to stay where she was instead of going home, she allowed herself to be taken away on being told it was time, and such words as she uttered, while they walked, were the politely indifferent words of one who expects nothing, and therefore doesn't take any particular interest in anything.

Behind her waddled the dog, sniffing occasionally at Jen's skirt, but otherwise behaving himself, a dog, Jen saw, now that he wasn't enveloped in his mistress's arms, of a long-backed, low-bellied build, with short legs turning outwards at their ends—rather, though not very, like a dachshund, and of no known breed.

What father made of the dog, Jen couldn't imagine. That there should be a dog at all with him on his honeymoon was astonishing, but that it should be this dog, so noisy and suspicious, was almost incredible. But then she had now lost, as it were, all count of father. Sides of his character had been brought out that afternoon by Netta of whose very existence nobody, till then, had dreamed. The acceptance of the dog certainly suggested infatuation, only it did seem to Jen, whose life had been cloistered, impossible to believe that a man so old, so gifted, so dignified, impressive and alarming, could suddenly change completely, and become the sport and plaything of a little girl. Father, being a sport and plaything? No, no,—in spite of the curious evidence offered by almost every word Netta had said, she couldn't bring herself to believe it. Not, certainly, in father's case. Other old men might, for all she knew, make fools of themselves, but father? No, it was too unlikely; he was merely being indulgent on his honeymoon, and putting up with the dog strictly for the present only. That dog, Jen felt convinced, would never see Gower Street.

Still, even a temporary putting up with it was strange. Everything was strange. Her mind fumbled, as she walked by Netta's side to the village, trying to arrange the pieces of the puzzle into some recognisable shape. She didn't recognise anything. At tea—after a while Netta had obeyed her exhortations, and drawn her chair to the table, and pretended to eat—the girl had dropped some odd bits of information in answer to questions, showing father in most unexpected lights. Jen had gazed, bewildered, at the pictures presented, for they included his presence in that omnibus—he who never went in omnibuses; stooping to pick up a parcel—he who never touched, much less stooped to pick up, such things; talking to the owner of the parcel—he who never talked to strangers; following the stranger—true, a most sweet stranger—when she got out, and offering her his umbrella because it was raining, and holding it over her, and actually seeing her home, and going in, and being introduced to an awe-struck sister-in-law. For it appeared that Netta had lived with her brother and his wife in Chelsea, and the brother was a journalist, and the sister wrote too, and they both were enthusiastic admirers of Richard Dodge, and nearly had a fit when he, the unapproachable, and unknowable, walked into their drawingroom.

These revelations of father's private activities astounded Jen; and most of all astounded was she to remember how having, after that first time, gone into the Chelsea drawingroom regularly every day, on each of these days he had come home to Gower Street and had tea with her as usual, and not betrayed by the smallest sign what, in a phrase which would have seemed fantastic used in his connection a month ago, he had been up to. That he had been up to a good deal should have been evident to her when he suddenly walked in with a wife, but her excitement and absorption in the consequences to her own life had left her no time to think. Now, listening to Netta, and looking back at his behaviour during the whole of this period, she was astounded. What *sang froid*, what competence in cunning! Butter, to use another phrase once unthinkable, hadn't melted on a single one of these many returns to tea, in father's mouth.

Oh, yes, said Netta, languidly answering the last of the questions, for there came an end, Netta having suddenly shut up like an oyster, to Jen's powers of asking—oh, yes, naturally she had been thrilled when she discovered who it was she was walking with that day.

No, not an idea. She had just taken him for a kind old gentleman, who hated seeing girls, without umbrellas, getting wet.

Oh, yes—of course she had been still more thrilled when he wanted to marry her.

Yes—quite soon he began to want to.

Yes—her breath was taken away. Funny, wasn't it, she remarked, listlessly fingering the dog's ears, to remember all these thrills now.

Yes, she had liked marrying secretly; it had seemed as if it would be fun.

Yes, he said it was because he wanted to avoid fuss, and she had liked the idea of springing it on her relations.

No, she hadn't sprung it yet. She didn't want to now, somehow. Funny, wasn't it, she here again remarked, how one didn't want to do things after a bit.

Oh, no, they wouldn't be worrying. They thought she was staying with a friend.

Yes—perhaps she had better. She would write to them from Brighton. There wasn't any point now—she couldn't think why she had ever thought there was a point. In springing the news on them, she meant, and seeing their faces.

She didn't mind, now, about their faces.

Funny, wasn't it, said Netta, a third time.

And she looked at Jen with ruminative eyes, the tear well got the better of, and, stretching out her hand towards her cup, drank a mouthful of tea, and after a pause remarked, irrelevantly, that her name used to be Baines.

Soon after this, Jen said it was time to go, and got up and took her hat off its peg, and put it on.

Netta made no objection. Really she was quite easy to manage, thought Jen, trying to persuade herself that everything was all right, and that there was nothing to worry about. A little firmness—mixed with kindness, of course—was all that was needed. She knew she had been firm. It remained for her now to hope she had been kind.

Doubts, however, as to this, combined with her efforts to make head or tail of father in his new aspects, caused her to be rather silent on the way to the village. Netta, for her part, was rather silent too. She had come asking for bread, and had been given what she regarded as a stone, so naturally she wasn't feeling exactly chatty, though she accepted the situation with resignation.

Stones, it seemed to her, were being handed out pretty freely these days, and she ought soon to be quite used to them, she told herself as she walked by Jen's side, dangling her hat loosely in her hand, and trying to prevent her head from hanging in too obvious a dejection. There was a motherly-looking old lady in the hotel at Brighton, for instance, who had instantly given her a stone when, disturbed into effort by Richard's unaccountable behaviour, she had tried to consult her as to what she ought to do about it. And now Richard's daughter, who had seemed so jolly and cheerful in that awful house in Gower Street, had given her one too, refusing even a single crumb of the bread of comfort and enlightenment.

Yet really her lot, considered Netta, did seem to be one which needed explaining. Even on her wedding day, sitting alone in that diningroom listening to the noises her new crowd was making in the hall, she had begun to suspect it needed explaining, and her honeymoon had convinced her that it did. But Richard, it appeared, mustn't be talked about. Directly one married a man, he became, apparently, unmentionable. See how they shut her up. The old lady had shut her up at once, and now this Jennifer had shut her up too, though she could have thrown more light on him than anybody in the world. But what, then, was a poor girl to do? she asked herself, her charming, ruffled fair head drooping in spite of her efforts to hold it up. And the strangest part of the whole business—enough, she was sure, to make the perkiest tail hang down—was the fact that of all the millions of people in existence, the millions and millions of other people in the world besides herself, only she should be obliged to go back that evening to Richard Dodge.

❦

When, finally, the chauffeur had been extracted from the *Jolly Shepherds*, and she was inside the car with the dog on her lap, her stepdaughter, who was standing at the door looking at her, not only had doubts, but qualms.

The girl was so young. She was so lovely. She had such thin little shoulders—shoulders far too frail, thought Jen, anxiously examining them, to bear the burden of responsibility for father's and his daughter's happiness. Two enormous Dodges flopping on to this girl, depending on her for their enjoyment of life—it did seem rather much to ask of her; and Jen, looking at her through the window of the car, had qualms.

Perhaps she might, after all, have let her stay the night, and telegraphed to father. She had wanted to so badly. What would it really, in all the years to come, have mattered that for a single night she was away from father? Ah, but it must be right to make her go home. Faced by a newly-made wife who doesn't want to, the only thing anybody could do was to insist that she should. The whole world would be unanimous that Jennifer had done right in sending her back to her husband.

Still, she had qualms; and what was more, when she saw the child sitting alone in the hired car, she wasn't at all sure that she oughtn't to go to Brighton with her, and see her safely into father's arms. Suppose something happened to her on the way? Suppose the strange chauffeur had drunk too much during his time of waiting at the *Shepherds*, and drove her into a ditch, or got off his seat and was rude to her?

But this Jen simply couldn't bring herself to do. It would be too like someone lately risen from the dead being caught and forced back into his well-known coffin. Where father was, there would always be for her a feeling of burial. No, she didn't quite mean that—she meant that he might—that she mightn't be able— Besides, there was sure to be some sort of a scene, either tragic or wrathful, and it was right and proper that married people should have their scenes to themselves.

"You'll take care of yourself?" she asked, the more anxious for Netta's welfare that she was doing nothing, herself, towards it.

"Oh, yes," said Netta indifferently, over the head of the dog who was sitting bolt upright, with a wary and hostile eye on the figure at the door.

"You don't think I've been unkind, Netta? I wouldn't be unkind to you for the world," said Jen, earnestly.

"Oh, no," said Netta, a brief smile, half wry, half patronising, and wholly resigned, flickering across her face at this. "You're an ignorant old maid," was the thought that lay behind the smile. "A funny, very nice I daresay, but quite ignorant, old maid. It's no good talking to *you*—"

And she put out her left hand, on which a wedding ring, too big for it, slipped up and down on the thin third finger, and gently patted her solid stepdaughter's arm.

"Goodbye, Jennifer," she said. "I'm sorry you're not going to live with us. It would have been—"

"Don't call me Jennifer," begged Jen.

"But I heard Richard—"

"Yes, but people who love me—I mean, my mother used to call me Jen. Please do."

"All right," said Netta, who now that she was actually starting had got her courage together again, and was holding herself up very straight inside the car, as a married woman should when, from her own car, she is conversing with a spinster in the road. "Goodbye, Jen. Enjoy yourself in your cottage all to yourself. You won't—" she leaned forward slightly, and the smile flickered again, but this time was more like a small grin, "you won't forget that if ever you want help and advice you've got a mother to come to now, will you?"

"Oh, Netta, I'm sorry if I've been horrid!" cried Jen at this; but before Netta could answer, the car started off with a jerk and she was left standing alone in the road, outside the *Jolly Shepherds*.

She walked home slowly. She didn't see Mr. Patterson greeting her from the inn door; she didn't see the interested, conjecturing eyes watching her from behind windows; she was too deep in uneasy thought, in distressing qualms, to notice anything or anybody.

Had she mismanaged Netta's visit? Ought she, instead of cutting her short with scandalised admonishments, have let her talk freely, and then see what could be done about whatever her trouble was? Of course it had been quite right to send her home—there was no doubt in her mind as to that; but she might, perhaps, seeing how young she was, and how apparently without anyone to go to for counsel, she might perhaps have been a little more—have been a little less—

"Oh, bother," exclaimed Jen, shaking off these troubled feelings, and walking more quickly. What could *she* do, if Netta were temporarily disillusioned? Probably all brides had a time of being disillusioned, and got over it, and settled down, and it would be most wrong if outsiders gave ear to them during their brief preliminary restiveness, and meddled in any way. Interference, she was sure, was a profound mistake—*any* interference, with anybody. The married must be let alone; and so must the unmarried be let alone. It was no more fair for the married to come to the unmarried, in search of bolstering up, and upset their peace, than it would be for the unmarried to go to the married, in search of company, and upset their husbands. She had been absolutely right to make Netta go back, and absolutely right not to go back with her. It wasn't just selfishness—why, who said it was?

Jen, opening her gate, paused a moment with her hand on the latch to wonder where such a word could have come from.

Selfishness? What, to restore a wife to her husband, and for oneself ask nothing of anybody except to be left in peace?

Selfishness?

Ridiculous.

CHAPTER X

Yet she had doubts; and they continued with her for the rest of the evening. Useless for her to pretend to sing while she got her supper ready; she knew she was only doing that to drown her doubts. Useless for her to carry the two chairs out after supper on to the path, and sit as usual in the sweet darkness, her feet on one, her head on the back bar of the other, and prepare to enjoy herself with the bats and stars; she didn't enjoy herself. Do what she would, she couldn't free her mind, she couldn't think of anything except Netta, and of what she might have said and done to her, and of what she had in fact said and done to her, and also of what father was probably saying and doing to her at that moment.

Well, but this was absurd, thought Jen, shifting uncomfortably on her two chairs—quite absurd, to let her evening be spoilt by something she couldn't help. And how did it help Netta either, that her evening should be spoilt? And what could *she* do, if people got married, and then didn't like it? But still the picture of father's frenzy, either of wrath or anxiety, and of Netta arriving tired, and having to face this frenzy before getting away to bed, while she herself, in her far-away safe garden, sat so cool and free, continued obstinately to blot out the stars.

She couldn't see the stars because of Netta. The girl seemed to have left her trail everywhere. She was in the air, she lurked in the corners, the whole place was full of tired young Netta who, in Brighton, wasn't being able to get away from father before he had had his say. No, and after he had had his say, had it to the last word, she still wouldn't be able to get away from him, because he, of course, would go with her. Father had a right now to go where Netta went, to pursue her into any fastness. There was no escape, no rest anywhere now for Netta.

Really marriage must be pretty awful, unless there was a lot of love about, thought Jen with a shiver, trying to imagine what life could possibly be like when there wasn't a door in it which might legitimately be locked. And when later she locked her own door, locked it at the moment she herself chose, without anyone either urging or prohibiting, the proud door through which no human being had a right to pass uninvited, and climbed up the stairs to her quiet, empty room, and knew that in it she was going to lie in peace till morning, her state seemed so extraordinarily blessed that she was more full of doubts than ever about her behaviour in the afternoon to Netta.

For mightn't she who, through having so little, had so much, after all have been kinder to someone in just the opposite case? Mightn't she at least have listened sympathetically, instead of turning the deaf ear of a shocked old maid to her attempt at confidences? Even, without any real harm being done, she might have let her stay the night, as she so much wanted to, and have got to know her better, and made, as she said, friends. A telegram could have been sent to father. He was going to have her with him for the rest of his life. It wouldn't have mattered that she stayed away from him for just one night.

But she hadn't done any of these things. She had hurried her off, with nothing to think over except admonishments, and at the back of the hurry there hadn't been so much the thought of father's anxiety, as of her own threatened peace.

Yes; that was it. About midnight, unable to sleep, her doubts dissolved into certainty. No good, thought Jen turning restlessly in her bed, no good trying to persuade herself that concern for father had come into it. It hadn't. All that was in that righteous sending-back was concern for herself. Selfishness, that is.

It did seem as if selfish were the word.

❦

But that, Jen remarked to herself next day, when, very wholesome again in the clear morning light, she sallied forth, spade under arm, to her daily digging, was the distorted view of the tired out.

She had been very tired when she went to bed. On the top of her usual hard day's work, which tired her anyhow, for she wasn't as much used to it yet as she hoped soon to be, had come the unexpected moral disturbance of Netta's visit. It had alarmed and exhausted her; and if you are alarmed and exhausted enough, she knew, you'll think anything, and quite easily persuade yourself that white is black. Which it isn't.

Therefore she pushed yesterday, and everything in it, out of her mind, addressing herself, as the sensible should, wholly to the actual moment, conscious that Netta and father had long ago said all they were going to say, and that whatever had happened between them was now over—vanished, too, beyond their reach, into the maw of yesterday. So she worked hard in the garden, which was beginning to look as if some day it might almost be neat, now that so much of it lay piled up in the churchyard; talked awhile to Mrs. Jones's little girl, who brought the week's washing about midday, and hadn't been quite so shy lately, sometimes consenting to perch like a half trustful, half frightened bird, on the doorstep, and pipe a few comments on the weather; ate her dinner in the porch, among the flickering shadows of roseleaves; rested afterwards by reading one of father's earlier works again, one of those written before she was old enough to type for him, and therefore not so familiar to her; became so much absorbed in it that she rested longer than she had meant to; and then, remembering that she had been in her cottage uninterruptedly now for nearly a whole week, she thought it would be interesting to see how much it had cost her, and she got out her fountain-pen and began totting up figures—just to give her an idea, just to see how she stood.

This, thought Jen ten minutes later, when she found she had lived for almost a week on less than fifteen shillings, was the perfect life. Exclude men and exclude meat, and one could flourish, it appeared, on almost nothing. At this rate she was going to be rich on her hundred a year, because if you only spend half your income, and on that half have everything you want, you are, unarguably, very comfortably off indeed. For a week she had been well-fed—a man wouldn't think so, and a servant wouldn't think so, and a butcher wouldn't think so, but it was true for all that, as was evident by the increasing vigour of her digging. Also she had been clean—well, not so very, because of there being no bathroom and hardly any water, but quite clean enough to go on with. And, finally, she had had a tight roof over her head—that is, it hadn't been rained on yet, so she didn't know for certain, but it looked quite tight. Oh, yes—she had forgotten there was another five shillings to add for the tight roof, but even so the week's expenses, including the rent, only came to a pound. One pound a week for everything; two pounds a week to pay the one pound with; no boots or clothes to buy for at least five years; why, it was *playing* at life.

Jen put down the pen, and tilted back the chair, and gazed with proud and happy eyes through the green curtain of creepers at the sunlit garden beyond. Yes, and it was what life might always be, if only one broke away from the tyranny of things and people, she mused, or had the luck, as she had had the luck, to be freed from them automatically. Things and people. Houses, servants, relations,—possessions, in fact, of any sort, including somebody's love. They smothered one; they devoured one; and long before one's natural end, if one let them have their way, one was utterly destroyed.

She tilted the chair slowly backwards and forwards, her hands thrust through her leather belt, her eyes reflecting the brightness of the afternoon, her heart filled with that security which is their portion who are living well within their means, and reflected that she would certainly have been destroyed in a few more years, if she had stayed in Gower Street. She hadn't a doubt about it. Look what an apathetic, bloodless creature she had already become, palely existing in father's shadow, fiddling away at his creations instead of trying to create something of her own, her life merely his life at second hand. There was nothing bloodless about her now, thank God, she thought, pushing up her sleeve and proudly contemplating her sunburnt arm. Father wouldn't know her again, and would dislike her more than ever in her new, shiny brown skin, and all her blisters. She could picture his reserved, withdrawn look when he saw her the day she would go to Gower Street to welcome him and Netta home. He detested sunburnt, blistered women; he detested women who weren't, if they couldn't be pretty, at least neat. She had left off being neat some days ago. Spades and neatness didn't get on very well together, and several of her buttons had come off in moments of more violent digging, and it was so nice without them, the feeling of sudden space, of lots of room for expansion was so agreeable, that she hadn't sewn them on again.

She would, though, before father saw her; she would try not to shock him too dreadfully. Even, she thought smiling down at her brown arm, on behalf of his feelings she would go the length of buying a pot of cold cream, and spend the night before she met him soused in it—though she didn't suppose it would be of much use.

And the smile still on her face, she looked up on hearing a slight noise outside the porch, and found herself smiling at Mr. Devenish.

❦

Devilish was the last person she wanted to smile at, and she stiffened into solemnity at once. Besides, what was all this coming and going in her cottage? More people had been to see her in a fortnight there than came in a year to Gower Street—oh, far more, because nobody ever did come to Gower Street except old Sir John Messager, when he dined once a month with father. Why, it was getting to be like Piccadilly. She would have to hire a policeman to regulate the traffic. And in an extremely discouraging voice, not getting up, she said, "Have you come to call on me?" and, suddenly remembering the sardine-tins, turned red beneath her sunburn.

"Good afternoon," was Mr. Devenish's reply—a lame one, he felt.

"Good afternoon," said Jen, polite now, because of her apprehensions. She half got up, and made a gesture of invitation towards the other chair. Those sardine-tins. Fool she had been, to put herself in the wrong. Because of them, he had a hold over her, Devilish had. He had come about them. She could see them in his eye.

"I thought," said Mr. Devenish, advancing into the room, "that being your temporary parish priest—"

"Yes," said Jen, nervously, as he paused; "yes." And added, desiring to placate, "I think it is very forgiving of you to come and call on me after my dreadful behaviour with your coat."

"Not at all," said Mr. Devenish, his coldness becoming marked.

Mr. Devenish was always cold, but sometimes he was colder, and this reminder that here sat the root of all the maddening domestic troubles he was going to have to deal with on his return to his own vicarage, made him colder. Besides, he hadn't come to call on her—he had come to administer a deserved rebuke. For, having written the letter to Ollier, and eased his anger a little in this way, it struck him that if he posted it the effect might be to bring him home at once; in which case his own period of peace and comfort in the marvellously run vicarage would come to an abrupt end, so that, on second thoughts, he laid the letter aside, instead of posting it. But he felt very strongly that something should be done, and the woman not be allowed to think she could behave as she chose with a churchyard; and by the afternoon of the day succeeding his discovery he could contain himself no longer, and went down to her cottage to relieve his feelings, and at the same time stop the scandal, by stern rebuke.

(That was because he was all acid inside from too much good food, and no work at all.)

Taking hold, therefore, of the chair she indicated, he placed it in such a position that its hind legs were out in the porch,—as far, that is, from the objectionable woman as it would go, and sat down, his shovel hat in his hands—shovel, because, however hot the weather, he declined to descend to undignified straw,—(Should she offer him tea? Jen asked herself. No, Devilish shouldn't get any tea,) and raising his pale eyes to her face (she had never seen such pale eyes; really they were almost white. Now what, Jen wondered, was that a sign of?), he resumed and finished the sentence begun when she interrupted him, and told her that, as her temporary parish priest, he thought it his duty to point out that in using consecrated ground as a refuse-dump she was not only infringing the law, but seriously overstepping the bounds of Christian decency; and he was about to proceed to request her to remove the disgraceful pile at once, when his words were arrested by something he suddenly noticed, against the wall behind her head.

Why he hadn't noticed it instantly on coming in he couldn't imagine, for it now seemed to fling itself straight into his face. It was a row of books. And such books; such superb books; the only civilised objects in the sordid interior. For there, on a shelf as miserable and makeshift as everything else in that room, bound with an admirable judgment, lettered with a no less admirable restraint, stood, in sober magnificence, father's complete works; and so striking, and so unexpected were they, flaming away at him over her head in that bare, dilapidated old kitchen, that for a moment they quite took Mr. Devenish's breath away.

"You have some very beautiful books," he therefore couldn't help saying, after a surprised pause.

"Books?" repeated Jen, nervously twisting round on her chair to look, as if hearing for the first time of their presence.

She had forgotten father's books. Perhaps she oughtn't to have put them in this room, for every eye to see. Perhaps—

"Oh—those," she said, with an assumption of indifference.

On the shelf, alongside of father's, were one or two others, of a kind she found indispensable to her happiness—a Shakespeare, a shabby Keats, the works of Max Beerbohm—but these, she knew, weren't the ones Devilish meant. He meant father's books; those specially bound first editions with which, at Christmas and on her birthdays, he had appropriately, and, he considered, adequately, rewarded her services.

"Classics, I presume," said Mr. Devenish, eyeing them.

"Yes," said Jen. "Yes."

And weren't they? With two continents periodically bursting into their praises, weren't they classics? True the continents didn't seem to read them much, judging by the sales, but at least they evidently knew they ought to.

Yes, of course they were classics, or would be, as soon as father had had time to be dead a little while.

Mr. Devenish eyed them for a moment in silence. From where he sat he couldn't read the titles, but they seemed to be a collected edition, probably of Shakespeare, and were so out of all proportion gorgeous, looked so exactly like some splendid fragment of a great library, that, prepared to believe the worst of this woman, he asked himself whether they could have come into her hands legitimately.

A hostile scepticism emanated from him, and filled the room. Feeling it flowing round her, Jen thought that perhaps, after all, she had better offer him tea—to distract him, to make him feel better disposed. Tea, the day before, had distracted Netta. Anyhow, during and after it she had ceased to talk improperly and tactlessly about father. Perhaps Devilish too would be improved by tea.

"How did you—where did you—" he began, his eyes on the books.

"Oh, they're prizes," said Jen, trying to sound careless. "Wouldn't you like some tea?"

"No tea, thank you. May I ask whose?" he inquired, his eyes unalterably fixed.

"Whose? Why, mine," said Jen.

"Really," he said, his voice charged with scepticism.

Prizes. Those. School prizes, he was asked to believe. Those magnificent volumes. And prizes *she* had won.

"Yes," said Jen. "Rewards. Do you doubt," she went on, nettled by the expression on his thin, down-cornered mouth, "that I deserved rewards?" How dared Devilish, she thought; how dared he doubt.

But it was plain that he did doubt, and the effect on her was to cause her, injudiciously and inopportunely, to boast.

"They're not ordinary books," she said, before he could answer her question, her head held high with proper, but injudicious and inopportune, pride.

"So I see," he observed, his mouth turned down.

"They're all first editions—signed, numbered, and bound, on purpose for me. Consider, then," she flung recklessly at him, "how deserving I must have been."

"I understood," said Mr. Devenish, declining to consider anything of the sort, "that you said they were classics. Might I ask—"

"So they are. Contemporary classics," Jen interrupted, beginning to feel rather as if she might soon be in a temper. Coming into her cottage like this, when nobody wanted him to. Being rude. Using one of her chairs to sit on and be rude in. Her chair. Her house. How dared Devilish?

But look—he wasn't sitting on one of her chairs, he was getting up off it, he was crossing to the bookshelf to examine the volumes more closely, in another second he would see their titles, and their author's name. What effect, she wondered, turning her head to watch him, would it have on him?

Not that she cared really, Jen said to herself. Why should she care a fig for Devilish? He had no say, thank God, in anything she did, it wasn't he who could give her notice to quit.

The effect on Mr. Devenish was distinctly bad. A smaller intelligence than his couldn't have failed to put two and two together. This, then, he thought as he stood in silence before the shelf, was her father. She was the daughter of Richard Dodge, the notorious atheist, and latterly, it was plain from his writings, the notorious libertine. A natural development, no doubt, thought Mr. Devenish. When a man hadn't got God—

In silence he stood before the books. Though he hadn't read a line of them himself, he was abundantly aware, from reviews, articles, and such mention as his brother clergy, with aversion in their voices, made, of their nature. And she, who of course must know how they were regarded by the God-fearing and decent, openly flaunted them in a cottage belonging to a priest!

Ollier couldn't have had an idea—one must do him that much justice—who it was he was letting into his cottage. Why, at any moment the man himself, the disgraceful Dodge in person, might come down and occupy it too.

For a moment he kept his back turned to her, ostensibly studying the titles. Now, he was thinking, he could hesitate no longer, and at the risk of shortening the Olliers' holiday, and having to leave the Cherry Lidgate vicarage and go back to his devastated home sooner than he otherwise would need to, he would immediately post the letter written the evening before. No longer dared he consider his own interests, thought Mr. Devenish, filled with an immense unacknowledged desire to get even with Miss Dodge by causing her to be turned out—duty must be put before his personal comfort and well-being. The information he would add to the letter would be far more serious and important than the information he had begun it with. Even Ollier would realise that something must be done.

"Devilish isn't taking it well," Jen said to herself, watching his back.

It was an expressive back. She remembered the anger visible in its lean lies that day in his study, as he stood with it turned to her, his finger on the bell. How very glad, how thankful she now was that she had worn his coat, and accordingly hadn't got his cottage. Short shrift, she felt, would have been made of her by Devilish if he had been her landlord. Out she would have gone, the very first time she dared so much as move a single chair of his furniture.

Then it occurred to her, as he still stood silent before them, that nobody yet had seen father's books on her shelf, except Netta, who naturally wouldn't mind. Devilish was the first stranger to be aware she had got them there, and to draw the obvious conclusion. His reaction to them was, therefore, important. From it she would be able to gauge the probable reaction of Alice. James didn't count, for he already knew what Dodge she was, but Alice didn't, and Alice and Devilish, Jen felt, were birds of a feather, and what Devilish disapproved of, Alice, she was sure, would disapprove of too, and what shocked Devilish would certainly shock Alice, and if Alice were shocked then she would worry James about it, whom she worried quite enough as it was. Really, when one came to think of it, Devilish ought to—

Suddenly her mind was irradiated by a great light. Yes, now—*why* not? she asked herself, everything else blotted out by the sheer brilliance of what she saw.

Dazzlingly clear to her was it in that instant that Devilish ought to marry Alice. *Of course* he ought to. They were made for each other. Why, living only four miles apart, he hadn't done it already, she couldn't imagine. It would be an ideal arrangement, because few people, she supposed, would be willing to marry Devilish, and for Alice it mightn't be easy either to find a mate; but being so much alike, both of them having so much of that bony quality which bruised softer people, and bones not being able to bruise other bones, they would probably get on wonderfully, and perhaps even produce a little bone to carry on their name—a merrythought, she said to herself, remembering the strange power of childhood to emerge, radiant and perfect, from quite unpromising parents. And then James, kind, gentle, sensitive James, would be released, then he would be able to do what he wanted, and never be scolded, and never be spirited away for a whole month to some place abroad just when his garden was so lovely. In fact, it was the one solution of James's troubles.

Swept by enthusiasm, she forgot to wonder what Mr. Devenish was thinking as he still stood silently scrutinising the row of books. The only snag she could see in the plan would be if he should have a wife already. She didn't believe he had, from the look of him, but looks weren't much to go on. No wife, it is true, had been visible, either in his own vicarage, or on James's lawn the day she found him there, but that didn't mean there wasn't one. Several photographs on his study walls had looked like wives. Any one of them might be an existing Mrs. Devilish.

"Are you married?" she longed to ask, she longed to get up and tug his sleeve and ask, so urgent did it seem that she should know.

What she did say was, stretching out her hand for the kettle—one of the conveniences of her kitchen being that in whatever part of it you were sitting you yet, without getting up, could reach anything—what she did say was, ignoring his recent refusal, "I'm going to make you some tea. I'm sure you would like some tea"—hoping that over their cups he would become more human, believing that he wouldn't, for reasons of decency, be able to say anything unpleasant about father while he was actually being nourished by her, and then, when she saw him softening, she would gently lead the talk round to wives, and find out if he had got one.

Mr. Devenish, however, took no notice of what she said about tea, but immediately at the sound of her voice turned round, and fixed his eye on her. "Have you read these?" he asked, indicating the books.

"Read them?" answered Jen, too much taken up by the brilliance of her new idea to mind now what he thought of her being father's daughter. "Why, I typed them. Except the very earliest ones at the beginning of the row."

"You *are* his daughter, then?"

"I've been brought up to believe it," she said, smiling—though instantly was serious again, and got up rather hastily, for there was that in Mr. Devenish's face which suggested the visit was about to come to an abrupt, and perhaps an explosive, end.

Now why should he explode? What difference could it make to him, who she was? She wasn't his tenant; he had no authority. How much better, instead of being angry about things that didn't concern him, to sit down quietly, and have some tea, and tell her if he had a wife. And as she faced him, it seemed to her that Rose Cottage got rather more than its share of people who were angry, or at any rate unbalanced. James and Netta hadn't been angry, but they had been unbalanced. Alice had been angry on the path, and now Devilish was being angry, or going to be in another second, in the kitchen. Really, when one came to think of it, nobody yet, except herself, had been peaceful in that house. Poor little house; poor little inoffensive, dear house. Why should its modest walls be compelled to reecho dissension?

On this occasion, though, they reechoed nothing, for Mr. Devenish said no further word, but, taking up his hat and stick, simply walked out.

She watched him go, astonished that anybody could be so absurd and so rude. Perhaps after all he wasn't quite good enough for Alice. Well, anyhow, this was the end of Devilish as far as she was concerned, and after this if she met him she would simply look as if she hadn't.

But she wondered whether perhaps it mightn't be as well to put the books away upstairs, where no one would see them.

❦

On second thoughts, however, Jen recognised this as weak. "I'll do nothing of the sort," she decided, jerking up her chin; and to show her independence, and how little she cared for Devilish, she turned the remaining sardines out of the tin she had opened for her dinner on to a plate, and marched off to the churchyard with the empty tin, and leaning over the wall placed it carefully on the very top of the snail-heap.

"There now," she said aloud, tossing back her hair and glancing up defiantly at the path on which Mr. Devenish was usually to be seen; and before going indoors again, she went for a brisk run up through the orchard on to Burdon Down, so as to shake him thoroughly out of her mind, and give her kitchen time to air. And up there it was so bright and clear, so immense and empty, and the turf was so springy, and the sun shone so warmly, and the larks sang so gaily, and everything seemed so free and happy, that she soon got rid of Devilish, and was free and happy herself again.

After all, why allow passing strangers to ruffle one's peace? If they came—unfortunately and surprisingly, seeing that the last thing she had expected in her new life was to have callers—they also went. Such was the strength of her position as a single woman that they were obliged to go, they had no right to remain. Doubtful was their right to come, but certain was their absence of right to remain.

Indeed, she thought, as she ran down the slope to her cottage half an hour later, refreshed and serene, gay and confident again, she was most safe. No one could be more unshakeably safe than a detached, respectable spinster, who was so poor that she had no responsibilities, and asked so little of life that she got it.

And pulling aside the creepers of the porch, it took her quite an appreciable instant to realise that the figure, sitting motionless in the kitchen waiting for her, was father.

❦

Father.

Now why—? Now how—?

She stood holding the creepers back, staring at him aghast. Somehow she hadn't supposed Netta would tell him that she wasn't in Gower Street, though why she hadn't supposed it she couldn't imagine, seeing that the first thing the girl would have to explain on reappearing in Brighton would be where she had been. Naturally she had told him, and here he was; and the vague fears that had floated round the cottage during Netta's visit became suddenly definite, clotted together, grew into things with cold, strong fingers that clutched at her heart and dragged it down into her boots, while the light of the brilliant afternoon at the same time seemed to dim out and go grey.

Awful effect, thought Jen, struggling to free herself of these sensations by making fun of them, on a child of the visit of its parent. But she couldn't free herself. She couldn't get any fun out of the silent figure staring at the floor. There was no fun anywhere, in either her or him. What had he come for? What could have brought him, except something that she was very sure she wasn't going to like?

He was sitting on the chair she had pulled sideways when she wanted to watch Mr. Devenish's reactions to the shelf of books, his hands folded on the knob of that umbrella beneath which Netta, on her fatal walk in the rain, had sheltered, his body so still that he might have been of stone. Indeed, a little while previously a mouse, peeping brightly out of its hole, had supposed he was of stone, and had come confidently out into the open and run right across his boot.

This had disgusted father, who was already quite disgusted enough. Mice, he had thought, withdrawing his foot; and no doubt cockroaches as well. But if the theory he was gradually forming were true, then of course, from Jennifer's point of view, the more cockroaches and the more mice the merrier; for, waiting in that squalid spot, and considering his grievance that he should have to be in it at all, and, what was more, should have to squander money on a taxi all the way from Brighton in order to be in it, he had gradually evolved the theory, his mind that day being biased, that Jennifer was doing this to punish him—punish him for marrying again, for slighting, as she would suppose, as all grown-up children easily supposed, her mother's memory, punish him by living sordidly, by starving publicly, while at the same time flaunting the fact—there were the books to prove it, placed deliberately in the most conspicuous spot, inevitably at once catching the eye and rousing the curiosity of the entering stranger—that she was Richard Dodge's only child. She desired, that is, father suspected, to hold him up to obloquy.

Naturally he didn't like this, and he sat considering his position with a mind considerably biased. It seemed to him that women were letting him down on all sides. It seemed as if he were surrounded by women going off secretly, giving him the slip—that he, of all men, should have lived to be given a thing so vulgar!—thickening his atmosphere with unpleasant surprises, darkening his sky with unnecessary worries, picking his life naked of tranquillity; in fact, behaving like locusts, thought father, who every instant that he sat there alone became more biased.

The image, however, displeased him; and he was brooding on the question as to whether his brain were not already becoming vulgarised, and whether, in his endeavour, by marrying, to purge his writing of too much love, he hadn't dropped instead into a different and worse coarseness, when he became aware, from a slight movement in the porch, that Jennifer had returned.

Without turning his head he knew that she was there, looking at him. Tiresome creature, he thought, his bias becoming suddenly excessive, yet so much harassed had he lately been that he hadn't the vitality to use words more violent; tiresome creature, putting him to all this trouble. Even if her motives should turn out not, after all, to have been vindictive, she was still a tiresome creature. Ungrateful, undutiful, disobedient—she was all these as well; but chiefly at that moment, after his long drive in the heat, did she seem to him tiresome, choosing the most remote, un-get-at-able place she could find, in which to make her absurd gesture of disapproval.

Well, she had made it, and now must at once go home. She wasn't going to be allowed to continue making it. Quite apart from his dislike of obloquy, it had become clear to him during his honeymoon from small things Netta had said, and from small things she had neglected to do, or failed to see that she was expected to do, that she was going to be incapable domestically, and his original desire to have his young wife to himself had now made way for an earnest desire not to. He was quite off young wives to oneself, if they couldn't house-keep. The house had to be properly run. He couldn't work if there were bad food and disorder. Jennifer must continue at her post.

Besides, Netta herself wished her to—or so he had gathered, from her vague and evasive remarks on her return from the secret expedition the night before. She had, during the course of the ensuing discussion, given him to understand that Jennifer's intention of living apart was a disappointment to her, that she had supposed, and hoped, she would be with them in Gower Street. Vague and evasive as usual, standing as usual as near the door as she could get—from the first she had stood and sat as near doors as possible—her head a little on one side, watching him like some bird poised for flight at the first sign of movement towards her, she had nevertheless conveyed to him that she would like Jennifer to live with them; and live with them, accordingly, Jennifer should. For plainly it was desirable to conciliate and fix Netta, who every day was becoming more strangely fluid and unapproachable, while yet remaining so timid and gentle that a man might well suppose he could do what he liked with her. And every day, too, to his increasing perplexity, she was becoming, so it appeared, less used to marriage, instead of, as was to have been expected, more so.

This wasn't natural. It was the last thing father had been prepared for. That reluctances should increase rather than diminish, surprised and disturbed him. And because he was weary, and activity in such heat, and cross-country journeys in such heat, and arguments in such heat, and women in such heat, all seemed to him very difficult and troublesome, a most unusual thing escaped him as he sat waiting—a sigh. And it was just as he was sighing that footsteps came quickly towards the cottage, and immediately afterwards Jennifer, he knew, was standing in the porch looking at him.

But he didn't look at her. He didn't move. He remained quite still, his eyes fixed on the floor. And such was his bias that day against all women, of whom the world seemed to him far too full, that though he had been irritated till then that she didn't come, he was much more irritated now because she had.

"This is—a great surprise, father," he heard her say presently; or, rather, stammer, which at least showed she had the grace to be ashamed of herself.

He remained motionless, as to his body. Never yet had he got out of chairs for Jennifer, and it wouldn't have occurred to him, even though he was in her house and not in his, to do so now. But he did turn his head slightly, and glanced at her from beneath his heavy eyelids; and in that brief glance he took in everything—the condition of her skin, and of her hair, and of her clothes, and he thought, as he resumed his contemplation of the floor, "Good God."

She let the creepers drop from her hand, and slowly crossed the threshold. As she came into the room, a strange suggestion of warm soil, of hot labourers engaged in turning it over, came in too, and father, who detested any sort of soil and every sort of labourer, was more shocked than ever.

"Good God," he thought again, really quite immensely shocked; and asked himself, as he sternly gazed at the floor, from what undesirable forebear of her mother's she could have inherited so dreadful a readiness to sink. Look at her; just look at his daughter; in less than three weeks, sunk. No Dodge that he could recollect had ever sunk. All Dodges died higher up than they began. It wasn't from his family that she had got it. He could only conclude that poor Marian's relations must have been even worse than he had sometimes suspected.

Or was it that she was sinking thus conspicuously on purpose? In order to hold him up to utter obloquy?

Motionless he sat, waiting, enduring, and shocked. Even when, after a moment's hesitation, she stooped and kissed the top of his head—for she thought it better to begin, anyhow, affectionately—he still motionlessly endured, accepting the kiss as an inevitable act of conventional dutifulness, merely making a slight backwards gesture of removal with his arm when it was over, so that so warm a woman should get a little farther away.

And she, as she kissed him, couldn't help thinking, through all her fears, how bald poor father was getting, and wondered what it could be like being bald and at the same time married to Netta—or rather she wondered what it could be like being Netta, and at the same time married to somebody bald. The bald should marry other balds, thought Jen, her mind slipping about irrelevantly in her confusion; though perhaps that was just what they none of them wanted to do.

"If I had known you were coming, father, I would have tidied up," she said, trying to sound natural and unembarrassed.

"And washed," said father.

The familiar tones. The familiar authoritative disapproval. All Gower Street come flooding into her cottage.

"And—washed," repeated Jen falteringly, feeling as if she were back again at being twelve.

She sat down on the chair Mr. Devenish had so lately sat in—poor

Devilish, he wasn't so bad really—and she sat because her legs felt as if they wouldn't go on standing. Not with dignity. Not, that is, without swaying. Better sit, thought Jen, abruptly doing it; in crises, much better sit.

Was this a crisis, though? For some reason father had come to see her, but that didn't make a crisis. There was nothing to be afraid of. He and she had finished with each other. Of his own act he had released her. Of course she wasn't afraid. It was only that her legs—

"Perhaps, Jennifer," said father, gravely incommoded by the workingman flavour clinging to her clothes, and wishing she would move her chair farther away, though it was evident that in that small space she couldn't, "you will explain why you are not at home."

"But I *am* at home," she said, collecting what she could of courage.

Yet, looking round, it didn't now seem quite as if she were. Father's presence made a surprising, a disconcerting difference. Curiously, the effect of it was to turn her little kitchen into something very like the back diningroom. In spite of the roses, still gaily nodding round the porch, in spite of the marigolds she had stuck that morning in a jug, still bravely flaunting on the windowsill, it suddenly seemed a gloomy place—a place of authority and obedience, of dominant sires and unquestioning offspring; a place, that is, belonging to father, instead of to herself.

"This *is* my home," she said, uncertainly; and father, as tartly as his fatigue permitted, replied, "Nonsense."

"It isn't nonsense," said Jen, struggling to keep her end up.

Whereupon, with another brief glance at her from under his heavy eyelids, he said, "That, Jennifer, is impertinent." And at the rebuke she shrank a further couple of years back into childhood, and felt as if she were only ten.

Well, this wouldn't do at all, she thought, giving herself a shake. She must stand up to him. He was only a visitor, like any other visitor, and presently, like any other visitor, he would have to go away again. She would talk to him on equal terms. She would be natural and unembarrassed.

Therefore, when he asked, "Why did you leave Gower Street without my knowledge or permission?" she was so much determined to get on to equal terms at once, that she answered, leaning forward—it incommoded him—"Oh, my dear father—don't let us talk of knowledge and of permission. Am I then a slave?"

Even as the words came out, however, she felt they were unfortunate, and when, after a pause during which she waited, rather huddled, for his answer, he remarked, more offended by her addressing him so unusually as her dear father than by her outrageous question, "It gets us nowhere that you should be insolent, Jennifer," she knew he was right, faltered that she was sorry, and shrank so far back into childhood that she felt as if she were now no more than six.

At this rate, thought Jen, very uneasy at the rapidity of her progress backwards, she would soon be in her cradle again. Already her legs seemed too short to reach the floor; already pinafores seemed to be fastening themselves round her body, and pigtails flopping about her ears. If she didn't take a firm and final stand, the next thing that might happen would be that he would order her into the corner, and that if he did she would go.

"The fact is," she said, making an immense effort, and speaking very fast, "it's almost impossible for children to talk naturally to their parents without sounding rude. Anyhow it is if the children are me, and the parents are you, father. Will you please believe that I don't mean to be rude, and that I'm only trying to say things really, for the first time in my life?"

He made a slight movement of one of the hands folded on the knob of his umbrella. It might have meant anything. She took it to mean acquiescence; but in that she erred.

"Why have you come, father?" she accordingly proceeded, persuading herself—her heart, though, remained in her boots—that the ground was now clear, and she could go ahead with talking naturally.

"Do you need to be told?" he asked.

"Yes," she said, sticking to it. "Yes. I do. You're on your honeymoon, you know—" it really was most alarming how awful naturalness sounded—"and so is Netta. Then oughtn't you both to stay on it, instead of keeping on coming to see me? Isn't that what people generally do? I mean, if they are on a honeymoon, don't they stay on it?"

He looked at her, and this time continued to look at her. She shifted on her chair, but wouldn't let herself not look back.

"Are you seeking information, or giving advice?" he inquired; and all the little unfurling tips of her courage seemed to curl up.

"Both, I think," she answered, struggling, in spite of this, to smile and go on being unembarrassed. The difficulty, however, of smiling at father! While as for being unembarrassed, her embarrassment was such that it burst out on her forehead in beads.

"No one would have come here if you hadn't come here," he said; which, of course, was entirely true.

"I suppose they wouldn't," she admitted. "But I had to come somewhere, father."

"In order to make your gesture."

"What gesture?"

"Of disapproval. Of punishment."

"Punishment, father?"

"Do you tell me, Jennifer, that this secret flight, this deliberately sordid hovel, is not for the purpose of registering your disapproval?"

"What of?" she asked, puzzled, trying to understand.

"Look at my books. Look at them—placed on purpose in the most conspicuous spot."

"Yes—of course they're there on purpose," she said, following his glance, perplexed, to the resplendent row. "They're so beautiful. Especially inside," she added, with some vague hope even now of placating him. "I've been reading them again, and I can't tell you—"

"Then don't," he interrupted. "Pray don't say you cannot tell me, Jennifer, and then at once proceed to attempt to. It is a foolish trick. I accept your statement that you can't." And with a movement of his hand he wafted her back into not being a day more now than three.

A toddler. A toddler, who in another moment would be put in the corner if she didn't do something about it.

She looked at him with fear in her face. It was amazing how father continued to be father. Who could have imagined that even here, in her own house, on her own ground, he still so completely would continue to be father? And why shouldn't his books be there? And what did he mean, talking of punishment?

"I think we're at cross purposes, father," she said. "You seem to have got hold of some queer idea—"

Again he interrupted her. "I am not accustomed, Jennifer," he said, "to be spoken to in the way you have since you came in." And he sat looking at her sombrely, moved by a desire, entirely new to him, to box her ears. He was not a natural boxer of ears—had indeed never applied his hand to anybody; but now this desire did stir in him, and only the excessive heat, and his own languor, kept him quietly in his chair.

"That's just it, father," she said. "It ought to have been done long ago. Though I don't know," she added, gripping her hands nervously together, "at what point exactly it could have begun. I was always so young compared to you. However much I grew up, you had always grown up more. Still, if only I had screwed myself up to it, by now we might have understood each other."

"Screwed yourself up. A pleasing expression," commented father. "And I assure you I understand you perfectly—or at least I supposed I did, till Netta told me you had left home without a word, and were in a hovel."

"A hovel? Oh, father—it's the sort of lovely little cottage people paint."

"It is a hovel, Jennifer."

"Oh, father—"

"And a hovel on purpose."

She got up and crossed to the door, suddenly feeling she must be near an exit. Her withdrawal, though slight, relieved him.

"I wish I knew what you are talking about," she said. "What do you mean by on purpose, and punishment, and all that, father? I had to find something. I found this. And I think it's lovely—or did, till you came into it."

"Thank you, Jennifer."

"I mean, till you came and made me feel how it looked to you. It *does* look different, since. But it won't, directly you've gone—"

"Thank you, Jennifer."

"I mean, I love it, father, and am happy in it—or was, till you came—"

"Thank you, Jennifer."

"—and somehow made me feel I oughtn't to be. Don't you want me to be happy? I know I want *you* to be."

"Thank you, Jennifer."

"Oh, don't be angry. I'm sorry it has been sprung on you. I didn't mean it to be. I was going to tell you about it after you were back in Gower Street—prepare your mind, and get you used to the idea. If Netta hadn't found out I was here, you wouldn't have known till I told you myself. And I've not neglected what I had to do for you. You must know I wouldn't leave things at sixes and sevens. The house is quite ready—or will be next week when you arrive. And I've finished the fifth chapter, and I've interviewed secretaries, and made a list of the best ones for you."

"Thank you, Jennifer."

"Oh father—please don't keep on saying Thank you, like that! Why are you so angry? You wouldn't be, if you gave yourself time to think. You know you don't want me at home, now that you've married again."

"Perhaps you will tell me in what way my having married again absolves you from your duties," he said.

"Good heavens, father," she couldn't help exclaiming at this, "is there no end to you?" And then was frightened, and stood leaning hard against the doorpost, staring at him while the tickings of the cheap clock on the wall sounded enormous in the stillness.

"I'm sorry," she said, after a scared pause during which he merely sat heavily in his chair, looking at her. "I didn't mean to be rude—" and immediately was excessively rude again; for on his informing her, in order to put a stop at once to all this nonsense, that he desired her to return without delay to her home, which was, as she well knew, her father's house, she appeared to lose all decent control, and began talking in a way he wouldn't have believed possible—a changed creature, he said to himself, as he listened in amazed distaste to the heated and garrulous flood suddenly let loose on him. Or was it that she was only a creature unmasked, and always, beneath her stolid gravity, her unquestioning obedience, this was what she had really been?

Silent and motionless father sat, not attempting to interfere with her self-exposure, merely watching the tousled and contentious person in the doorway, who was pouring out nonsense over him. Such nonsense, too; such grievous nonsense. Stuff about beauty, and independence, and the bliss, he gathered, of nothingness. To have nothing, to be nothing—it appeared to amount to that—was the only true freedom, according to his absurd daughter. If she had declared that to be dead was the only true freedom, it would have made quite as much sense.

But, pitiably and confusedly as she talked, and insulting and ungrateful as her implications were, it did somehow emerge from the welter that the theory of a vendetta for his remarriage was incorrect, and she was here simply because she liked it.

This, however, if anything made it worse, considered father; to enjoy going down in the social scale, and enjoy neglecting her person—enjoy, that is, to put it in the only way it deserved to be put, pigging it, seemed to him, that hot, rank afternoon, worse than vendettas. For vendettas, after all, were things that passed, things which might be expected to burn themselves out, whereas this dreadful pleasure in base things, seeing that base things abound and accordingly can be had for the asking, would have no end. Unless, that is, she could be brought to her senses.

❦

Yes; unless she could be brought to her senses.

It oughtn't to be difficult, he thought, trained as she had always been in submission; but what an occupation for a tired man, on a hot afternoon! He was very tired. He had been tired before he started—heat, hotels, and honeymoons being enough to tire any man, he told himself, explaining away his profound and unusual fatigue,—and the drive, over rough roads in the oven-like taxi, hadn't made him less so.

It seemed to him hard, as he sat motionless while she gesticulated and blustered in the doorway, that he should have to bother about Jennifer's senses. Why she should choose this moment to take leave of them, just when he had Netta on his hands as well, he didn't know. He supposed the explanation was that women had no idea of honour, and wouldn't hesitate to let a man down at any moment, should they feel like it. Unfortunate, then, that one couldn't do without them; most unfortunate. But when they were Netta, they held the whole beauty and youth of the world in their little cool hands; and when they were Jennifer, they made it possible for a man to do his work in quiet and comfort; so there one was,—dependent. It was unfortunate. And it became acutely unfortunate if, being Netta, they appeared to wish to keep beauty and youth to themselves, and edged off to the nearest door whenever one tried to approach them—she should have told him of this habit before he married her, thought father in an aggrieved parenthesis—or if, being Jennifer—well, just listen to Jennifer, thought father.

"You see," she was saying, a little more quietly, having raved herself, it was to be presumed and hoped, out, "it's really every bit as unreasonable for you to ask me to give up what I'm doing and go and live with you, as it would be for me to ask you to give up what you're doing and come and live with me"—a new view indeed of the relation of creator and created, of bread-earner and bread-eater, he thought; though, of course, she had her hundred a year. That miserable hundred a year was at the root of all the mischief. Marian should never have left it to her. It steadied women to have no money.

"Do you suggest," he said, determined to remain calm, conscious that anger this hot weather would be bad for him, "that your and my conditions are equal, and our relative positions the same?"

"No, I don't. You're somebody, and I'm nobody," she answered—pat as you please, thought father, curiously annoyed to be told by her that he was somebody. Somebody, indeed. If she had said everybody, now …

"But even," she went on, "though I'm so entirely nobody, in my little way I've a right, as you've married again, to my freedom."

Ah—there they were, the words to be expected, the immemorial words. Right to freedom. Words bound, thought father watching her icily, to occur sooner or later in the speech of persons whose ambitions outran their talents—usually disaffected female relatives.

"A right to your selfishness, you mean," he said, "and to your incredible ingratitude." For what could be more grossly selfish than this digging of herself into an indolent solitude, and what more grossly ungrateful for her creation by him, and her preservation by him, and for all the comforts of his house? True, she apparently didn't want the comforts of his house, but she couldn't get away from the fact that he had created her, and, having created, also preserved her; for if he hadn't she wouldn't now be here, insulting him. Much harm could be caused by creation, thought father, looking at his daughter with sombre eyes.

He spoke, however, calmly, determined that nothing should stir him to the agitation of anger. The continuous heat, the unaccustomed and bad hotel food, the constant strain of being with someone so young as Netta, someone so far away from him in actuality, and yet apparently so close, was very trying to father. He hadn't felt so old for a long time. Years ago he had felt old, after Marian's death and before Jennifer was sufficiently trained in domesticity to prevent his missing his wife, but he got over it, and by the time he embarked on his courtship of Netta he wasn't old at all. A man in the prime of life he had been, when he started courting Netta. What had become of his prime of life he didn't know. There seemed very little of it left. No doubt it would return with the cooler weather, and the resumption of regular work in Gower Street. But for the resumption of that regular work the presence of Jennifer in the house was indispensable. Good God, thought father, goaded by this knowledge, why must she give all this trouble? Ultimately she would have to obey and go home; it was unthinkable that she should seriously defy him. Then why, if it must be ultimately, couldn't it be now?

"Suppose I said things like that to you?" she asked, in answer to his last remark. "You wouldn't like it a bit, would you, father. You'd think it awful. But you expect me to receive them quite meekly when you say them to me." And she told him, too deeply involved now in plainspeaking to hesitate about going in for a little more of it, that so far from feeling she ought to be grateful, till she left his house she hadn't known what happiness was.

"A nice thing for a father to hear," he said, his eyes smouldering, forced, by fear of the effect on him of anger, to continue calm.

"I'm only trying to be honest."

"I should prefer less honesty and more decency," he rapped out.

"Yes—and what a barrier that has always made between us!"

"I know nothing of barriers. But I do know that you will return home immediately."

"What—and hang round you and Netta for the rest of my days?" she answered, trying to talk easily, to take it as rather a joke on father's part. "Why, you know in your heart that that's exactly what you were afraid I might do."

"Jennifer, I expect you to leave this place at once, and go home," was all he said, holding on to himself.

"Do you seriously think I will?" she asked; and then, suddenly terrified lest by some awful, not to be shaken off compulsion, she might, after all, obey him, lest, disciplined as she was, she might after all give in and sag back into being his helpless child again, she cried, flinging out both hands as if to ward him off, as if to prevent his getting hold of her, "Oh, but you're a selfish, selfish, wicked old man, and stark staring mad into the bargain!"

❦

He made a half movement, as though to get up, but found he couldn't. He stretched out a shaking hand towards his hat lying on the table and tried to reach it, but found he couldn't do that either. He looked at her with eyes so bloodshot with rage that she shrank back into the porch.

"How dare you—" he began, clutching his umbrella as though, if he could only get at her, he would strike her; and then broke off, and said in a voice totally bereft of anger and rather frightened, "Jennifer, will you give me a little water?"

The change was so surprising that she looked at him a moment uncomprehendingly,—almost instantly, however, alarmed by what she saw, flying to the cupboard to get a cup. She didn't possess glasses in that meagre establishment, except one upstairs in the bedroom for toothbrush purposes, and hastily snatching a cup off the shelf, she dipped it into the bucket.

"Don't you feel well, father?" she asked, giving him the cup, spilling half the water in her anxious hurry.

"It is—very warm," he gasped, trying to take it from her with both his uncertain hands.

His umbrella had fallen to the floor; his face was congested; his eyes were alarming. In the end, she had to hold the cup herself to his lips, watching him drink with a face of deep concern.

Poor father; she had behaved outrageously, making him angry after his long drive, when she might just as easily have explained things nicely and politely,—hedged even, not been so uncompromising and rude. He had his troubles, she was sure, being so fond of Netta and Netta not being so fond of him. And the weather was against him; and the hotel food was what he would be certain to hate. But it would all be perfectly all right once he and Netta were in their own home, and settled down. Everybody settled down. Netta would adapt herself, and it was only just now, just at the beginning that—

She hung over him, not knowing what to say, not knowing what to do, wondering whether she ought to loosen his collar, hoping that she oughtn't to, because she didn't believe she would ever have the courage to lay familiar fingers on father's collar. But of course she would if it were necessary—of course she would do anything—

"Air," murmured father, indicating by a movement, as he finished drinking, that she should go a little farther away. "There is no air."

There was indeed no air. The heavy, dead-still afternoon was declining into a heavy, dead-still evening, and for the first time since she had been in her cottage it felt as if there might be a thunderstorm. She and father in a thunderstorm, thought Jen; she and father, marooned together, cut off, ringed in by lightning, while Netta away in Brighton got more and more anxious—or didn't get more and more anxious, which would be worse.

Doubts as to Netta's being anxious crept into her heart as she hung round father, and filled it with concern on his behalf. Poor father. Not to be well, and to have a wife who didn't mind, seemed rather a miserable state of things.

Well, but perhaps Netta did mind—or would, when she knew about it. She herself mustn't, thought Jen, begin yearning over him. There was no reason whatever to yearn. The most successful of men, a man just married to an enchanting wife, a man still on his honeymoon—ridiculous to start worrying over him.

But he looked so much congested. He looked so old. …

"Let me help you out into the porch," she said, taking him gently by the elbow. "It's cooler there."

He was too languid to resist. He didn't want her near him, but he couldn't do without her; there, said father to himself wearily, as she got him on to his feet, you had his life in a nutshell.

He leaned against her, and to Jen it was the strangest sensation, having father clinging to her for support. Not yet ever had he touched her, except, night and morning, in a brief, perfunctory kiss. Aloof and unapproachable, he had passed along the years of her childhood and her growing-up without so much as a pat on her shoulder, or a stroking of her hair. Now he was clinging to her, and clinging to her so heavily that she needed all her sturdiness to guide his footsteps out into the porch. And again she felt a yearning feeling, which again she tried to argue away.

"If you will walk with me to the gate—" he began.

"Ah, but don't go yet, father—you mustn't, really," she said anxiously. "I'll bring a chair out, and you can wait a little, till you feel better."

It was as if she hadn't spoken. He continued to move on, leaning heavily against her, and by the very heaviness of his leaning propelling her forwards with him, shuffling along in silence, and she perforce being obliged to shuffle along too.

The taxi man, who had been asleep in his seat, woke up at the sound of their combined shuffling, and got down and came to the gate, and opened it for them. He had tried to assist the old gentleman to get out of the taxi, and had been pushed aside; he now met with no opposition on his trying to assist him to get into it—on the contrary, the old gentleman left it all to him, and if he hadn't been a strong young man in good condition, he couldn't have done it.

But he didn't like the way his fare, once in, dropped on to the seat, and shut his eyes.

"Feels the 'eat," he said, looking at him a little dubiously, not sure he wanted a fare who felt the heat as much as all that; for he had heard of fares who, when you glanced round at them through the window, had left off being fares and turned into corpses, and he was anxious to avoid getting landed with one of these.

Father, however, shut his eyes only because he wished, for a space, to see no more. This odious and suffocating spot, this child to whom affection and gratitude were empty words—let him see, and hear, and know no more of them. His one desire now was to get back as quickly as possible to his wife—thank God he had a wife, and one who, however temporarily shy and elusive and unused to the give and take of marriage, was yet so exquisitely at the beginning of life that there was nothing she wouldn't still have time to learn.

But, sitting there in the taxi with an effect of being huddled, and his head drooping, and his eyes shut, father's appearance was most alarming, and Jennifer, as she stood at the door watching him, became a prey to violent misgivings. Suppose something were to happen to him on the way? Suppose, bumping along over the downs all those miles to Brighton, he were to faint, or have a stroke, or something awful?

"Feels the 'eat," said the taxi driver a second time, who now didn't like the look of his fare at all. "Oughtn't to be out by 'isself, not an old gentleman oughtn't, not this sort of weather."

"Oblige me by starting," said father, suddenly opening his eyes, and fixing them for an icy instant on the red face of the offensive young man.

"Oh, but wait a minute—you've forgotten your hat and umbrella!" cried Jennifer. "Don't start yet, father—wait a minute while I go and fetch them—"

And she ran back to the house, and snatched up the hat and umbrella, and snatched her own hat, too, off its peg, and pulled out her money from its secret hiding place behind the potato sack.

She was going with him. She couldn't possibly let him go alone in the state he was in. She would never forgive herself if anything happened. And it wouldn't take very long—she would be back that night—there must be ways—after handing the poor old dear safely over to Netta—

Slamming the door behind her, she flew down the path again and scrambled into the taxi beside him. "You can start now," she called to the driver, who meanwhile had climbed into his seat. "I'm going to see you safely to Brighton, father," she said, turning to him, whose eyes remained statuesquely shut. "I can't let—I couldn't *bear* to let you go alone."

❦

Father's face became a mask. He leaned in his corner as far from her as possible, and petrified into complete silence. She would come with him, would she, taking up what little air there was; she would come off jollying—positively that was the word he was moved, by his wrath, to descend to—jollying to Brighton, thrusting herself in on his honeymoon, using as a pretext his momentary indisposition, an indisposition entirely due to her own behaviour; but she couldn't go to Gower Street, she couldn't go home, and simply do her duty.

Let her, then, come. Not a word would he speak to her. Ten thousand times rather would he have been ill alone in that taxi than be boxed up in it with Jennifer. And what was she going to do when she got to Brighton? In those clothes? Wearing that disgraceful hat? Did she suppose she could stay the night at his hotel? Where he was having his honeymoon? Why, it wasn't even decent.

Thus father thought in his wrath, and knew it was useless to rap on the window and tell the driver to stop, because the driver now evidently regarded him as a sort of patient, a person who is humoured rather than obeyed—an old gentleman, the fellow had called him, father remembered, trying not to remember it; and Jen, her solicitude being met by total silence, after a few miles began to think that perhaps she had been a little impulsive.

It was all very well going with father if he were ill—one would then, of course, do anything for him; but if he weren't ill, it did seem rather a pity to have left her cottage in such a hurry, with its door unlocked, and anybody able to get in.

Yes, she had been impulsive; she saw plainly that she had when father presently sat up quite straight, and looked out of the window on his side with apparent interest at passing objects. He had recovered, and could quite well have gone back by himself. And he detested her being there; she could feel him detesting it, feel his detestation proceeding from him in great cold waves.

Still, now that she was about it she had better see it through, thought Jen, in case he had a relapse; but it was a melancholy fate to be making a journey she needn't have made to Brighton, only for the purpose of making another journey, and a probably costly and difficult one, away from it again.

And so, in silence, they got to Brighton, and began to drive along that endless, and to Jen horrifying, front; and father thought, "I shall not say a word. I have done with words to this woman. Let her find her way back to her hovel as best she may." And Jen thought, seeing herself every moment more enclosed by houses, and feeling that father was now quite well, except for his hostility, "*What* a fool I've been to come!"

❦

Still, she decided that having come, she would speak to Netta a moment, before beginning to search for ways of getting home, and tell her about father's little attack. He really had looked most frightening, sitting all congested in that chair, not able to get out of it, not able to say what he was trying to say, not able even, as for an instant he had evidently wished, to hit her. Netta must keep a watchful eye on him; she must take care of him—in fact, Jen said to herself in a flash of uncomfortable candour, there were no limits to the care she wanted taken of father by somebody else.

She followed him into the hotel—he hadn't said a word as he got out of the taxi, and passed through the revolving doors without looking round—admitting that it must be true that she was selfish. But then so was he, so was everyone, and it was no good worrying about it. Indeed, selfish for selfish, father was by a long way the selfishest of the two when it came to choosing between herself and him, she thought, close on his heels in the revolving door, so close that the hall porter, seeing them being disgorged almost simultaneously, correctly surmised that she was accompanying Mr.

Dodge, and was astonished that anyone accompanying him should look so much like a tramp.

"Lift," mumbled father, shuffling across the hall, looking neither to the right nor to the left, and making signs with his umbrella. "Lift."

"Mrs. Dodge asked me to give you this, sir," said the porter, intercepting him and handing him a letter.

"Mrs. Dodge? Is she not upstairs?" asked father, pausing surprised, and staring at the handwriting on the envelope.

"No, sir—gone out, sir."

Gone out? Just when it was dinner-time?

Puzzled, and too much astonished to be annoyed, father clumsily transferred his umbrella to his armpit, and opened the letter then and there and read it; and having read it, he fumbled to get it back into its envelope, and, in the fumbling, it, and the envelope, and the umbrella, all fell to the floor.

The porter hurried forward to pick them up, and so did the lift boy, and so did Jennifer.

"Oh—you are there, Jennifer," said father, looking at her with an odd, dazed look, as though he were trying to make her out in a mist.

"Yes, father—yes—"

She drew his arm through hers without a word, and helped him into the lift; and when they reached his floor, and it stopped, and he made no movement to get out, she gently urged him into the corridor, and led him along it to the suite he had taken—"Number fifty—round to the right," the lift boy had said in answer to her question; and his steps grew slower and slower the nearer he got to it, and he seemed to move with more and more difficulty, and she knew, without his telling her, that Netta had left him.

CHAPTER XI

About this time James, having been for nearly a fortnight in Switzerland with Alice, and still being over a fortnight off from the date she had fixed for their return, grew restive.

He was on the Lake of Lucerne, and he was on it because this was where Alice, as it appeared, in her depressed condition least minded going. So there he was, in a small place called Hertenstein,—a very beautiful small place, consisting only of shady paths, soft green slopes, and two quiet hotels. And in one of these hotels, the one away from the landing-stage, round a wooded promontory on the edge of a tranquil bay, James presently grew restive.

Up to this point, absorbed in the realisation of the havoc he had wrought in Alice, his time had been taken up by dismay. She hardly spoke, never said Bosh, and her hand was heavily bandaged. When, thus bandaged, she tried clumsily to do needlework in the hotel garden beneath the plane trees at the water's edge, it naturally attracted a good deal of attention from the other visitors—mostly old ladies of inquiring dispositions; and on her saying, in answer to their questions, that she couldn't tell them what had happened, they began to make small jokes, after the manner of people being bored in hotels, and the invisible hand became known as Miss Ollier's Mystery, and James felt it very much.

For it was true of James that he wouldn't hurt a fly, and was of those who on their walks step out of the way of ants; so that to have hurt his sister, actually hurt her physically so much that her spirit seemed quite broken, caused him to spend most miserable days in Hertenstein—a place, he couldn't help seeing even so, made for honeymoons and love. And Alice, perceiving she could do anything she liked with him, anything at all, by simply saying nothing and not looking well, abandoned the direct methods she had hitherto gone in for, and became daily more silent, and more apparently patient in the bearing of pain.

Just to begin with, her wrenched finger had really hurt very much and, overcome by this strange new sensation, she who had hardly ever had a pain before, as well as by horrified amazement that James, so gentle, so easy to manage, should suddenly have turned into a wild beast, she had genuinely broken down, and been for the first time in her life a poor, whimpering woman. But long before she reached Lucerne she couldn't honestly have said that her finger troubled her any longer, and all that remained of her whimpering was indignation that he could ever have brought her so low. It had taught her a valuable lesson, however, humiliating as it had been, searing as its remembrance was, for it had shown her the quickest and easiest way to keep control of James.

So she kept control of him by her silence, her low spirits, and her bandage, the danger of the situation being too great to bother about the particular means she used; because, thought Alice, if he could become so much excited over whether or not Miss Dodge were given apricots, it was plain that, however astounding it might be from the point of view of the credible, he was already attracted. And though it was a mystery how he had managed to become attracted when he had only seen the woman, to Alice's certain knowledge, for a few minutes the day she arrived, or indeed how, having seen her, he could have become attracted at all, yet this thing had happened, and the peace and happiness of their life together had somehow to be saved from destruction.

At any other time, with what disgust would Alice have turned from these mean methods. She, who was all for open and above board fighting, and no nonsense about it, and the best man winning, was now driven by necessity to lay hold of the surest weapons; and the surest weapons obviously being to continue as she had begun that day at the gate, except that never again would she whimper, she stuck to her bandage, and whenever he asked her how she felt said, with a crushing absence of reproach, that her head ached.

For a fortnight James was very unhappy. His tender, conscience-stricken heart was so much troubled that he could think of nothing except the state to which he had reduced poor Alice. From his mind he excluded all thoughts of Jennifer, and concentrated entirely on Alice—giving himself up to her, spending his time devising means of helping to make her head leave off aching, sitting with her, reading aloud in his gentlest voice, taking her for walks, and drives, and steamer excursions. He began each day by taking her for a little walk, she neither refusing nor agreeing, but silently going, and bringing her back punctually for luncheon because, being *en pension*, he knew she wouldn't, with her frugal mind, want to miss a meal which had been paid for. He began each afternoon by taking her for a little drive, or a little outing on a steamer; and during these excursions, as indeed at all times, he did his utmost to distract her thoughts from what he imagined must be himself and his gross brutality over that basket.

Vain, however, were his efforts; useless his solicitude. Poor Alice didn't seem able to be distracted. Briefly she would glance at the views he pointed out, or at the flowers he picked for her; briefly she would say they were pretty, using the same word for the Rigi or a marguerite. And then, remarking with a sigh that her head ached, sink back into her distressing silence.

James was much worried. But he would have been even more worried, as well as unpleasantly surprised, if he had known that what she was thinking of, when she thus withdrew into monosyllables, wasn't him at all, but his tenant. For clear it was to Alice that Miss Dodge must go, and that not an instant longer than could be helped must she stay in that cottage, and her thoughts were entirely taken up by considerations of ways of getting rid of her.

The thing bristled with difficulties. How get rid, decently, of a woman who had paid her rent in advance, and given no visible cause of offence? Day and night Alice cudgelled her brains to find an answer to this question, even once or twice, hard pressed by the knowledge that time was passing, praying about it.

The ideal, of course, would be for him to find the cottage empty when he got back, and himself in the presence of a *fait accompli.* He wouldn't dare say a word, Alice was pretty sure, because any comment he made would merely expose how far his folly had gone. That it couldn't have gone very far she was also pretty sure, for even folly needs time, and there had been no time at all, really. What were twenty-four hours? The whole of that black period in their lives which had begun with the woman's first appearance in Cherry Lidgate, and ended with his savage assault on the basket, was covered by twenty-four hours, most of which he had spent in bed. Nothing could possibly have happened, except in James's own thoughts, Alice was certain. The woman herself couldn't possibly know what he was so idiotically feeling about her—Alice thanked heaven at least for that much.

But this quiet emptying out of the cottage before they got home was an ideal, she was afraid, beyond her reach. If only she could think of a way of doing it! If only she were cleverer! Not that it didn't do her credit that she wasn't, thought Alice, for the cleverness needed for a job like that would be of the crafty, Jesuitical sort that she abhorred—in the matter of ordinary cleverness she was as well endowed, she considered, as any woman. Still, she did feel that if she somehow could manage to be Jesuitical for just long enough to pull this thing off, the result would be so gratifying that it would more than make up for a temporary lapse. Indeed, in her relief she would find it quite easy to forgive James everything, and magnanimously refrain from any further allusion to what he had done. Also, she would at once shed pretences, bandages, and the rest of the humiliating wiles—oh, how more than thankful she would be to do that!—and return to being the frank, honest, devoted sister of happier days; and perhaps even she might reach the stage, a little later on, of laughing with him about it all.

Yes, she even considered this possibility, though on second thoughts she put it aside as improbable. To laugh would be overdoing reconciliation, Alice decided. She never had laughed with James about anything. They weren't on that kind of footing. Besides, she was by nature no laugher, and really couldn't begin at her age to try to be one.

Then suddenly one afternoon, thinking of these things, she sighed impatiently—a real sigh this time, not one of those designed to keep James sorry; for what was the good of planning what she would do or wouldn't do after Miss Dodge had been got rid of, when she still hadn't the remotest notion how the getting rid of was to be accomplished? And

James, looking at her sideways—they were resting on the grass in the shade of one of those fruit-trees which make the slopes round Hertenstein beautiful with bright apples, and at the end of the lovely, glancing lake they could see Pilatus, the colour of an opal, crowned with pale clouds over against the hot blue of the afternoon sky—James, then, looking at her sideways on hearing this sigh, the latest of many he had heard now for a fortnight, and seeing her knitted brows, which seemed now continually knit, and her gloomy expression, which seemed now incapable of clearing, said to himself that it was perhaps no wonder nobody had ever wanted to marry poor Alice. And he fell to thinking, for he was tired and discouraged after his prolonged efforts to help her to recover, how it would wear a man down to be constantly with a woman he had injured, and obliged to hear her sigh; and how he could imagine such a man at last, having done everything in his power to make amends, and the sighs still going on, taking to his heels, and chucking the whole thing.

He could imagine, that is, another man doing this; not himself. He was a clergyman, strange as it often seemed to him who would so much preferred to have been a market-gardener, and clergymen didn't chuck things, and take to their heels. It wasn't, of course, of himself that he was thinking.

❦

Yet almost at once, even as he lay there propped on one elbow quietly nibbling a blade of grass, it did turn out to be of himself.

That last sigh of Alice's seemed to wake him up with a jump to realities. He looked at her as if a veil had been snatched from his eyes—sighing away there, frowning away there, in a setting of such beauty that she ought to be singing Magnificats to God for allowing her to see it.

Why should he stay with her any longer? These glowing solitudes of Hertenstein, solitudes made so clearly only for love and kind words, these whispering woods, these romantic waters—what was he doing, wandering among them with a sister who wouldn't speak? He had devoted himself unceasingly, he had left nothing undone to induce her to forgive him, and all his endeavours only led her to a deeper silence, and a more impenetrable gloom. Why, then, he asked himself, now gnawing rather than nibbling the blade of grass, should he not leave her, and go home?

God knew he had pressing business awaiting him at home, thrust on one side because of Alice and her needs—the pressing business of putting things straight between himself and his neighbour. Wasn't that most urgent? Wasn't that of the utmost importance? Besides, Alice would get well quicker if he went, and didn't constantly remind her by his presence of the shameful incident of the basket. Once or twice he had noticed her talking quite briskly to the other women in the hotel when he came upon her unexpectedly, as if it were his presence which caused her low spirits, and his absence which relieved them. What point, then, was there in his lingering on?

There was no point, thought James, filled with a sudden suspicion that perhaps she was really quite well already, and only wore the bandage so as to make him go on being unhappy. If this were true—it seemed incredible, but a thousand little things at once occurred to him which appeared to confirm it—then all the rest of her behaviour, her silences, her sighs, her resigned unreproachfulness, was also put on so as to keep him unhappy. And in that case she was cruel, and deserved to be left. Oh, but he would leave her anyhow, if she deserved it or not, because he was tired, tired of her, sick to death, and could and would endure no more.

Thus did rebellion, on that grassy slope above the Lake of Lucerne, take hold of James, and by the time they got up and began walking back to the hotel to tea—sick he was of the hotel, and tea, and perpetually walking back with Alice to it—his mind was made up. He would go home. He would get away as soon as ever it could be managed without Alice knowing. Duplicity? Very well. Conduct unbecoming in a clergyman? So be it. Nothing but duplicity and unbecoming conduct would get him out of this, James felt, and accordingly they would have to be gone in for wholeheartedly. For what excuse could he make that she wouldn't instantly brush aside, if he began trying to make excuses? And what use would it be to say straight out he wanted to go home, seeing that she would then go home with him? It was essential that he should see his neighbour, at least the first time, without the feeling that Alice was just round the corner, and might appear any moment. He must, he must see his neighbour alone. He had kept her out of his mind because of having to make amends to Alice for what he had done, and he knew that only by not thinking of Jennifer could he properly attend to Alice; but now that he suspected the hand beneath the bandage was as well as it had ever been, and that the headaches and low spirits were all put on, he flung the doors of his heart wide open, and Jennifer—had she not told him her sweet name was Jennifer?—came flooding back into it like light, like warmth, like a man's hope of heaven.

In a state of great private upheaval James walked beside Alice that afternoon, who, if she hadn't been so much preoccupied by her own problems, would surely have noticed his unusual silence. With no one in his life had he felt as he felt with his tenant—so safe, so happy, so utterly at his ease. And she was, besides—ah, here was the glowing core of it—the only person in the world he had ever kissed, really kissed, as a man should kiss a woman. What could make a stronger link between them than that wild, unpermitted moment in the orchard? He and she alone knew of it. Could either of them ever forget? Wasn't it burned into their hearts? Great and glorious was it to have been so close to another human being—a peculiar, and to him till then unexperienced, bliss. If he had offended her, he was sorry, but never, never, thought James, recovered now completely from his first dismay lest he had been a cad, would he be sorry for what he had done. Back to her he must go, and as quickly as possible. Flight, swift and sudden, was the only way—flight, and a letter to Alice, to be given to her after he was safely off, explaining.

Explaining what, though? It was difficult. He must think it out. Explaining that he was more needed at home now than at Hertenstein, he supposed, his forehead as much furrowed as Alice's, and furrowed by, if he had known it, precisely the same problem.

Yes, he supposed that would be the only way he could put it—adding a suggestion that Alice should stay where she was as long as she liked it and felt it was doing her good, and he would send her all the money she wanted.

But it was difficult. She wouldn't accept that he was needed at home.

She would wave that aside as nonsense, and say Bosh. While as for sending her all the money she wanted, didn't that seem rather like buying her off?

But after all, he said to himself, his moral fibre considerably loosened or he couldn't have consoled himself by thinking such a thing, many a man before him, set on getting away from some impossible woman, must have done the same thing.

❦

He quailed, however, before the vision that presented itself of Alice's face when she read the letter he would leave for her, and before he could feel brave again he had to conjure up the picture of that other face, the face that transformed itself into beauty by just smiling.

Then, indeed, he did for a moment feel very brave, and as if there was nothing he wouldn't do or dare so as to get back to Jennifer, to his friend, to his—oh, why not say it?—to his dear love; and since it was most necessary he should be alone a little in order to think out ways of accomplishing this, after he had deposited Alice at her special table under the trees by the lake, where her friends were already collected, instead of sitting down beside her as usual he said he would like, it being so hot, to bathe before tea, if she wouldn't mind having tea without him, and, before she could answer, he walked off.

Alice did mind. It was most irregular for him to want to bathe at that hour. Of course in such weather it was natural and proper to bathe, besides saving the expense of baths in the hotel, but it did seem very odd to wish to do it at tea-time. James had bathed that morning before breakfast; what did he want with it again, just when he ought to be having tea? And what a way to behave, going off without giving her time to say anything!

Darkly she watched his retreating figure, wondering whether he really were going to bathe, or whether it was just an excuse to leave her. It might be that. It might be that he was beginning to get out of hand again, and was no longer feeling as penitent as he did at first. She hoped this wasn't the explanation, for indeed she could go no further in pretences—she was weary enough, as it was, of perpetually, in his presence, having to seem ailing, and indeed she didn't feel she could bring herself to manage to seem worse.

It was therefore a relief to Alice to see him, after disappearing into the hotel, come out again with a towel over his shoulder, and go along the right path to the bathing place. What she didn't see was that the moment he was round the first corner out of sight, he struck up through the woods, and doubled back by another path to the hotel. At top speed James, while Alice, relieved, was quietly drinking her tea, made for the side door of the hotel, so that he could get in without anyone knowing. Duplicity? He was afraid so. Conduct unbecoming in a clergyman? Well, but what was he to do? He had to get hold of a Bradshaw, and couldn't ask the concierge for one while Alice was about; for clear it was to him that the first thing to be done, when one wished to go away, was to look up trains.

So that, arrived rather out of breath in the lounge, after a furtive glance round to see if he was being noticed, he went to the concierge's desk to borrow a Continental Bradshaw, and immediately, at this very first stage of his plotting, became involved in lies. For when the concierge, who naturally had all trains at his fingers' ends, asked, as he handed him the Bradshaw, if he could help him, James, who felt that until the man actually saw him go he mustn't know he was leaving, had to say it wasn't a train he was looking up, but just the address of an hotel; and when the concierge, still bent on helping and full of hotel addresses, asked, Which hotel?, James, his ears red, one eye on the open door into the garden through which he could see Alice sitting by the lake, in a terrible hurry to get away with the Bradshaw to his bedroom lest she should happen, for any reason, to get up and walk towards him, had to say he couldn't remember.

This was distressing, not to say grievous, in one whose lying was made so much worse by his being a clergyman, but what was he to do? After all, he hadn't wanted to be a clergyman; he had been coerced into being one. Wasn't it just simply coercion, to bring up a soft boy to the idea of the Church, to train him to look on it as inevitable only because there was a nice living waiting for him to drop into? Even when he was at Cambridge reading for orders, so little did he want to be a clergyman that he used secretly to pray that the old vicar then at Cherry Lidgate would live to be a hundred. But he hadn't. He died punctually at the right moment; and in James was shovelled to the old man's shoes, and the result was that almost everything he did, and quite everything he wanted to do, at once became unseemly.

What he was doing now, for instance, thought James, rushing up the stairs two steps at a time, the Bradshaw under his arm, and not using the lift in case one of the inquisitive old ladies, adrift from her moorings in the garden, should chance to be in it, was certainly unseemly, and in a very high degree, and what he was going to do next, slip off home without a word to anybody, was still more so.

He didn't care. There was a point in one's life when one could stand no more. He had reached that point. And just as he got to the top of the stairs, and was congratulating himself on being safe at least so far, who should he bump into, as he hurried round the corner into the passage leading to his bedroom, but the hotel manager, and what should he say, jerking it out in the surprise and stress of the encounter, but *Damn*.

The manager, a neat, bald man, wasn't shocked because of being a Swiss, to whom one English word was as good as another, and all were indifferent so long as bills were paid, but James was. Here was his moral fibre loosening with a vengeance. He hadn't said damn since he was an undergraduate, and even then he had said it most sparingly. For it to jerk up to the surface so naturally the moment he was taken by surprise, seemed to show that inside him he must be full of such words, only waiting to be released.

"I *beg* your pardon," he said, crimson and shocked.

"Not at all, not at all, Meester Ollier," the manager reassured him, all smiles, supposing he was apologising for the bump. "It is me who say pardon. Please—a moment, yes?" he went on, putting out a plump, detaining hand, as James was about to hurry on.

"What is it?" James asked nervously, a man obviously bursting with impatience.

But the manager noticed nothing, being bent on explaining, with much smiling deprecation, that he had only that day realised Monsieur was a clergyman of the Church of England, and therefore without loss of time he was in the act of coming to seek him, when they so fortunately met, in order to ask whether he would be kind enough to conduct Divine Service in the drawing-room of the hotel, for the benefit of the English visitors, on the following Sunday.

"Why, that's tomorrow!" exclaimed James aghast, pressing the Bradshaw tight beneath his arm, poised for flight.

Tomorrow. If he got away that night, he would be at home tomorrow. He hadn't thought of such an immediate getting away, but if he did, if it were possible, it would save him from the hypocrisy of standing up in his surplice among all the armchairs of the drawing-room, looking as good as gold while his heart was full of duplicity, and in the name of God shriving Alice and the old ladies.

Aghast he stared at the little bald man. No, no—he couldn't be pursued like this by Divine Services into the recesses of what was supposed to be a holiday, he couldn't be caught, tripped up, by his calling, reminded with the effect of a slap in the face that he was a clergyman first and a man afterwards, just when he so passionately knew it was exactly the other way round.

"Monsieur need have no fear," the smiling manager, observing his dismay, assured him. "True it is not long time, but the drawingroom shall be prepare, and a altar arrange and garnish. Everything will be 'andsome, and as it is expect."

❦

In his room, locked in his room, the towel still hanging over his shoulder, as it had been when he left Alice, ostensibly to bathe, James dragged a chair up to the window, and began feverishly studying the Bradshaw.

He had had to say yes to the manager; impossible for him to refuse. Alice had brought his cassock and surplice and stole with them, so that he hadn't the excuse of not being able to officiate because he hadn't got them. So like her to bring them, he thought; so like her to insist, even on a holiday, that he shouldn't for a moment forget his profession. He had found the whole rig-out laid on his bed the day after they arrived. He was trapped, entangled in his own canonicals. Probably Alice herself had put it into the manager's head to ask him to hold a service; or else she had put it into the old ladies' heads that what they wanted was a service,—the smiling little man had said something about a general wish.

General wish! As though in their hearts they any of them really wanted to be shriven, and wouldn't feel utterly lost and cold, deprived of their comfortable, familiar little sins. Why, it would be like taking their bedroom-slippers from them, poor old things, and leaving them to pad about bleak stone floors with nothing between them and reality but their naked soles. And what, James thought, in his exasperation playing with the idea of breaking his word, and letting the drawingroom be prepared and the worshippers assemble, while he himself slipped away to Lucerne and England, was all this shriving, anyhow? If anybody needed shriving it was himself, with his duplicity and damns, not these poor old ladies. Alice, perhaps, might be the better for a little of it, but even that was doubtful, seeing that her conduct towards him was only, she would say, the result of his conduct towards her, and therefore inevitable and justified. The whole thing was ridiculous. He was being kept there entirely for the sake of forms,—empty forms to which no one paid real attention. He was sick of forms. He was sick of having to pretend he wasn't sick. Really it was a terrible, a horrifyingly lonely thing, thought James, gripping his head in his hands and staring at the Bradshaw on his knees, to be all by oneself in the middle of other people's determinations and conventions, and having to behave as though they were one's own, having to put on one's surplice every Sunday and talk as if one agreed, and talk as if one upheld, when all one wanted—

Well, he knew what he wanted, and the first step towards getting it was to find out trains. With nervous, hurried fingers he began flicking through the pages of the Bradshaw in search of trains of escape. He was caught now till Monday, but on Monday he would be off—or perhaps even on Sunday he might manage it, after he had kept his promise and done his duty. Trains, trains, James muttered to himself, feverishly hunting, and soon discovering that there was only one, and that it left at the most difficult hour imaginable. For here he was in Hertenstein, twenty minutes by steamer from Lucerne, with no way of reaching the station by land except an endless motor drive in and out of the many convolutions of the lake, and the single through train to Boulogne left Lucerne soon after nine in the evening, and the steamer on which he must be, if he was to catch it, left Hertenstein at half past eight, and though everybody else in the hotel dined at seven he and Alice, by her wish, didn't dine till eight, so that by the time he ought to be going round the promontory to the landing-stage, she would be almost exactly in the middle of her pudding.

Could he leave her at such a moment? Wouldn't it be quite hopelessly conspicuous? And Alice prized puddings. She looked forward, he knew, all day to the evening pudding, there being none for luncheon. What excuse could he find for getting up and leaving the table, which would seem to her valid enough to permit her to finish her pudding unperturbed?

His determination began to wobble again. Just Alice's pudding, and his dislike of interrupting her enjoyment of it, was enough to set him off hesitating. The details of flight, on really looking into the matter, were so difficult. He couldn't think of any way of starting that wouldn't defeat its own ends. A sudden pain, for instance, if he were at dinner to descend to pretending one, would only bring Alice too to her feet. He couldn't even have a sudden pain in peace. She would follow him with remedies, she wouldn't be able to resist a chance of doctoring him, although it meant throwing off her carefully kept up apathy. And she would besides, he knew, beneath her brusqueness and severity, be genuinely concerned, because, beneath everything, in some strange, Alician way, she was genuinely fond of him.

No, no—he couldn't do that, thought James, staring at the Bradshaw on his knees, his hands gripping both sides of his head; he couldn't pretend he had a pain, and worry Alice. His flight would have to be quite unprepared-for, probably before breakfast, and then hanging about Lucerne till the train left in the evening.

But—again he wobbled—Alice could look up trains too. It would be the first thing she would do, when she found he had gone. And if she did, she would soon discover that he couldn't have got farther than Lucerne, and would come after him.

What would happen then? Wouldn't it all be highly unpleasant and painful?

Ah, but this was very absurd, he said to himself, with a quick movement brushing the Bradshaw off his knees, and getting up and beginning to walk, tormented, about the room. Any other man would go back to his business, or whatever he wanted to go back to and perhaps called business, and no female relation would dare try to stop him. This was the punishment for years of softness, of giving in, of shirking the moment which most growing-up children must reach, when they either have to beat off their relations or be smothered. So much worse, so much more painful all round, to beat people off when they were comfortably settled into thinking they had got hold of you for ever. Worse for them, and worse for you too, thought James anxiously, for you were so far more aware of the hurt you are going to inflict, and you knew what you didn't know in your early youth, that patience and lovingkindness are of greater value, in the long run, than a freedom that is got only by smashing one's way out.

The long run! Perhaps; but he wasn't in the mood for the long run, he said to himself, walking quickly up and down the narrow room, his hands deep in his pockets. He dared say by the time he came to die it might seem better to have stuck to patience, but he wasn't dying, he was very much alive, and let Alice, for once, be the one to go in for lovingkindness. Besides, he detested tyranny; he detested it so much that he had let himself be tyrannised over chiefly from fear lest, in resisting, he should become a tyrant himself. Not that there had ever been much fear of that, James admitted. He hadn't enough grit for the tyrant business, and saw no value whatever in the upper hand.

But Alice's upper hand, which had ruled him so long, weighed on him now too heavily, and he would have no more of it. Jennifer had been right—how much he adored thinking of her as Jennifer!—when she said that no one could be free till they had got rid of the concentrations of home life. He would at once set about purging his home life of concentrations. He would show Alice he intended from henceforth to do as he liked, and he would clear the ground for this demonstration by giving her the preliminary shock of his unannounced departure, after which other shocks wouldn't perhaps seem quite so bad.

One had to begin. And who knew whether, by the time Alice rejoined him at Cherry Lidgate, he and Jennifer wouldn't have—he and Jennifer mightn't be—God, if that could only come true, and Jennifer would make him safe for ever by marrying him!

"Who's there?" he called out quickly, snatching up the Bradshaw and stuffing it beneath the bed-cover; for someone was knocking at the door.

❦

It was the concierge.

"Mees Ollier," he said, on James opening it an inch, and looking out with a flushed and startled face, "she ask for de Bradshaw."

James's face became more flushed and startled; in fact it was a picture of alarm. Alice wanting the Bradshaw too? What in the name of—

"Did you say I'd got it?" he breathlessly inquired; and the concierge, who had his likes and dislikes, at once reassured him.

"I say 'e not dere," said the discerning man. "I say 'e borrowed. I say 'e come back soon. Please—'ave you finish wid 'im?"

Overcome by so much intelligence and friendliness, James gave him five francs on the spot. He gave tips freely, the concierge and the rest of the hotel had discovered, and it had much endeared him to the staff.

With a grin of understanding, the concierge watched through the crack of the door while James, who thought he had shut him out, went to the bed and extracted the hidden Bradshaw from beneath the coverlet. Something was being done here that the Mees mustn't know about—"*Une vielle fille tout à fait assommante*," was the concierge's opinion, who had been spoken to by Alice rather as if he were a dog, and therefore grinned with both understanding and sympathy when he saw that monsieur had hidden the Bradshaw.

"Dere is a letter for monsieur in de bureau," he remarked, when James came back and handed it out to him.

"What on earth didn't you bring it up for, then?" James asked, his heart giving a great bump, for suppose it was—why shouldn't it be?—from Jennifer? So few people wrote to him. Bills and business went to Alice. Who could it be, if not Jennifer—Jennifer, answering the hurried note he had sent her after he left?

"Mees Ollier see it," explained the concierge. "She say, 'My bruder gone bathe. Give it me.' I say, 'It is forbid, Mademoiselle. De 'otel never give letters except to de personne dey belong.' I not bring it up," he went on, permitting himself another grin, "because monsieur 'ave gone bathe."

Excellent and admirable man. Was there ever such resourceful intelligence and friendliness?

James gave him another five francs. His heart beat warm and grateful. He forgot Alice's ominous demand for the Bradshaw in his excitement.

"*Merci—merci beaucoup*," he cried, pressing the great coin into the man's warm hand; and shutting him out quickly he went over to the window to see if Alice had gone back into the garden.

Yes. There she was. Sitting once more in her usual place among the old ladies under the plane trees. And tea was being cleared away, so that it must be time he got back from his bathe, or she would be beginning to look at her watch.

Not that he cared two pins now for Alice's watch, except that, if he were late, she might come up there searching for him; but he did violently care about that letter, and he was going down at once to get it. So, turning away from the window, he caught up the towel he had had over his shoulder when he went, ostensibly, to bathe, and poured water over it in his washbasin, so that it should be wet, wrung it out, flung it once more over his shoulder, and ran downstairs.

That letter. He would hold it deep in his pocket, tight and safe in his clenched hand, while he sauntered out to Alice and explained he had come back from bathing by another path. If she mentioned there was a letter for him in the office, he would carelessly inform her that he had read it, and it was from a Cambridge friend. She knew he still had one or two of these; it was quite possible, though unusual, that they should write. And he would be able to say anything, to carry off anything, with Jennifer's letter throbbing hidden in his hand. The old ladies, Alice, the duplicity of the damp towel, the lie about the Cambridge friend—nobody and nothing could touch him, or make him feel guilty and ashamed, while there, in the hand thrust deep in his pocket, throbbed Jennifer's letter.

❦

But it wasn't from Jennifer. Directly he saw the handwriting he knew it wasn't, for though he didn't know hers he did know Devenish's, with its minute squiggles scratched into the tiniest of spaces.

Extraordinarily disappointed, feeling as if he didn't care now about anything, gone completely flat, he went slowly out into the garden towards the group under the plane trees, dangling the envelope listlessly by one corner, not bothering to open it, not in the least interested to find out what the fellow wanted. Besides, he would be seeing him soon now, much sooner than Devenish had any idea of, and anything he wanted to know could be settled then.

But if James wasn't interested, Alice was, and very much so. She had been thinking of nothing but the letter since catching sight of its end sticking out of the pigeonhole with their bedroom numbers on it in the bureau. The concierge—rude man, she had at once reported him to the manager—had refused even to let her look at it, and she had been impatiently waiting for James to come back from his bathe to find out who it was from. He, of course, chose this day of all days to be late, but she forgot her vexation when he at last appeared holding it in his hand, and dropping her usual apathy called out, while he was still far off, "Is that for you, or for me?"

Well, she knew the answer, James thought. It was odd, seeing that he himself was secretly plotting, how every fresh evidence of dissimulation on Alice's part gave him another small shock; but it did. Perhaps it was because he was so much accustomed to her sturdy, inflexible honesty that he couldn't get used to this dreadful habit of play-acting and laying herself out to take him in.

"I'm sorry I'm late," was all he would say when he got close, behaving as if he hadn't heard her question.

The old ladies, who had been twittering together, according to their custom, since luncheon, and deftly tweaking out each other's feathers, so that by tea-time they invariably felt a little irritated and bereft, and as if there were nothing left to pride themselves on, welcomed James with real delight. Here was someone who invariably restored their ebbing confidence that they were important. He knew—they were certain he knew and appreciated—what well-born, well-brought up, well-connected, nice people they were really. He listened sympathetically and with interest when they told him about their rich and eminent relations, and he believed what they told him. Unlike his sharp-nosed sister, who seemed to believe nothing without actual proofs, he believed unquestioningly in the generals, colonial governors, millionaires, and other distinguished persons who were their cousins, or had been their husbands. And he was a clergyman; and he was a man; though it was funny—they often, when Alice wasn't there, remarked on it—how easily one forgot that he was either.

"Ah, *here* you are!" exclaimed the oldest of all, beaming at him, and snatching up her workbag off the chair beside her, so as to make room for him.

"No—come and sit by me, Mr. Ollier," pleaded another.

"No—this is where he always sits," declared a third.

"We thought you were lost."

"We hear you're going to have a service tomorrow."

"Mind you preach us a good sermon."

"Mind you show us how wicked we are."

And as they began all to twitter at once, James, smiling in a general, vague way, sat down without attempting to say anything.

He wasn't in the mood for the old ladies. Depressed by his disappointment about the letter, and by his uneasiness that Alice too should have asked for the Bradshaw, he didn't want tea, and didn't want to be talked to, and didn't want to be reminded of that service next day. Indeed, he felt rather like a sort of Parsifal, unwillingly hemmed in by flower-maidens grown grisly.

Poor old things, though; he mustn't be unkind, thought James. But it really was amazing to think that each of them, except Alice, who was the only spinster of the party, should at some time or other have been loved, and turned into a mother.

Just fancy, thought James, much depressed by this reflection. Was it possible, he asked himself, that love, splendid love, with its high hopes and exquisite emotions, should end in twittering old ladies and, he supposed, their counterparts, growling old gentlemen? Just fancy, thought James, much depressed at the thought.

"Who's it from?" Alice cut in, holding out her hand for the letter, her underlip contemptuous, as it always was when he was made much of in her presence. These silly old women. Little did they *know*, Alice thought.

He had, after all, chosen a seat next to Alice. From habit, and also because he wasn't in the mood for the old ladies, he sat down next to his sister; and they nodded at each other, as much as to say, What devotion,—disappointed, for they hadn't much to amuse or interest them, but making the best of it, while they privately wondered how he could. For, after the first day or two, Alice hadn't been much liked, and the general impression was that James's untiring devotion was unaccountable.

"I think it's from Devenish," he said listlessly, in answer to Alice's question.

A waiter, who had followed him out, began arranging tea in front of him. The sun shone in little patches through the leaves on the checked blue and white cloth, and the metal teapot, and the rolls and cherry jam. It flickered over the figures round the tables, lifting a nose here into prominence, and a throat there. The water of the lake gently gurgled against the steps of the terrace. The warm, sweet afternoon was full of the scent of ripe fruit and drowsing roses. And two young people, rowing across the cove in a little boat, held their oars out of the water a moment and drifted silently, while they watched the peaceful-looking group over there in the shade, and thought, for the hundredth time that perfect day, what a delicious place the world was, with everybody in it so kind and so happy.

"And they're quite old," remarked the girl.

"We'll be happy too, when we're old," said the boy. "We won't ever have left off. You'll see."

"Aren't you going to open it?" Alice, under the trees, at that moment was asking James, unable in her curiosity to keep up her pose of indifference.

"Oh, it'll keep," he said, languidly.

"There might be something important in it about the parish," said Alice, annoyed.

"What should there be?" inquired James, his eyes on the two young people out there in the boat; for the boy had just leaned forward and brushed a swift kiss across the back of the girl's neck—"No wonder," thought James, his heart giving a responsive thump; that, surely, being the sort of thing one should be doing when one was young, instead of sitting festering among old ladies.

"What should there be?" repeated Alice, with quite a good deal of her old tartness. ("She's perfectly well," he said to himself, noticing it, "and I'm off.")

"How can I tell till I've read it?" he asked.

"Poor man—let him have his tea in peace," protested an old lady; and the others immediately joined in, and the air was full, for the next few minutes, of an immense twittering and fluttering of ancient wings, while Alice sat silent, her underlip contemptuous.

She could afford now not to mind how the silly old women went on over James, for all of a sudden, during his absence at the bathing place, she had found the answer to the problem of how to get rid of Miss Dodge without his knowing, and the relief was so great that for the moment she didn't mind anything. Between two mouthfuls of tea it had flashed on her—and such a simple answer, too. A little drastic, perhaps, and not what she would have chosen if she had had a choice, but a real solution. Why not, this voice of inspiration had asked, give James the slip, and get home first?

Yes; why not, indeed? All she would have to do would be to find out what train left in the early morning, and go by it before he was up, leaving a letter with the concierge for him, and by the time he got it be well on her way to Bâle and England. By the time, too, that she had finished her tea she knew exactly what she would put in the letter—the servants, she would write, were giving trouble, and she must sacrifice the rest of her holiday, but he wasn't to sacrifice his on any account; he must stay on at Hertenstein till the end of his freedom from parish duties, and not think about her. So would she seem to be unselfish into the bargain, which, though not important, was all to the good. And though he might, of course, come after her, she didn't suppose he'd be so foolish, for nothing would give his infatuation for that dumpy danger, Miss Dodge, away more completely. Also, even if he were to, she would have had the start of him, and have been able to turn the woman out before he could possibly catch her up. Quite easy to turn her out once she was alone with her, and had a free hand. She no longer cared in the least about the paid rent and the absence of actual offence, nor did it any longer trouble her that it would mean more untruths, for she had got used to them by now—and besides, when one was in danger one couldn't bother about things like that, temporary things which would re-arrange themselves automatically directly the woman was gone.

And having finished her tea, she thought she wouldn't waste a minute, but at once get a Bradshaw—naturally she wasn't going to ask the concierge about trains, for no one must know she was leaving till she had actually left—and choose which one she would go by.

Great was Alice's satisfaction and relief of mind as she went indoors and asked the concierge for a Bradshaw. Even when she couldn't immediately be given one, even when he was rude to her about the letter he refused to hand over, she wasn't seriously disturbed. An immense relaxation of spirit was upon her, a relaxation so complete that she wasn't really annoyed now either by the way the old ladies fussed over James. Let them fuss, she thought, almost complacent, for the first time for many days feeling calm; let them pet him if it amused them, and behave as if they thought he needed protection.

So he did need protection, but not from his sister, not from the one person in the whole world who knew how to take care of him—as she was about conclusively to prove. Few men, judged Alice, had been more lucky in their sisters; and she was so generally pleased that when James, feeling the old ladies' hostility to her, and not caring to be exalted at her expense, held out the letter and said, "Would you like to see what

Devenish says, Alice, while I have tea?" as she took it from him she very nearly smiled.

❦

She took it, and opened it, and at once became absorbed. Her head bent, the sheets—there were three—spread out on her lap, she heard nothing more that was being said round her, for the first sentence began, after the preliminary *Dear Ollier*, with, *I think you ought to know that that woman who is in Rose Cottage*—and having read this Alice became lost to the world.

James at once forgot Devenish, with whom he had never had anything in common except his collar, and began drinking the tea, which he didn't in the least want, and listening to the old ladies with as much of his usual polite attention as he could, while his eyes followed the disappearing boat. "There goes Love," he thought wistfully, mechanically helping himself to cherry jam.

Yes, there it went—a blessed little boatful of it, gliding away over the golden water, the boy and the girl alone in their rightful bliss, while here he sat just as if he weren't a man at all, just as if he were nothing but some sort of stuffed image the old ladies liked to have about them, and on Sunday mornings dress up in a surplice, and pretend was a priest. And presently, when he had finished his tea, and the beastly cherry jam—he was bored stiff by the cherry jam, the sickly, stony stuff he had had to eat twice a day for over a fortnight—he would have to go up to his room and begin thinking out his sermon for next day, while those two happy ones in the boat—

But here a fresh wave of rebellion leaped, swift and hot, in his heart, for out there on the still water the boy had again leant forward and kissed the back of the girl's neck; and this time not hastily, as if afraid of being seen, but, farther from the shore, and alone, as they probably felt, between golden water and golden sky, for quite a long while.

This was more than flesh and blood could stand—James's flesh and blood, anyhow—and he cried out to himself that he'd be hanged if he'd write a sermon, and he'd be hanged if he cared that he had promised to officiate on Sunday, and he'd be hanged if he would stay another day in that hateful, beautiful place, where every leaf whispered of love, where youth kissed sweetly as youth should kiss, while he, who was young himself, got nothing but cherry jam and old ladies. Let them find someone else to put inside his surplice on Sunday. Let them get one of the old bearded crocks who must be crawling round the lake in crowds that month on their anaemic holidays, to mumble over them. Why should it be him, he would like to know? Why, of all the thousands of clergymen, should he be the one to be caught and clapped into a surplice, and forced to put off the most urgent business in the world? He would chuck the whole thing. He would pack his bag, and go that very night. He would leave it at the concierge's office while Alice was dressing for dinner, then accompany her as usual into the diningroom, then, when the time for catching the steamer had come, just get up from the table, say, "I'll be back in a minute"—his final he, he hoped—and simply not be back in a minute. No pretences of illness, no sudden pain which would bring her after him to see what was wrong; simply just get up, and vanish.

"That's the way to do it!" he exclaimed, crumpling up the paper object which some of the visitors called a serviette, and some a tablenapkin, the ones who called it a tablenapkin being much shocked at the ones who called it a serviette, and the ones who called it a serviette not even being aware that they thereby placed themselves irrevocably beyond the pale. "That's the way!" James exclaimed, throwing down this papery producer of impassable gulfs, and so much inflamed by his resolve that he didn't know he exclaimed aloud.

His face was flushed; his eyes behind their spectacles shone; he pushed back his chair; he jumped up.

The old ladies began to twitter in chorus.

"What way?"

"Do what?"

"You're not going already?"

"You've only just come—"

"You haven't had your second cup yet—"

"And only half a roll—"

"Now, Mr. Ollier, don't be in such a hurry to leave us—"

"We've hardly seen you all day—"

God, they were like moths; like crowds of soft, fluttering moths, choking up a man's mouth and eyes and ears, thought James, standing staring down at the pale old faces, and startled that for the second time that afternoon he had used, outside a prayer, the name of the Deity. That was swearing. And he had said damn, too. He, a clergyman, swearing. Well, but he had never wanted—

"Where are you going, James?" inquired Alice, coming to life, and looking up at him, he thought, oddly.

The letter was open on her lap—three sheets of it. She seemed to have finished reading it, but he didn't want it, he didn't care in the least about Devenish and his letter.

"He's going to write his beautiful sermon for tomorrow," one of the old ladies answered for him, taking him under her wing, protecting him from the way that sister spoke to him. As if he were a dog, she spoke to him. Really, just as if poor Mr. Ollier were nothing but a dog.

"Oh. Yes. Of course," agreed Alice. "I hope it will be a good long one," she added—oddly, James thought again.

He neither assented nor denied; and going back to the hotel went upstairs, locked himself in his room, and at once began to pack.

❦

"I'm a liar and a hypocrite, I swear, and I'm obviously quite unfitted to be a parson," said James to himself, collecting his things with such a rush of joy in his heart, now that his mind was at last made up and he was really off, that he had to shut the window in case he should begin to sing.

It would never do to sing. No man sings who is writing a sermon. Even the most artless of the old ladies down there in the garden would suspect he was doing something else, while as for Alice, she would be up knocking at his door like a shot.

So he shut the window, and got busy.

Fortunately he and Alice—her idea—had divided the money they had brought with them, each being in charge of half, so that in case of theft, and Alice appeared to be unable to believe they would escape it abroad, there would still be the other one's half to fall back on. He had spent a good deal of his, what with five-franc tips and odds and ends of that sort, but there was enough left, he found on counting it, to get him home, even if he hadn't had his return ticket, even if his blood hadn't been up, and he ready to borrow from the concierge, or travel in a truck, or walk.

What a shilly-shallier he had been! What an afraid fool, thought James, throwing his things into the bag, rejoicing in his vigorous, made-up mind, and whistling shrilly for a moment till he remembered he had better not. Seeing the boy kiss the girl had done it. That had been the last straw, more than his flesh and blood in its present state could stand. Fate, James laughed, squeezing his sponge dry, had sent the boy out in the boat, and impelled him to kiss the girl, solely that a figure in a black coat having tea on the shore might finally be freed—and he dried his toothbrush with such a passionate energy that the towel tore.

Oh, they were most natural and proper, the longings he glowed with, having for their aim, he now clearly knew, marriage, or at least an attempt at it. Who, he asked of the dull hotel bedroom, who that intended trying, at least, to marry Jennifer, was going to sit quiet, and eat cherry jam like a good boy, and then, all nice and obedient, write a pretty sermon for dear old ladies, and keep on steadily doing nothing except what was expected of him, and wait with his sister in Hertenstein till such time as she chose to take him home? Who indeed? asked James, derisive of his former self, triumphant. Worms might, but not he; no more of that sort of thing, thank you. Though what would happen when he got home, half dead with excitement and wild hopes, and Jennifer turned him down, and Alice arrived twenty-four hours after him, as she well might in her anger, and how life would then shape itself for him, he hadn't an idea. There would be fighting in it, of that he was sure, and scenes most unseemly in a vicarage; but he'd go through with it; he'd fight. For Jennifer, refusing to marry him, would still remain his friend, she would always be there, next door in Rose Cottage, and always would back him up, he was dead certain, in resisting tyranny. And later on when she had had more time,—for the whole thing, he knew, had been most madly sudden, and it would be natural for a woman to turn down a man who hadn't even courted her—later on, when he had been able to show how real, how deep his love was, her sweet friendliness might grow into something warmer, something which, if not love, and he really didn't know why she should love him—he said to himself, with a glance at the dragonfly he saw in the looking-glass, might yet make her not mind marrying him. She might get used to him, that is; she might learn not to mind his face, and the sorts of things in him which so much exasperated Alice, and had the effect on other people of either making them at once very familiar, or forget he was there. She was different from anyone he had ever met. She was simple, and close to him, and dear. She had the most heavenly voice. He had kissed her. She was his darling friend.

❦

By six o'clock James had packed everything, and was sorry he had begun so early. There were still two hours before dinner, and here he was imprisoned in his room, because if he left it Alice might come in, and seeing his things had disappeared, and seeing the bag, might fairly conclude that the one contained the other.

He therefore began walking up and down, and every five minutes looked at his watch; and since courage ebbs when there is nothing to do, his courage, if not actually ebbed, was certainly a little reduced by seven o'clock, while doubts began blowing hither and thither through his mind in chilly, small puffs.

Not doubts as to the desirability of what he was going to do, but doubts, rather, as to his manner of doing it. Oughtn't he, after all, to wait till after Sunday? Oughtn't he to go through with the service arranged, and avoid unnecessary humiliation for Alice, and disappointment for the old ladies? Whatever day he left, since he was leaving secretly he would still get home first, still see Jennifer alone. Really, the more he thought of it the more he was afraid this was what decency demanded, if the word decency could be used in connection with surreptitious flight.

But he had packed his bag; it seemed a pity to unpack his bag. And, a prey to a fresh access of shilly-shallying, James stood in the middle of the room, fingering his doubtful chin, and putting himself in other people's places.

This time he was jerked back to determination by Alice herself; for as he stood uncertain, his forehead furrowed, his eyes staring at nothing, he was suddenly caught into attention by a small white object which apparently was being pushed, with the greatest care, under his door, and watching it with astonishment he presently perceived, when it had got in a little farther, that it was a letter.

Devenish's. Devenish's, being returned to him. But—why returned in this odd way?

Motionless he stood, watching the thing coming slowly through on to the mat. How queer of Alice.

She was outside there, then, stooping down performing this strange action. He mustn't move. He mustn't let her know he wasn't sitting at his table in the window, as she supposed, writing his sermon. Perhaps she gave him back the letter this way so as not to interrupt him, for she had an exaggerated respect for sermons and their composition, and always behaved as if they were the most important things in life.

Still—why couldn't she have waited till dinner, and given it back then?

James watched, standing entirely motionless, for his room was small, and even in the middle of it he wasn't far from the door, and if Alice heard him moving she would probably want to come in; and it wasn't till, listening intently, he heard tiptoe footsteps go away along the corridor, that he, himself on tiptoe, went cautiously to pick the letter up.

It was from Alice. It wasn't Devenish's letter at all. It was a folded note from Alice, saying she wouldn't disturb him at his work, so she let him know this way that her head ached rather badly, and she wasn't coming to dinner. She would go to bed, and didn't want to see anybody, so he mustn't bother to come to her room.

"*Well*," thought James, letting it fall from his fingers, and staring, astounded, straight in front of him. "Of all the providential—!"

❦

Every movement now once more full of life and purpose, all his doubts gone, convinced that Providence, in spite of his lies, was taking him under its wing, he dashed to the table and wrote the letter he was going to leave with the concierge for Alice, which needn't, as things had turned out, be sent up to her till next day, and from his pen the words he was writing, most of them untruthful, dropped with an almost gay, and quite astonishing, glibness.

What a start,—what a comfortable, roomy, safe start he was being given! Jennifer wouldn't have known him, so gleefully determined was his face as he gummed the envelope, banged it tight shut with his fist, jumped up from the table, locked his bag, got his hat and coat, and felt in his pockets to see if passport, ticket, and money were all there.

It was queer how well making up his mind suited him, and being excited and happy. It seemed to change his face entirely. If he hadn't had those enormous spectacles on, anybody who saw him at that moment would have thought him a quite attractive young man, with rather a funny face, it was true, but such an alive one that its very funniness was endearing.

Nobody did see him, however, on this his first excursion into good looks, for, finding that it was nearly eight, and deciding to cut dinner and start at once so as to make dead sure of not missing that steamer, he had the luck, on stealing downstairs with his bag and letter and coat and hat and stick, a man, to the most casual glance, obviously departing, not to meet a soul—not even, on searching for him, the concierge.

This didn't at first seem so lucky, but on second thoughts was perceived to have been so.

"Now where on earth's that fellow?" he wondered, anxious and hurried, when he reached the bureau in the hall and found it empty.

No sign of him. No sign of anybody. And as it was impossible to hang about waiting, he seized the pen which lay always ready for arrivals to fill in the police forms, scribbled across the top of the envelope of the letter he had written, *Please send this up to Miss Ollier tomorrow morning with her breakfast, and on no account disturb her tonight*, put a five-franc piece on it, shoved it where, in a minute or two, he knew, it would be under the concierge's nose, and disappeared through the swing doors into the dusk of the deserted garden, as swiftly and silently as the shadow of a bird on the wing.

It was, after all, lucky, he realised, as he slid along close against the wall above which, on the first floor, the old ladies in the diningroom had reached the last lap of their evening meal, and were finishing up their orange juice and Evian water, that the concierge hadn't been there, for so he had had no need to tell a single soul that he was leaving. Alice would pay the bills; he would send her more money directly he got home; and only their table-waiter would notice that he wasn't there, and by the time it began seriously to surprise him, he, James, safe on the steamer, would have got clean away.

Why, what a lark this was! Quite apart from the high issues involved, it was such a *lark*, he thought, as he stole swiftly, a broad grin on his face, through the dusk. He hadn't felt so jolly and reckless since he very nearly got drunk once in his first year at Pembroke. If only Jennifer were with him, as she was with him the last time he shrank into the shadows, it would be perfection, but even as it was it seemed very near it—the excitement, the thrill of kicking loose, the still more acute thrill of not in the least knowing what would happen when he saw Jennifer again, and what would happen when Alice saw him again. And how exquisite the setting of his lark was! There couldn't have been a more beautiful moment for escape, just when the gentle evening was putting day to bed, thought James romantically, and drawing soft curtains of darkening woods and solemn waters about its cradle. He wasn't in such a hurry but what he could notice and love this. Usually he was sitting with Alice in the glaring light of the restaurant, eating the sort of dinner he most disliked, while this was going on outside. What he had been missing every night, stuffed away there in that hot room!

But all that was over, and here he was, out in the delicious dusk, heading straight for Jennifer and freedom, and this little path winding round the curve of the bay, this little path which a moment ago had been a garden path, with roses and petunias set each side of it in great stone vases, and now had strolled off, like some sweet wanton, beyond the reach of orderliness, this little path, beginning here beneath the overhanging trees and beside the still waters, was going presently to end in the path through Jennifer's garden, leading him to her feet.

It was, therefore, a most blessed little path, thought James, and he would for ever love it; and when he got round its final curve and was out of sight of the hotel, and could see the red lamp hanging above the landing-stage glowing quite close through the branches, his heart was so full of one thing and another that he felt a great desire to stand still a moment, and take off his hat, and bless God, and thank Him for having kept him safe so far.

But he didn't quite like to do that, because of still being that which he had admitted he was two hours earlier, a liar, a hypocrite, and a person who swore, so he continued on his way with all his thanksgivings choked up inside him; and entering that thick grove of chestnuts which so pleasantly shades the garden of the Hertenstein hotel facing the landing-stage, and seeking a seat to put his bag and coat on till the steamer should arrive—he could hear it thugging in the distance down the lake, though he couldn't yet see its lights, for it was hidden in the bay where Vitznau is—he found the seats all filled by people drinking their after-dinner coffee in the cool of the trees, so had to go to the other end of the garden, near where the steamer would come in.

And there, where the dusk beneath the deep shade of a chestnut had clotted into darkness, he found a seat with only one person on it; and putting his things down, and mechanically lifting his hat, for dimly he could see it was a woman, he wouldn't have noticed the indistinct figure further if it hadn't made a sudden movement, a pronounced sudden movement, and half started up.

So then he did look, peering surprised into the shadows; and it was Alice.

CHAPTER XII

For a second James's heart stopped beating, only to race on again at twice the speed. Alice? Alice, who had just written that she was going to bed? And he putting down his bag and rug, plain evidences of intended flight, on the very seat she was sitting on!

Alice, for her part, at first didn't say a word. She was too much amazed to do anything but stare up in silence at the shadowy, unmistakable form. What was he doing there? Had he, in some incredible fashion, in spite of her having been so careful, discovered that she was going home, and did he, then, mean to accompany her?

The thugging of the steamer was much nearer now. In a few moments it would have arrived. Something must be done. He couldn't, he mustn't, be allowed to go home with her. But why did he want to? Why, in the name of all that was dark and mysterious, wondered Alice, did he want to?

"James, what are you doing here?" she managed at last to ask, fear and anger in her voice.

"What are *you* doing here, Alice?" was his answer; and in his voice too was fear and anger. She had somehow spied on him, and with astonishing abandonment of honour and decency had written him that lie about going to bed—just so as to trap him, just so as to catch him in the very act of departure.

"You said you had a bad headache. You *wrote* it," he went on, in a voice of astonished aggrievement that she, the honest Alice, the woman who used to be straightforward to the point of discomfort, should have stooped so low. And his anger flaming high at the thought of such intolerable hypocrisy, he was going to accuse her roundly of lying, when he caught sight of something he hadn't immediately noticed in the darkness: Alice, too, had a bag and a rug.

Speech left him. He stood staring at these objects, the bag on the ground at her feet, the rug, neatly strapped round an umbrella, on her lap, aware that they could only mean one thing; like himself, she was taking to her heels.

Now, what was going to happen? Now—oh, good God—what was going to happen?

He sat down. He sat down on the farther end of the seat. Perhaps he might be able to think better, sitting down. And he wouldn't let himself pull out his handkerchief and wipe his forehead, though it badly needed it, because he wasn't, if he could help it, going to let her see how deeply he was agitated.

Yet he was, naturally, immensely agitated. Was she, then, really coming with him? Was he not, then, to have a moment, a single instant, to himself, either on the journey or when he got home? Were his footsteps to be dogged, wherever he went and whatever he did, while he was engaged on this most delicate and precious of missions? Oh, but it was simply monstrous, this tyranny! And monstrous had been the weakness and subservience on his part which had made it possible.

There was the steamer, thugging very loud and close. In another minute it would have arrived. "I'd like to know, Alice," he said, turning on her, his voice shaking with anger, "why you told me, *wrote* me, an untruth."

"I'd like to know, James," she flung back at him, "what you are doing here. I've asked you once already. Perhaps you'll explain."

"Explain? I'm doing what you are—waiting for the steamer."

"You intend to go home?"

"Don't you?"

"You were going to leave me, if I didn't happen to have had the same idea, stranded in the hotel?"

"Wasn't that how you were going to leave me?"

"Bosh. A man isn't stranded. A man—"

"Oh, shut *up*!" cried James, descending with a plunge to the manners of the nursery, to the level of a rude small boy tugging his sister's pigtail. And as he said it, said the incredible words, he was rushed through by such a blast of defiance that he felt that every window in the world had been flung open, and a bright, tearing wind was whirling all the timid slaves, all the afraid people crouching behind them, violently on to their feet.

Alice twisted round at her end of the seat, so as to face him. What was that? What had he said? Had she really heard plainly? "Do you think I'm going to allow you to speak to me like that, James?" she inquired; and though he couldn't see it, he knew exactly the thin line her mouth went into as she snapped the question at him.

He laughed. He jumped up, and laughed. He thrust his hands in his pockets, and stood defiantly in front of her, and laughed. James laughing. James daring to laugh.

"Allow?" he said. "I'm going to speak to you just like that, whether you allow it or not. When you say Bosh, I shall say shut up." And he added—positively, she couldn't believe she heard it—"Don't be a fool, Alice."

Before she could say another word a bell rang, and there was the steamer right upon them, and shadowy figures were detaching themselves from the deeper shadows of the trees, and James, snatching up his things, ignoring hers, leaving her to manage as best she could, strode away to the landing-stage just as if she weren't there.

"Why, he isn't even a *gentleman*," was Alice's comment, as, incandescent with wrath, she hurried after him, carrying her things herself. Or did he—and he was such an idiot that he quite possibly did—perhaps imagine that he had frightened her, and that she would stay behind?

Frightened her? She had yet to find the man who could do that. But evidently it was what he did think, because just as she was following him on to the gangway he turned and saw her, and said, over his shoulder, "You don't seriously mean to come, Alice? How can you leave the hotel without paying the bill, and without the luggage?"

To which she answered, pushing along behind him, "How can *you*?" And when they were both across the gangway and on the steamer, she added, "It's your job to pay bills and see after luggage, and if you'll take my advice you'll stay here and do it."

"You must be mad," almost hissed James, glaring at her.

"Not more than you are," quite hissed Alice, glaring back.

In this way they cast off from Hertenstein, taking no notice of each other in the matter of buying the tickets to Lucerne; and James went and sat in the bows, and Alice went and sat in the stern; and both their bloods were up to fever pitch. And Alice, in the stern, asked herself, tingling with indignation, whether it would be possible for any one who had just heard him talking to her, to guess that he was a clergyman and a gentleman. And James, in the bows, asked himself, tingling with indignation, whether, then, there were no lengths to which she wouldn't go to get her way. And he thought of the unpaid hotel bill, and the manager, who had been so polite, being forced to the conclusion, till money could be sent him from England, that the English clergyman and his sister were a pair of common swindlers.

❦

What a journey that was. At Lucerne they walked the short distance from the lake to the station without speaking, though James did this time take her bag from her and carry it. And because he did this, Alice at once concluded he was sorry, and marched at his side holding her head very high and stiff, reflecting sardonically on the absence of staying power in her weak brother. Always she had been able to get the better of him, and always she would be able to.

But it seemed that he wasn't after all really sorry, for when, still without speaking, they got into the train, having put her bag in the rack for her he went off with his own things, disappearing without a word along the corridor.

Alice wasn't going to stand that. She had had time on the steamer to think, and had decided that the long hours together in the train should be spent clearing James's mind about the tenant of Rose Cottage, and her own intentions in regard to her. These intentions were fixed and unshakeable, and, seeing that here he was coming with her, the sooner he knew them the better.

But how could she clear his mind if he were in another compartment? Besides, it was rude, it was unbrotherly, it was careless even of her safety, to leave her alone at night in a foreign train, where anything might happen to a woman.

So she went after him, when she realised he wasn't coming back, lurching along the narrow corridor, her bag and rug getting very much in the way, for of course she wasn't going to leave them for some foreigner to loot, and then lurching along another corridor, and another—corridor after corridor, the whole length of the train, without finding him. At the door of each compartment she stopped, and supported herself against the sides while she scrutinised its occupants to see if he were one of them, being stared at in return with unconcealed hostility by passengers afraid she was going to crowd in, and not running him to earth—would it be believed?—till she had passed through the entire train, and reached the restaurant car.

In that melancholy spot—melancholy, because dinner was long over, and only bare tables were left—she found him sitting leaning his head on his hand, with a bottle of Perrier water before him. Perrier water! So like James, she thought, putting her bag and rug firmly on the table, and squeezing herself into the chair opposite him.

"I'm sure, James," she began, "that you must be sorry for what you said, and I've come to give you an opportunity of apologising."

And James just stared at her through his big spectacles, the spectacles which seemed to magnify his eyes till he might have been, she thought, some kind of an insect instead of a Christian clergyman—stared at her, and said nothing.

Evidently, she thought, he still was feeling rude. This was tiresome, because it would lengthen her task. He couldn't be allowed to go on not being a gentleman. It was a necessary preliminary to what she had to say, that he should apologise for having left off being one, and time would be taken up making him see this.

But, after all, she had the whole night before her. He wasn't going to be able to escape her. And though the journey would no doubt be very tiring if she were obliged to talk during its entire length, talk she would, sooner than not bring him back to decency, and from decency to the right frame of mind in regard to Miss Dodge. For Miss Dodge, whom she had planned to get rid of quietly, would now, owing to James's incomprehensible behaviour in coming too, have to be got rid of openly, with him there and knowing all about it, and therefore he must be made to understand the necessity for her ejection.

Easy enough, surely, thought Alice, with Mr. Devenish's letter to show him what sort of woman they had got as their tenant. Easy enough, surely, when he knew she was the daughter of that dreadful Dodge, whose books simply couldn't be seen in a God-fearing drawingroom. And look at what she had done to the churchyard! Surely, when James knew all this, he would recognise the inevitability of her departure; nor was it really possible, really it wasn't, thought Alice, that he could have any feeling for the woman of the sort she, Alice, had once or twice been inclined to suspect. Really the time was too short, and really the woman was too plain. There were limits to possibilities. Her imagination, Alice assured herself, had badly run away with her about Miss Dodge.

She must, however, find out why he was making this sudden secret journey before she laid her own cards on the table, and since he was in such an extraordinary mood, so totally unlike any mood she had known him in except during that brief business with the basket, she proposed to begin by making it plain that she would stand no nonsense from him, neither now nor ever, and that she altogether declined to put up with a rudeness which would be bad enough in a child to another child, and was disgraceful in a clergyman to a lady.

So when she said she was sure he must be sorry, and wanting to apologise, and James just stared at her without a word, and, judging from his expression, and his flushed face, and rumpled hair, was still feeling highly abnormal, she decided that perhaps the best thing to do would be to put aside, for the moment, the question of his manners, and proceed at once to Devenish's letter. Better get straight to the point. Better wait with her demand to know how he dared leave her alone, with foreigners, at night. So, pushing the rug on the table on one side, she undid her bag and drew out the letter.

"I think you ought to see this," she said, holding it out.

He took no notice.

"You haven't yet, you know," she reminded him, still holding it out. "And it was written to you, not me."

He took no notice. And he took no notice either of the letter or of her because of the immense restraint he was putting on himself not to cry out, "What the *hell* do I care about Devenish?" And he did still try not to swear; he did still try very hard not to swear.

"You'd better read it," said Alice, continuing to offer it. "I had hoped to spare you worry—" (He thought, his whole nature temporarily changed, "What is she getting at now?") "—but as you'll reach home at the same time as me, I can't. That's why I wished to go home first—so as to spare you worry—" (He thought, staring at her in silence, his whole nature turned to distrust, "Oh, *aren't* you an angel!") "It's about Rose Cottage," finished Alice.

Instantly, at this name, his face went all different. It was so remarkable, the instant transformation of defiant hostility into an alarmed, an anxious interest, that it now was Alice's turn to stare; and stare she did, and slowly became certain, beyond any further doubt, that Rose Cottage, or rather the woman in it, was at the bottom of everything. No use telling herself it wasn't possible; it only too evidently was. No use wasting time wondering how ever, or why ever, it had happened; it only too evidently had. And before her during this night in the train, this one short night, these few hours left her in which to win or lose, lay, she realised, the struggle of her life.

❦

She lost. Long before Bâle, where they were turned out of the restaurant car because at that place it was taken off, she had flung all her cards on the table, and long before they left Bâle he had flung all his. In the corridor, outside the compartment where she had first had a seat, but a seat now filled, she found on going back to it, by an enormous Frenchman who knew nothing of her claims, and cared nothing, on her pointing out that if he didn't give it up she would probably have to stand all night,—in the corridor outside the now crowded compartment, she and James held on to the window-bar, their bodies swaying with the swaying of the train, their souls, so it seemed to Alice, in whose memory this journey remained as a nightmare, gripped together in a life and death struggle, and each was every moment more certain that the triumph of the other one meant death.

Above the roar of the train they shouted—had to, if their words were to be heard; and sometimes they shouted singly, and sometimes they shouted together, but always they shouted—had to, if their words were to be heard.

"*Mon Dieu, ces Anglais! Qu'est-ce qu'ils ont, donc, ces deux affreux Anglais?*" complained the French passengers inside the compartments nearest the noise.

And Alice, though she felt, horribly, that she was losing, though she felt her strength going for the first time in her life, and her breath giving out, and her throat growing sore, still struggled, still went on beating herself against what she gradually was forced to recognise was a rock.

A rock! James, a rock? Wildly she laughed, her laugh ringing out sudden and shrill, and very uncanny—"*Mon Dieu, qu'est-ce qu'elle a, donc?*" muttered the French passengers, who had at last managed to get used to the shouting, but woke with a start at the laugh.

And once, later, when the train was getting near Rheims, and it had been daylight for hours, and they had long known how ghastly each looked, wildly she wept, bursting out into a flood of stinging tears—"*Oh, là, là,*" groaned the French passengers, shifting, exasperated, in their seats, "*il ne manquait que ça*"—weeping, and weeping, as she clung to the window-bar, her thin body so much shaken that James marvelled how it could contain such passion, such terrifying will power, without shivering to pieces before his eyes. All, too, directed to self-destroying ends, he thought, enraged that he was forced to pity, determined that he wouldn't be got at, touched, weakened. For wasn't she bound, in trying to destroy him, to destroy herself? And hadn't she, unless she could bring herself to let him go with a blessing, destroyed herself already?

"Good God, Alice," he said, when, the train slowing down to quiet at Lâon, he had no need for a moment to go on shouting, "good *God*, can't you see that what you've got to do is to be friends with Jennifer, and then we shall be happy all round?"

Jennifer? "How—how dare you!" she gasped.

"Dare what? Dare tell you we can be happy all round?"

"Dare to say God to me," gasped Alice, beside herself at his calling the woman Jennifer. "You swearing—you, a clergyman—"

"Oh, damn being a clergyman!" cried James, very loud; so loud that, had there been any English or Americans in that coach, the train being at a standstill they must have heard him.

And the French passengers, their eyes heavy from want of sleep, watching the uncontrolled and formidable pair still at it in the corridor even though it was now another day, supposing them to be husband and wife, and marvelling at the sorts of persons the natives of Britain married, groaned in profound disgust, "*Quel ménage!*"

❦

There was an exhibition going on at Lâon, and people got out there, and there was more room in the train, and James was able to find an empty compartment.

Once or twice during the night, during a lull in the violence of their struggling, he had tried to persuade her to sit down, to sit on the bags and rugs rather than not sit at all, but she had refused. Some idea possessed her probably, thought James, of standing up to him physically as well as morally, even though she were to die for it; but the long hours on her feet had the inevitable effect, and when at last there was room, and he took hold of her and helped her, whether she liked it or not, to a seat, she was so much exhausted that having tumbled into it she found suddenly she could say no more. Not one word more. She was finished. James had won.

"Unless," thought Alice, giving up, letting her head, helpless with fatigue, drop sideways against the cushions, "somebody helps me, there's nothing left for me now in life. Here's the end of everything for me. I shall be poor. I shall be alone. And no one will help me, because there isn't anybody. It's a hideous, hideous shame."

And from between her closed eyelids burning tears welled out, tears still burning with incredulous horror at the terrible things she had had to listen to; and they fell unhindered down her face, making marks along it, for it was all dirty with the smoke and soot of the night in the corridor; and where they passed they left pale lines behind them, like little lanes of misery, irregularly winding.

And James, watching her from his seat opposite, thought, "Oh, isn't it awful, isn't it awful—?"

But still he stuck to his guns, still he was determined not to be weakened, still he held on unshakeably to what he knew was his one chance of life.

❦

From this point to Boulogne they were silent, exhausted both of them by their own violence, and in silence at Boulogne they went on to the boat, and in silence sat side by side together on deck.

He didn't leave her now. He carried everything, and did all he could for her comfort; but neither of them spoke any more. What was there left to say? Nothing, thought Alice. She knew there was nothing, because no words existed, at last she was convinced, which could change what was going to happen.

With closed eyes and sunk head, she considered the bleak, immediate future. The instant James got home, he was going to Rose Cottage to ask Miss Dodge to marry him. He had said so. He had declared that all heaven and all hell shouldn't stop him. Heaving and grinding through the night in that terrible train, he had shouted it over and over again at her, like a madman he had kept on shouting it. Now he was quiet; now it was finished; now she knew exactly what she had to expect—her miserable homecoming, left alone in the house she had tried to make so perfect for him, in which he and she, so she had believed, would spend their pleasant, honourable lives; alone, and desperately miserable, while he, a stone's throw away, would be being happy with another woman. James, doing her this wrong. James, her brother to whom she had absolutely dedicated her life.

Well, it didn't matter. What did it matter? The only thing that really mattered at that moment was to be able to lie down in a bed, and sleep. And too tired to feel anything any more, the rest of the journey was nothing but a blur for Alice, led off the boat to another train, asked for keys she couldn't find by people in uniform who tried to make her read lists, taken to another swaying, heaving carriage. On and on she went, with nothing before her, nothing, nothing, but defeat, poverty, and a hideous, frightening loneliness.

It seemed a lot of trouble to be taking, she thought—all this long journey and effort and fatigue, just so as to get home to only that. Was there no one, then, in the world to save her? Was there no one in the whole world who would say, "I need you"? Wherever they stopped, she saw so many men and women at the stations, so many people crowding everywhere; you'd think, she said to herself, staring at them red-eyed, there might be one among all these people for her—a single one who might want her, who would save her by wanting her. She only needed just one.

And she sunk her chin on her chest and thought, This comes of not marrying. If she had married, she couldn't have been left. Brothers, who were sufficiently ungrateful and selfish, were able to leave one, but not husbands. Husbands had to stay, thanks to the law, unless they were prepared to face disgrace. Whatever happened if they were clergymen they had to stay, and she would only have considered a clergyman.

Why hadn't she? Why had she let her youth slip by, without putting out a few feelers?

But she knew the answer to that: it was because of her devotion to James.

And now look at her.

London. More exertion and trouble. Another train. Fields, brown and dried up by the long heat of the summer, where a minute ago chimneypots had been. Woods growing dusky, for it was towards evening. Villages. Church bells ringing, when the train stopped. Church bells? Yes, it was Sunday; so it was. But they would get home so late that it would almost be Monday—too late, much too late, for James to go to Rose Cottage that night. He couldn't do it. It wasn't decent. No one, especially no clergyman, made offers of marriage in the middle of the night. He would be obliged to put it off. He would have to sleep on it. And perhaps, when he had slept on it, when he had had just a little more time to think it over, he might feel different, and after all might—

A weak ray of hope, weakest and wateriest of rays, but still hope, filtered into the darkness of her mind. She opened her eyes, and looked at James in his corner opposite.

Out went the ray again. She had only to glance for an instant at his face to see that here there was no room for hope. He was beyond her reach. He was—where was he? wondered Alice, dismally. In what strange land, in which she had never travelled, was James now wandering, while she stayed here alone?

❦

He was staring out of the window, but obviously didn't see anything. Equally obviously his unhappy sister, and the terrible journey, and the shattering quarrels of the last twenty-four hours no longer existed for him. He had forgotten her. She had passed out of his life. And he was thinking—Alice shuddered and recognised it, though she had never before seen any one thus thinking—of love.

It seemed hardly decent to look at him. His intent, irradiated face was no fit object for a sister's gaze. Every mile they drew nearer the end of their journey it became less fit, in its increasing, tremulous excitement. The expression on it was dreadful to Alice. Love the sunderer, the destroyer, the obliterator, she thought, had swept him away from her, and left her alone to freeze.

She turned away her head. She couldn't look at him. She was nothing, and nobody. Let her die.

❦

The church clock was striking eleven when they arrived at the Vicarage, and as the taxi pulled up they heard the strokes slowly and solemnly falling, great drops of sound, on the night.

"It's very late," said Alice, making a last faint effort.

But why make it? She knew it was useless. And indeed, before she could get out of the taxi, before she could free herself from the rug, he was gone.

Round the front of the house, through the dark garden, along the path to the churchyard, down to Rose Cottage, like a man in a dream ran James, and Alice sat in the taxi in front of their home, a crushed and miserable woman.

Well, she had better go in, she supposed. She couldn't stay in the taxi all night. But she did feel as if there were no point in anything, either in going in or staying out, as she disentangled herself from the confusion of the rug, and walked slowly up the path, and began trying to fit her latchkey into the lock of the front door. Bed; bed; all she wanted now was bed. To hide in the dark, not to think. …

Mr. Devenish, passing through the hall at that moment, was himself about to go to bed, tired after all the praying and preaching inseparable, for him, from Sundays—he occasionally sombrely reflected on the expression Day of Rest—when he heard the faint sound of fumbling at the lock, and paused with one foot on the bottom stair, and turned his head, and gazed in the direction it came from with surprise.

This surprise increased a hundredfold when the door was presently opened from outside, and there stood Miss Ollier, blinking in the bright light. Her clothing and hair were, he observed, disordered. Behind her was, he observed, a man carrying bags. Very naturally, he stared.

He had had no word of this. The letter he had written, and which he had since regretted—for why hurry the Olliers' return?—could hardly yet, he judged, have reached their Swiss address. He had only posted it on Wednesday night. It couldn't have left London till some time on Thursday. The resort was remote, not one of the big towns with frequent and swift deliveries. If Miss Ollier's appearance was due to his letter, then all he could say was that it established a record, both of efficient postoffice work and of rapid railway travel.

Whatever it was due to, however, she should have let him know they were coming home—he hadn't yet observed Ollier anywhere, but he, of course, must be at hand. They should have telegraphed. Though it was their house, he, at their request, and in order to oblige them, was its occupier, and courtesy required at least a telegram. Therefore, for the moment, he found no words to say, and waited, his foot on the bottom stair, to be given an explanation.

None was forthcoming. The man with the bags put them down just inside the hall, but didn't go. Apparently—now that the door was open Mr. Devenish, who had begun to be a little deaf, could hear an engine running—he wished to be paid. He, clearly, was a taxi driver, and clearly, therefore, this wish was justified.

Miss Ollier, however, didn't pay him. She seemed unaware that he wanted anything, or that anyone, except herself, was in the hall. Without a word, without a look, she crossed it and entered the study where Mr. Devenish had just been finishing his evening, and neither turning on the light nor shutting the door, sat down at Ollier's writing-table, and at once began to cry.

Mr. Devenish, being a gentleman, himself paid the taxi man and got rid of him. Then, following the distressed lady into the study, and switching on the light and shutting the door, he remarked that he was sorry to see her like this, and inquired if he could do anything. And it was all the more to his credit that he should express sympathy and offer help, in that he was exceedingly annoyed that he had so injudiciously, and against his own interests, stirred the Olliers up, and even more was he annoyed with the Olliers, for thus disconcertingly, and against their own interests, reacting to his stirring.

Yet in spite of this he asked quite kindly if he could do anything, and at the sound of his voice, with an air of heavy surprise, Alice raised her head. She had entirely forgotten, in her misery, that Mr. Devenish would be at the Vicarage. She hadn't given him a thought. And he, looking down at the swollen face and crumpled figure, found it difficult to believe that this was the trim, the efficient, the selfpossessed Miss Ollier he, if but slightly, knew.

Being in adjoining parishes, naturally from time to time he had met her. Once or twice he had taken tea, too, with her and her brother, and she and her brother had once or twice taken tea with him. On those occasions she had seemed to him a little overbearing, and inclined to take the lead—not very womanly, that is, of manner, though undoubtedly of a perfect womanliness in that most womanly of spheres, the right ordering of her household. In Ollier's house, he could see even on those brief visits, everything moved on oiled wheels. Method was, in all things, apparent. An organising brain of the highest class was manifest behind the delicious scones he was offered, the dazzling brightness of the silver teapot from which his cup was filled with excellent tea, and the silent decorum and smart starchedness of the maid who ushered him in; and now, since he had been living for a fortnight himself in the admirable Vicarage, he knew that not only was the house a model of cleanliness and punctual comfort, but the woman sitting there crumpled up before him had the finest appreciation, most rare in her sex, of what was meant by really first class cookery.

"Do not tell me," Mr. Devenish had said to himself, after a single day spent with Alice's food, "that any of this excellence is due to Ollier. He is a dreamer, and an ass. He doesn't know the difference between cabbages and truffles. The person who is the mind and inspiration of this house is his sister—" and not only the mind and inspiration, but, in spite of her outward hardness, the heart and the soul too; because no one, in Mr. Devenish's opinion, without real gifts of imagination, real sensitiveness of feeling, knew what cooking, at its highest, could be.

So he looked down at her, genuinely concerned to see a person of such gifts brought so low, and she, hearing his voice, looked up at him all swollen-eyed, and said, "I forgot you would be here—" and tried to hide with her handkerchief that she was crying.

She couldn't, of course, hide it, and he drew up a chair, and sat down beside her.

"You are, I see, in great distress," he began. "If I can help you in any way—"

Here he interrupted himself to ask, looking round, "Where is your brother?" For it seemed to him that Ollier ought to do his share in this helping.

Alice made a funny noise, half gasp, half sob. "*Where* is he?" she said, her brimming eyes on Mr. Devenish's face. "That's just what is so horrible. He's at Rose Cottage."

"At Rose Cottage, my dear lady? Do you mean where—"

"Yes, yes," cried Alice, her face all pulled anyhow by emotion. "Just think of it—he's gone there to ask her to marry him."

"*That* woman? Your brother wishes to marry *her*?"

Mr. Devenish gazed at her aghast; and, oh, the comfort of that incredulous face, the deep, reviving comfort of the amazement in that voice! Here was someone who understood, who felt as she did; here was someone in absolute agreement with the sorts of things she herself was thinking about Miss Dodge.

Her red eyes looked up at him over the edge of her handkerchief. Who would have imagined, she thought, choking back a sob, that in Mr. Devenish she would find a comprehending friend? He had always seemed to her such a dry man. When, during that dreadful journey, she wildly searched her mind for someone she could go to, who would help, who would sympathise and be on her side, she had only been able to think of Lady Higgs, and she wasn't going to be much good, because she didn't like troubles. How much better, now, was this! How much better—through all her grief she recognised it,—in serious trouble, was a man. A real man, that is; not a poor, unbalanced creature like James.

"I am much shocked," pronounced Mr. Devenish, after a pause.

"Isn't it terrible," wept Alice.

"Terrible indeed. He got my letter?"

"Yes."

"And in spite of that—?"

"Yes."

"But how can he, a priest of the Anglican Church, marry the daughter of a notorious atheist, and a dissolute atheist into the bargain, judging from his books?"

"I asked him that. I said all that," sobbed Alice. "And he answered that he would leave the Church. He said—he said—he hadn't ever wanted to be a clergyman, and would be glad to come out of it and be what he called—what he called—an honest man. Oh, he's mad—quite mad—he has only seen her once—the day she—she came here and asked about the cottage. Yes, and once for a second or two besides—but I was there—he didn't even speak to her. He gave her—he gave her—some fruit I was taking to Lady Higgs. He wrenched it—wrenched it—"

"My poor friend," said Mr. Devenish, laying his hand on hers. "My poor, poor friend."

Sobs had choked her. It took her some moments to recover a little. Strangely helpful to that recovery was Mr. Devenish's hand; strangely comforting the feeling it gave her of not being alone, of having someone kind with her on this the worst night of her life, someone who saw, as she did, what a disgraceful brother she had, disgraceful to himself, to her, and to the Church whose consecrated priest he still, whatever his future plans might be, was.

"So very unattractive, too," remarked Mr. Devenish, pursuing his own thoughts—the words dropped like oil on Alice's wounds—"and I should say a good deal older than he is. Now tell me," he went on, her sobs having quietened, "as much about it as you feel you can."

And still keeping his hand on hers—why not, poor creature, poor devoted creature?—he listened attentively while, with many pauses, with many fresh tears having to be wiped away, she unrolled the whole story.

❦

Just at its beginning she slurred things over a little, leaving Mr. Devenish with the impression that from the first she had been against the woman having Rose Cottage, but otherwise Alice was quite truthful; and as she proceeded, and got to the night in the train, and wasn't able not to cry bitterly again at the recollection of its horrors and humiliations, Mr. Devenish held her hand more firmly; and when she reached the end, the hideous moment when after all, in spite of her hope that James wouldn't really go to the cottage till, anyhow, next day, he jumped out of the taxi, not caring what became of his sister, leaving her, exhausted as he knew she must be, to disentangle herself as best she could and get into the house in the dark alone, Mr. Devenish gave her hand a brief extra pressure, laid it gently on her lap, and leaning forward and stretching his arm across to the table by the fireplace, poured out some whisky from the tray on which still stood the remains of the final refreshment of his day.

"You are to drink this," he said with authority, holding it out to her,—the comfort, the comfort to Alice at that moment of having someone taking care of her!—and he rather wished, now, that he hadn't eaten all the sandwiches. If he had known, he would have left one or two. But they were so good; so extraordinarily good. …

And when Alice obediently had taken the glass and drunk, though she very much disliked whisky, he poured some out for himself, regardless of having already had his usual evening allowance, because he was going to ask Alice to marry him, and felt he could do it better on whisky.

For clearer and ever clearer had it become to Mr. Devenish, as he sat listening to her narrative, that Ollier's folly was his own opportunity. How he had envied the man the possession of this wonderful sister! Now, of his own free will, the idiot was letting her go; more—he was actually driving her away. Well, she wouldn't have to go far; she would only need to step from one vicarage into the next, and the worries, and the perplexities, and the discomfort and semi-starvation which was all he had had, till the last half hour, to look forward to when he got home, would vanish as if at the touch of a magic wand. Miss Ollier was the magic wand. Miss Ollier would bring her cook with her. Indeed, she would bring her entire staff.

"I have heard," Mr. Devenish therefore began, having put down the emptied glass and again taken her hand, "your brother call you Alice."

"Yes," said Alice, wiping her eyes. "It's my name."

"May I too?" he inquired.

"Of course," she said; and suddenly felt a little strange and hot.

There was something in Mr. Devenish's voice—something different. Ought she to draw her hand away? But it seemed a pity to do that. And perhaps it was only the whisky.

There was a brief silence, during which Mr. Devenish was wishing that he also could be her brother, and needn't have to be her husband. Mr. Devenish was not, by nature, a man readily disposed to become a husband. True he had been one once, but he had never really liked it. It might be as well, he thought, looking at her, to tell her this, so that from the first she would know she mustn't expect—

But no; hardly. Not now, at any rate. A woman, he understood, invariably wished to be woo'd for what she called herself. Not very sensible of her, for there must be many men like him, who felt that this side of her was an obstacle to be got over rather than a reward to be striven for. Far better, surely, to prefer to be woo'd, as he willingly would woo, for her power to do those things Miss Ollier—Alice, he supposed, now—did to such perfection, and not trouble about that ill-defined quality, herself. Still, he couldn't at this moment ignore it. If never again, he must for this once conduct himself in such a manner that she should imagine it was all he wanted.

So he pulled himself together, and said, "Alice."

"Yes?" said Alice, feeling queer, and sitting up straighter. Something was going to happen. She was sure something was going to happen.

"I love you," said Mr. Devenish.

"I don't believe it," said Alice.

He stared at her blankly. What? What was this? And she hadn't said these astounding words shyly, she had said them with all that positiveness, that curtness, he had so frequently noticed in her, and not admired.

Her face was violently flushed. She pulled her hand away. "I've had enough worry and trouble today without this," Alice said, beginning to cry again.

"Do you call it worry and trouble when a man wishes to marry you?" he asked, a good deal knocked out of his stride.

"They never do," said Alice, stiff with integrity, holding both her hands pressed tight against her waist, as if afraid something might happen to them if they were loose.

"I do," said Mr. Devenish. "I wish to marry you."

"Why?" asked Alice.

Really.

He got up. He began to pace up and down the room. Of all the foolish questions. Bad enough for a man to have to propose, but to be asked to give reasons. …

Was it possible, was it possible, that he was going to be refused? Here he was, offering to rescue her. That's what it came to—rescue, from an intolerable plight. And all she said was, "Why?"

"Alice," he began again, stopping in front of her.

"Yes?" said Alice.

"Don't you realise—"

He paused, and she said, again curtly, "Realise what?"

"That I—I'm very fond of you," he got out.

"Why?" asked Alice, a second time.

"Why? Why? Well, why shouldn't I be?" asked Mr. Devenish, becoming definitely rattled.

"Because it seems to me unlikely," said Alice, sitting bolt upright, her hands clutching each other, bristling with determination to be honest with him if she died for it. She felt as if she might die—this, coming on top of what she had already been through. "Most unlikely. Nobody ever has been yet. Not like that. Not—not in that sort of way," she said, forcing herself to look him in the face.

"Then isn't it time someone began?" asked Mr. Devenish, rallying.

"High time, I should say, considering my age," she answered, brusquely.

This brusqueness. Could one marry brusqueness? But the vision of his disordered home flashed before his eyes. Yes, one could marry brusqueness.

"Do you know how old I am?" she asked.

"You make it very difficult for me," he said.

"Would you have me lie?" she asked.

Then Mr. Devenish, feeling her slipping from him in some extraordinary way, grew desperate. "I won't," he said, standing over her and raising his voice, "I won't and can't go away without you—without your promise to be my wife. Do you mean to say you would let me go? And condemn me to being alone and miserable for the rest of my days?"

"You've been alone ever since I've known you," said Alice, "and you haven't seemed miserable."

"Seemed? Seemed?" cried Mr. Devenish. "Does a man go about shouting to the housetops that he is miserable? I said nothing, because I knew you were indispensable to your brother, but now that he himself is turning you out—Alice, mustn't we rescue each other?" And there was suddenly such real feeling vibrating through Mr. Devenish's voice, such genuine supplication, that Alice couldn't help thinking, in spite of her dreadful fear that it was far too good to be true, that he did, perhaps, mean what he said.

She stared up at the tall black form standing before her, trying to take it in. Was she, then, saved? Was it possible that what she had so shiveringly faced in the train as never, never going to happen, had happened, and there was somebody in the world, after all, who wanted her?

"Do you *really*—" she began, her voice trembling.

No, she couldn't go on, she couldn't say it. She was going to cry again. Yes, so she was. And how silly, how really imbecile to cry when she was so very—when she was just—

"Alice—"

"Do you—really and *truly* want me?" she managed to get out, looking at him in a kind of agony.

"Want you!" exclaimed Mr. Devenish.

And at the way he exclaimed, at the authentic ring in it of longing, Alice couldn't but be convinced. And at the way, convinced, she looked up at him with her swollen eyes, something stirred in his heart, that heart left empty for so many years,—something kind, something sorry, and, after all, affectionate; and he stooped down, picked up both her hands, and kissed them.

Time passed. For Alice, it flew; and for Mr. Devenish too at first, in his relief and real thankfulness, it didn't seem altogether slow. But after half an hour, when he was getting used to his good fortune and already felt as if he had been engaged to Alice Ollier for months, it began to drag a little; and after a further half hour be definitely thought it would be a good thing, now, if he went to bed. He was tired. He had had a long day, and the strain of its unexpected ending was telling on him.

But he couldn't very well go to bed and leave Alice to sit up alone for her disgraceful brother, nor would it be possible, he began to perceive, for him to go to bed at all in this house, so long as he was alone in it with Alice. Her brother must be there. Doubly essential had it become that he should be there, now that Alice and he were engaged.

As this grew gradually clear to him, Mr. Devenish grew gradually annoyed. His pressure on Alice's hand, which he had been affectionately and gratefully holding, relaxed. It is impossible, when one is tired, to take the same interest in a situation as one did before one was tired, and his interest accordingly relaxed, and so did his pressure on Alice's hand. Why didn't Ollier return? It was now, he noticed on looking at the clock on the chimneypiece, half past twelve—a shocking hour for a priest still to be proposing. And apart from the shockingness, the want of consideration of such behaviour was beyond all—

"Perhaps I had better bring the kitchenmaid as well," Alice was saying, continuing to examine the happy details of her exodus from Cherry Lidgate. She had been doing this now for nearly an hour and a half—chatting, chatting, not giving a thought, apparently, to the remarkable and disturbing absence of her brother.

"Certainly bring the kitchenmaid," said Mr. Devenish, with one ear listening for sounds of Ollier's arrival. Surely he must soon come in. If he didn't, would he, Mr. Devenish, have to go and fetch him? Was it possible that he would presently be engaged on so peculiarly distasteful an errand? Yet how could he go to bed in that house, alone with Alice? "Certainly bring the kitchenmaid," he said, abstractedly.

"But oughtn't I to leave someone? Just to look after James at first?"

"He should have thought of that before," said Mr. Devenish, obscurely. And he added, being every minute more annoyed at the way he was being kept out of his bed, "Where do you suppose he is?"

"Where? Why, I told you. He's at Rose—"

"Quite, quite. But look at the clock, Alice."

Alice looked at the clock. "Good gracious, how *late*!" she exclaimed, astonished. "I thought you had only just—it feels as if we had only just—"

"Anything *but*," said Mr. Devenish emphatically, annoyance plain in his voice.

"Are you tired, Cyprian?"—yes, she had already learned to call him Cyprian, and it was surprising what tenderness there was in her inquiry. All thawed inside, Alice was; all warm, and softly fluid, after her long, ice-bound years of spinsterhood. This was her man, her husband, her real job,—found at last.

"I think *you* must be," he answered, moved, a second time, by something touching about her, and for a moment renewing the pressure on her hand; for he was not yet as completely exasperated by their situation as he was half an hour later.

Half an hour later—getting on, that is, towards one o'clock—he had let go of Alice's hand altogether, and was sitting with his arms folded across his chest. He recoiled from the thought, but it did look as if he would have to go out into the night and fetch in Ollier. There was a nice prospect for a clergyman—having, in the small hours of the night, to fetch in another clergyman from the most highly undesirable lovemaking. True that if it hadn't been for this wish of Ollier's to propose to Miss Dodge, he himself wouldn't have got Alice. But of what use was Alice to him at one o'clock in the morning? The warmth of a man's appreciation and admiration naturally cools at such an hour. No man can continue relieved and pleased throughout a whole night. Things pall. Alice palled. After one o'clock, everything palled.

"Hadn't you better go to bed?" he said, breaking into the flow of her talk.

It was amazing to him how she could still go on chatting. One would have supposed that she would gradually cease, from sheer physical fatigue. And she seemed entirely to have forgotten her brother, and that he was the reason why they interminably sat there. Nor did she seem aware of the difficulty they would be in if he didn't soon come back. Women were shallow. And tough; incredibly tough. After the journey she had had, at the hour at which they had now arrived, still to be able to flow on so briskly about housekeeping plans and arrangements—

"You'd much better go to bed," he said at last, definitely cross.

"Do you want to?" asked Alice, surprised. To her the evening appeared only just to have begun. She could have sat there talking for ever, there was so much to say, and all of it so wonderful.

"Of course I want to," almost snapped Mr. Devenish.

"Oh, then, let's go at once!" exclaimed Alice, getting up quickly, full of solicitude and unselfishness. "You go on, Cyprian, and I'll put out the lights."

"Don't be foolish, Alice," he answered, very cross indeed. "Till your brother comes in, I'm bound to wait up for him. How can you and I, alone in the house, and especially now that we're engaged—"

He didn't finish, and she stared at him a moment, and then turned red; but happily, triumphantly red, for actually, and for the first time in her life, she was in a situation in which, it appeared, she could be compromised. Never before had her reputation had to be considered. It was sweet—oh, it was sweet to Alice, ridiculously sweet, she saw, but so very sweet, to have to be careful, to have to think of such things, and avoid the risk of being compromised.

Now did she indeed adore Mr. Devenish, who had brought her to this happy pass, and the deepest, the truest affection welled up for him in her heart. "Goodnight, then," she said, standing before him, delighting in obedience, in womanliness, in the new, delicious sensation of her good name being in danger. "Good-night, then, Cyprian." And she wondered, though hardly daring to wonder, "Will he kiss me?" For till then Mr. Devenish had only kissed her hand.

Yes, Mr. Devenish did kiss her; not in the least as lovers kiss, but she didn't know anything about that. He got up from his chair, and kissed her briefly, perfunctorily, on the brow, and Alice was quite satisfied.

"It's *unpardonable* of James to stay out so long," she said, looking up at him full of sympathy for her poor tired Cyprian, but also, now that she knew what proposals of marriage were like, full of sympathy for James. Had not she and Cyprian lost all count, too, of time? If James were as careful of Jennifer's reputation—in her own happiness she called her Jennifer quite naturally—as Cyprian was of hers, then he'd soon be in now, and one mustn't grudge him his happiness, poor James; and after all, it was his determination to marry Jennifer that had given her Cyprian, and she couldn't be angry with him really.

"It really is unpardonable. But you won't have long to wait now," she assured him, glowing with the happiness both these men had given her, as she went out of the room.

Still pleased, and the clock pointing to a quarter to two. What, Mr. Devenish asked himself sombrely, could women possibly be made of?

Half an hour later he felt it was to be endured no longer, this waiting and waiting, and nothing happening. Highly disagreeable as it was to have to turn out at that hour and find his way in the dark to Rose Cottage, he was afraid this was precisely what he was going to have to do. He couldn't sit up all night. He must have some time, at least, in a bed; and after a few moments of further hesitation, during which he hoped against hope that Ollier might yet appear, he went reluctantly to the hall, and took down his hat and muffler, and reluctantly put them on.

The church clock shivered out the quarter as he let himself out of the front door, and proceeded to find his way in the dark, through the garden, to the churchyard. He knew the path perfectly in the day, but imperfectly in the night, and he remembered there were certain tombstones, askew with age, which in places leant awkwardly across where he had to pass.

Really this was a monstrous errand he was on, thought Mr. Devenish, picking his way. Nothing he had had to do in his whole life had been as distasteful. Was Alice worth it? Yes, he supposed she was. On the whole, even then he supposed she was, though heaven knew what disgraceful love scene he was going to be forced to interrupt because of her, nor what words he would find to say when he had interrupted it.

Unpleasant; in the highest degree unpleasant, he said to himself as he came, for all his caution, into contact with one of the crooked tombstones. But he did at last get safely inside the Rose Cottage garden, and at once was struck by the darkness and the silence surrounding the house.

They had very carefully shut themselves in, thought Mr. Devenish, and very carefully seen to it that no ray of light should get through the windows; and more afraid than ever that what he was going to interrupt would be discreditable, he decided that he ought to make as much warning noise as he could, in order both to save them embarrassment and himself the necessity of condemning. He didn't want to have to condemn too much. Carried beyond a certain point, condemnation might preclude him from marrying Alice. He couldn't marry into scandal.

Advancing, therefore, with great strides, kicking his feet loudly against the bricks of the path as he strode, he pulled aside the thorny curtain of creepers choking the porch, and lifted his hand to strike imperiously against the door.

It struck nothing. The door was wide open. And he had used such force that he nearly fell, head foremost, into the dark kitchen.

❦

Mr. Devenish was much taken aback. Jarred, too; jarred considerably.

"Ollier!" he called, too angry to make any bones about shouting. "Ollier!" he called again; and paused to listen.

There was no answer. They were upstairs, then, and upstairs was, Mr. Devenish knew, in such circumstances the very last word of impropriety. Yet, as he stood listening in the dark, for not being a smoker he had no matches, and couldn't strike a light—as he stood listening, and wondering whether it would be his horrid duty to go upstairs after them, he gradually became convinced that no one besides himself was in that house. Neither Ollier nor Miss Dodge were there. The quality of the silence made this at last convincingly plain.

But where were they, then? And what ought he to do next?

He felt his way out again, groping with his hands, his feet proceeding as carefully as a blind man's.

In the garden the darkness wasn't so complete, because of the stars. Perhaps, he thought, they were somewhere under the trees. The door of the cottage being open suggested that they had gone outside, urged thereto by a last flicker of decorum, outside not being quite so improper at that hour as inside, though there wasn't much to choose between them. And he called, turning his head first this way and then that, "Ollier! Ollier!" And again, when he left off, there was nothing but silence.

Then Mr. Devenish, worried now, walked down the path leading into the lane, so as to peer out and see if, lost to all sense of time and decency, they might be strolling there, and he found the gate wide open, swung right back on its hinges as if someone had pulled at it violently, and rushed through.

He himself went through, but slowly, and stood in the lane and again called, "Ollier! Ollier!" and again paused, and listened.

Not a sound. Not a sign anywhere, of anybody or anything. Dead night-silence in the lane; the hour of deepest sleep heavy upon it; and here also there was an effect, overwhelmingly convincing, of emptiness.

Mr. Devenish retraced his steps, and being a tidy man carefully shut the gate behind him. He also took the trouble, for he hated doors to be open which ought to be shut, to fumble back through the creepers and shut the door of the cottage; then, making his way through the churchyard to the Vicarage, confessed to himself that he was nonplussed.

They had gone. They had evidently bolted. But why? Why disappear like that, insisting on being openly scandalous, when there wasn't the least necessity for flight? He and Alice would have been ready to help them with their countenance and goodwill. Nobody could have said anything if he and Alice had shown they had no objections to her brother marrying this woman. Of course they had, privately, many objections, but as they themselves were going to be married it was far better that Ollier too should marry, and be independent of Alice, and not make a fuss, as he otherwise might, over her leaving him. The only pity was that his wife should be Miss Dodge.

What, by the way, had become of Miss Dodge the last few days? He remembered suddenly that he hadn't seen her lately, and tried to recollect when it was that he had last noticed her working in the garden. Certainly he hadn't seen her that day, and he doubted whether he had the day before. Had she, then, been preparing indoors for her departure, knowing that

Ollier was coming to fetch her? Had it all been a secret understanding, and a plot?

But why should the cottage door have been left open, unless in the hurry of unpremeditated flight?

These questions, however, were now of little importance to Mr. Devenish, faced as he was by the distressing fact that without Ollier in the Vicarage, and with Alice in it, he wouldn't be able, short of grave scandal, to sleep there himself that night. If he did, the servants would of course know in the morning, and equally of course the parish would know immediately afterwards, and presently, when it became public that he was going to marry Alice, it would only be taken to mean, in the depraved lower-class language, that he was being forced to make an honest woman of her.

An honest woman of Alice. Really, thought Mr. Devenish.

He proceeded very slowly towards the Vicarage garden. Abhorrent as was the prospect to him of not being able to go to his comfortable bed, still more abhorrent to him was the faintest breath of scandal. Where, then, was he going to sleep? Out of doors? On a tomb? He asked these questions of the indifferent night with much bitterness, and began, being tired and cold, to blame Alice for having come home. She should have let her brother do his worst without her. She hadn't prevented the worst, in any case—all she had done, thought Mr. Devenish, rendered unfair by fatigue, was, in her officiousness, to prevent his own going to bed.

It was now half past two. His situation seemed to him altogether desperate. Creeping into the house like a burglar, he snatched his coat off a peg and stole out again, and sat down on a seat outside the drawingroom windows, buttoned up to his ears, his hat well down over his eyes, considering what he could possibly do.

It took a good deal of considering, and it wasn't till nearly half past three that the wife of the landlord of the *Jolly Shepherds* was dragged slowly up out of the depths of sleep by great knockings on the inn's front door, and waking her husband, who swore, told him he must go down and see who it was; and he did, and it was Mr. Devenish.

"Can you give me a bed?" asked the reverend gentleman—quite different-spoken now from what he had been when last Mr. Patterson saw him and he would hardly say good morning.

"No," growled Mr. Patterson, hitching up the trousers he had hastily pulled on over his nightshirt. And he thought, rudely, Damn his eyes.

Parsons. Keeping on coming. This was the second one he had had knocking him up that night. Young Vicar, looking as if he had gone potty, had crashed against the doors and windows just as he was having his first sleep, wanting to know what had become of the Rose Cottage lady. Well, young Vicar, he was different; he didn't mind so much getting out of bed for him, though at first, knowing he had gone away for a holiday, Mr. Patterson had taken him for a ghost. Young Vicar belonged to the parish, besides being a nice, harmless young gentleman. No, he didn't mind him, and had spoken soft to the poor young fellow, and told him what he knew, which was that the lady had been seen driving through the village in a taxi with an old gentleman a few days before, and hadn't been back since. Owing bills, too, she did. Not that anybody was worrying about that—they knew she hadn't gone for long, because she had left all her things, and she wasn't that sort of lady, either. No, he didn't know where she had gone. She had just been seen driving away late one afternoon with an old gentleman. That's all.

This he had told young Vicar that very night, who, after staring hard at him a moment, turned away without a word, and started walking off at a great rate along the road to Amberton, as if he meant to catch her up. Catch her up! And she gone three days.

Well, it was plain enough what was the matter with young Vicar, and he didn't wonder at it with that sister of his nagging away at him, and he wished him luck, poor young gentleman; but what the hell was the matter with this one? He was the parson, Mr. Patterson recognised, who was taking on young Vicar's job while he was away. Then why didn't he sleep in the Vicarage? What did he want to come to the *Shepherds* for, in the small hours of the night, asking for a bed?

“Mr. Patterson,” said Mr. Devenish—Mr. Patterson, eh? and only yesterday passed him in the road without so much as a nod—“I really must have a bed.”

“What’s wrong with the one at the Vicarage?” growled Mr. Patterson.

“Miss Ollier is in it—I mean,” amended Mr. Devenish with anxious haste, horrified at his slip and at the immediate grin it produced on this unpleasant man’s hitherto surly features, “she is in the Vicarage. She arrived tonight, quite unexpectedly. Her brother isn’t there. I’m sure you’ll understand that I can’t possibly sleep—”

“Come in,” said Mr. Patterson, throwing the door open. “We’ll put you up, sir. I couldn’t sleep with ’er myself neither.”

CHAPTER XIII

Gower Street, on that Monday morning of an August dustily declining into September, was looking its worst, and so was everything and everybody in it, including James, as he trudged down it soon after nine and thought he had never seen such a dreary street, nor any that seemed less able to leave off.

He was calmer now. Exhausted bodies, he found, put a check on excited minds, and he had reached the stage of just doggedly plodding forward to his goal, which was Jennifer. And because footsore and travel-battered young clergymen are infrequent sights in the London streets, passers-by stared at him curiously, and boys on bicycles swerved in their efforts to see him to the last, and the taxi driver who put him down at the corner of Bedford Square judged from his crumpled condition that he must have been having a prolonged night out, and, deducing his calling from his collar, was shocked.

James didn't care. James couldn't care, because he didn't notice. He noticed nothing except the numbers of the houses, and walked peering up at them through his spectacles, his face haggard, his eyes bloodshot with fatigue, a man with only one idea—to find Jennifer. From the dreadful moment when he was faced by her empty cottage, and all his flaming hopes and longings were flung back at him frustrated, he had hardly known what he was doing. Fear lest something awful should have happened had sent him wildly striding through the night, instinctively making for London. Over the dew-drenched downs, through sleeping villages, along deserted roads, James wildly rushed, and when he got to Amberton, and found there was no train before the workmen's train at six, whipped by fear and love he pushed on ten miles farther, to the mainline junction.

He was going to Gower Street. He was going to find out from the servants there where her father was, and then, wherever he was, go after him. She was with him. The old gentleman she had been seen driving through the village with was her father, and never, never had she gone of her own accord. Detestable tyrant. Devourer of lives. Wanting everybody dangling round him—his daughter, as well as his wife. He had forced her to go against her will. He had fetched her away, whether she liked it or not. Oh, but two could play at fetching! Under her monstrous father's very eyes James would fetch her back again. Even if he had to carry her. Even if he had to carry her in his arms, against his heart …

Wildly James rushed towards London, wildly his brain whirled among the agonies of thwarted love; but by the time he reached the mainline junction he was, naturally, calmer, for he had come twenty miles altogether by then, and they had calmed him.

Indeed, so much was he calmed that he was able to perceive, as he sat huddled in a corner of the 4.54 express to Victoria, and knew he would be in London by seven, that if he had gone to bed quietly in his vicarage the night before, and caught the quick morning train from Amberton, he would have arrived in Gower Street very nearly as soon as he was going to now, because of the impossibility of knocking at people's doors before breakfast.

But he couldn't, of course, have gone to bed. Last night he had been past reason. He could no more have kept still and waited, than any other bereft, tormented lover. Besides, it didn't matter that he had walked all those miles unnecessarily, because nobody was there to jeer at him. He had, thank God, eluded Alice, and could ache with fatigue, and hardly see out of his eyes, in peace.

The clerk at the hotel at Victoria, where he went on arriving, in order, first, to discover the number of the Gower Street house, and, secondly, fill up the time till he might decently knock at its door by having a bath, hesitated about letting him in, because of not being accustomed to bloodshot clergymen. The taxi driver, whom he dismissed at the corner of Bedford Square so as to approach the house inconspicuously, eyed him with almost insulting disapproval. The very beggars, to whom he mechanically gave pennies, thought poorly of him. And a woman with a baby on her arm, from whom he bought, hardly knowing what he did, a bunch of white heather, mocked his abstraction by taking the money and keeping the bunch.

James noticed nothing. Intent on one thing only, protected by his singleminded absorption from every hostile criticism, he proceeded, immune, along the dismal street. A piano-organ grinder proceeded along it with him, pushing his organ beside him close to the kerb, because James, thinking it was a penny, had dropped half a crown into his outstretched cap, and such softies being rare the man was hopeful of getting another half-crown out of him. So that to have driven up to the Dodge house openly in a taxi would have been obscure to the way James did ultimately arrive at it, for the organ grinder stopped the moment he did, and played him up the steps to a tune of loud and furious hopefulness.

James didn't hear. He was far too much agitated by the fact that here he was at last, on the very steps his Jennifer's feet for years had so patiently trodden. But the house heard, and the effect on it was instantaneous, for hardly had he reached the top of the steps, and was stretching out his hand towards the bell, than the door was violently pulled open, and a servant came out in such haste that she bumped right up against him.

"Now you clear *off*!" she shot out, before she realised what it was she had charged into.

"I *beg* your pardon," said James, who always begged other people's pardons for them, snatching at his hat and very nearly losing his balance, for the servant, who was Minnie, was solid, as well as on this occasion swift, and James wasn't at all firm on his feet after all he had been doing with them.

"Oh, sir—I'm sure, sir—I 'ope, sir—" gasped Minnie, entirely overcome by the discovery that this which she had bumped into and told to clear off had nothing to do with the piano-organ but was, however much the worse for wear and tear, an authentic priest of the Church. "Oh, sir—" therefore gasped Minnie, who so much longed for clergymen, and never got them in that house, and here, the very first time one did come— She almost wrung her hands.

"Don't you want it to play?" asked James, for the first time realising that he was being accompanied by loud music, and that this seemed to be the cause of the servant's emotion.

"It's the master, sir—'e can't stand them 'urdy gurdies—drives 'im off 'is 'ead, sir," panted Minnie, flustered out of her senses by the clergyman here, and the piano-organ there, and both having to be attended to, and she not knowing which to begin with.

"The master? Is Mr. Dodge at home, then?" asked James, his heart giving a great thump. If that were so, inside that door, only a few yards away from him—

"Oh, yes, sir—'avin' 'is breakfast, sir," distractedly explained Minnie; and abandoning James for the moment, she ran down the steps, sixpence clutched in her hand, to silence the horrible noise going on at the kerb; and he, left there alone with the door ajar, before he knew what he was doing had pushed it open, and was inside the house.

❦

Well, that was a strange thing to have done, thought James, astonished. To come into another man's house like a thief, like somebody after the umbrellas!

His heartbeats choking him, he admitted it was strange, regrettable, indefensible, but even while he admitted it he was triumphant, and turning round quickly, he shut the hall door behind him.

There. He had burned his boats. The servant was out, and he was in. Now he had said goodbye for ever to being a gentleman, and had done something so incapable of being explained away that he needn't even try to, and could go ahead, unhindered by scruples, on the same glorious, heady lines. Having got in so far, he asked himself, why not go in still farther, and search for Jennifer in person? Why should he not, instead of waiting to be found, go and find?

Yes—why not, indeed? thought James, swept by the overwhelming courage of the usually timid once they are thoroughly roused. He had to do something. He had put himself in a position in which he must immediately act. The servant would be back in a minute. Directly she had silenced the piano-organ, which seemed to be defying her and playing more furiously than ever, she would hurry into the house the kitchen way, and rush up into the hall in a great and justified fluster, to demand what he supposed he was doing there.

He looked round him with the eye of an attacker, seeking the most vulnerable spot. What a place, he thought—what a frightful place for anyone to be shut up in, when all the gardens of England were full of phloxes! It was like the entrance to a tomb, that dark, narrow hall, lit dimly by a coloured glass window at the head of the stairs; a place fit only to keep corpses in. That his living Jennifer, should be, however temporarily, incarcerated there, inflamed him still more with the spirit of conquest and deliverance. Quick, quick—let him do something quick. That first door on the right must be the diningroom, and in there the head corpse—thus in his excitement did James think of his future father-in-law—accordingly was having breakfast. The servant had said her master was at breakfast, and round the bleak family table he was gathered with that secondary corpse, his wife (who was no doubt thinking regretfully of the days when she was still above ground), in a state of iced fury because of the piano-organ, while Jennifer, his Jennifer, created if ever anyone was for sunlight and freedom and the wind in her hair, waited on them. Could one think of a fate more monstrous on a radiant summer morning, than to be entombed in Gower Street, pouring out coffee for corpses?

James strode over to the shut door. He was going to walk in, simply say, "I've come to fetch Jennifer," pick her out of her chair, draw her hand through his arm, and walk off with her before the corpses realised what was happening. If they did, if they dared emit a single sound, he would turn on the head corpse, say, "You have a wife of your own, sir—what do you want with mine?"—and so out, haughtily, irresistibly, into the street, and neither God, man nor devil should stop them.

But just as his hand was on the doorknob, he heard something that made him twist round quickly.

Footsteps. Hurried footsteps. Running down the stairs.

Through the rattling of the piano-organ he heard them, through any noise London could have made he still would have heard them, for they were Jennifer's.

He stood transfixed. His heart seemed to give one great thump, and then stop altogether. Jennifer, to be the one to find him there? Jennifer, to be herself immediately found? Oh, but how wonderful—what a miraculous swift end to their troubles, what sudden utter plain-sailing into safety and bliss!

She came flying round the corner of the landing, not looking at anything except her feet, her face very grave, intent only, it appeared, on getting to the bottom quickly, and she ran as though, if he had been standing at the foot of the stairs, she would have run, inevitably, straight into his arms.

In an instant he was there, waiting for her, his arms stretched out to catch her, and never, never let her go again; but she, at the last moment becoming aware, in spite of her bowed head, of someone in the way, jerked back on her heels just in time to save herself from bumping into him, and flung out quick, startled hands to keep whoever it was off.

"James—" she whispered, staring with all the shrinking amazement with which one stares at a ghost, "*you?*"

He couldn't hear what she said, because of the piano-organ, but he saw her lips move, and then remain parted as she stared at him with an expression he was far too much swept by joy to notice.

"Oh, Jennifer," he exclaimed, saying the first thing that came into his head—and such a first thing, when he had thought of so many beautiful ones for this great moment—"how *tidy* you look! I've never seen you so tidy, and proper, and very nearly as though you were a clergyman's wife"—And the piano-organ at that moment coming to the end of its tune, in what seemed the profound silence immediately falling on the world, his words sounded as loud as if they had been shouted.

Clergyman's wife. Clergyman's wife. The house echoed the startling words.

She leaned down quickly from the stair on which her flight had stopped, and caught him by the sleeve. Instantly he seized her hand, and held it fast on his arm.

"Hush—" she whispered, glancing fearfully over her shoulder. "You must go away at *once*, please."

"Of course," he answered, not hushing at all, gazing up at her beatifically, swimming in happiness, in what seemed to be a bath of warm, rosy light. Marvellous moment—just as it was, complete and marvellous. There were moments even more marvellous waiting on its heels, he knew, but meanwhile this first one, this first sight and sound and touch of Jennifer—how perfect. "Of course," he said, transfigured as he gazed at her, a James no one living had ever before seen. "Directly you're ready, darling, we'll go."

"Oh, hush, *hush*—" she urgently whispered at that; and as he didn't and wouldn't hush, but at once opened his mouth to say more, she came down the last stair, and distractedly drew him across the hall by his sleeve into the room he had guessed was the diningroom.

And so it was the diningroom, but there was nobody in it; no corpses, nor any signs of them, except the remains of breakfast on the table, and that only for one. If he had gone into this room defiantly announcing his intentions, as he had been on the brink of doing, they would have fallen rather flat, thought James, so happy that he could laugh at himself.

She shut the door behind them, and with a sudden twisting movement of the hand he held tight on his arm, dragged it free. "There," she said, panting a little. "Now, what have you come for, James?"

"Why, you, of course. What a silly question!" he answered.

"For goodness sake *hush*," she said, standing well away from him, very stiff and straight. "If father were to hear—"

"Let him," said James.

"But he would be most terribly upset."

"Do I mind?" said James, taking a step forward, which got him no nearer, for she at once took a step backward, towards the breakfast table.

"Have you left off being a gentleman?" she retorted.

"Yes," he said. "That night under the apple-tree. And what are fathers, Jennifer? Nothing at all, compared to husbands."

"There are no husbands here."

"But there are. There is. There will be. Directly you—oh, Jennifer, do you mind smiling, my darling? I don't know you with this strange, Gower Street face."

"James, don't say darling."

"What—when I love you so terribly?"

"Nonsense. You can't. There hasn't been time. And will you please go? It's most important you should. Father—"

"No time? Why, ever since that night—"

"You should be ashamed of that night."

"But I'm not. I was at first, but I haven't been for a long while. It was most wonderful. It showed me there's only you in the world for me—"

"James, I can't listen to such talk. Will you go, or must I ring the bell?"

"Darling, she won't come. She's outside. I shut her out with the organ-grinder."

"You shut her—?"

"Now listen, Jennifer—you don't really think I'm going, do you? Without you?" And talking very fast, so as to get it all in before the strange, intimidating expression on her face should become more strange and intimidating, before the unapproachableness of her attitude, the, as it seemed to him, incredible hesitation about letting herself be rescued, became worse, he began pouring out explanations, protestations, all the things he would have supposed were so evident, so simple—telling her that he had come to take her home, first to her home, and then, when she had got used to the idea, to his; that he knew it had happened very suddenly and that she would probably need a lot of time to think it over, but be would wait for years if only she married him in the end, and meanwhile let him see her every day, and show her how utterly, how deeply he adored her; that when one had a father like hers it was most necessary to counteract him with a husband; that once they were married they would be indescribably happy, because he was certain, however much appearances were against him, that they were made for each other; that she mustn't waste another instant, but go away with him at once from this ghastly prison; that he couldn't imagine why she had allowed herself to be brought back to it; and—"Oh, Jennifer," he finished, holding out both his hands, "I can't possibly live without you—I can't, I can't. So what are you going to do about it, my darling?"

To which she, standing bolt upright, and apparently quite unmoved by his passion, looked him unflinchingly in the eyes, and answered, "Father can't possibly live without me either. And he came first."

❦

Father. Father. She was obsessed by father. Did she suppose that father was going to be allowed to grab and keep his daughter, as well as his wife? "We'll see about that," James thought, setting his teeth.

But there was something almost granite-like about her face, something that suggested to him, icily, that against this obsession he might be going to have to beat for hours and hours in vain. Not for more than hours and hours, and all well, of course, in the end, he assured himself; but what hideous waste of time, when here they were, free to walk away together that very minute, and no one to say a word!

His courage did, at this point, begin a little to sag. For courage, for the uttermost brightness of unconquerable courage, he had to have Jennifer on his side. If she wasn't on it, if she held herself even for a few minutes aloof, virtue, he felt, would be bound to go out of him.

"I never heard such nonsense," he said very loud, so as to drown his growing fear. By now they ought to have been well on their way to the station. It was like a nightmare that they weren't, that they were still standing in that hideous room, with all those yards and yards of carpet between them which he couldn't, somehow, cross. "Really, Jennifer—when he's got his wife."

"But that's just it. He hasn't," she said.

"How do you mean—he hasn't?" he asked, sharply.

"She's gone."

There was a tiny silence, like the quick intake of a breath. "Gone?" he then said, rather shakily. "Gone, Jennifer? Gone where?"

"Gone back to her relations. For good. She has left him. So I—"

She made a slight movement with one hand, and broke off. Let him finish the sentence. It wasn't difficult. And, having finished it, let him go. For what, she asked herself, looking down at the congealed bacon near which her hand was resting, could one do in this silly life, in this silly, silly life, when every step one took seemed to leave out and hurt somebody, except harden one's heart? Upstairs father, left out and terribly hurt, dependent on her now more than ever, to whom she was bound by every tie of decency and pity, down here James, in this distressing condition—what could one do, faced by such dreadful dilemmas, except shut one's eyes and stick to the person who needed one most? James was nothing to her, really—how could he be? He merely, mixed up beyond disentanglement with her brief sojourn in bliss, represented all the things she loved. She had done with those things now, and she mustn't go soft and sorry over him just because he wanted to marry her, and couldn't. It was vital that she shouldn't go soft and sorry, and make things worse for everybody—no, nor go soft and sorry over herself, either. For was it a reason, because a woman once had known delight, that for the rest of her life she should lament? Let her be grateful for those short weeks of glory, and come back from them to work as one comes back from a holiday. Her path was plain and straight. She could never desert father. She would die first. And that being so—

"You see how it is, don't you, James?" she therefore said, forcing herself to speak in the most matter of fact voice, and standing by the table as before, a very poker of a stiff, unbending woman.

She leaned, though, heavily on her hand. She was finding it difficult to keep her eyes fixed steadily on his. They wanted to waver. They wanted to slink away, while she hit him.

And she began again, "You see how it is, don't you. If I couldn't leave father before, I can ten thousand times less now. He's old. He's pitiful. He keeps on having queer attacks. He has only got me in the world. You must see for yourself that it's unthinkable. I'm very sorry. I can't tell you how much I wish you didn't—you hadn't—"

Now her voice was beginning to waver, as well as her eyes. It mustn't. It shouldn't.

She leaned harder on the table, and took a fresh breath. "We're starting work again this morning," she went on, steady again. "Just as if nothing has happened. He oughtn't to, he's not nearly well enough yet, but he insists, and he's coming down at ten to begin. You can imagine, can't you, James, that if he were to find you here, and think that perhaps I—that you—that we—"

Now her voice wavered so much that it stopped altogether. It seemed to trip and fall flat on the rock of his silence. Not fair of him; not fair, she thought rebelliously. He should help. He should play the game. If she could, he could. …

"James," she said, making another effort, her voice quite small now. "I wish you wouldn't look like that."

And after a moment, as he continued to look exactly like that, "What am I to do between you both?" she asked, with the gesture of one who is at her wits' end. "What am I to *do*?"

And after another moment, as he still said nothing, she answered the question herself by going over to him and, with a faint sigh at her own collapse, laying her head on his breast.

❦

After all, it had been on it before. Dragged there by violence, it is true, but still on it. It did make a difference. It wasn't as if it were the first time. And she simply couldn't bear to see his face any longer, she must at all costs, if only for a moment, wipe out its despair.

Queer, she thought, feeling oddly at home in this position, while he held her close and murmured incoherent words of love into her hair, how quickly one got used to breasts. That first time under the apple-tree, what rage, what hot humiliation; and now this second time—well, just look at her, thought Jen, shutting her eyes; no fuss, and everything as natural as natural. It couldn't last, she knew; it mustn't last. But just for this little fleeting moment, these few seconds snatched from the very edge of danger, let them comfort each other, and clutch at Love.

And James thought, desperately kissing her hair, "Whatever comes next, I've had this—" and told her, almost ordered her, not to mind, not to be too unhappy, because things could never be so bad for her again with him loving her and waiting for her, that everything would come right some day, that all she had to do was to be patient—only desisting from this line of consolation, on perceiving that it involved nothing less than the death of father.

And Jen thought, giving herself up to the brief, delicious relaxedness of her mind and body, "I expect this is my ultimate undoing, but I don't care. After this, I shall never be free, but I can't help it. James will begin, directly father leaves off—" in her turn pulling herself up on realising, with a shiver, that father couldn't leave off unless he died.

And Minnie thought, coming to clear away, and finding the strange clergyman, who had so mysteriously disappeared from the front steps, locked together with her mistress in the kind of embrace that could only mean marriage, and neither of them taking the least notice of her, not even seeming to know they were being observed, "Well, if this won't finish off master!"—and hastily withdrew, overcome, into the hall.

And father thought, upstairs in his bedroom, propped on pillows, and a little incommoded by the weight of the breakfast-tray on his knees, which Jennifer, hurrying away to stop the piano-organ, had neglected to remove—father thought, his gaze fixed abstractedly on the half-empty jar of honey, "I shall re-write that fifth chapter. It needs purifying."

For father, who was that day going to begin work again, to re-enter the serene land, untouched by trouble, where imagination sits and broods on beauty, while physical contact with it doesn't exist, was all for purification. He was as one who, awaking from a nightmare, finds himself safe and sound and sensible, in his own quiet bed at home. Two days in that bed, being waited on by Jennifer—she was doing very well; showing a good deal of devotion; anxious, no doubt, to atone for her past behaviour—two days in that quiet, accustomed, single bed, and three whole nights by himself, had done wonders for him. At first within an ace of complete collapse, he had had to be soothed with sedatives, but very soon became far more soothed by what Wordsworth called, writing of inward eyes, but really, father couldn't help thinking, describing marriage when it has left off, the bliss of solitude, and was able to turn his back for ever on Brighton and its painful associations, and be brought home; and after a week-end of healing rest, he was going to get up that morning, and resume his customary life.

He contemplated the prospect with relief and thankfulness. In work alone were true joys to be found. These other so-called joys, involving fatigue, involving ceaseless unrewarded exertions, and a base, excited, torturing dependence on someone else's goodwill, were, father now perceived, what the vulgar, so he understood, described as all my eye and Betty Martin—a curiously senseless expression, but in its very senselessness aptly descriptive of his own brief excursion into imbecility.

Work was the only real happiness—creative work, at once one's armour and one's delight, one's protection and one's fulfilment. He was athirst for it. He was returning to it not only undamaged, except perhaps a little in his body, as was only natural when a man, for so many nights, had been tormented instead of asleep, but with a mind finally cleared of confusion, finally aware of true values, discriminating, perceptive, and wise as it had never been, and of course completely purged of that tendency to luxuriate in sensual images which the reviewers had lately been complaining about.

They would have no further reason to complain. The tendency was killed in him for good; and killed, he recognised, thanks really to that girl. Now he could see, and frankly he acknowledged, that she had done him a positive service by leaving him. Wives, reflected father, half sitting, half lying on his pillows, and not very comfortable because of the heavy tray on his knees, should leave more frequently. The Brighton doctor had warned him against agitation or emotion of any kind, even including annoyance and small angers; but what agitation, emotion, annoyance or anger, could there be for him now? The cause of them had gone. Nothing and nobody else could affect him. Into the safe kingdom of his work he was returning like a prince temporarily dislodged by a mob of turbulent, absurd desires, and there, restored and strengthened, his brain better than ever, he would apply himself to the drawing forth into gracious life, one after the other, of the beautiful and balanced books he felt were quietly waiting, curled up in his mind, to be born. Jennifer was there to attend on their birth and type them. She too was to re-enter her kingdom. She too was probably purged. Where was she, by the way?

He interrupted his thoughts, and looked round the room, surprised not at once to see her. How odd of her not to have come back, he said to himself, realising that it was a long while since she hurried away to stop the piano-organ. He also realised that the piano-organ had been silent for some time, and he was puzzled, and, in spite of the Brighton doctor's warning, annoyed.

He was still more annoyed when, stretching out his arm to ring the bell for her, he shifted his knees, and the tray immediately slid sideways with a great clatter of plates knocking against each other, and the tea upset into the honey. How very odd and careless of her, thought father, surveying the mess irritably, not to remember she had left him there, with this great, heavy thing on top of him.

But his annoyance became acute when, instead of his daughter, the cook Minnie appeared in answer to his bell.

The cook. The cook, penetrating into his bedroom. What next?

"I didn't ring for *you*," he said, sharply, the angry blood rushing to his face.

"I know, sir. I'm sorry, sir. But I thought if I could do anything—" panted Minnie, who had run up two flights of stairs from the hall, and was all red and flustered.

"It's not your business to wait on me," he snapped; and then, suddenly remembering the Brighton doctor, controlled himself, and said more calmly, "Will you please ask your mistress to come up."

"She's engaged, sir," said Minnie, unintentionally apt. Not for anything in the world would she interrupt what was going on in the diningroom. She had scampered upstairs herself, sooner than disturb the Church at its lovemaking. Her master wouldn't survive this, she was sure, now that he hadn't got his own flibberty-gibbet of a wife to fall back on, but she couldn't help that, it was Miss Jen's turn, and nobody should interfere with it.

"Engaged?"

Father stared.

"What do you mean,—engaged?" he asked, controlling himself hard. "What, pray, are the duties she can be engaged in which could justify—"

"It ain't duties, sir," panted Minnie, as he paused. "It's just—well, she *is* engaged."

And suddenly realising the full, peculiar appropriateness of the word, panic seized her, and she was so much scared, so certain that the moment her master also realised it he would have a fit and be finished off, that, sooner than stay there and be forced to sheer murder by answering his questions, she simply turned tail and bolted.

Then father could control himself no longer. His anger leaped out, bright and sharp-edged, like a sword from its scabbard. It was the last keen sensation, as it happened, that he was to know.

He leaned forward, and with both his hands, and all his strength, gave the breakfast-tray a great push on one side, and succeeded in freeing his legs.

This in itself was very bad for him. The Brighton doctor had specially cautioned him against any and every physical exertion. But he didn't stop to think of that.

The cook, flouncing off without answering him! Jennifer, sending up insolent messages! What was the house coming to? What did these women suppose they were there for? Engaged, indeed. Engaged, when he rang, when he needed assistance, when she knew she had left him pinned beneath a tray. He would go down and see for himself what was the nature of this engagement. He would go down and show her that just because he hadn't been very well lately, she wasn't to suppose he could be treated as a cipher, and that talks with tradesmen could come between him and the answering of his bell. He would dismiss Minnie. He would—

Getting out of bed and shuffling into his slippers, father began, with trembling fingers, to tie the cord of his dressing-gown. Fuming, muttering, the veins standing out alarmingly on his temples, he started off across the room towards the door, but before he had got half way a strange desire seized him—strange, considering the impetuous energy with which he had just got out of it, but enormous and quite irresistible, to go back to bed again; to lie on it, that is, for a minute or two, and rest before walking all that long way to the door. The room was so big. The door was so distant. His knees didn't seem to be holding him up very well. His head felt as if it were much too full, and would, unless immediately supported by a pillow, burst.

Not so much frightened as compelled, father retraced his stumbling footsteps and dropped down full length on the edge of the bed. Yes—that was better; much better. Queer, how shaky he was still. He would lie there quietly a moment, and not get angry. Foolish to get angry. No sense in it at all. That fellow at Brighton had been quite right. He mustn't; he wouldn't. Too much depended on keeping himself serene for his work. Ridiculous to allow a cook—ridiculous just because a cook didn't answer—and a daughter sent up word that she was—that she was—

What was it Jennifer said she was?

He groped round in his pulsing brain for the word. From the tipped-over teapot a slow trickle of tea approached over the edge of the upset tray on to the counterpane, and towards his hand as it lay heavily flung down beside him. He looked, lying there with his mouth open and his eyes shut, like an ancient baby, which had had its bottle, and was going to sleep. And he thought, his hand making a feeble movement, as though it were about, with the old familiar gesture, to rub his nose while he searched his mind, "Now what was it Jennifer sent up word she was doing?"—but, finding no answer, be gave it up.

For why should he bother? It didn't matter. Jennifer didn't matter. Nothing mattered. Cooks, daughters, wives, words—they came and went, they came and went. Like waves. Like tides. They ebbed and flew—

No, it couldn't be flew. Now what, thought father, his hand once more slightly stirring, now what was the word that invariably accompanied ebbed?

Well, never mind. He gave up again. It didn't matter. Just lie quiet, and sleep for a few minutes. Really he couldn't be bothered any more. Nothing mattered; except, perhaps, a pillow. One wanted a pillow. When one was going to sleep, one wanted a pillow. But that was about all.

❦

Such were the last articulate thoughts of father, who, after that, dropped off, as he wished, to sleep, and after sleep dropped off, as he didn't wish, but it was of no consequence because he wasn't aware of it, to death.

He was alone when he died; but this too was of no consequence, since he didn't know it. James had just gone. Jennifer was coming up the stairs. Minnie, cowering in the kitchen, whither she had fled for cover, was shakily peeling the potatoes for his lunch.

To the end of her days Minnie bore about with her, hidden in her heart and never breathed to a soul, the dark and dreadful conviction that it was her fault that he died.

And so it was.

AFTERWORD

Jennifer Dodge is one of the 'two million surplus women' of the years between the end of the First World War and the beginning of the Second. This was the figure commonly used by commentators at the time, referring to one of the apparent effects of the casualty rate of the Great War: there were far fewer men to marry. The number was approximate – the 1921 census suggested there were actually 1.75 million more women, and this number had scarcely changed by the 1931 census – but the 'type' was certainly embedded in the mindsets and bookshelves of many readers of the period. And Jennifer's father, for one, doesn't like the phenomenon.

> Father didn't like old maids; not to be shut up alone with, most of every day, in the back diningroom as well as at meals, and he couldn't help feeling relieved to think that this stretch of his life was over.

Even though he is only 'shut up' with one such 'old maid', she is plural because, to father, she represents not just the specific but the general. Unmarried women were a topic of much debate and conversation in the 1920s and 30s, with an unprecedented number of guides attempting to commiserate, congratulate or remonstrate with those who had reached their mid-twenties without having secured a husband – let alone their thirties, as in Jennifer's case. Some were brightly showing these women how to make the most of it. Others, such as Charlotte Haldane's unpleasantly titled *Motherhood and Its*

Enemies (1927) took a less encouraging approach. She divides women into several categories, including:

1. The sexually normal, whose career leads in due course to mating and motherhood.
2. The originally normal, doomed to permanent virginity with or without the necessity to support herself economically.
3. The professional or 'vocational' prostitute, who lives either on or chiefly by the economic support of men to whom she does not bear children.
4. The 'amateur' prostitute, who while substantially earning her own living relies on men for providing her luxuries and amusements. She either may or may not bear children.

If we take Haldane's classification seriously – which takes some stretch of the imagination – Jennifer could arguably have been slotted into categories 2 or 3, at the start of the novel. While her father labels her an old maid, she certainly at the same time 'lives either on or chiefly by the economic support of men to whom she does not bear children' – albeit this man is her father, while Haldane is presumably thinking of a less filial relationship.

Like many unmarried women at the time, Jennifer is expected to serve relatives of hers who are or have been married. Father's relationship to her is so overriding that he is known as 'father' by the narrator as well as Jennifer, and he even takes over the title of the novel. Many dependent spinsters in novels of the period were dependent on their family not just for room and board but for the framework of their identities. In May Sinclair's *Life and Death of Harriett Frean* (1922) and F.M. Mayor's *The Rector's Daughter* (1924), for instance, the heroines give up their chances of marital happiness to devote themselves to their mother and father respectively. In Sylvia Townsend Warner's 1926 novel *Lolly Willowes,* Laura is expected to sacrifice herself completely to the role of aunt in her brother's house until, like Jennifer, she flees to the countryside – where she finds a novel way to reimagine her identity. In 1929's *The Bachelor Woman and Her Problems*, Mary Scharlieb says of the unmarried aunt in the house:

> Is she not the one human being above all others on whom we can rely and count, just the one not too much involved in her own joys, sorrows, inevitable duties and engagements, to be able, indeed delighted, to come forward to give a helping hand and a sympathising glance in all the trials and perplexities of the world?

Is she not, Scharlieb implies, devoid of personal identity, and ready to have one formed for her? By extension, this aunt role is filled by any unmarried woman in the house who should be all-to-pleased to perform it. Not for nothing was a company called Universal Aunts created in 1921, offering to do 'anything for anyone at any time'. Father certainly expects Jennifer to continue in this role.

Elizabeth von Arnim had very little experience of being a single, dependent adult woman in a household. She was married twice – both marriages entitled her to use the title Countess; both marriages were unhappy. She wrote wryly in *All the Dogs of My Life* that 'perhaps husbands have never altogether agreed with me'. Von Arnim left her domineering first husband Henning August von Arnim-Schlagenthin and, after his death, married the Earl John Francis Russell. This marriage seems to have been even worse, and she later described it as 'years of acute misery'. Russell died shortly before *Father* was published, though she had been separated from him for over a decade by that point. His final act was to leave all his papers, including von Arnim's love letters, to someone she referred to as 'one of his women'. Though she would use these painful memories as inspiration for novels such as *Vera* (1921), she treats the position of an unmarried woman in the home differently from the unhappy wife. While both could be subjugated,

❦ ❦ ❦

perhaps only the unmarried woman was expected to be grateful to be wholly dependent on the people who housed her – while being extremely, fragilely dependent. It can end at any point on the other person's say so, even if not her own.

As *Father* opens, and father has just ensured there is one less unmarried woman in the world, Jennifer is considering one dominant feature of being a single, dependent woman in the 1930s: a lack of spatial autonomy. Throughout the novel, Jennifer sees her escape into independence through the lens of the rooms and houses that surround her. Even in the first few pages, her longing to have her own life is powerfully shown through an imagined collapse of the building around her:

> Through and beyond father she saw doors flying open, walls falling flat, and herself running unhindered down the steps, along Gower Street, away through London, across suburbs, out, out into great sunlit spaces

Jennifer doesn't have grand ambitions. She only wishes 'the smallest, cheapest, and remotest place', and to subsist on the £100 a year that she inherited from her mother. It should be noted that this is three years after Virginia Woolf stipulated £500 a year as necessary for a woman (alongside a room of one's own) in *A Room of One's Own*, which von Arnim reviewed. While Woolf was writing about the sum she thought needed for a female artist to explore her creativity, Jennifer is looking solely for escape – and, perhaps with a less upper-middle-class mindset than Woolf's, is willing to find this escape on a much lower sum than Woolf's £500. By some calculations, £100 in 1931 would be approximately £6,500 today – that is; less than half the figure that is considered the 'poverty line' in the UK.

In order to get to her own, independent home, though, she must get the permission of another man. In one of many very funny scenes in

❦ ❦ ❦

Father, Jennifer conducts an interview with a vicar who can offer the lease of a cottage – but does so wrapped in his coat, which infuriates him to the point of refusal. It is, of course, not the last time we'll see him. Thankfully the second home she interviews for, Rose Cottage, does end up being hers – albeit due to an angry reaction by Alice towards her brother James, who is the kind and seemingly weak-willed vicar of the parish.

Alice is a fascinating counterpart to Jennifer in the novel. She is several years older than her brother and rules him absolutely. As well as speaking firmly to him on all occasions and silencing him with "Bosh", she – like father – rules him spatially. Alice will not let James have control over who might tenant Rose Cottage, even when the decision comes to her cost. She dictates where he can drink coffee; she takes him as far as Switzerland (this setting is particularly poignant as, when von Arnim was writing the novel, she was preparing to sell a much-loved home in Switzerland). And yet she, like Jennifer, is a dependent relative. In Charlotte Haldane's taxonomy, she would also fit into type 2 or 3. Though Alice has an antagonism towards spinsters – 'Alice didn't trust unmarried women an inch. Naturally they all wanted a good home, and not having to pay for it' – she is in precisely the same position. She and Jennifer are two sides of the same coin. Alice is selfish, rude, and unkind, but she also recognises her dependence on a male relative. Personality can only make so much difference to Alice's outlook and position within a social framework where gender is the most important characteristic:

> Her whole life would be torn up by the roots if anything happened to James – anything finally severing, like death or marriage. Why, she would be done for. She would just sink into an unconsidered spinster, with neither authority nor background; and, if it were marriage which severed, she would be unpleasantly short of money into the bargain. Outrageous, of course, that it should be so, but that

❦ ❦ ❦

was life all over – men getting everything, even if they were fools, and women's only chance of proper recognition and power being in connection with, and through, the creatures; unless one were one of these women with so-called gifts, one of these artist-women, but she thanked God she wasn't that sort. And quite apart from the fact that she owed her comfortable home and position, and her freedom from money cares to James, having ruled him since he was a baby he had now become necessary to her very existence – something to care for and to bully, to goad and to guard, something belonging to her, an object in life. What she would do without James, Alice, in her softer moments, couldn't imagine.

We can assume that what money James has would go to his older sister on his death, but she wouldn't be able to keep living in the vicarage (which would be tied to the job), nor would she maintain her position in society if either death or marriage meant she was no longer in her current house and role.

Jennifer, however, is delighted to 'do without' these things. As though to hammer home Jennifer's dissatisfaction with the status quo of housing, she spends the first night on a mattress that has been dragged outside. Gardens and outdoor spaces recur throughout Elizabeth von Arnim's most famous work – few readers could forget, for instance, the descriptions of the paradisiacal Italian landscape in *The Enchanted April*. During her lifetime, Elizabeth von Arnim's books were published as 'By the author of *Elizabeth and Her German Garden*' and she was synonymous with this character who said 'the garden is the place I go to for refuge and shelter, not the house'. Jennifer's longing for the rural, for the anti-London, is what motivates her fleeing – but when she gets to her new home, the house is as important as the garden. Perhaps putting the mattress in the garden is a way of showing her power over the space – no longer tied to spatial dichotomies put in place by other people.

Yet, when father appears, he is not cowed by her independence.

❦ ❦ ❦

Indeed, he expects her to return. Jennifer sees such a close link between one's environment and power dynamics that she is confused that father should still be the more powerful: 'Who could have imagined that even here, in her own house, on her own ground, he still so completely would continue to be father?' Perhaps every reader would have imagined this, von Arnim's ironic tone suggests – but we hear the sentence in Jennifer's voice as well as the narrator's. She is genuinely surprised, because she is affected by environment to such a degree that it marks her physically. When James tracks her down at her father's house, he says. "I don't know you with this strange, Gower Street face". Similarly, when father arrives at Rose Cottage, 'All Gower Street came flooding into her cottage'. So powerfully does he represent a certain place that he seems to bring it with him.

The difficulty of spatial independence for unmarried women is not solved by *Father*. Instead, von Arnim creates convenient engagements and an even more convenient death. The reader is satisfied; we would have been unhappy had the novel ended otherwise. But, while Jennifer and Alice move into marriages, arguably replacing one dependency with another (however happily, at least in Jennifer's case), von Arnim leaves obliquely in the background all those single, dependent women who still don't have a room of their own.

Simon Thomas

Series consultant **Simon Thomas** created the middlebrow blog Stuck in a Book in 2007. He is also the co-host of the popular podcast Tea or Books? Simon has a PhD from Oxford University in Interwar Literature.